Old Mill Road

L. V. Gaudet

ISBN 978-1-9992823-3-2
Library and Archives Canada
First edition published October 2019
Printed by IngramSpark

Cover art by Erskine Designs
https://www.facebook.com/pg/erskinedesigns/posts/
https://erskinedesigns.weebly.com/

Discover other titles by L.V. Gaudet:

Garden Grove
The Gypsy Queen
Old Mill Road

<u>The McAllister Series:</u>
Where the Bodies Are
The McAllister Farm
Hunting Michael Underwood
Killing David McAllister

To my readers.

There is safety in pretending a thing is not real.
Even when every fibre of your being knows that is a lie.
There is safety in forgetting.
In a way.

You can't escape the dream

Table of Contents

1 -The Kids' Discovery

A choked guttural sound hung between them. The four kids stood in a circle looking down at it. Darkness was already creeping across the sky, chasing the late afternoon sun away. The gloom was made darker by the shade of the tall trees surrounding them. Glimpses of open grass could be seen through the trees ahead where they entered the woods.

"I don't think we should tell anyone," David said. He was the oldest of the group, a virtual adult at ten.

"We have to," his younger brother Ian insisted.

"They'll think we did it," David warned. "We could go to jail."

He looked at Felicia for support, but she would not look at him. Felicia would not look at anything but the thing on the ground.

"You all have to swear to not tell anyone. Ever." David looked at each of them.

The third boy and youngest of the children, Nick, whimpered.

I don't want to go to jail, Nick thought, fear surging through him despite the numb shock. That's where they put bad people like Uncle Harvey. Uncle Harvey scares me; a lot.

Nick looked at his sister Felicia for help, but she was oblivious to the terrifying thoughts in his head. He looked at David and Ian. They seemed to have forgotten he was there.

I don't want to go live in jail with Uncle Harvey. Nick looked back at the gruesome spectacle on the ground before them and started to cry.

Felicia just stood there next to her little brother, her face ashen, shivering although it was still quite warm and sticky with the humidity left behind by the waning hot day.

She knew they would not put them in jail like adults. They were only kids, after all. And how could anyone possibly think they did this? But she did not say that.

She did not say anything at all and just kept staring down at it with a sick feeling.

Felicia put one arm around Nick to comfort him. He leaned into her gratefully and huffed as he tried to get himself under control.

Ian shook his head. Not in disagreement, but in utter shock at finding themselves here in this place at this moment; facing this.

"Nobody is saying anything," David said. The look he gave them all bordered on angry defiance, but still the chilled shock they all felt.

"Fine. If you swear to keep the secret, then don't say anything. Otherwise, you have to tell me you are going to betray us all."

The only sound was Nick's soft whimpering and sniffling.

No one met David's eyes. No one looked up from their terrible secret.

The breeze picked up, the gust of wind invading the woods to rustle the leaves, picking up and swirling any loose leaves it found and letting them fall as they would. It teased at Felicia's hair, making it dance for a moment, and then the gust of wind was gone.

Felicia shivered harder under the onslaught of the wind despite the lack of chill on it.

Someone walked over my grave, she thought. It made her shudder.

"Come on Nick," David said, looking at him seriously, "you have to stop crying or they'll know something is wrong. We can't leave here until you stop."

Nick coughed and blubbered, trying to make the tears stop.

A crow stared down at them from its perch on a branch, their only witness, and then took flight to vanish over the trees.

The sky grew darker, the sun lowering on the horizon, as they stood there mutely staring like worshipers at a grisly shrine.

Finally, with Nick's tears under control, they nodded their wordless agreement, turned, and melted into the fast darkening woods, looking more like spectres than living children.

This will be their secret.

2 - Vanished

Home from school, the screen door loudly banged closed behind David. He dropped his school bag just inside the door, kicked off his shoes, and ran for the television in the living room.

"Don't slam the door," his mother's voice called from somewhere in the house.

Ian came in after him, closing the door more carefully than his older brother, and joined David lying on the floor watching cartoons.

"Psst."

David looked around for the source of the sound.

"Psst."

He got up and walked to the kitchen doorway. Felicia was on the other side of the screen door, waving at him with a finger at her lips. He walked over.

"What?" he whispered, a little annoyed. His irritation quickly vanished when he saw her face was discolored and her eyes were red and swollen from crying.

He slipped out the door, careful not to let it bang on its spring-loaded hinges, and pulled her aside out of sight of anyone inside, full of concern for both her and their secret.

"What's wrong?" David asked.

"I don't know." Felicia looked at him with eyes filled with sorrow and fear, her voice choking on the words.

"What do you mean you don't know?" David squinted at her with an expression that suggested he did not believe her.

Of course you know what's wrong, otherwise you wouldn't be crying, he thought. He said nothing, knowing she would speak if he kept silent.

"Everybody's gone crazy," Felicia whispered. "Mom just keeps crying. Dad is stomping around yelling at everybody, strange people keep coming and going from the house. They whisper and stare at us with weird looks. No one will tell Nick and me what's going on."

David arched an eyebrow at her, his question unvoiced. He did not dare ask.

Did you tell? His mind screamed it. He tightened his lips to keep from voicing those three terrible little words.

Felicia whimpered.

"Dad was yelling at someone on the phone, at Mom, and at us. The police came to the house. Dad rushed out to meet them outside before they could come to the door. He yelled at them too."

Felicia's face was pale, her skin waxy, and she looked like she was almost too weak to stand.

Like she's sick, David thought. He shook his head slowly. This is serious. You do not yell at cops, everybody knows that.

"Do they know about what we found yesterday?" he asked, almost unable to, afraid of the answer.

"I-I don't know," she sobbed. "I-I'm scared. So is Nick."

Felicia's mother's voice carried to them on the wind, calling her to come home. She sounded off, strained.

"I have to go," Felicia whispered.

David watched her run across from the back yard to the front street and away down the road toward home. She ran with that awkward gait of a girl whose growth needs to catch up to her long lanky legs.

*****

The next day David banged the kitchen door open just as he always did when he came home from school. This time he did not let it bang closed.

His mother was about to yell out of habit to not slam the door, but he beat her to it, closing it softly. Dropping his school books on the floor by the door, David called out.

"I'm going to Felicia's."

"Be back before supper," his mother's voice called back.

Ian gave him a curious look as David passed him coming in the door, always arriving that moment after David.

Catching the door as David let it go to slam closed, Ian closed it quietly, left his stuff by the door, and retreated to the living room to plop on the floor and watch cartoons.

David hurried across from the back yard to the front street and down the road, following Felicia's path home yesterday.

*****

As was customary, David went straight to the back of the house. The doors to Felicia's house were closed. There would be no whispering through the open screen door like at his house.

David frowned at the house.

"Odd. Felicia's mom usually has only the screen doors closed on a hot day like today to let the breeze cool the house."

He stepped up to the back door and knocked, waiting.

When no one answered, he knocked again.

The place had an empty feel to it, like it was deserted.

David walked around to the front. The front window curtains were drawn tight. He tried knocking on the front door.

"There should be someone here."

Still, there was no answer.

He walked around the house inspecting it, standing on tiptoes and trying to look in the windows, and finally pulled an old small wooden crate sitting by the back shed to a spot beneath a window. He stepped up onto the crate. It wobbled for a moment. When it settled, he stood on his tiptoes and pulled himself up by the window ledge. He could just see inside.

What he saw did not look right. The house was not as tidy as usual. Felicia's mother was well known around town for being too neat for the liking of the town gossips.

It was nothing major that was wrong with the house, just little things that he could never remember ever being out of place when he was in the house. The large vase that always sat beside the living room end table with decorative sticks of some kind was tipped on its side; its sticks spilled half out. A shirt or something, he could not tell what, lay discarded on the floor. Past the kitchen doorframe, he could just make out one end of the kitchen table.

He craned his neck, stretching to see further into the kitchen. He got down, shifted the crate, and climbed back up to see part of the kitchen through the doorway. Two flies buzzed around an unfinished dinner there. The chair was pushed back as if someone had gotten up and left in a hurry. It sent a chill down his back.

That was the last he saw of Felicia and Nick and their family.

3 - Waiting at the Old Train Station

Twelve Years Later

The train rattles past the old train station without slowing down. Trains don't stop here anymore. The station is nothing more than a rotting wood platform partially covered by a sagging roof which now has many large holes and missing boards and a small ticket office. The rusted old padlock barely holds the door closed, the latch's old screws sagging loosely in the worn wood.

Two young men wait in front of the old ticket office, though no train will ever come again. They are men, barely, just starting out their adult lives.

Pacing restlessly, Ian scuffs his toes against the rotting timber of the platform, silently hoping it does not give way beneath his weight.

David is sitting calmly on one end of the wooden bench. The other end looks like it had been chewed off by rot; the half-seated frame looking soft, cracked, and unlikely to hold a man's weight. He watches his younger brother pace.

"They're building homes up there on the old Mill Road," Ian says, "a whole development."

He turns and looks at David, his expression grim.

David looks at him with a surprised look.

"Wow," he says, "I'd forgotten."

"Yeah, me too. It's been a lot of years."

David shakes his head, amused. He chuckles.

"Man, were we dumb," he says.

"Uh-huh. Bunch of dumb kids." Ian doesn't look amused. "They'll find it you know."

"So?" David's lip curls up in a half smirk, unconcerned over the possibility of their childhood secret being discovered.

"What if they figure out we were there?" Ian's forehead crinkles with the worry plaguing him. He can't help it. He grew up scared of being blamed for it; the memory of it tormenting his sleep and turning dreams into nightmares.

"What if they think we had something to do with it?" he asks.

"We didn't. We were just a bunch of kids. Nobody would suspect kids." David shrugs and sighs. "Besides, they don't put kids in jail."

Ian chuckles. It is an unsure and nervous sound. "Yeah, but we sure thought they would."

"Yeah."

Ian looks at his brother with a dark look. "But they could now, couldn't they?"

"They wouldn't. We were just kids then. Besides we didn't do anything. We just found it."

"It could have been us," Ian presses. He can't shake the hollow fear that filled him the moment he saw that billboard sign near the turn off to the old Mill Road announcing the coming new development.

"It could have been anybody," David says. He doesn't want to talk about this anymore. He wishes Ian would just drop it.

"We were there. We didn't tell anyone." Ian looks tired, almost sick. "Hell, man, it was just a kid."

They are interrupted by a crashing through the bush. Both men turn to look in the direction of the noise.

Ian looks startled, like he might flee at any moment.

"They're here," David says.

Ian shakes his head, a puzzled look on his face.

"It's the wrong direction. Why would they be coming through the woods?"

4 - Nick's Return

The deafening growl of the large machines scraping away at the raw open wounds in the earth do not drown out the sharp cracks of trees being violently crushed and their sturdy trunks snapping as they are torn down by heavy machinery. Their large treads leave deep patterns in the damp hard-packed mud as they trundle about, unstoppable. The background noise of chainsaws and large mallets used to cut taller trees down can barely be heard in the cacophony.

A dented white trailer sits parked haphazardly on the grass at the edge of the black scraped ground. A hastily crafted makeshift boardwalk, two rows of two by four planks laid end to end, lies mud-spattered across the black expanse of raw mud extending from the trailer to a grassy area populated by thin mostly dead trampled long grass where an assortment of trucks and cars are parked.

On the edge of this parking area a group of middle-aged and greying suited men stand around looking important, waving and pointing at the construction area with what looks like rolled plans and blueprints in their hands. A couple of them are even wearing hard hats, an unnecessary accessory since they won't get close enough to dirty their nicely pressed suits and fine leather dress shoes, let alone risk bumping their well-coiffed heads.

One of the suited men pauses, looking hard at a young man driving a bulldozer across the field. The machine lurches in jerking lumbering movements like the operator is drunk or a child.

"Say, isn't that Rueben's boy?" he asks no one in particular.

The man beside him stares at the driver, thinking.

"Yes. Yes, I think it is," he says. "What was his name again?"

"Wow, I haven't seen them in years," the first man says. "Nicholas or Nick, I think. They moved away, didn't they?"

"Or ran away," the second man chortles. "I heard there were some problems with the wife's brother."

They are brought back to the conversation at hand by the others of their group, planning the construction of the new development on the old Mill Road.

*****

The young man driving the bulldozer is unaware of the men's sudden interest in him. He keeps glancing at the woods bordering the field they are tearing apart.

"I never understood why my family packed a few bags and left after a phone call interrupted dinner that night."

Nick focuses his attention back on the tractor, the engine growling and the gears grinding as he shifts them, changes direction, and presses forward with the blade scraping a fresh raw wound into the ground. The top layer of grass and soil wrinkles and gives, being scooped up against the dozer blade to slough off to one side in a crumpled broken ridge of ruined mud and grass. He looks at the woods again.

It had been a strange day that day twelve years ago.

He vaguely remembers discovering something bad in the woods with his sister and their friends as a kid. He doesn't remember what they found, but he does remember the police coming to the house, his dad yelling a lot at everybody, his mother crying, and his sister's very strange behaviour.

"I can't explain why, but I don't think we ever told anyone what we found. I only remember that something happened, not what was said or what happened."

Nick's memory is more a grainy impression than a real memory, lost along with so many other memories to time and the confusion of a child's mind.

Even now, his dreams are haunted by hazy images that mean nothing to him; disgusting insects crawling through moss and dead leaves rotting in the dark woods, a face that looks strangely soft and putty-like; a face that is not really a face. A face that is not all there, like it was in the process of being made or un-made by a special effects creator. The face would call his name, its dead eyes weeping, mouth twisted in a grimace of pain and fear.

This is why Nick came back.

He stops the tractor, putting it in reverse, and turning it. The machine bounces and jogs over the rough ground made rougher by his inexperienced work. He stops the tractor, looking at his handiwork, the ruined ground ahead of him, hoping no one notices what a mess he's making of it.

The woods pull at his attention again.

"Something happened to my family that day; something that changed them forever. I'm not sure what, but I know something terrible lies hidden in the woods along the old Mill Road."

He vaguely remembers a silent pact of secrecy made by frightened children, a pact his sister's haunted eyes staring back at him every time he looked at her never let him forget. Whatever it was it had to remain a secret. He could not remember what that secret was and could never bring himself to ask Felicia. Whatever it was, it had tormented her every day since.

When he learned of the development being built in the area, he once again tossed a hastily packed bag in the car and drove. It was not hard to get a job on one of the work crews. Workers were being brought in from all over for this project. They did not even bother to check his background. Otherwise, they would have known he lied about his training and experience when they hired him. Harder, was trying to drive a bulldozer he lied about knowing how to drive.

"Hey!"

The angry yell snaps Nick's attention back. He stops the machine, the tractor rocking with the sudden jolt, and looks.

"You almost ran me over!"

"Sorry," Nick calls down, looking startled. He nods his hat to the man below.

The guy glares at him, shaking his head in disgust as he walks away.

Nick puts the tractor in motion again. He works the blade, the blade's awkward jerky motions making the whole tractor rock, positions it too high, and starts the forward motion again, doing a poor job of scraping away the top later of earth.

*****

A man stands at the edge of the woods some distance away from where the heavy machinery is tearing the woods apart to make way for the development. He is skinny, worn, and weathered looking, dressed in old clothing that are as old in style as they are in wear. He has the look of a grizzled man who has seen too much, his age lost somewhere in the years of unpleasant experiences. His long greying hair and beard only make him look scruffier.

No one notices him standing in the shadows of the trees.

He watches the young man driving the bulldozer with obvious inexperience. He sees the two suited men take notice of the young man and tenses as he watches them, knowing they are talking about the young man. He relaxes when they return to their conversation with the other suited men, ignoring the young man again.

He backs away, melting into the woods, and vanishes.

5 - Something in the Woods

David and Ian run hard down the overgrown long unused road leading away from the old abandoned train station, their breath coming in ragged gasps, legs aching from the effort, faces pinched with strain and fear.

They are so absorbed in the effort of running that they do not notice the approaching car ahead of them.

It is an older car, well used, and looks filled to capacity with young men. Music blares from it and its tires crunch on the broken chunks cracked out of the old road that has not been maintained since the train station it serviced was abandoned. The car stops ahead of them and waits for the running men.

David and Ian almost run headlong into the front grill, Ian dodging it last minute while David puts his hands out and deflects off the hood. He gives the occupants a grin and raises his arms over his head in victory, pretending it was on purpose.

The men inside the car laugh at the two brothers.

"What are you running from?" the driver asks, leaning out his window to address the two out-of-breath men.

The brothers look at each other, trying to catch their breath. David leans on the car and Ian bends over and grasps his legs to keep himself standing.

"What (gasp) the hell (gasp) was that?" Ian asks between ragged gasps for air. You can hear the strain of fear in his voice, although he tried to hide it.

"Bear?" David gasps. His voice holds the tension of fear too, but not as much. He is not just older; he has always been braver and more reckless than Ian too.

Ian shakes his head. "That was no bear," he puffs.

"You being chased by monsters?" the driver, Mike, laughs at them. The others in the car laugh too.

"Oooo, the old Mill Road Monster is going to get you," Mike moans in his best spooky voice.

This makes everyone in the car laugh harder.

Ian and David give Mike an unimpressed look.

They have all heard the same tales as kids. Tales they told each other in the darkened corners of rotting abandoned outbuildings, trying to outdo scaring the wits out of each other.

There is one story that has been told for generations, of a strange and frightening creature living in the woods. Those woods border the old Mill Road for miles past the old mill that gave the road its unofficial name on one side and the train tracks and the abandoned train station's long unused road on another. This creature is rumoured to be the cause of the occasional mysterious disappearance of pets, farm animals, backpackers, campers, and children.

Disappearances in the area are uncommon, but that did not stop the stories. One such story is that the strange creature and some rather brutal unexplained deaths at the mill just off the old Mill Road are the reason the mill was abandoned many years ago.

The rear car door nearest to David and Ian swings open with a grinding squeal and the young man who opened it leans out with a grin.

"Are you coming?" he asks.

These young men are who David and Ian were waiting for at the old train station. Men they grew up with. This is going to be a typical day in a small town with nothing better for the young men to do than hang out and maybe get into a little trouble.

The brothers get in, wedging themselves into the already overpopulated car, relieved to be getting out of there.

"Where are we going?" David asks.

"Down to the old Mill Road," Mike calls back over his shoulder as he guns the engine, turning the car around too fast in the narrow roadway. "We're going to go check out the construction going on down there."

Ian looks back the way they came, still unnerved by the noises they heard in the woods.

6 - What I Found

Tractors growl as they prowl the construction site, clearing and digging. They stopped clearing away trees to expand the field further into the woods for the time being, waiting for the surveyors to mark the way deeper into the trees. The first thing they need to do is rough in the sewer and water lines, while surveyors stake out where other things are to go. The men and machines work around each other, always conscious of the fragility of the soft bodies and danger of the hulking metal machines.

Two men are surveying the next section to be cleared ahead of the tractors that will tear out more trees and bush. They will be added to the growing pile pushed in a line on one side of the construction site awaiting removal.

One surveyor stands across the field with his tripod while the other steps over rough ground of raw mud to the line of trees, carrying a long pole. When he reaches the trees, he stops and gets his bearings, moving when his partner signals that he is not in the right spot. He moves step by step, watching his partner across the field, stopping when he gets the nod telling him he is in the right place.

With one final look back at his partner, he turns and steps past the boundary line where the woods dare not encroach on the field lest the farmer who once ploughed it tear down the wayward plants beneath the turning blades of his tractor.

He moves on, step after step, the trees closing around him dampening the sounds of construction. He pauses to look behind him to make sure his path is straight and true and is half surprised he can still see his partner and the moving tractors through the trees.

"Funny how things get more quiet the moment you step into the trees," he says, thinking how it almost feels like he just stepped into another world, one that is separate from the one where the construction is going on only a few yards away.

It's like looking through a window.

He spies one tractor moving amateurishly at the hands of the driver and shakes his head wryly.

"Where do they get these guys?"

His partner's waving arm catches his attention and he waves back. His partner is impatiently waving him to keep going further into the trees.

He nods. "Good, he can still see me." He moves deeper into the woods. He turns again, walking backwards to keep an eye on his partner's signal and to make sure he can still see him.

There, the signal to stop. He stops and stands his pole on the ground. Grasping it with both hands, he pushes down, working it into the previously untouched earth. The ground is hard, matted with decades of roots and grass.

He shifts his weight, drawing one foot back to step back and get better leverage, and immediately feels the pressure on his heel.

His eyes widen just a little, knowing immediately that he has snagged his foot on something, putting him off balance. His first instinct is to grip the pole for support to stop from falling.

It is useless. The pole barely pierced the surface of the ground. There is no steadying support there.

Still gripping the useless pole, he feels himself tilting unavoidably backwards, unable to right himself. He twists his body, reacting without any thought except, *I'm falling.*

The momentary vertigo is disquieting.

He hits with a softer impact than he expected, the sponginess of the ground a relief, landing on the rotting remains of a large tree that is slowly melting into the earth where it lays. His head is lower than his body, lying sprawled over the fallen tree.

He looks around to get his bearings. Ferns and other undergrowth grow up around the tree as if seeking to hide it. It is mostly branchless; just a few rough stumps sticking out where the largest branches once extended from the trunk. The ground beneath is uneven and he wonders with relief at how he missed landing on the two large rocks.

"If I fell on those, I could have seriously injured my back."

He looks down, or rather up at the odd angle he lays in, at his body. Termites are swarming in a frenzy at the sudden disturbance of their home, crawling crazily over him. His first thought is that they are ants and he starts slapping at himself, naively afraid of being bitten. He rolls partially to get his hands under him, squirming to reposition himself to get to his feet.

"What the hell?"

Something lays in the concave dip of a hollow in the ground almost beneath the tree.

He manages to sit up, still twisting his body to reposition himself so he can stand, eyes glued to the almost unrecognizable thing.

He examines it, drawn to solving the puzzle of what this thing is.

"Dead animal," he mutters, feeling a mix of interest and disgust at the decomposed remains that are so close to his face.

Two small bones are all that are left of the smaller bones; bare of flesh and with the appearance of having been nibbled on. The mass seems to have partially become one with the ground. Mostly it is curled in on itself like a sleeping animal curled for warmth. In the mass he can make out bare yellowed bones, a few bits of flesh at the joints and beneath skin that tightened and discoloured as it mummified. It has been ravaged by scavengers, the perfect symmetry of the remaining bones ruined, half of them missing and some pulled away, dropped where the thief left them when startled into bolting without its meal.

He wrinkles his nose at it. It has the unpleasant odour of very old garbage left to rot. It has rotten past the putrefaction stage, most of the remaining soft tissue having liquefied and seeped into the ground, but his imagination fills in the details of what he thinks it smells like.

He wonders at the other substance. Fur? Some kind of hair? No, it doesn't look like fur or hair.

He realizes with a sick feeling.

Cloth. Rotting cloth; or what is left of it. It looks brittle, like the slightest touch would dissolve it into powder.

He gets to his feet, taking a step back. He looks over the bones again, now seeing it for the first time.

They are human. Small.

A child, his now panicked mind flashes the thought at him and it feels like a rude intrusion.

He looks around, needing to confirm. He roots through the rotted leaves, ferns, moss, and other low growing plants.

He finds it. A child sized human skull.

It hits him like a sledgehammer blow to the stomach, even though he already knew. He has found the long-abandoned remains of a child. What he does not know is that it is in the exact spot four children found a similar body years ago.

Afraid to leave it, worried he won't find it again but afraid to stay near it as if death might somehow be contagious, he hesitates uncertainly. Picking up his fallen surveyor pole, he jabs it into the ground near his grisly find and makes his way back to the field.

He breaches the line between forest and field and an uneasy relief floods over him. He half hopes it will somehow prove to be some kind of weird trick.

His partner is still standing at his tripod, looking at him with annoyance and wondering what the heck is going on.

He ignores him, moving along the flatter ground running parallel to the woods while he can and cutting across the rough ground when he has to, stumbling over the rough ruts left by the tractors. He heads towards the trailer office and haphazardly parked workers' vehicles.

He is halfway there when he spies the foreman across the field.

With a heavy resignation, he changes direction, heading for him. Across the field his partner is trying to signal to him, but he is oblivious, his focus only on that foreman.

The foreman turns to him when he reaches him.

"What's up?" Duane asks, frowning at the disturbed look on the surveyor's face. His first thought is that he found something, that their stakes have been moved and they just wasted days digging in the wrong places. Sometimes that happens on a jobsite, usually the victim of restless kids.

"I have to tell you something," the surveyor says, "in private."

Duane shrugs and motions him to the trailer across the field. They head for the trailer, the surveyor keeping a three-foot distance from the foreman as if it will somehow protect him from what he found.

After a brief moment inside the trailer the two men exit, retracing the surveyor's previous trip to the woods. His partner watches them with confusion.

With the surveyor uncertainly leading the way, they make their way in until they find the fallen tree, the surveyor pole marking its location.

"There," the surveyor says, hoping the foreman finds nothing. Right now he would rather the embarrassment of being made to look like a fool than to have what he found confirmed by another.

Duane walks closer to the pole, studying the ground.

"There's nothing there." He turns and looks at the surveyor with an unhappy look. "Is this a joke? It's sick, buddy, if it is."

Heat rushes through the surveyor and a flush rises in his pale cheeks.

"What? How?" he manages. He half steps, half stumbles forward, his legs feeling like wood logs. He is relieved, afraid, and shocked all at once.

How did he not see it? he thinks. *It was right there. Did I imagine it?*

He walks close to the downed tree, standing next to the foreman and not seeing anything.

"I don't understand," his voice comes out weak and shaky.

He just stands there, paralyzed in the moment, and then manages to make himself move. He walks around the tree with dread pouring into his stomach like a ball filling with ice cold water.

The sight shocks him just as much this time as it did the first. He stares, his expression troubled and face paling with a grey pallor.

Duane shrugs and follows him, walking around to the other side of the fallen tree. He looks down and feels the tightness grip his stomach. He grits his teeth and shows little other reaction.

He nods. "Ok, let's go back."

The surveyor looks at him, thinking, *That's it?*

The two men walk back out of the woods in silence, each lost in his own thoughts.

Had Nick seen the two men going into the woods, he might have watched with a tense sense of unease. But he was too busy struggling with the controls of a tractor he does not know how to operate.

They reach the trailer that serves as an office.

"Go sit in the trailer until you collect yourself, then go home," Duane says.

"Are you shutting the site down?"

Duane looks around at the men and tractors working. If there was anything resembling evidence, it's long gone. Besides, the body has obviously been there for a long time and scavenged by animals and birds.

"No. I'll call the cops after we shut down for the day. Might as well not lose an extra day's work if they shut the whole site down."

The surveyor retreats to the office and Duane looks out over his domain.

He is in charge of the site, the men and equipment, and making sure the job comes in as close to on time and on budget as he can. He has a sense he should be worried about the delay this will cause, but he isn't, not very much anyway.

I grew up in this town, he thinks. I grew up hearing all the rumours and the old stories kids tell each other to scare the wits out of each other. Like everyone who grew up here, I grew up hearing the stories about the old abandoned mill down this road; stories of a monster living in these woods and of kids and pets vanishing, their remains found years or even decades later, if they are ever found at all, victims of the old Mill Road monster.

*****

Acting Sergeant Malcolm Colbert's police car dash radio crackles to life.

"We have human remains at the construction site on Road Three Fifty-Seven." The dispatcher's voice is crackled and tinny. "We need a car to attend to the scene."

Malcolm abandons his pursuit of dinner and turns the car around. He picks up the radio, talking into the handset.

"Acting Sergeant Malcolm Colbert here. I'm on it."

"Fire and ambulance will meet you there," the radio crackles and goes silent. Dispatching a fire truck and ambulance is a precaution in case the person is not dead.

*****

Malcolm arrives at the jobsite before the ambulance and fire truck that are each coming from different nearby towns where they are housed. He drives across the field to the temporary trailer that acts as a site office.

A man sitting outside the office waiting watches the squad car bounce over the rough ground and tire tracks of the workers' vehicles meandering through the grass.

Malcolm parks on the grass next to the trailer and a lone truck and gets out of the car, walking over to the foreman. They exchange nods and first name greetings.

"Malcolm."

"Duane."

"So, where's the body?" Malcolm asks.

"In the woods," Duane says, thumbing the direction behind him.

"Lead the way."

It takes only minutes to arrive at the spot, but it feels interminably long to Duane. He stops short of the fallen tree.

"There."

"I don't see anything," Malcolm says.

"It's on the other side."

Malcolm walks around the fallen tree, half expecting it to be a joke. He is sure he would have seen any body lying on the ground by now.

Malcolm stops on the other side and studies the ground. It takes a moment to see it, the body blending into the low ground vegetation and rotting leaves.

The cadaver, what is left of it, is small and curled up into a foetal position as if trying to find warmth in the last moment of life.

He is not entirely sure it is human. He has seen plenty of pictures but has not seen human bones up close and in person before.

"You sure this is human?"

"Look under those leaves," Duane points.

Malcolm uses his foot to push the leaves back, not wanting to touch anything just in case.

There, nestled beneath the safety of the leaves, is a child-sized human skull.

"It's a person," he says unnecessarily.

Malcolm is unaffected by the whole thing. The bones are old, what little flesh remaining having become one with the ground beneath it.

"Whoever it is, this kid has been here for a very long time."

He thinks back, not remembering anyone reported missing in the area. He would have remembered a kid being reported missing.

He nods. "Okay, let's go."

They both start back to the open field.

"Won't be needing that ambulance," Malcolm mutters. "It doesn't matter. It's policy."

The ambulance and fire truck will come and they will pronounce the obvious, he thinks, calling the details in to a doctor to give them the verdict on the victim's living status over the phone. Then they will leave, but I'll be stuck sitting here waiting for the coroner to come remove the body. There will be a perfunctory crime scene investigation. But from the look of it, this crime scene is years old and likely won't reveal anything except maybe some scat from whatever scavengers fed on the bones recently.

They arrive back at the trailer.

"You go on home," Malcolm says. "I'll have a car come around and take your statement."

Duane nods, grateful to not be stuck here waiting too. He gets in his truck and leaves before Malcolm can change his mind.

Malcolm opens the cruiser trunk to get the roll of yellow police tape, walks back across the raw ruined ground, and starts wrapping and unrolling the police tape across the tree line, blocking the area off at the edge of the woods.

He hasn't eaten in hours and the sooner this gets done, the sooner he can eat. His stomach growls at him unhappily at the thought of the food it is missing.

The ambulance arrives first, and Malcolm leads them across the rough ground to the body, where they pronounce the child dead via a cell phone call with a doctor in the next town before the fire truck arrives on scene.

Their job done, the rest of the first responders are free to go. Malcolm walks back to the vehicles with them.

"Are you in for a long wait?" one of the paramedics asks.

"Could be. The coroner has gone home for the day by now. Bringing her back would be a call back. They'd have to pay overtime. I might have to get you to bring me a sandwich," Malcolm chuckles.

He watches the ambulance and fire truck drive away then gets into his car.

"Time to start the waiting game."

He picks up the radio and calls in, signing on with his car number.

"One deceased confirmed. Fire and ambulance have left the scene. The scene is very cold, years old. Do you have an E. T. A. on the coroner?"

"The coroner's gone home," the voice crackles at him from the radio. "I requested a call back, but it was denied. You won't be seeing her until the morning."

Malcolm's gut grumbles hungrily again. He looks down at it, rubbing it to try to silence its protest.

"Are there any cars free? Anyone who can relieve me for an hour to get something to eat?"

"Sorry. The queue is full. If anything else comes up tonight we're going to have to ask for a loaner. I'll try to send someone your way as soon as a car comes available."

"Can you bring me a sandwich?"

"You know I can't leave the switchboard."

Malcolm sighs heavily and replaces the radio to its holder.

With a frown, he settles himself in his car for the long night of waiting and watching what might be a years old crime scene. He has to slap himself a few times, get out to stretch and walk around a bit, trying not to doze as he sits there alone in his car through the night with his unhappy stomach grumbling at its hunger.

Across the field yellow police tape ruffles in the breeze, draped and ugly, marking off the area where field meets forest at the edge of the construction site. It was put up hastily. Everything had been done hastily after the events of a few hours ago.

7 - Suspicion

David and Ian sit together at a worn table in the dimly lit beer parlor, the only one in their little town. Dusty's is a throwback to an earlier time, the décor having never been updated in the decades of its existence. Glasses of draft beer on the table between them catch the light, making it seem brighter within the confines of the golden liquid.

The group dispersed hours ago.

"I just can't believe it," David says, "little Nicky, here."

"And working at the site of the new development on the old Mill Road," Ian finishes for him.

They recognized Nick almost immediately when they saw him working at the construction site.

"Do you think he remembers?" Ian asks.

David shakes his head thoughtfully, his eyes lowered against his own memories trying to peer out through them.

"He was the youngest. Maybe. Probably not. They moved away. It's pretty easy to forget when you aren't around a thing."

"Do you think it's just a coincidence then?" Ian asks. "He suddenly shows up, there of all places, when they start tearing the woods apart?"

"I always wondered what happened to them," David says, his eyes getting a far away look.

"When did they move away?" Ian asks. He searches his memory but cannot remember.

"That next night; the day after we found it in the woods," David says. He stares at his beer as if it somehow holds the past like a crystal ball. He remembers that hollow feeling of loss when he discovered his friends' house empty of all signs of life and the sick feeling that something was terribly wrong all those years ago.

His first thought was that whoever or whatever had done that to that kid saw them in the woods the day before. That he, or it or whatever it was, had gotten them and that he, Ian, and their family would be next.

Rumours flourished in the weeks that followed, but no one actually knew what happened to Felicia and Nick's family. They just vanished. They never came back for their belongings and, after a while, the house and its contents were quietly sold off.

At times over the years he even crazily thought that maybe the monster that was supposed to live in the woods down by the old mill is real. That it got Felicia and her family. Of course, it's not and it didn't. It's just old stories kids tell to scare each other like Scary Mary coming out of the mirror.

"She came to the house after school the day after we found it," David continues. "She was crying. She said everyone in her house went crazy, that the cops were there. She was scared. They never came to school the next day."

His eyes look hollow now, as if he'd lost something from sight long ago and has been looking for it ever since.

It is a look Ian hasn't seen in his older brother's eyes in a long time. David is always so confident and unconcerned about everything, unlike himself who is a worrier and tends to second-guess everything.

David's reaction to thinking about Felicia makes Nick wonder if that confidence is nothing more than a shell David hides behind.

"I went to their house after school," David says, his voice almost catching as the emotion fills him like it is happening all over again. "They were gone. It was like they just vanished or were taken or something. Dinner was still on the table." He pauses. "I remember that. I'll always remember that. Dinner was still on the table."

He looks up at Ian now and Ian can see the torment in his brother's eyes.

It's the same look he came home with as a boy when he walked into the house two days after their discovery in the woods, the day he learned Felicia and Nick's family left. David had just been really quiet and it scared Ian. Finally, that night he told Ian what was wrong, about Felicia and Ian's house and how it seemed as if they had just been suddenly taken by aliens in the middle of eating supper. Vanished in the middle of living.

They both thought immediately of their secret then, the thing in the woods, but did not say so to each other.

They never said so to each other, but they just knew; they had a pact of secrecy never to talk about it, not even to each other. And they never did, until now.

David and Ian both look down at their beers, needing to look away from each other.

"I always thought you'd marry her when we grew up," Ian says.

They both lapse into silence.

Someone enters the bar. The brothers look up to see who it is. Their faces change, brightening somewhat, when they recognize the face that has changed so much over the years and yet stayed much the same.

"Hey! Nicky! Nick!" David calls, waving him over.

The young man turns, squinting to see who is calling him, his eyes not yet adjusted to the dim interior after the bright sun.

"Hey," he calls back, waving back at them, approaching uncertainly.

These guys seem to know him, but Nick does not know who they are. It is that awkward moment when you know the other expects you to remember them, but your mind just draws a complete blank.

"Come, sit down," David waves him to sit. "What brought you back after all these years?" Something in David's friendly expression is off, guarded.

"Work," Nick says as he joins them.

He tries to place their faces, their voices. A sense of familiarity is coming to him. The hair color of the one who called him over, his lazy half grin that suggests he is up for getting into any kind of trouble. The familial resemblance between the two and the other's quiet observation of everything around him like he prefers to thoughtfully observe rather than actively participate, teases at his memory.

David looks around, catches the waitress's eye, and signals her to bring another round of draughts for the table.

"Just going where the work is, eh?" David says.

"That's about it," Nick answers, studying his long-ago friend as if his face might give up some deep secret.

Too many years have passed. Nick was too young and the years and his mind's need to protect itself had melted away too many of his childhood memories. He just is not breaking through that barrier to place who these two young men are.

Nick was the youngest of the group, him and Ian playing together while his sister Felicia and David were friends. Felicia and David's was that complicated kind of friendship of the older siblings, pushed together to keep an eye on their younger brothers, finally becoming friends and confidants while David secretly crushed on Felicia and she wisely ignored her knowledge of that crush.

Forced together, all four became friends despite the age difference that is small now that they finally breached that barrier into adulthood but seemed like an enormous gulf of time as kids.

"Hey, look who's here," a voice calls from across the room. All three young men turn to look at a figure shuffling towards them from the shadows beyond the end of the bar lined with bar stools. It is an older man, accustomed to spending a great deal of time here and somewhat inebriated.

"Little Nick," he slurs, clapping the young man loudly on the back. He cocks his head at him. "You're not old enough to drink, are you?" he slurs with a wink, whispering too loudly.

Nick glances quickly at the waitress as if she might actually kick him out if she overheard.

"It's all right," David smirks at Nick's anxious look. "This is Dusty's; it doesn't matter if you are legal. Dusty's doesn't kick out paying customers, even if they are under-aged."

Nick nods at him with a slightly sickly grin. He heard as much from a few of the work crew at the construction site but was sceptical of its truth.

"Your family move back?" the drunk asks.

"No, I'm just here for work. I got a job on that construction project up the old Mill Road; then I'll be moving on."

"Un," the drunk grunts. "Always wondered what happened to the lot of you after that trouble with your uncle. What was his name?"

"Harvey."

"Yeah, ol' Uncle Harvey."

"What trouble?" David asks, his expression unreadable.

Nick shakes his head, holding his silence.

"He just got out of jail back then, s'what I heard," the drunk tells them. "Killed some kid. Got off light because they couldn't prove it wasn't an accident. But we all know he did it. Didn't get enough time for it s'far as I'm concerned." He glares around the room as if Uncle Harvey might appear at any moment.

"Heard he was skulking around your house making trouble. Ol' Joe said he hit your mom, threatened her or somethin' the night your family packed up and left."

David studies Nick's face, watching it work.

Nick's face twitches with the effort of holding something back.

David exchanges a meaningful glance with Ian, a look that Nick catches and is not happy about. He wonders what they know that he does not.

Nick is stunned by the old drunk's revelation.

Uncle Harvey killed a kid? he thinks. He is a bad man, volatile and dangerous. But, to kill a kid? Is it true? If it is, this is the first I heard of it.

Uncle Harvey always terrified him.

There has always been rumours about Uncle Harvey, Nick thinks. He was more than the black sheep of the family; he was the wolf in sheep's clothing. Hushed whispers were exchanged in quiet corners when they thought no one was around to hear. It has always been said that there was something wrong inside of Uncle Harvey. Something broken and sick in a way that he was not to be pitied like you are supposed to with the mentally ill, but that he was to be despised and avoided.

No, I don't believe it, Nick thinks. He cannot let himself believe it. Even crazy Uncle Harvey could not be that bad. That would mean I'm related to a child killer. What would that say about me?

Nick turns his attention to his two new acquaintances.

These guys know me, but I don't know who they are, he thinks. They look the right ages, so I probably went to school with them, maybe even played and hung out with them. They know something they aren't saying, and I'm pretty sure it's about me and my family.

Their familiarity comes into focus and some broken memories come back to him, memories of playing with a friend, Felicia following along grudgingly and angry about always having to watch him, and the other boy who hung around with them. He was older and hung out more with Felicia than with him and the other boy.

He looks at the brothers and finally sees the resemblance to those boys in the young men. Their names come to him, Ian and David, but it comes with a feeling of unease.

They never left, he thinks, so maybe they know the secret that haunted Felicia all these years and made my family move so suddenly we didn't even take time to pack. Maybe they know the secret in the woods. He looks down, keeping these thoughts to himself. Maybe they were the other kids in the pact of secrecy I only vaguely remember. I need to find out, but right now I need to get out of here so I can think.

"Look," Nick says, getting up from his chair too quickly to be casual, "I've got to go."

"We'll come with you," David says, getting up to follow.

Nick is not happy about this.

I have to talk to these guys if I'm going to learn anything, but right now I need to be alone, he thinks. I need to digest everything.

Nick walks out without waiting, hoping David and Ian will just let him go. David follows on his heels. Ian jogs to catch up after hurriedly tossing some money on the table to pay the bill.

David catches up to Nick before he reaches the door and follows him out. He comes in close to Nick as soon as they are outside, putting himself into Nick's personal space, slinging one arm around Nick's neck in a rough familiar hug and pulling him closer, dragging him along with him as he walks at a fast pace to put off Ian catching up to them.

The rough gesture makes Nick feel threatened.

"Do you remember?" David whispers harshly to Nick, putting his mouth next to his ear so Ian won't hear as he tries to catch up.

"What?" Nick pulls back, trying unsuccessfully to pull free without making a scene.

David holds him firm.

"You know what," he hisses. David is not buying Nick's confusion. "That day in the woods off the old Mill Road."

David releases him and they stop and stare at each other, a stare-down to see who will win where there can be no winner.

Ian catches up to them, immediately sensing the tension between them. He stands back a few paces uncertainly, watching the tense standoff and wondering what is going on.

"I don't know what you're talking about," Nick insists.

"It's no coincidence you suddenly appear when they start digging up the woods, and working on the jobsite." David's stance is accusing.

"What are you here for?" he demands. "Are you trying to find it?" He stares at Nick, feeling that he is keeping something very important a secret. "To expose your uncle or to protect him?"

"You don't know anything," Nick mutters, getting angry.

Exactly what is David accusing me of? he wonders.

"No, I don't," David spits. "All I know is that my friend and her family vanish after we find a dead kid in the woods, nobody would tell me anything, and suddenly you come back years later when the body is sure to be found." He glares at the younger man, breathing heavily, ready to pounce on him and pound the answers out of him.

The anger over the pain and feeling of abandonment so long ago comes rushing back over David. They did not even take time to pack, to sell the house ... to say goodbye.

Nick's mind whirls at breakneck speed. He tries to see the memory that David's words should have brought but cannot.

Was that what we found in the woods? A dead kid? We found a dead kid? Is that what the old drunk was talking about? But my uncle was in jail then, wasn't he? He was released after we moved, wasn't he?

He feels the urge to shake his head to clear the confusion and fights it.

Didn't that drunk guy say Uncle Harvey just got out of jail for killing a kid? He thinks. If that's what we found in the woods, it couldn't have been the same kid my uncle was accused of killing.

"So why did you come back Nick?" David asks again, staring at him intently.

David is pressing him for an answer and not allowing him time to think. He needs to think, to process this. He has no idea what to say.

"Come on David, just leave him alone." Ian tries to pull David away.

"Fine!" Nick snaps at David, blurting it out without knowing what is going to come out of his mouth. "Yes, I'm here to find the body if that's what it is, before anyone else does. I'm here to find it and get rid of it. Maybe if I get rid of it everything will be ok again. It has never been okay. Nothing has been okay since that day."

Nick's mind keeps working wildly. He has no idea what he just said, his mind caught up in trying to remember something, anything, about what happened so long ago.

A body? He thinks, still trying to process it. We found a body in the woods and that was the secret that haunted Felicia all these years?

What did David mean when he asked if I'm trying to find it? Does that mean whatever we found then is still there? That we left it in the woods?

I've always known Felicia knew more about whatever happened than she let on, although she always denied it, saying she didn't remember or that nothing happened. But I always knew she knew more. It was in her eyes.

After a while, Nick gave up asking and could only watch her suffer in silence.

David stares at him in a mixture of contempt and need.

"Felicia," David asks, "how does she feel about all this?"

Nick shifts his stance as if getting ready to make a break for freedom. He looks at David again, trying to figure out what he just said. He didn't quite hear the question.

"I've always wondered all these years," David continues, his anger melting away to leave him feeling suddenly exhausted at the thought of Felicia. "She took it harder than all of us when we found the body. Where is she? How is she doing?"

He studies Nick, noting how edgy he is.

Now Nick knows what David asked. He was asking about Felicia.

"She's fine. She's around, not here." Nick's eyes shift as if he is worried someone might overhear them.

"What happened?" David presses. He feels the need to know like a physical force. "All those years ago, when your family disappeared, where'd you go? Why?"

"We just moved, that's it, we moved." Nick is being defensive. He is on edge and becoming more so with the questioning.

A group of young men passing by them stops and calls out to them.

"Hey, did you hear?"

"What?" David turns to them, calling back.

"A body's just been found up at the old Mill Road construction site, a kid or something."

Nick's face pales.

Ian blanches, turning to David for support.

David clenches his jaw, thinking.

David and Ian are thinking the same thing, *Is it THE body?*

Nick is unable to think at this point. He is still trying to process and make sense of what he just learned, and the passerby's words have not sunk in yet.

News in small towns travels faster than the news happens. At that moment, a police cruiser pulls up beside them. The driver's window rolls down and the occupant leans out casually.

"Hey, you're Nick, right? Know where your uncle is?" he asks Nick, "Your Uncle Harvey?"

"Why?" Nick asks with a tremor in his voice.

"No reason," the officer says, "just looking for him."

The officer does not have to tell him. He knows. The words of the young man moments ago do not sink in; they come crashing down on him.

A body has just been found up at the old Mill Road construction site, a kid or something.

Nick knows they would have found something incriminating with the body. Either that or they suspect Uncle Harvey just because he is Uncle Harvey. He remembers Uncle Harvey, although he has not seen him in years. It is one memory from his childhood he could not forget. His mind clung to it, vivid and living. He still scares him after all these years.

Why is the officer asking as if I might have seen him? he thinks. Is it a dig? Why would they think Uncle Harvey would have come back here with me? Why would they think he would come back at all? This is the last place my uncle would ever go if he went to jail for killing a kid. Everyone knows your face in a small community. People never forgive child killers.

The cruiser's radio crackles to life with the news that Harvey has been located and brought in for questioning. The low volume is audible only to the officer in the car, not to the men standing outside it.

"I'll see you boys around," the officer says meaningfully, staring directly at Nick. He drives away.

David turns back to Nick, studying him.

"So, old Uncle Harv maybe is the one that killed that kid we found all those years ago," David says to him. The statement is so loaded it is dripping with unsaid meaning.

There is something in Nick's look that tells David he is hiding something about his Uncle Harvey. As kids, Nick never could keep a secret. His face always gave him away. Apparently, it still does.

What are you hiding? David wonders to himself.

"Look, I really have to go," Nick says. He turns and walks away, ignoring their calls to come back.

"He's hiding something," David says. "He knows something he's not telling us."

Ian shrugs.

"Why is this bothering you so much, David? Why do you need to dig it all up again? I'd rather it stay buried and not have to think about it."

"I'm going to find out what it is," David declares.

"Well, I'll see you later," Ian says and turns to go home.

"Later." David just stands there watching Nick go.

8 - Memory Lane

Nick is torn. Part of him is telling him to go back. David and Ian have answers. But he does not know what questions to ask.

He walks fast, thinking, not paying attention to where he is going. The only thing he knows is that he does not want to go home.

Home is not even a home. His childhood home here had been sold years ago.

For now, with nowhere to go and little money, he is sleeping in his car. Even that feels like a safe refuge right now.

It is also utterly depressing, isolating.

I wonder what the house looks like, Nick thinks.

Without thought to where he's going or his intentions, he finds himself taking a walk down memory lane. He wanders the town with an address in his head until he finds it, his old childhood home.

He had to look up the address before coming because he did not remember it.

Finding the address, Nick stops and stands there, staring at the house. Nothing about it is familiar. It jogs no memories.

He tries his best to remember what happened when he was just a kid. Nothing comes.

"Is it the right house? Thirty-two Galving Road. The address is right. Is the house wrong? The house is brown. Should it be blue?"

A memory teases at the back of his mind but will not come.

"Wasn't there a swing set?"

Nick looks at the house for any signs anyone is home. It appears to be abandoned, temporarily at least. He walks around to the unfenced backyard and sees only a tired looking birdbath and a bunch of tall flowering plants that look more like weeds gone wild than flowers to him.

He walks right up to the house. He feels in the back of his mind that this might not be the right thing to do, that whoever lives here now might be creeped out by this. It does not stop him.

Nick looks in the window. Nothing inside looks familiar, but why should it? After all these years, the house must have gone through at least one family. They would have changed the wallpaper, the furniture. He moves on to another window and then another. Nothing he can see inside stirs any feelings of familiarity.

He moves on, wandering the neighbourhood. He passes a few boarded-up houses. An abandoned leaning barn can be seen rotting across a field.

The neighbourhood itself and the old schoolhouse bring back some fuzzy memories, but mostly just a vague sense that it should be more familiar than it is. The main street changed little over the years, but most of the buildings only have the same sense of vague familiarity as the school. A store is boarded up, the front glass window broken in one spot, where a ball or rock was likely thrown through it.

After wandering for a while, Nick finds himself walking down the old Mill Road towards the construction site. He sees another abandoned home on the edge of a farm lot across the field, the barn rotting behind it.

When he reaches the construction site, he sees the ruined raw wounds the tractors made clearing the field and trees. The broken trees are piled along one side, twisted and mangled, like a giant beaver dam.

Nick stays back, backing into the shadows of the trees at the edge of the woods at the entrance to the site.

Police tape still marks off an area at the edge of the woods across the field where the tractors had last been tearing the trees down.

A police car sits silently, the occupant guarding the site.

"That must be where the body was found. Whatever was there must have been removed by now. What are they guarding then?

There were no police when I left work. Whatever happened, however the discovery was made, it must have happened after the jobsite closed for the day."

His attention is drawn from the police car and back to the yellow tape flapping in the wind.

"Who would have been digging around in the woods at the edge of the site to make the discovery?"

He looks up the road, its destination vanishing as it winds between trees on both sides. If he keeps going along that road Nick will reach whatever is left of the old abandoned mill.

He turns around instead, heading back the other way. He wanders back through town, trying to find any familiarity in anything.

Nick finally stops when he finds himself at the old abandoned train station.

"There sure are a lot of old abandoned places. This town was dying before I was born."

He mounts the platform and sits on the partially rot-eaten bench in front of the ticket office. He just stares off into nothing, as though waiting for that long-ago train that will never come again.

In the woods beyond the train station, the dry timber of the branches of a fallen tree crackles as something moves, stepping on the dry dead branches and moving over the fallen tree.

Nick hears the cracking of branches but takes no notice, his thoughts elsewhere.

"I have to tell Felicia about the kid they found." Nick mulls it over uncertainly, reconsidering.

"Should I tell her? How will she take it? No, maybe I shouldn't.

It might make her come back here. That's the last thing she should do. This place is poison to her. She has a right to know. But will it only make her worse? Will it only destroy her more; bringing old horrors back to life for her? Definitely, I shouldn't tell her."

He is torn between needing to learn more, knowing his sister knows more than she would probably ever tell, and wanting to protect her. He sees her tormented eyes before him, the sadness that never leaves the curve of her mouth.

"I should tell her."

9- Detective Liam Tobin

The sun has risen on Malcolm Colbert's squad car. He sat there all night watching the scene where the body was found. He stirs from nearly dozing at the sound of an approaching vehicle.

He looks around. The van is bouncing over the rough ground towards him and parks next to him. The coroner and crime scene technician finally arrived, coming out together from the city.

Malcolm gets out of his car stiffly and stretches.

"It's about time you got here."

The coroner nods to him while the technician goes to the back of the van to get his equipment.

She looks around and spots the police tape across the field.

"Good thing I brought boots," she says.

The coroner turns back to the van, pulling out a pair of rubber boots and replacing the flat shoes on her feet with the boots.

She and Malcolm turn as the crime scene technician comes from the back of the van. He looks like a scientist extra out of an alien abduction or virus thriller. He is suited in white head to toe with heavy black boots and gloves. The front of the head covering is a large plastic window. On his back is an air tank. He is pushing a gurney piled with a cadaver bag and bag of supplies towards them.

He stops and looks at them.

"What? I was told this one was ripe."

The coroner and Malcolm shake their heads at him with amused expressions.

"It's old," Malcolm says. "Too old to be ripe."

The tech pulls off his head covering and tosses it on the gurney with a grin. He shakes his head. "Can't breathe worth a damn in that thing anyway."

"All right, where's the body?" he asks, looking at them.

"In the woods, not far in," Malcolm says.

Malcolm leads them across the field and into the trees to the remains, the coroner and crime scene tech struggling to drag the wheeled gurney with them.

When they arrive at the site the surveyor's pole still is standing where he jabbed it into the ground. Malcolm points the body out to them.

Wordlessly, they do a perfunctory search of the area for evidence.

The tech takes the gear off the gurney and pulls out a camera, walking around taking photos of the body and the surrounding area.

While he is doing this, the coroner pulls on thin surgical gloves and kneels, studying the body without touching it.

Returning the camera to the bag, the technician lays the cadaver bag on the ground next to the body. Each taking a position on opposite ends, he and the coroner carefully start lifting the remains to put it in the bag intact. It seems as if it will come away in one piece at first, and then it falls apart.

They exchange a look over the body.

Malcolm watches as the coroner picks up the pieces, shoving them into the body bag. A shovel is used to remove the remaining flesh that stayed behind, melted to the ground beneath the bones, depositing the detritus into the body bag with the rest of the remains.

They do another search of the area for any potential evidence they missed, and the technician zips up the body bag. They lift it, slinging it up onto the gurney. He sets the gear on top of it.

"The site is old," the coroner says. "I didn't really expect we would find anything, and we didn't."

"Except the cadaver, what's left of it," the tech says.

She gives him a pained false amused grin. "Let's get this back to the lab."

Malcolm fights a chuckle, feeling more punchy with hunger and fatigue than amused as he watches the two awkwardly carry the gurney holding the body bag with the loose bones back over the difficult terrain, lifting it higher to get around some of the bushes and fallen trees. It isn't much better going over the rough ground the tractors chewed up. With the cadaver under the gear, the tech has to keep grabbing for the equipment to keep it from falling off. They finally reach the vehicles, load it in the back of the van, wave, and drive off.

Relieved to be able to leave at last, Malcolm drives wearily home.

*****

An hour after Malcolm leaves, another car arrives. A suited man steps out. Detective Liam Tobin. He stands there, taking in the jobsite, the motionless tractors, and the lay of the area.

He walks along the grassy edge bordering the raw open wound of the field the tractors tore apart, then along the edge of the woods to the police tape stretched across the barrier of trees. Without pausing, he ducks under it and walks into the woods.

Tobin has no one to guide him and no pictures; only the description of where the body was found. He spots the abandoned surveyor pole still standing and finds the fallen tree and the location that previously held the body without too much trouble.

Crouching down, he examines the ground where fresh scrape marks reveal where the body was removed.

He carefully turns over a clump of rotten leaves nearby, delicately extricating a few leaves, one of which breaks as he does so.

He picks at the downed tree, noting its sponginess. He picks away a piece of rotting bark to reveal the scurrying termites beneath.

He has seen scenes like this before. The odds of finding anything relevant are nearly nonexistent. He looks anyway, turning over clumps of rotting leaves.

Tobin gets up and wanders the woods around the tree.

Satisfied, he returns to his car and drives to the police station.

*****

Malcolm arrives for the start of his next shift to find a man he doesn't recognize sitting in the office, one knee crossed over the other, casually sipping a coffee.

He takes in the man's suit, the traces of now dried mud and detritus on the bottom of his shoes, and the tired lines around his eyes and mouth.

"Are you from dead cases?" Malcolm asks. They both know what he means. Cases get old, they get stale, and they sometimes get closed and sometimes never do. They get cold. There are a few scattered detectives whose sole function and purpose is to chase down those dead cases left sitting in limbo. C. C. I. Cold Case Investigations.

It is a job without reward for the most part. Years can be spent chasing down a cold case without ever resolving it.

"I am," Tobin says, introducing himself without moving to get up. "Detective Liam Tobin." He holds out his left hand to shake hands, his right still holding the coffee cup.

Malcolm steps forward and shakes his hand awkwardly, having to bend down a little and use his left hand to do it. "Acting Sergeant Malcolm Colbert."

The detective nods acknowledgement.

"Good luck," Malcolm says. "There is nothing there. Do you need me to take you to where the body was found?"

Tobin shakes his head. "I already visited the site."

"Did you find anything we missed?" Malcolm asks doubtfully.

"I'll tell you what I found," Tobin says. "Witnesses."

"Witnesses?" Malcolm is shocked.

"Unfortunately, I don't think they'll tell us anything now." Tobin says.

"Why? Who're the witnesses?"

"Termites."

"How does that help us?"

"Speeds the decomposition," Tobin says. "The body was planted at the base of a termite colony. What do insects do best? Decompose anything around them to dirt faster than the elements alone. That tells me the body likely has been there for less time than it would superficially appear. And it's older than that."

"How long is that?" Malcolm asks.

"Maybe ten," Tobin says. "With the termite colony there, I'd say the body was there less than five."

"Weeks?" Malcolm asks, shocked at the idea the body is so recent in its advanced state of decomposition. His mind is already playing back through time searching for any calls on missing children and coming up empty.

"I didn't think termites ate corpses," he says.

"Ten years," Tobin chuckles. "Termites are not interested in bodies. They soften up the tree, moisture sets in, and that speeds up the decomposition of the body and the dump site."

Malcolm nods as if he understands.

"So, what's your plan?"

"I managed to get a hold of the coroner before she left town. Got to have a quick informal look at the body; what's left of it. The body and dirt it sat on were a jumbled mess." Tobin shakes his head with disappointment at what he feels was sloppy work moving the cadaver. "They took lots of photos, at least. I got a look at those. Had her send me digital copies. With the amount of color leached into the bones, they've been there or someplace like it for years."

"I don't see how that's possible," Malcolm says. "There hasn't been anyone missing around here in years. It's hard to believe a body, especially a kid, could just go missing unnoticed and sit there so long without anyone ever finding it. You get kids playing around in the woods sometimes. Hunters. Heck, it's not the first time that area was surveyed for the construction going on."

He looks a Tobin seriously.

"I just can't wrap my head around how that cadaver could have sat there so long without anyone coming across it. This is a small town too. Nothing happens in a small town the whole area doesn't know about. If any kid went missing it would get around town fast, and around the next town and the next."

"You don't think the victim is local," Tobin says.

"No, I don't. There is no way. It's a kid. If anyone lost a kid, I would know. Even if they were just passing through, who loses a kid and doesn't ask for help? Doesn't tell anyone?"

Tobin nods. "A person asks for help if they can."

Malcolm looks at him with alarm.

"You think this could be a kidnapping victim? Maybe someone passing through and lost this kid or had to get rid of the body?"

"I don't rule anything out," Tobin says.

"Know anywhere I can stay while I'm here?" he asks.

"Dusty's is about the only place around, if they have room. They only have a couple rooms and one is usually taken by Paul Doughan when he gets drunk and his wife kicks him out for a few days."

"How often is that?"

"Every few days."

"I'll go check it out," Tobin says, getting up.

Malcolm starts for the back room where the lockers are.

"I'll be around if you need me. If not here, then out on the road somewhere."

Tobin nods and leaves the building.

When Malcolm comes back out, dressed in his uniform and gear, he sees Tucker McKinley coming into the building. He is in uniform and carrying take out from Dusty's.

"Lunch?" Malcolm asks.

"We have company," Tucker says. "Harvey Lawson is in holding."

Malcolm nods. "Probably just as well. I bet we aren't the only ones that will see him as the most likely suspect. He lawyer up yet?"

"No. Says he doesn't need one because he didn't do anything."

"They all say they are innocent."

"Until they are guilty."

"See you around," Malcolm says. "I'll be out driving around." He grabs the keys to one of the cars and leaves.

Tucker walks to the back room with the holding cells. "Lunch is here." He does not sound happy about it.

10 - Uncle Harvey

Harvey's motionless prone form on the metal bed of the holding cell belies the anxiety and turmoil that fills him. His eyes are open just a crack, enough to see but give anyone who looks at him the impression he is sleeping.

Harvey looks worn and weathered, dressed in old out-of-style clothing. His scruffy hair and long beard add to his worn image. He has the ageless look of a grizzled man who has seen too much, lived through too many unpleasant experiences, and does not fit in well with civilization.

That impression is fitting for the man who seldom leaves the woods where he lives alone in a small cabin that looks as derelict as the man.

Harvey is a bit of an odd bird and is not generally comfortable in the company of other people, something of a reclusive oddity, and a man of unnerving silence.

There is not a person alive who knew Harvey that did not harbour some fear of the man, even if only because they did not know how to break through that shell to the man inside.

The smell of greasy food from Dusty's still clings to the air.

Harvey listens to the sounds of the building beyond his cell. The officer who brought him in is out of sight in the area beyond the holding cells. He hears the squeak of his chair and his footsteps as he walks to the coffee station, the gurgle of him filling his coffee cup, and his footsteps back to his desk. His chair squeaks again as he sits down to drink his coffee and wait.

The officer is impatient. The chair shifts and squeaks again and his footsteps come towards the holding cells.

Harvey does not open his eyes or move a muscle, continuing the charade that he is sleeping.

He hears the officer's uniform fabric rustle, his footsteps come to a stop, and the soft rustle of the uniform and a tired sigh as the man leans against the wall.

"Are you sure you don't want a lawyer?" Tucker asks, his voice exasperated and bored at once.

"No, I'm good," Harvey says without moving anything but his mouth or opening his eyes.

His unconcerned casual attitude only serves to aggravate the officer more. He bristles.

"Twice in the history of this town a child's body has turned up in the woods, and both times you just happen to have come back to town around that time," Tucker says. "With your past, aren't you even a little concerned about going to prison? You know what the other inmates will do to you. Even they don't like child killers." He sneers at this, trying to get under Harvey's skin.

"I didn't do it," Harvey says calmly, still not moving or opening his eyes.

Tucker steps forward, whipping out and extending his baton in one swift stroke, banging it on the holding cell bars loudly. The sound can be heard through the whole building.

Harvey casually opens his eyes and looks up at him.

The officer glares down at him hatefully. He has no doubt the man in the cage killed this child and the other one found years ago in the same area.

Harvey moves slowly, swinging his legs around and sitting up on the hard bunk.

"The first one they determined an animal was responsible. This time..." Harvey shrugs. "They'll figure it out soon enough and you will have to let me go."

Tucker's stance shifts menacingly. He grips the baton as if he might beat the prisoner senseless if not for the bars between them. Child deaths and child killers always hit the officers hard. In that moment, Tucker wishes he is the kind of man who could beat a sick bastard like this to death. He tightens his grip on the baton in frustration, feeling useless. It would not bring the child back even if he had been that kind of man.

"Cut him loose," a voice behind the officer interrupts.

The officer and Harvey both turn to see a man wearing a suit minus the tie standing at the entrance to the holding cells area. Tucker gives him a cold look.

"Are you his lawyer?"

"Detective Liam Tobin." He does not bother to flash his badge, expecting his sense of authority to be authority enough. "I've been put on this case."

Tucker considers demanding to see his badge.

"He called in the feds?" he asks, referring to his boss.

The unfamiliar detective nods. "He did. He had to."

"We picked him up on suspicion he has something to do with the kid in the woods."

"We're letting him go," Liam says. "We are not filing charges. Yet."

After giving the detective a sour look clearly signalling his feelings about it, Tucker grudgingly puts his baton away and turns to unlock the cell door. Opening the door, he stands aside, holding it open.

Harvey bows to him graciously as he exits the cell, careful to keep his distance from the officer. He does not want to give him any justification to grab him and slam him down on the ground like he knows he is itching to do.

Tucker glowers at Harvey, keeping himself in check. As much as he wants to beat this child killer, he will not touch him without cause.

Harvey walks out of the holding cells area past the detective without a glance back.

"Don't leave town," Liam says. "We will want to talk to you again."

Harvey gives him a wave without turning and heads for the building exit.

"Why the Hell are we letting him go?" Tucker growls. "We haven't maxed out the time we can hold him without charging him."

"Just giving him a little rope to hang himself with," Liam says with a grin, watching Harvey leave.

"Why were you holding him?" Liam asks.

Tucker looks at him in surprise. "He's our suspect."

"The only suspect?"

"Yes, of course."

"Why him? Who is he?"

Tucker puffs up his chest a little, leaning forward. He does not do it intentionally. It is a reaction to this stranger, an outsider, questioning him as if his team is doing something wrong. Not by Liam's tone, but by the questions and his nature of being an outsider.

"That was Harvey Lawson. He's always been trouble. Got arrested for some mischief years ago when he was still young. It happened before I was on the job, but everyone in town heard the story. Just when he got out of jail for that, sentence served and showing up back here in town, the body of a child was found in the woods. Of course he was found out for it, just showing up like that. There were no kids missing and no murders or anything, then he shows up and so does a body."

"It was a murder then? There was proof of that?"

"I'm sure there was. We just didn't find it. But it's strange, isn't it? That he shows up and just then a body is found?"

"Yes. Strange." Liam wonders at what the officer is not saying. It could be coincidence, it could not be.

"He has lived here since?" Liam asks.

"He went to prison for a few years for the murder before it was overturned. Harvey Lawson has been living here ever since. He's always been weird. Odd. An outsider even though he was born and raised here, his family farming here for generations."

"Do you have a lot of trouble with him?"

"Enough. We keep an eye on Harvey. Try to anyway. He's secretive. Hard to figure out what he's up to."

"You don't trust him."

"Hell no. He's too strange. There's always been bits of trouble involving Harvey. Nothing big, but enough. Disagreements. He's always been trouble."

"If our friend here is guilty this time, he will show us," Liam says.

11 - David

David cannot stop thinking about Felicia. What does she look like now? He is sitting on the couch in his living room brooding over it. "If Nick came back, does that mean she will too?"

Ian comes in and sees the troubled look on David's face. He sits in the chair across from him, studying him.

"You really think Nick came back to make trouble?" Ian asks, thinking that is what David is dwelling on.

David looks up at him.

"What? No. I mean yes, but that's not it," he says.

"Do you think they found it? That that's what it is?" Ian asks.

"They must have," David says. "I haven't heard of any kids going missing. Have you?"

Ian shakes his head no.

"So, if they found a kid, it has to be the one we found back then," David says. "Nobody ever said anything then about finding a body. You aren't still worried they'll put us in jail, are you? We were only kids back then and all we did was find it. They wouldn't even know we found it. How would they?"

Ian pales at the thought, looking guilty.

"What?" David asks, catching the sick look of guilt.

Ian swallows, trying to think of how to say it.

"What did you do?" David's tone sounds like a father trying to coax a confession from a child he knows is guilty of the crime but wants to hear him say it.

Ian reluctantly meets his eyes.

"I think I left something behind with the body," Ian says weakly. His knees feel like they will crumple beneath him at any moment.

David's expression hardens. He is more angry than shocked.

"You just figured this out now? All these years, how did you just decide now that you left something behind? How do you know?"

"I always knew," Ian says guiltily.

David glares at him.

"Why didn't you say something back then? You knew we were all freaked about getting caught. We could have gone back for it."

"You would have made me go back. I was scared."

"And all these years," David persists, "all these years and you never said anything, never went back for it. You left evidence that we were there, and you didn't do anything about it."

"You said kids can't go to jail," Ian says defensively. "You said they would never think we did it because we were kids. I was afraid to go back. I didn't even think I'd be able to find the place again."

Ian stops talking, out of excuses. He hangs his head in shame.

"I lied," David snaps. "Kids have killed kids before. We were there. They could have suspected we did it."

He glowers at Ian, who just looks back guiltily. Finally, David sighs. There is nothing we can do about it now. Maybe whatever it was is not even there anymore.

After so many years, it is a shock to think that there could be anything left of the remains to be found, that they had not been eaten by scavengers or rotted to nothing in the damp undergrowth of the woods.

"So, what was it?" David asks. "What did you leave behind?"

Ian looks down, suddenly feeling embarrassed.

"A toy," Ian says.

"A toy." David's expression is a mix of relief and concern. "What kind of toy?"

"An action figure," Ian says.

David can't help it. He bursts out laughing so hard tears come to his eyes and he doubles over.

When he is finally able to get control of himself again, he straightens up and looks at Ian with that lopsided half smirk of his that is a sure sign he is plotting mischief.

"An action figure. How do you know you left it? I mean, how sure are you?"

Ian shrugs. "I realized it was missing the next day. I was playing with it when we went to the woods. I stuck it in my pocket. The next day I couldn't find it."

"So, you don't even know where you lost it," David says. "We were all over the place. You could have lost it anywhere."

He bursts into a new round of uncontrollable laughter.

Ian just stands there looking at him. He feels sick. He can't help the nagging fear that if they found a toy with the body, they will somehow link it to them. To him.

"What if they find it?" Ian asks.

David looks at him, his eyes tearing from laughter, but his face turning grave.

"How many toys were probably lost in those woods over the years? Kids have always played in the woods. It doesn't mean anything. There is no way they could link it to us."

"But what if they do?"

"Even if they did, they would probably just chalk it up to kids playing in the woods. They wouldn't have any reason to suspect kids did it."

"The woods are pretty big," Ian says unhappily. "I don't know. It seems like a pretty big circumstance for some kid to just happen to lose a toy at the exact spot a dead body is found."

"That's if you lost it there. We were all over those woods that day. You could have lost it anywhere. You are worrying for nothing. It probably wasn't even in the same spot."

Ian looks down, fidgeting, and meets David's eyes again.

"I need to know."

"Fine," David says. "Let's go."

"Where?"

"Where they found the body."

A chill seeps into Ian at the thought. He wanted to do this a moment ago, but now he doesn't.

David gets up, walking to the door, and stops, staring at him.

"Are you coming?"

"I'm coming," Ian says, regretting it already.

He follows David out stone-faced and trying to hide how sick he feels inside.

When they arrive at the construction site on the old Mill Road, David drives in and parks the car by the office trailer.

The site is still closed after the discovery of the body and theirs is the only car there. Tractors are scattered around the field seemingly randomly, others are parked in a line on one side as if on the edge of a great black wound of ruined dirt road. Across the field they can see the flickering of the yellow police tape tied off along the stretch of woods, fluttering in the wind.

David and Ian stare at it mutely, each with his own thoughts.

Trying to look braver than he feels, David speaks a little too loudly. "Okay, let's go."

He pushes his door open and gives Ian a let's go look.

They trudge across the field to the woods, walking along the tree line until they reach the police tape. Ducking under the tape, they disappear into the trees.

The woods feel like they close in around them, making outside noises a muffled distant reality. David leads the way, stopping when he thinks they are near the spot. He looks around.

"It's got to be around here. Look for a downed tree."

"It's been twelve years," Ian says. "There might not be much left of it."

"So, look for anything that might suggest it was a tree."

"There's a pole sticking out of the ground over there."

David looks and sees it. "Let's check it out."

They walk to the surveyor's pole, looking around it. David toes at the ground, shifting a layer of rotting leaves. Kneeling, he takes a closer look at a depression next to the soft remains of what once was a tree lying on the ground. The ground is disturbed, the scrape marks still clear.

"This has to be it." David looks around as if for witnesses.

Feeling hollow inside, Ian searches around for the small toy lost over a decade ago. He avoids looking at the scraped bare soil where the cadaver of a child was found.

"It has to be the same body," David says. "I'm sure it's the exact same spot."

"I'm not finding it," Ian says. "What do we do now?"

"Go home. There's nothing we can do. Let's go."

Ian gives one last back and follows David out of the woods to the car. They drive home in silence.

12 - Felicia

It is dusk and the shadows are deepening across everything. It is that time at the end of the day when frayed nerves might jump at nothing and an overwrought mind plays tricks.

David wanders the edge of the woods just beyond where the now idle heavy equipment was clearing brush. Yellow police tape ruffles in the breeze, draped and ugly, marking off the area. No one is guarding the scene now. He knows he won't find anything, but he needs to look anyway.

His eyes scan the area, seeing trees, rocks, and brush that are no longer there, replaced by the ugly black scar and heavy machine tracks where the brush had been torn out and the ground scraped flat. He sees the rise and fall of the uneven ground, the shadows cast in the late afternoon sun of many years ago.

On the edge of one side of the cleared area, the mangled trees and bushes are piled up like a freak show dam built by an insane giant beaver.

Slowly walking across the area, eyes studying what is no longer there, he stops with a sharp intake of breath.

It's there. Just beyond the edge of ruined ground and a little ways in the trees, there will be a slight hollow beneath the shelter of a downed rotting tree that had not yet been dug up. The body would be nothing more than sun-bleached bones scattered by animals if it were still there at all, still exposed to the sky as they left it so many years ago.

David ducks under the police tape and enters the darker shadows of the trees.

Not far in, he spots it, the rotting remains of a large tree melting into the ground where it lays, ferns and other undergrowth devouring it as they grow in its place. The branches are mostly gone now; just a few rough stumps sticking out where the largest branches once extended from the trunk. The tree once lay straight, partially leaning and not quite touching the ground except at its base. It lay across the top of two large rocks, rough ground, and other fallen deadwood, and was partially caught up in the branches of other trees as though they had reached out to catch their fallen brethren, snagging its branches with their own and forever frozen in time in that position.

Now the tree lies on the ground, their hold finally released, limp and sagging with the rise and fall of ground and rocks beneath it. The top side looks chewed down and soft with the rot as it slowly melts back into the ground it once grew from.

With a nervous swallow, David walks around the tree to the other side. Although the tree sags into it, the hollow is still there. That spot where they found the body.

He knows without a doubt it is the right place. He has seen the image in his mind every day. It is burned into his memory as fresh as that first day they saw it.

There is nothing here now, but he can see the body in his mind's eye as if it is still present and preserved exactly as they found it. The face of the child stares back at him, not all there, dried skin covering a section from the nose down on one side of the slack jaw. The rest is part flesh covered, part pale bone, as if the skin and tissue were slowly melting away like an ice cube left in the hot sun. The rest of the body is lost in the dimness of childhood memory, only the grisly face staring at him, clear and accusing. He can't tell if it was a boy or girl.

"It's been a long time," a soft female voice comes from the shadows.

Startled, David spins around. He stands motionlessly staring, silent, and his mouth open with surprise.

He stiffens, trying to place the voice, knowing immediately who it belongs to, yet somehow disbelieving it.

She steps from the shadows.

His eyes roam over her, absorbing her. She looks even more beautiful to him than he imagined she would.

She is an older version of the Felicia he crushed on as a kid. More mature, curvy, somehow softer than the bony girl he knew. Her eyes hold the aged look of someone who has lived a hundred years and seen too much trauma, the lines of her mouth an indefinable subtle sadness.

"Felicia," David whispers.

"What are you doing here in the woods?" she asks, her voice soft, undemanding.

"I-I'm," he stammers.

"Looking for something?" she asks as she closes the distance between them.

He can smell her now; her subtle perfume is perfect for her. She is perfect. He never forgot her in all those years. There had always been something special between them, something that told him they were meant for more, to be more than just friends.

"What are you looking for David?" His name almost caresses off her tongue. "The body? It's gone. Are you scared? Worried? Worried they will find out we found it all those years ago and kept it a secret?"

He swallows hard, his throat a large dry knot. He can hardly breathe; it feels like he will choke on his own throat.

"Are you scared they will find out what we did?"

"We-we didn't do anything," he gasps.

"Are you sure? Do you remember? Who do you think killed that poor boy?" She blinks at him. Her eyes locked onto his, drawing them in, trapping them, trapping his stuttering heart.

Felicia moves; walking around him, stopping behind him, so close he can feel her presence although he can no longer see her.

David is spellbound, unable to move. He swallows.

"Old Uncle Harvey?" she whispers softly, her breath tickling his neck with her closeness. "Bad bad Uncle Harvey? Do you think he did it? Do you think you will find something after all this time to incriminate him? We all knew he was a bad man, that he did bad things, didn't we? Everyone in town said so."

Her body barely brushes against his as she circles him, her perfume wrapping him in its heady blanket. She stops in front of him, looking at him with her head slightly tilted as if he were some odd bird she is trying to think what it might be.

She walks again, stopping behind him once more.

It is pure torture for him every time she moves from sight. He wants to turn, to keep her in view, but is afraid to move. If he moves she might be gone, nothing more than a whisper, his imagination playing with him.

A part of him keeps harping deep inside that she is not there, not real, that he is dreaming her.

David shakes his head, unable to think. His heart cries out for her, his hands want to reach for her. His lips want to ask her a million questions.

Felicia takes his headshake as a 'no', that he does not think Harvey murdered the child. Her eyes narrow as she studies him.

"You don't remember much from that day?" she asks.

David's mind can only focus on one thing, Felicia. The rest of that day does not exist, just her.

"I remember we found it. We were all scared and decided to keep it a secret. You came to my house. You'd been crying. Then you were gone ..." he trails off.

"Gone. Weren't we all gone that day, one way or another?" Felicia asks.

Her hands are on his shoulders now, her body not quite touching his as she stands behind him, whispering softly close to his ear.

David feels tingly and weak at her nearness, numb. His body feels like it is melting to soft goo. He is exhilarated and terrified all at once. It is what he has dreamed of all these years, only he wishes she would stop talking about the dead kid. It is ruining the moment, making it feel too surreal, and wrapping them in a dark blanket of anxiety.

"You remember, don't you," she pauses, "what we did, what we all did that day?"

"We did nothing," he stiffens, confused.

"We ... did ... NOTHING!" she starts softly then screeches.

She is on top of him now, shrieking, her nails raking at him, fists pounding on him, attacking him in a vicious wild frenzy. He shakes her off, turning to look at her, stunned by her unprovoked attack.

Something hits him in the side of the head, hard. His head swims, dizzy, his eyes becoming unfocussed. Pain crashes through his head with a second blow. He staggers; falls to his knees, trying to stay upright. He can't see, just a wild blur, but he can feel the warm dripping wetness of blood flowing from his head.

"I DID IT!" Felicia screams at him. Even in her fury, her voice is beautiful to him. He blinks, trying to look past the fuzz at his long-lost friend and first and only love. Yes, even at such a young age, unknowledgeable about love, all those years ago he had known that he loved her.

David falls forward, unable to keep himself upright on his knees, on his hands and knees now. His arms are strangely weak. He struggles to keep his head up, to keep looking at her, his eyes focusing in and out of the haze that is pressing in around him.

Felicia's voice comes at him, sharp, angry, accusing.

"I did it! I killed the boy! It was all my fault!" Her voice rises in pitch as she shrieks at him, her small fists frantically reining blows on him.

Finally, the attack stops. David feels dazed, in mind and heart. He doesn't know what to think, what he knows.

He manages to pull himself upright again, still on his knees. Standing is too much for him right now. He looks around for her, but his eyes are unable to focus. His head feels so very heavy.

Something bites at him, biting him in the back with a searing pain as he wobbles there on his knees. It bites again and he cries out with it. He can hear her, see the blurry image of her circling around, stopping in front of him. He looks up at her, pleading with his eyes. It bites at him again. This time from in front, and again and again, searing pain shooting through him each time. He falls backwards, lying on the ground. He can feel a sticky wetness of quickly cooling warmth on his back and chest.

Felicia stands over him, staring down at him.

"Don't you get it?" she demands quietly. "Uncle Harvey was scary, but not a bad man. He was never a bad man. Poor strange and frightening Uncle Harvey. He went to jail already you know, before the boy in the woods, for killing a kid. But he didn't do it. He went to jail so no one would find out it was my fault, it was all me. That was the first time. Now he's going to go to jail again, for this child, to protect me."

She sobs.

David's heart beats, he feels just that one lub-dub, tries to look at her. His lips move, trying to talk to her.

She looks down at him, calm now, sad. Tears roll down her cheeks.

"Why David, why?" she whispers. He is dying. She knows it and he knows it.

"Felicia," he whispers her name.

"It's ok," she whispers. "Uncle Harvey will look after me again. Look." She shows him the weapon in her hand.

The knife and her hands are covered with his blood. Her hands are trembling.

"This is his," she says. "They will think he did it. He will go to jail for your death too."

"No!" David's mind cries out. His lips try to cry out too, but they are breathless, dying.

She thinks Harvey will take the fall for his death too. She does not know Uncle Harvey is sitting in a jail cell, having been arrested for that long-ago murder. He knows. He wants to tell her, aches to tell her.

He wants to save her from this. Protect her. His Felicia.

His mind races; a million questions running through it, playing back the memories even as the blackness engulfs him. The blackness and the cold. *Uncle Harvey in jail for killing this child long ago, covering for Felicia. But, did she really do it? Or is she covering up for her younger brother Nick?*

Ian steps out from behind the looming bulk of a bulldozer.

"You shouldn't have done that," Ian says.

Felicia spins and glares at him.

"He was going to find out," she says.

"Your Uncle Harvey is in jail, you know. They picked him up this afternoon for killing the boy in the woods."

Her eyes widen, realization dawning.

"What do we do now?" she asks.

13 - You Can't Escape the Dream

David wakes up with the worst headache he has ever had in his life. Pain shoots through him. He can feel each and every stab wound. He tries to moan, his breath catching and gurgling in his throat. His arms are wooden, lacking feeling.

I can't move, he thinks weakly. David thinks he should be thinking it wildly and wonders why he is not. He is dying and he wonders at how it is that he feels nothing about it.

The grass is digging into him, but it feels wrong. The ground feels wrong. Where is the mesh-like density of the grass? The cool hardness of the ground?

His mind brings up the image of the dead child's face in the woods and it becomes his own.

He wills his hands to move and finally they do. He feels himself for the blood he knows is soaking his clothes and pooling on the ground around him. He feels nothing, his numb hands move with a slippery sound, rubbing against sheets.

Confusion.

Where am I? He opens his mouth and tries to voice the words in his head. He thinks his mouth moves, but it is so dry, his lips and mouth, his throat. No sound comes out.

He tries to open his eyes. They feel so heavy, like he is waking from a deep sleep. They are scratchy and dry; gummy and crusted over with sleep sand.

David finally cracks his eyes open and his surroundings swim with fuzziness. He blinks and the room slowly comes into focus.

He is in his own bedroom.

"Wha? How'd I get here?" He can't make his thoughts clear. His whole body is one big cramping ache. He feels like he put in a killer day of hard exercise or work. Every muscle and joint in his body is stiff with pain that seems to pulse with his heartbeats.

But his heart is beating so fast. The pounding in his head throbs with it. It is racing so fast. It makes him feel sick. His whole body starts shivering. He is so cold.

He sits up woozily, the room spinning and his head too heavy to lift. The motion causes the pain in his head to slice sharply, making his stomach nauseous. He tries to focus on breathing.

Why am I breathing so slow? My heart is racing so fast? The thought comes but feels jumbled in his head.

David groans. He manages to get to his feet and his whole body feels weak. His hands tremble. He staggers to the bathroom, turning on the light.

The light is like a knife stabbing him in the eyes. The room spins wildly. He paws at the switch clumsily, turning the light off.

He staggers unsteadily to the sink, turning the faucet on, and leans down to the sink. He uses his hands as bowls, alternating scooping water from the running taps to his mouth, sucking the water back. The more he drinks the thirstier he is.

Finally he stops, splashing the cold water on his face and neck. It is soothing. The water in his stomach makes it feel worse. His stomach clenches with nausea. He holds onto the sink with one hand to steady himself, turning the water off with the other.

David tries to pull himself together, to not vomit. Who knows what that will do to all the stab wounds?

"The stab wounds! How am I standing? How am I even here?"

David swoons, his legs almost giving out.

He looks down at himself, feeling himself, his stomach, his back.

He is still wearing the same clothes as yesterday. They are dirty with mud and old leaves, dishevelled. But there is no blood, no holes.

Confused, he looks in the mirror. His face is pasty and looks more like rubber than skin. His eyes are droopy, his hair a mess, and his eyes bloodshot. He can't think, can't concentrate.

"But," David manages the one word, thinking. The last thing he remembers is going to the field on the edge of the woods where they are tearing out the woods; down the old Mill Road.

He found the tree where they had found 'it' years ago. The body in the woods.

And then...

And then Felicia. Beautiful Felicia. As perfect as he had imagined she would be.

But she was not perfect. She was wrong. Inside of her. She acted weird and then she killed him.

The realization is dawning on him. "Did I dream it?"

Obviously you dreamt it, you idiot. You wouldn't be looking at your grubby face in the mirror if you didn't. And with that thought, he turns and drops, barely making it in time to vomit into the toilet.

David is suffering the worst hangover of his short adult life. The last moments he remembers are mixed between reality and dream, churned in a soup of alcohol that left him with alcohol poisoning.

He feels relief even through the chills, shivering, pain, and nausea.

His whole body heaves with it, retching and belching out the vomit into the toilet, his stomach and with it his whole body convulsing violently with the need to puke out the poisons.

She didn't try to kill me, his mind whirls through the hot flashes, icy washes of sweaty chills, and pasty wet shivering wracking his body.

Was she there at all? Is she here?

His mind loses the thought, unable to focus, his body too busy purging to let him keep thinking on it.

David finally stops dry heaving and lets his body limply sag to the floor. The cool linoleum is soothing against his sweat-chilled body burning with the heat of the toxins poisoning it. He lays there curled up and shivering, the room spinning drunkenly, his whole body feeling like pain-filled rubber melting into the floor.

The dream was not like the usual dream about it, the body in the woods, and Felicia. This is a new twist. A new dream.

The old one still haunts his sleep now and then. Something is in the woods. Something that wants to devour them all. It is the reason the body is there. They all run but cannot get anywhere. David, help me, Felicia screams and she falls. Somehow, she is lost in the rotting fallen trees and the bushes and the thick undergrowth. Felicia, where are you? He calls out. He cannot find her. When he does, she is the body in the woods. The face that is only half there, part dried leathery flesh and part bone. And then it is coming again, and he is running. Nick and Ian are there somewhere too. He can hear them calling, the sound of them crashing through the woods. But what if it is not them? What if it is something else he hears charging through the trees, snapping them off? David keeps running, but he is getting nowhere. He cannot escape.

You cannot escape the dream.

*****

David is in the kitchen sitting at the table slouched over it with his head resting on his arms and a plate with dry toast next to him when Ian walks in.

"You look like hell," Ian says. "You were pretty hammered last night. I'm surprised you made it home. Where did you go after we left Dusty's?"

"Just wandering around," David says, his voice muffled by his arms.

"You didn't go to her house again, did you?" Ian asks. "You know there's nothing there to see. She's never coming back. Even if she did, the house isn't theirs anymore."

"I didn't go to their house," David says, not moving.

"Are you sure? After we went to the woods and you tying one on after, I thought . . ." He pauses. "I hope not. The people living there don't want you coming around anymore. Last time they said they won't call the cops anymore. I don't think that means they aren't going to deal with you hanging around there some other way."

"I didn't go to their house," David repeats, his voice rising with annoyance.

"So where did you go?" Ian asks.

"Just wandered at bit and came back here."

Ian shakes his head. "You came back and grabbed the whisky and left again."

"Fine," David mutters. "I went back down the old Mill Road to check out the construction going on. Then I came back and took the whisky. I wanted to be alone."

Ian nods his head, understanding. David went back again to see if there was any sign of the body they found as kids.

"They didn't find it," he says.

David finally looks up, bleary eyed, staring at Ian in confusion.

"The body they found clearing trees up the old Mill Road. It wasn't the same one we found," Ian says. "It's a new body. It has to be. There's no way it could have still been there. Animals would have scattered it, eaten it. Coyotes would have eaten the bones and left nothing behind but their shit."

"Now look who's all sure of himself," David mutters. "Yesterday you were sure they'd find that stupid toy and pin it on us."

Ian gives him a hard look.

"You really are an asshole when you drink," he says.

David just stares. He does not know what to say, can't focus his thoughts.

"Jesus, look at you," Ian mutters. "You drank yourself into oblivion. You've got alcohol poisoning, don't you?"

David just groans in response, his head sinking back down to bury his face in his hands again.

"Have you eaten anything?" Ian asks.

David thumbs towards the uneaten dry toast.

"You'll feel better after you eat," Ian says. He rinses out the remnants of yesterday's coffee from the pot and fills the coffee maker with fresh water and grounds, turning it on to brew. With the coffee started, he gets out a box of cereal and pours some into a bowl. He gets milk from the fridge and splashes that in too, making the cereal swim in a white pool. He sits down and devours the cereal while waiting for the coffee to finish brewing.

"Get me some coffee, will ya?" David mumbles.

Ian shakes his head. "Coffee's a diuretic. That's the last thing you need. Drink some water."

"No, it's not," David counters.

"Yes, it is."

"Stop being my mother."

"Whatever." Ian pours himself a coffee and leaves David to suffer alone.

Ian leaves to shower and get dressed while David just sits with his head resting on the table, his head pounding to the beat of his heart. They both pound dully, his body feeling like a lump of overstuffed soggy dough.

Cleaned up, Ian goes through the kitchen, heading out the door. He is dressed in his coveralls for work.

David does not even look up.

Ian walks away from the house, down the street and around the corner, heading to the gas station where he works as an attendant, pumping gas and selling whatever the station happens to have for sale. The products in the store can vary somewhat, depending on what the owner happens to get a deal on. The gas station is one of those little multipurpose affairs. They have two aged gas pumps, one more than many other middle of nowhere small towns have, and a small store carrying everything from motor oil and overpriced hair sprays, to cheap quality toys and road maps, to junk food and sporadically stocked overpriced grocery products.

David finally manages to chew and swallow his dry toast, his stomach roiling unhappily.

He downs a double dose of acetaminophen, not caring that he is overdosing himself on it, and pours himself a coffee. His stomach lurches again, threatening to go into another bout of severe vomiting.

It is evening before David feels alive enough to do anything.

*****

David roams the small town, looking for Nick. It doesn't take long. There are not a lot of places he can go without leaving town.

He finds him in the only place the small town has where people can congregate outside of church, the hardware store, and the community centre. Dusty's.

As old and rundown as it is, Dusty's is more than a small town bar. It is the only place in town where you can go to sit down to a restaurant type meal since the old chicken place closed down when the owner passed away from a massive heart attack brought on by clogged arteries. It is the town pizza place, where you can order a pizza for pickup. It is the coffee shop where you go for the company, not the coffee. While the old farmer men tend to gather at the old hardware store, everyone else tends to gather at Dusty's. During the day, Dusty's has more of a coffee shop feel. After the night lights come on, Dusty's is the run of the mill old town pool hall bar.

David walks into Dusty's to find Nick sitting alone in a back corner booth. The moment he spots him, David heads straight for Nick.

Nick sees David walk in and regrets going there.

"I should have known," he mutters under his breath, "after the other night."

David walks to his table and sits down, not bothering to ask if it is okay to join him.

Nick glances at him and looks away, feeling awkward about this man from his past who he does not know and grilled him with distrust the other day just sitting down and joining him like a friend.

David smiles at Nick with that kind of smile that feels false. It is not insincere, that would be implying he is trying to pretend he is being friendly.

The waitress comes and David orders a hamburger and fries with a beer to wash it down. His stomach churns sickly at the thought of putting food in it. He waits until she walks away before speaking.

"You haven't answered my question yet," David says.

Nick stiffens. "You didn't ask me anything."

"You know what I mean," David growls, looking around and toning his voice down to casual again. He stares at Nick intently.

"Why did you come back? Why all of a sudden now? Working there of all places?"

Nicked shrugs, his motion tense. "Construction. You go where the work is."

"Bull," David sneers. "I saw you driving that tractor. You have never driven a tractor before. You are no construction worker. You are a liar. Why are you here? Why at the moment another kid's body is found in the woods? Just when your Uncle Harvey comes back too, just before the body is found."

The waitress comes back at that moment with David's beer.

"Your food will be along shortly hon," she says, putting the beer down in front of him on the table.

David looks up at her with his disarming smile and she smiles back, giving him a genuine smile.

"Thank you," he says.

Nick takes advantage of the intrusion, getting up. He tosses money down to pay his tab, turning to David.

"Leave me alone."

He walks out, leaving David and a bewildered looking waitress watching him go.

Ian walks in as Nick is on his way out. The two exchange a look in passing, Ian's curious and Nick's annoyed.

Ian looks around, spotting David, and heads over. He nods to David and the waitress as he approaches.

"Burger and fries, and beer, please. The usual," he says to the waitress. "Thank you."

He slides into the seat across from David.

"Short shift today?" David asks, referring to Ian's ordering a beer with what should have been his dinner break.

"Closed early," Ian says with a shrug. "No idea why. Harry was on the phone in the garage. Then he came into the store and told me to go home. Said we were closing early."

"I thought I'd find you here. You here with him?" Ian indicates the now empty entrance door where he passed Nick.

"I joined him for a bit," David says noncommittally.

"You won't get anything from him that way," Ian says, "by trying to bully it out of him. Nick has always been stubborn that way."

David laughs.

"What do you know about him? You haven't seen him since you were little kids."

"As long as you," Ian says. "He was my friend. I knew him better than you did. Every time you played one of your mean pranks on him, he shut down into himself. You saw it as weak. But he is the youngest of us all. That was his strength, his way to cope."

David studies him for a moment.

"You don't think he remembers, do you?"

Ian shakes his head. "No, I don't."

He looks David in the eye and looks away. He never could look David in the eye as an equal. He has always felt somehow less than him; the younger brother who could never be as good as his older brother, the star of the family, David, who has always been older, smarter, better looking, stronger, better at everything.

*****

Nick walks away from Dusty's angrily.

"Why won't they just leave me alone? I don't remember. That's why I came back. I need to find out what happened. What happened twelve years ago that tore my family apart? That turned Felicia into an unhappy empty shell?

Maybe if I find out, I can somehow fix her."

In his anger he keeps on walking, not paying attention to where he is going. Then he starts walking with a purpose. He heads across town to the old abandoned train station.

This is a place they went often as children. His hope is that visiting his childhood home, the places they went to as kids, will bring back the memories that everything else failed to bring back.

All he has is the nightmares, disjointed and frightening.

"You can't escape the dream," he mutters.

He arrives at the old train station. It is still bright enough, but the light is getting old, the sun is far in the Western sky and starting to set. It is at the point before the sky blazes with the reds and oranges of sunset. The lowering light only serves to accent how decrepit the train station is. The deepening shadows have grown long; the ragged holes eaten into the rotting wood are stretched longer in the shadows, deeper with the darker shadows, more pronounced.

He pauses a moment before mounting the steps to the platform. For a moment, he doubts they will hold his weight even though this is not his first time here since returning.

Nick mounts the steps. They creak beneath his weight and he imagines he feels them sagging beneath his feet. They do sag, but not as much as he thinks.

The wood planks of the platform creak with his weight, softening in the damp of the cooling early evening.

He walks across the platform to stand on the edge above the tracks, his toes hanging over, a short move from falling. The tracks run as far as the eye can see in both directions, vanishing in a straight line of distance in one direction, and around a curve behind the trees in the other.

He looks one way and then the other up the tracks thoughtfully. Then he crouches down and sits on the edge, his legs dangling.

Nick just sits there for a long time. Not thinking. Thinking. Thinking about everything and nothing.

He has an urge to stick his hand in his pocket. To pull out what is there. To look at it. To throw it away into the bush never to be found again. Maybe that will make the nightmares go away. Maybe that will make Felicia better.

In his pocket is a small toy. An action figure small enough to hide in his fist. He and Ian had been playing with them that day so long ago. The day everything changed.

It is one of very few things from their life here that he was able to bring with him. It was in his pants pocket still when his mother came into his room that night.

The night they found something in the woods.

He doesn't remember much of that night. He remembers feeling like nothing will ever be okay again. He remembers Felicia's haunted eyes. The telephone ringing. His mother crying.

The police came and his father yelled at them. Felicia ran off and his mother went crazy about it, running outside and calling her. Calling and calling. He remembers that.

He remembers being woken in the middle of the night; his mother grabbing clothing and shoving it into bags, clothing from his drawers, from the floor. She shoved clothes at him, telling him to get dressed.

They were the same clothes he had worn that day.

Nick remembers how strange that was. His mom, who kept the house cleaner than any other mom, who always made sure everyone wore clean pyjamas every night and clean clothes every day.

That moment made him more afraid than anything he can remember in his entire life.

His mother, tears in her eyes, looking frightened, urging him to put on dirty clothes while she frantically grabbed random things, shoving them into a bag.

He remembers that moment more vividly than any other memory.

After that is a blur, lost in the fog of time.

He found the toy in his pocket after they were already driving through the dark night.

Felicia sat next to him in the back seat of the car, already lost. She did not bother looking out the window or looking back.

He knows these two things only because he reminded himself every time he looked at that toy. It was a very confusing time in his life.

If I throw it away, he thinks, maybe all this will have never happened.

It is the same thought he has had for as long as he can remember. Since he was just a kid, when anything you imagined was supposed to be possible. Every time he looked at that damned toy. The adult version of the same thought he had throughout childhood. That somehow this is the toy's fault. That getting rid of it would make Felicia be Felicia again.

He stares into the distance at nothing.

"What did we find, Felicia?" he asks quietly. "What happened to you?"

"I thought I'd find you here."

The voice startles him. Nick turns to see the grizzled middle-aged man who looks older than his age. He stares at him, knowing he should know that face, but does not. Then he knows. It comes with a sinking sick feeling in his stomach. Uncle Harvey.

A chill runs through him. He stiffens. Fear.

"Don't be afraid of me, Nicholas," Harvey says. "You've always been afraid of me. Haven't you? Oh, but they call you Nick, don't they? How is your mother?"

"Fine," Nick manages. "She's fine."

"Good," Harvey nods.

Nick just wants him to go away.

"What kind of stories your mother must have told you about me," Harvey says.

Nick can see the smile through his unkempt beard because of the way his eyes crinkle at the corners.

"It's okay Nick. I know. Your mother doesn't like me. She doesn't approve of me. She believes what they say."

He stares at Nick, his expression serious.

"I did not kill that kid," he says. "I've never hurt anyone."

"Then why did you go to jail?" Nick asks. "You went to jail, didn't you? That's what everyone said. They said you went to jail for killing a kid. They said you got out, and then all of a sudden mom and dad pack us up and move in the middle of the night. They didn't even take most of our stuff.

It's like they were running away from something."

Harvey nods. "You are right."

He kneels down and sits on the edge next to Nick.

"There have always been stories around the old Mill Road," Harvey says. "Did you know that? They go back as far back as anyone can remember.

Do you know there is an old abandoned mill down that road? That's where it got its unofficial name, because the old mill is down that road."

"Yeah, everyone knows about the mill. It's one of those old waterwheel mills. Everyone says it was shut down because there were some pretty gruesome murders there."

"Do you believe that?" Harvey asks.

Nick shrugs. "Not really. It probably just was not very useful anymore. Everything is made in big factories now."

"It was shut down so long ago, I doubt anyone even knows why it shut down," Harvey says. "You are right, it is a small mill. Maybe it outlived its usefulness. The creek may have dried up, or it might have just been too old, in too much disrepair. Or it just became obsolete. Why it shut down doesn't matter. Kids will make up all kinds of stories to scare each other."

Nick nods, remembering now how David had always been pulling pranks and telling him scary stories. He never liked David because of it.

Harvey continues.

"There were a number of grisly deaths and disappearances surrounding the mill a long time ago. Some bodies were found at the mill itself, some in the woods around it. After a while, nobody went down the old Mill Road. It was as if by not going down that road they were somehow putting a talisman between them and the mill.

Some say it's haunted, you know."

"I'm not surprised," Nick says.

"Have you ever been there?" Harvey asks.

"No."

"It was children, you know," Harvey says. "The deaths, they were children, smaller farm animals, and pets. The most vulnerable. The easy prey. A lot of animals went missing first; sheep, goats, chickens and ducks, and pets. Not all were found. At first, they thought the coyotes were getting the animals that disappeared. It made sense. It was a bad time for coyotes. The deer and other animals were unusually scarce. Domestic animals were the natural choice. Hungry beasts will eat. The ones that were found only made everyone believe more that it was coyotes. They were ripped apart, partially eaten.

But then kids started to disappear. One and then another and a third.

They trapped and shot the coyote packs after the first. It didn't stop more animals and kids from vanishing. Or their bodies from being found dismembered and partially eaten."

"That's all made up," Nick says.

Harvey shakes his head. "No, it just happened so long ago that most folks around here don't remember. After that people, kids mostly, made up their own stories about the old mill down that road."

He looks down at his feet, fidgeting with his hands.

"A kid disappeared not so long ago. You were just little then, so I guess it seems like a long time ago to you. Folks around here wanted someone to blame. They blamed me. I just got out of jail for something small, just doing stupid stuff because I was little more than a kid and thought I knew it all, so I guess that made it make sense to them. People need to make sense of a thing, especially when it's a kid."

Nick looks at him. Harvey does not turn to look back at him.

"Did you do it?" Nick asks.

"No. But that didn't stop folks around here from making up their minds. They decided I was guilty and I went to jail. Enough people spoke as witnesses against me, saying they saw me do things I never did, that I was convicted."

"So, how long did you serve?"

"Long enough. I got twenty-five years, I was doing hard time, but then a few years in the sentence was suspended and I was released. Months later the conviction was overturned, and I was an innocent man in the eyes of the law."

He doesn't bother telling Nick that every day in the penitentiary was pure hell. He was a target. Everyone hates a child killer. He almost died more times than he could count. Finally, they had to put him in protective custody. That's civil speak for locking him into a tiny cell with no windows, nothing but a hole in the floor to crap in, and no view of anything outside of that tiny cell barely large enough to fit a grown man.

That was even worse than having the other inmates threaten and attack him daily. He had wished he was dead.

"Just not in the eyes of everyone in town," Nick says.

"No," Harvey says.

"That was when we moved away, wasn't it?" Nick asks.

His heart is racing. Finally, in talking to this man who he had hoped to avoid and never have to speak to, he might finally get the answer to one of hundreds of questions churning inside him.

"Yes," Harvey says, his voice sad and far away as if lost in a memory from the past. "When they let me out, that's when your parents packed up and moved."

That day still burns in Harvey's memory, a day of heartbreak and anger. He was released with nowhere to go but home. The first thing he did when he got out was call his sister.

He was free, walked out the door of the penitentiary by a lone guard and left there out front to find his own way to wherever he will go. Free to go home but with no way to get there and no money. He had looked down at the cheque issued to him from the corrections department, the balance of his pitiful canteen account; seventeen dollars and fifty-six cents. A check as useless as the change they gave him to make a phone call if he needed someone to pick him up.

They gave him enough for a couple of phone calls. Apparently, the first person you call usually does not work out.

They were right.

He called his sister. She got angry. She cried. She told him never to come back and to stay away from her and her family. And then she hung up on him. He managed to tell her he was coming home anyway in the brief awkward silence before she hung up.

He did not know if she had even heard it, until he got home. They had cleared out in the middle of the night as if running away. Running away from him.

It cut deeper than any knife he had been threatened with in prison could.

His second call did not work out either. He ended up walking and hitchhiking all the way home.

"Well, I just wanted to see how you are doing," Harvey says as he gets up stiffly to stand. "Looks like you are doing all right."

"I'm fine," Nick says.

Harvey studies him for a moment.

"If you need anything, you know where to find me."

I won't be looking for you, Nick thinks.

But what he says is, "Thanks."

Harvey sighs heavily and walks away, leaving Nick to his own thoughts.

Nick sits there for a while, just thinking.

He had been mulling it over since the other day, leaning first one way and then the other, back and forth. It will be in the news, online. It was in today's local newspaper. By tomorrow it will be picked up by other news agencies from the wire services. She will find out anyway. Maybe she will take it better hearing it from him.

It is time to tell Felicia about the body that was found.

Nick pulls out his cell phone, gives it a long stare, one last moment to put this off, and calls Felicia.

He waits while it rings, hoping she does not answer. A second ring drags out, interminably long. A third and he is second-guessing, thinking he should not do this. A fourth ring, he is torn. "Don't hang up, you have to do this."

A fifth ring. Nick is relieved. She did not answer. He is about to hang up when he hears the tell-tale click and the sound of dead air.

The pause is too long. He wonders if the call disconnected or if she really did answer.

"Hello." He finally hears her voice coming through the phone.

"Felicia, hi," he says.

"Hello Nick." Her words are formal. She talks like that a lot. Going through the motions of communicating with others, not feeling the familiarity most people do with those they are familiar with. She has always been distant like this, for as long as he can remember. Ever since that day, he is sure.

"I came back," Nick says. "To where we lived before, as kids."

There is a heavy pause. He is thinking how to word this. "To where we lived before Mom and Dad moved us in the middle of the night."

He waits for her to respond, listening to the stretch of silence. He starts wondering if she is still there or if the call was dropped. Or if she hung up on him.

"Felicia? Do you remember?"

"I remember," she says. There is an uncomfortable silence. "Why would you go there?"

"I heard they were going to be building a bunch of houses here. The little town is finally getting bigger. They were hiring for the construction site. It was an easy job to get."

"Why would they want to make that town bigger?" Felicia asks. Her voice is bland, lifeless. The words form a question, but in her tone, it is more of a statement. "Why would anyone want to live there? You did not go there just for a job. Why are you really there?"

Nick blushes, the heat of it rising in his face. He is glad there is no one around to see.

"I had to find out what happened. You won't talk about it. I was hoping I would find answers here."

"You are being stupid, Nick. There are no answers. Why are you really there? Mom and Dad got it into your head that you have to fix me; that you are somehow responsible for me. Well, you are not. There is nothing to be fixed."

"What did we find, Felicia?" he asks. He had stopped thinking about asking her that years ago, knowing it would do no good. She would never tell him.

"Nothing, Nick. We found nothing."

Nick scrunches his face, feeling the pain of dealing with her that he always felt. The pain of knowing she is suffering inside, and he is helpless to fix it. He breathes in and out, getting himself under control.

"We did find something," he says. "In the woods; you, David, Ian, and me. We were all there in the woods and we found something; something bad. Whatever it was, we swore to keep it secret. That night everything went crazy, Mom and Dad, everything. Something happened then and they packed us up in the middle of the night and ran away." He pauses, breathing again, trying to keep his voice calm.

"What happened Felicia? Why did they take us and run away? What did we find in the woods?"

"Stop it Nick," Felicia says.

"I can talk to David and Ian. They are still here. David wants to talk to me about it. He has been after me about it since I got here. What does he know, Felicia? I bet he will tell me what he knows."

She laughs into the phone, her laugh as lifeless as her voice.

"David? What has he ever known about anything? He was a kid, just like us. He probably doesn't even remember anything from that far back. Just like you, Nick. You can't remember either.

Why are you doing this Nick? For something that you can't even remember? For what? Some bad dreams? Dreams mean nothing."

"Well then I guess I'll just have to talk to Uncle Harvey, ask him what he knows. He is still here too."

"No, don't talk to him." It's the first time Nick heard emotion in Felicia's voice. The shock of it numbs him for a moment. It scares him. It makes him decide he needs to talk to Uncle Harvey.

Uncle Harvey must know something and Felicia does not want him to tell me, he thinks.

"Then tell me what you remember," Nick says. "What did we find?"

"No."

There is another long silence between them, and Nick is sure she hung up. Then he hears her breathe.

"Felicia, someone found a body. Up the old Mill Road where they are building the new houses."

This time there is an audible click and he has no doubt she hung up.

Nick feels nauseous.

"What have I done? I shouldn't have told her."

There is a crackling sound some distance in the bush.

Nick turns to stare towards the darkening trees. Amid the deepening shadows the sun is descending in a blazing wash of orange and red low on the horizon. Soon there will be no more light in the sky.

He holds his breath and listens. The sound does not come again and he wonders if he imagined it.

"Probably a bear, if there is anything there at all."

Nick finally gets up, crosses the rotting platform, and descends the steps.

He stops, looking around in the darkness. He has nowhere to go except to maybe his car. He starts walking.

14 - How to Catch a Killer

"I never liked these small-town cases. These small towns are too cagy for me. They don't trust outsiders and guard their secrets jealously."

Detective Liam Tobin is sitting at one of the desks in the small-town precinct building going over files of reports. The building is not as old as half the buildings in the town. Being a small town that has always been small, there are buildings like the church, feedlot, some of the houses, and the old abandoned train station that are more than a hundred, two hundred, years old. Some of the out-of-use buildings in the rural area surrounding the town, left abandoned to be swallowed up by the land like the old mill, are even older. Others, like the precinct, are the 'new' buildings at sixty years or newer.

This town has a larger precinct building than a town this size would warrant, an accident of best-laid plans that never came to fruition. The town is too small to have its own local police force and just happens to be somewhat centrally located for the regional force servicing the rural area and scattered small towns in its jurisdiction. It was also supposed to triple its size in manpower, with plans in the works to build new homes and a new school, a mental hospital that would have a section geared to the special needs of the criminally insane, and a new federal penitentiary within the detachment boundaries. All of these were to be scattered throughout the towns, increasing the population. The houses were pushed back and the rest cancelled, and so was the added staff for the detachment.

The door opens and Malcolm comes in, stopping in after hours spent cruising around on patrol.

"It's a quiet night out there tonight, not much happening," he says, seeing the detective in the building. "You're working late tonight."

Liam is used to working on the road, working and sleeping odd hours on cases like the body found in the woods.

He is an expert in this particular kind of crime. He is a cold case expert.

Liam stops his inspection of the files, turning to face Malcolm.

"There is a lot of history in these old towns," he says. "Did you know there was a similar case in this town years ago?"

"Everybody's heard of it, whether they grew up here or are new to town."

Liam nods. "No story dies in a small town."

He gets up, taking his coffee cup with him, and goes to the coffee pot.

"Coffee?"

"Yeah, I could use one."

He grabs a second cup from a tray with a paper towel lining it and clean coffee cups sitting upside down ready to use. Filling both cups, he pours in powdered coffee whitener and sugar and stirs them. He remembers how the officer takes his coffee.

It's just one of those perks of the job. When you have to pay attention to catch the smallest detail, keeping all those insignificant pieces of the puzzle front and center in your mind, recalling them at a moment's notice when something new comes up and you have to be prepared to find out where, if anywhere, it might fit. Remembering how someone likes their coffee becomes as natural as knowing how you like your own.

He brings the coffees over and hands one to Malcolm.

"Thanks," Malcolm says, taking the coffee and sipping at it carefully, not sure how hot it will be. Their old twelve-cup coffee maker is the type of cheap small appliance you can find in many homes. It is also well past its prime and has become prone lately to making coffee that can be hotter than it was ever designed to do, in which case it usually tasted something like you might imagine burnt tar might taste like, to tepid at best.

"What do you know about this older body found?" Liam asks.

"Not much," Malcolm says. "It was found in the woods along the old Mill Road. Somewhere between Mill Road and the old train station. The body had been there a long time. It was found because the weather turned. After months of drought there was a lot of rain for weeks. The body softened up, soaking up the moisture. It got moist. A moist decomposing body smells like nothing you can imagine."

"Oh, I can imagine," Liam says. "Most of the bodies I see aren't much more than bones. But sometimes we come across one that had been preserved for a while. Maybe kept in a freezer or mummified. Sooner or later a frozen body thaws out. Mummification fails, too, when the conditions it lay under change. Dry, they have surprisingly little odour despite the slow rot of decomposition even the best unintentionally or inexpertly mummified bodies are subject to. But get them moist, and all that slowly decomposing bacteria comes to life with a horrific stink. The decomposition of the body speeds up too. Of what is left of the body, anyway."

"Learn anything about this new one?" Malcolm asks.

"Not yet," Liam says. "Most of the reports haven't come in yet. All I have is the preliminary findings. Toxicology will take some time yet. I might not know anything for weeks."

"You are pretty calm about it," Malcolm says.

"It's not exactly urgent," Liam says. "The remains are old; years by the discoloration. Four to six by my guess with the dry conditions you had around here and the protected spot it was in. That fallen tree would have given it good cover. That and the raised ground would have kept it dryer. The only surprising thing is scavengers hadn't spread it out more or consumed it entirely."

"Wouldn't it be rotted to nothing but bone? I mean, the small bit of flesh and connective tissue, wouldn't that have rotted in that time?"

Liam shrugs.

"Sometimes what the body does is a mystery. If it dries out right, flesh and connective tissue can become like leather. That can last for years, decades even under the right conditions, without ever completely rotting away. Archaeologists have dug up remains mummified by an accidental act of natural conditions thousands of years old that still had flesh and connective tissue.

The other body rumoured to have been found years ago was old remains too, I bet. I would stake my career on it. There are no reports of missing persons in the right time frame in the area, and no other bodies, so it was probably a one off."

"Is that what you are looking for?" Malcolm asks, "The old files for that other body?"

The detective nods. "If there is a history of this sort of thing, I want to know everything I can about it, even if it turns out to be a false rumour." He shakes his head. "There doesn't seem to be any files here that go back quite that far. They must have been sent off site for storage somewhere. I checked with the location the old files are archived at, but they have no record of it."

"I have an idea where you might find out," Malcolm says.

The detective looks up with interest. "Where?"

"The retired sheriff. All of the files were sent for temporary storage before we relocated to this building. It might have been around that time. Maybe they were sent someplace else. Something like this, he would not have forgotten where the files went."

15 – Felicia's Response

"Why are you telling me this, Nick?" Felicia still has her finger on the hang up button of her cell phone, staring straight ahead at nothing. Her face is blank, expressionless.

She frowns. She had done so well locking all this away these last few years. Her eyes widen as it dawns on her.

"Nick, you went back there." Of course he did. He told her so. It just didn't get through her numbness until now.

Her heartbeat quickens. She has become so used to feeling nothing at all that this is a strange sensation to her. She feels heat rising up her body, her muscles tensing, and a sickening tightening in her stomach.

Suddenly she has to pee urgently.

For the first time in a very long time Felicia feels fear.

"I have to get out of here."

She goes to her bedroom, pulls down a large duffel bag from the closet shelf, and starts shoving clothes into it. There is not a lot there. If there is one thing Felicia is good at, it is running from her past. She grabs another smaller bag and packs that. Finally, she packs a medium sized suitcase with a long handle and wheels with her laptop and other things.

Done, she loads it all in the car.

Felicia returns for one last look around. She looks forlornly at her plants.

"They will die. There is nothing I can do to help that, but they are only plants," she reminds herself.

She goes to a closet and pulls out a small pet carrier, setting it by the door. She collects a leash, empties the two small dishes of dry kibble and water in the kitchen, stacking them and shoving them inside an opened bag of cat food, and places it next to the carrier. She returns to the kitchen, grabbing a large garbage bag, and goes to the bathroom. Quickly scooping the nuggets from the litter box, she flushes them and wraps the bag around the box, bringing that to the door.

Felicia hauls the food and litter out to the car, returning for the final time to her home.

She stops just inside the door and looks around.

Felicia feels nothing at abandoning her home and its sparse contents. This is not new for her. She has felt like she has been on the run most of her life; ever since that fateful day when they found *it*. Ever since their parents packed them up in the middle of the night and fled.

"Kitty," she calls. "Here Kitty." She never bothered to name the cat. That would be committing to keeping him around. Felicia is not so good at making long term commitments.

It takes a few moments before the shy cat braves making an appearance. The small cat pokes his head around a corner, staring at her warily.

Felicia kneels down, holding out her hand and snapping her fingers.

"Here Kitty, here Kitty Kitty."

The cat steps out and approaches tentatively, sniffing at her fingers in case there is a treat hidden there.

She rubs his back and head before picking him up and putting him in the carrier.

"It's time for Kitty to find a new home."

Felicia leaves with the cat in the carrier, placing it in the back seat of the car.

She gets in and drives away.

16 - The Day They Found It

Twelve Years Ago, When They Were Kids

Felicia's long-legged stride showed her annoyed insolence at having to spend her time outside school following her little brother around. The four kids roamed the neighborhood, the two younger leading the way.

"Come on Nick, this is stupid," Felicia complained.

David looked at her out of the corner of his eye. Like her, he was stuck playing babysitter to his little brother Ian. At ten years old, and the oldest of the group, David would rather be out hanging around kids his own age than with his brother and his friend.

Living in a small town with loosely scattered properties on its outskirts had its advantages, but it had its disadvantages too. Among them was the wildlife. On any given day, you could look out to find deer devouring your vegetable garden, rabbits chasing each other, or squirrels using your swing set and trees as their own jungle gym.

But it was also bear country; and raccoons, which were brazen creatures that treat your trashcan like a buffet and could be quite nasty if cornered. And there were badgers and foxes and, if you went far enough, coyotes or wolves depending what side of town you were on. The wolves claimed the forest to the West and tolerated the coyote pack on the East like warring gangs in an uneasy truce. The bears were usually more nuisance than dangerous, but there was always one every year that became too habituated to people and the easy access to their garbage and bird feeders.

The wolves were not so much of a problem. They tended to stay clear of people and their property, preferring to hunt game away from humans.

The coyotes were more of a concern. Their larger ears and longer noses setting them apart from their larger cousins, the coyotes were less shy of people. While the wolves' long low mournful howls could be heard in the distance, the coyotes shorter yipping calls could sound like they were right outside your yard.

Although rare, there has been the occasional cougar sighting too. It was not unheard of for cougars to stalk their prey, including pets and children, right in their own yards.

This was why David and Felicia were both made to follow their younger brothers around, Felicia suffering David's presence because their brothers are friends. The younger kids were free to roam and explore, staying out of their parents' hair, while their older siblings had the duty of keeping the younger ones safe.

Nick and Ian kept going, oblivious to David and Felicia's annoyance. The two younger boys were on a mission, exploring for hidden treasure.

Felicia scowled at the boys ahead.

They soon found themselves at the old abandoned train station. If there was one thing about small towns, it was the abundance of old buildings both in town and in the surrounding area.

Nick and Ian mounted the rotting stairs to the platform above, deftly stepping around boards that looked like they had been chewed by rot to sit loosely on the platform. They both went straight to the edge and looked up and down the tracks running off into the distance.

Felicia mounted the steps too, slowly as if it was a chore, and sat on the bench against the small ticket office. It didn't look like it would hold even her slight weight, but she has been here many times before and knew it wouldn't fail.

David followed in the rear and leaned against the ticket office.

"You know, the real treasure is at the old mill," David said, directing his words to the two younger boys across the platform.

Ian and Nick turned to look at him.

Felicia rolled her eyes with an annoyed look.

"Let's go there," Nick said eagerly.

Ian eyed his brother suspiciously. David has pulled enough tricks on him over the years.

"I don't think we should," Ian said. He pulled on Nick. "Let's stay here."

"Come on," David cooed. "Or are you too scared? It's just an old mill where pirates used to keep treasure."

Nick's eyes fairly gleamed. "Come on, Ian, let's go to the mill."

He didn't wait for Ian to answer or for David to lead the way. Everyone knew where the old mill was, even though no one went there. He almost danced across the platform and down the steps.

Ian reluctantly tagged along.

David started following the younger boys, then stopped and turned back to Felicia.

"Coming?"

She scowled at him and got up, following the group.

David smirked as he turned away; a small lopsided smile, one corner of his mouth turned up, that was both disarming to those who didn't know him and a sure sign he was up to no good.

Nick led the way, cutting through the edge of the woods to the old Mill Road. They climbed over downed trees and skirted thick brush, following a deer trail through the trees.

"You know the story about the old mill, don't you?" David asked casually.

"About the pirate treasure?" Nick looked at him eagerly.

"About why the mill got shut down," David said, one corner of his mouth turned up in a lopsided grin.

Felicia glanced at him and looked away. Everyone has heard that story. It was a rural legend that some people died in some gruesome and horrible way at the mill and they closed it down because of it. Depending on who told the story it could have been a horrible accident, murder, a wild animal, or – and this was the more popular version – they fell prey to something completely evil and not entirely real; the old Mill Goad monster.

The mill was an old waterwheel mill on a dried up creek. The building was small and probably would not hold more than a few people. Felicia knew this from stories she heard about it. She has never actually gone down the old Mill Road as far as the mill and has never seen the mill. Felicia did not know of anyone who has ever gone there or seen the mill.

This won't be good, Felicia thought. She never liked David before their brothers' friendship, and their responsibilities for their respective younger sibling, forced them to spend a lot of time together.

The time they spent together gradually grew from awkward to grudging acceptance, to a friendship born of familiarity, like cousins, only they are not related at all.

"Why was it shut down?" Nick asked, getting sucked into David's trap.

David spun on him, leaning down into his face for dramatic effect.

"Because there were bodies all over the mill," he crooned. "The floors and walls were painted red with their blood. It was the worst killing in the history of the world. A mass killing, blood and gore and body parts everywhere!"

Nick backed away, his face full of fear, eyes wide and staring at him raptly, absorbing it all and not liking it.

"The night it happened it was a full moon, and no one saw or heard a thing. No one even knew why they were there in the middle of the night. Some say," David paused for dramatic effect," they might have been Devil worshipers there to summon demons." His voice trailed off in a soft hiss on the S. "But, to this day, some people still say you can hear their screams echoing in the sky at midnight on a full moon."

Nick swallowed a hard lump in his throat. His heart was racing, pounding so hard in his chest that it felt like it would pound right through him and fall out.

"He's going to have nightmares, you idiot," Felicia complained.

She stepped between them, slapping David roughly on the arm with a stern look and wrapped one arm protectively around Nick's shoulders. She led him away without a look back.

David could not help the mischievous grin.

Ian looked from David to Nick and saw the fear in Nick's eyes.

"Come on," David said, heading towards the old Mill Road again.

Nick looked behind him quickly and then at his feet. He turned and looked behind them.

"I don't want to go to the mill," he said.

David smirked. "Are you scared?"

"Leave him alone," Felicia said, scowling at David. "Come on, Nick." She walked away with Nick, heading back.

"What?" David tried not to laugh, his arms spread in supplication.

Ian walked past him, not looking at him, and followed Nick and Felicia.

David watched them go for a moment, and then jogged to catch up.

"I don't want to play anymore," Nick muttered. He shoved his hands in his pockets and fingered the action figure that made a small lump in one. Both Nick and Ian had an action figure they were playing with earlier in their pockets. He kept on walking.

"That's fine with me," David said, happy to go home.

Ian felt bad for David scaring Nick and felt he had to play peacekeeper. He caught up to Nick and leaned in, whispering in his ear.

"Come on, let's get him back. See if he can keep up. If he loses me, he's in big trouble."

They exchanged grins and took off in a sprint through the woods, veered sideways off the dear trail, jumped and dodged, moving quickly. Their small size allowed them to move better through the denser trees than their older siblings could.

"Hey!" Felicia yelled, startled by their sudden bolt. "Nick, come back!"

They did not slow down.

She turned to David, angry and concerned.

"We're going to lose them! Do you know how much trouble I'm going to be in?"

"Me too," David said.

David and Felicia sprinted after them and vanished through the trees.

Nick and Ian got carried away, taking the game too far. By the time they tired out, they were lost.

Nick stopped first, panting heavily, and looked around. His grin dropped away quickly to be replaced by a frown.

Following, Ian stopped next to him, gasping and panting to catch his breath. He looked around.

"Where are we?"

"I don't know." Nick's brow furrowed with worry.

They heard a cracking sound somewhere in the bush and both turned, scanning the trees and bushes for the source.

"What was that?" Nick asked.

"I don't know," Ian said breathlessly.

"Do you think it's a bear?" Nicked stared at him with wide eyes.

Being a worrier, Ian was pretty sure it is a bear, but he did not want Nick to be scared.

"It's probably Felicia and David," he said instead, as much to push his own fear away as for Nick's benefit.

They could hear David and Felicia calling them some distance away.

Nick shook his head. "Listen to their shouts. It was closer than they are." He swallowed. "A lot closer."

"What do you think it is?"

"A bear maybe? It sounds big."

"We should make noise," Ian said. "Bears don't like noise."

"What kind of noise?"

Ian shrugged. "We could call David and Felicia. Let them find us."

Nick nodded, liking this idea. He did not want to admit he was scared.

The boys started calling out David and Felicia's names, yelling as loud as they could.

"I hear them," Felicia panted breathlessly, "I think it's coming from that way."

Not to be outdone by a girl, David nodded knowingly and changed course.

Felicia and David made a lot of noise pushing their way through the woods, dry branches crackling beneath their feet and snapping on trees.

"Shhh," Ian shushed Nick, looking around nervously.

Nick stopped yelling, looking at him.

"What?"

"Listen."

They both listened.

There were the usual sounds of birds and squirrels, the wind blowing through the leaves with a dry hissing sound. They could also hear the sporadic calls of Felicia and David, calling them and the sound of branches breaking as something charged through the woods.

"It's David and Felicia," Nick said. "They're getting closer."

"The other sound," Ian whispered. "Listen. I'm sure there is something else out there too. It's coming from another direction."

Nick listened, not hearing it. He looked at Ian.

"Are you trying to scare me?" Nick asked. "There's nothing out there but David and Felicia."

"No," Ian said. "I'm sure I heard something."

The crashing sounds came closer and so did Felicia and David's calling.

Nick started calling back again and minutes that stretched too long later Felicia and David came blundering through the trees, finding them.

"There you are," Felicia panted, her face stern. "You know we have to stay together nick." She rounded on him angrily, towering over him.

David doubled over, panting and gasping, trying to catch his breath. He looked around, trying to get his bearings. They were completely turned around and he had no idea which way to go.

"Sorry," Nick said sheepishly. "Can we go home now?"

Felicia looked around. Nothing looked familiar.

"Which way is home?" Ian asked, looking a little scared.

"It's this way." David pointed the way, hoping he was guessing right. He did not want to admit he did not know, or that he was scared too.

"It's this way," Felicia countered. She started out in another direction without waiting for him to respond.

"How do you know?" David asked.

Felicia pointed up to the sky without looking back.

David and Ian both looked up while Nick focused only on following his sister.

"Look at the sun. It's getting late," Felicia said. "The sun sets in the west. That way is west. The road should be this way."

David grinned. It was good enough for him. "I knew that."

Ian and David hurried to catch up.

They walked for what felt like hours, pushing their way through the bushes, trying to find an easier path, climbing over fallen trees when they blocked the way.

A downed tree sprawled on the ground blocked the way, its branches barren and poking up in dry brittle sticks. Felicia walked around the tree.

Nick stopped dead in his tracks, looking down, a puzzled frown on his face.

It took a few steps for Felicia to notice he stopped following. She stopped and turned to look at him with a frown.

"Come on Nick, I want to get home."

Nick just stood there staring down.

"What is it?" Felicia asked, annoyed. "Let's just go."

"It's-," Nick started, but trailed off.

Ian caught up to Nick and stopped to inspect what he was staring down at. He blanched.

"Gross," Ian complained. "Is it from Halloween? It's not even close to Halloween."

David stopped next to them, staring down at Nick's find.

Felicia only looked more impatient staring back at them.

"Whoa," David gasped, staring down in a mix of awe and shock. "I think it's real." His stomach churned and a sick chill slowly filled him with the shock of what he was staring at.

Felicia finally came back to see what they were staring at. She joined them, staring down at the thing on the ground. All animation left her face at the sight of it, leaving her face expressionless.

The four kids stood around looking down at it.

The downed tree Felicia walked around moments before sprawled across the ground, its wood going soft with rot looked chewed on by some giant creature in spots, but that was just its decomposition in death. Ferns and other undergrowth grew up around the fallen tree. Termites crawled around on it, following one another in a drunken path, moving in and out of a crack splitting down part of its length where the tree cracked from the force of the concussion in its fall when strong winds snapped off the dead brittle wood of its trunk near its base. The tree laid across the top of two large rocks, rough ground, and other fallen deadwood, its top partially caught up in the bottom branches of other trees as though they had reached out to catch their fallen brethren, snagging its branches with their own and forever frozen in time in that position.

Next to the tree was a hollow depression in the ground.

Lying in that hollow was the thing that changed everything.

Nick started sobbing and moved closer to Felicia. She instinctively put an arm around his shoulders. She did not want to touch him. Somehow, that familial contact felt wrong with what was happening.

Ian gagged and put a hand to his mouth to try to keep himself from vomiting.

"It doesn't smell like anything." David looked from one to another, looking to each of them for understanding. "It doesn't smell like anything. It can't be real. It should smell."

"It doesn't smell because it's all dried up." Felicia's tone was as expressionless as her face.

It has been dry for weeks, the region locked in a drought that has baked the crops in the fields, dried up small streams and creeks, and left everything dry and brittle.

The image will be burned into their memories forever.

The face of a child stared back at them. It looked strangely soft and putty-like but hard and waxy at the same time; a face that wasn't really a face and not all there. Dried thin skin covered a section from the nose down one side of the slack jaw. The rest was part flesh covered, part pale bone, as if the skin and tissue had slowly melted away like an ice cube in the hot sun before going hard. It was a face that was not all there, like it was in the process of being made or un-made by a special effects creator.

Closer inspection showed the softer flesh was not so soft. It had the subtle wrinkling of leather; dried from the wind and the sun and the dry rainless air. Insects crawled through the moss and dead leaves that rotted along with the corpse, drying into a dark mass with it. They wriggled and crawled through the face and the body that had partially melted into the ground with decomposition, feeding off the leathery flesh.

The grisly face stared back at them blindly, its jaw hanging slack in a lopsided demented death grin. Clear and accusing. They could not tell if it was a boy or girl.

David knelt down, inspecting it more closely.

"Shit," he muttered. "This thing is real."

He got up slowly and stared at the others in sickly shock. They stared back in dumbfounded disbelief that devolved slowly to mirror his look.

"We aren't supposed to be out here," David said. "We will be in trouble just for being here."

David also had the irrational fear of somehow being blamed for the dead kid in the woods, although they only discovered it. Like getting caught with your hand on the cookie jar when you were only replacing the lid you found sitting on the counter and did not touch the cookies.

That fear was a hot lump in his stomach like no fear he has ever had before.

A choked guttural sound hung between them. The four kids stood in a circle looking down at it. Darkness was already creeping across the sky, chasing the late afternoon sun away. The gloom was made darker by the shade of the tall trees surrounding them. Glimpses of open grass could be seen through the trees ahead where they entered the woods.

David looked at each of them, forcing them to meet his steady gaze.

"I don't think we should tell anyone," David said.

"We have to." Ian stared at him in increased alarm.

"They will think we did it," David warned. "We could go to jail."

He looked at Felicia for support, but she would not look at him. Felicia would not look at anything but the thing on the ground.

"You all have to swear to not tell anyone. Ever." David looked around at each of them sternly.

Nick whimpered.

I don't want to go to jail, Nick thought, fear surging through him despite the numb shock. That's where they put bad people like Uncle Harvey. Uncle Harvey scares me; a lot.

Nick looked at Felicia for help, but she was oblivious to the terrifying thoughts in his head. He looked at David and Ian. They seemed to have forgotten he was there.

I don't want to go live in jail with Uncle Harvey, Nick thought, looking back at the gruesome spectacle on the ground before them. He started to cry.

Felicia just stood there next to her little brother, her face ashen, shivering although it was still quite warm and sticky with the humidity left behind by the waning hot day.

She knew they would not put them in jail like adults. They were only kids, after all. And how could anyone possibly think they did this? But she did not say that.

She did not say anything at all and just kept staring down at it with a sick feeling.

Felicia put one arm around Nick to comfort him. He leaned into her gratefully and huffed as he tried to get his hiccupping sobs under control.

Ian shook his head. Not in disagreement, but in utter shock to find themselves here in this place at this moment; facing this.

"Nobody is saying anything," David said. The look he gave them all was bordering on angry defiance, but still the chilled shock they all felt. "Fine. If you swear to keep the secret don't say anything. Otherwise, you have to tell me you are going to betray us all."

The only sound was Nick's soft whimpering and sniffling.

No one met David's eyes. No one looked up from their terrible secret.

The breeze picked up, the gust of wind invading the woods to rustle the leaves, picking up and swirling any loose leaves it found and let them fall as they will. It teased at Felicia's hair, making it dance for a moment, and then the gust of wind was gone.

Felicia shivered harder under the onslaught of the wind, despite the lack of chill on it.

Someone walked over my grave, she thought. It made her shudder.

"Come on Nick," David said, looking down at him seriously, "you have to stop crying or they will know something is wrong. We can't leave here until you stop."

Nick coughed and blubbered, trying to make the tears stop.

A crow stared down at them from its perch on a branch, their only witness, and then took flight and vanished over the trees.

The sky grew darker, the sun lowering on the horizon, as they stood there mutely staring like worshipers at a grisly shrine.

Finally, with Nick's tears under control, they nodded their wordless agreement, turned, and melted into the fast darkening woods, looking more like spectres than living children.

This would be their secret.

*****

Felicia's lanky legs moved with a new angry stiffness. Her whole body was stiff with it as they trudged mutely through the forest, following her lead.

David glanced at her now and then. It was killing him to stay quiet. He needed to say something to her but did not know what to say.

Ian and Nick followed mutely behind them, lost in their own horror with the image of the dead kid swimming before their eyes and making them stumble constantly over the rough terrain.

David saw something ahead. It was a beacon of hope. A lightening of the darkness of the tree branches, an opening to the sky.

He pointed.

"A break in the trees. I bet it's the road."

Seemingly ignoring him, Felicia changed direction towards it.

After a stretch of time that felt much longer than it was, they were rewarded when they broke free of the trees into the grassy expanse running alongside the old Mill Road. If they continued in the direction they were going, they would have eventually found themselves somewhere back along the edge of the woods some distance from the abandoned train station and away from town.

They made their way across the ditch and started walking down the road towards home.

They walked in silence for some time. Only the crunching of stones along the edge under their feet marked their existence.

Finally, Ian broke the silence.

"What about his family?" Ian asked. "Or her if it's a girl? Someone is looking for this kid. They have to be worried. If they don't find the body, they will never know what happened to their kid."

Nick looked at him and then at Felicia. He avoided looking at David. Ian said what he was thinking, and he knew David would just say something rude about it.

David opened his mouth to speak but Felicia beat him to it.

"You got a good look at it. Did it look fresh to you?"

"No," Ian admitted.

"I heard nothing about any missing kids. Did any of you hear anything?"

Nick and Ian both shook their heads, softly murmuring, "No."

David almost said what he was thinking. Sure they did. The whole town did. A while back when Felicia and Nick's uncle Harvey came back some years ago before he went away again. He just got out of jail. Everyone said so. It was right around that time, right after he got back, that the body of some kid was found in the woods.

Just like today.

Felicia knew David too well and heard the same rumours about her uncle. Hell, she heard them in a way no one outside of her house would have, straight from her own mother's mouth. Her mother who hated her uncle Harvey.

She gave David a warning look and he closed his mouth.

"A kid who is still missing," Felicia added.

"No," David admitted sullenly.

Felicia looked at each of them solemnly.

"Whoever that kid was, nobody around here is even looking for him or her. Nobody but us knows."

"And whoever left it there," David said quietly. But they all heard.

Already, Nick was wondering if this was real. If they really saw the decomposing body of a child left in the woods. Was it months ago? Weeks? Days? Years? Was it a game they played and he only imagined it?

There was safety in pretending a thing is not real. Even when every fibre of your being knew that was a lie. There was safety in forgetting. In a way.

Ian was just numb. Numb with fear that somehow whoever or however that kid came to be there, whoever was responsible for his death, or hers, would know they were there. That they found it. That he would come after them.

An icy chill filled Ian and he was surprised he did not urinate on himself.

David had to continually force himself to not look back. To just look straight ahead as they walked on.

"We can't tell anyone," David said. "Ever. We can't even talk to each other about it."

Only Felicia knew what was going on in her mind as they walked home with the darkness deepening around them.

When they reached Felicia and Nick's street, they split up in two groups, going to their own houses.

David and Felicia shared one last emotionless look as they parted.

17 - Uncle Harvey

Today, Uncle Harvey's Cabin

Uncle Harvey's cabin is a rustic creature, separated from town by a good but walkable hike through the woods. It is a much longer drive through the twists and turns of backcountry roads that, if one is not familiar with, would leave anyone looking for it lost. The roads are not always passable by conventional vehicle. There are times when his only access to town is by snowmobile or off-road four-wheeler.

The cabin is in disrepair, like an abandoned old mountain-man cabin. A grisly wind-chime of polished bones from various small carcasses clatters with a mournful hollow sound in the breeze, as if forever mourning the deaths of the creatures that died to give it life.

A rabbit and a quail are tied together by their back feet and hanging limply, the last remnants of blood from the fresh kills still dripping to soak into the dirt beneath them. The blood stench would attract predators, except the dirt they drip into is a large mud-lined cookie sheet. The bloodied dirt will later be used to fertilize part of the garden where greens requiring more nitrogen grow, and to deter some of the animals like deer and rabbits that feed on the garden. The scent of blood will attract other animals too, but they do not usually eat the garden.

Another, mud-less, cookie sheet with a puddle of blood on layers of previously dried blood sits drying in the open air to be made into blood meal, a high nitrogen fertilizer. A weaker blood meal is used for the garden so as to not burn the plants with too much nitrogen.

Concentrated blood dried into blood meal can be set out as poison when the coyotes become too troublesome. When ingested by dogs, blood meal can cause vomiting and diarrhoea, and even severe pancreatitis, leading to death. As a high nitrogen fertilizer, it can also be used to make a homemade bomb.

Like the cabin, the fence surrounding the vegetable garden is in poor repair, doing little to stop animals seeking to devour the under cared for vegetables surviving within.

Harvey has not slept well since being released from the holding cell and looks even more worn and weathered than before.

There are no phone lines to the cabin and standard cell signal is spotty at best, if you can get a signal at all.

Uncle Harvey is on the phone inside his cabin, the voice crackling weakly in his ear. He runs his hand roughly through his scruffy hair and down his beard. The stress of the phone conversation is taking its toll on him.

"Why are you still out there?" The voice on the phone asks in a stressed voice. It is impossible to tell through the crackling feed if it is a man or woman talking to him.

"Unfinished business," Harvey says. "Besides, this is my home."

"It's not a home. It is an old cabin. Is it even liveable?"

"I've lived in it long enough."

"I told you last time not to go back there. Small towns don't forget."

"I was innocent then," Harvey says, the strain in his voice revealing more annoyance than the stress on his face. "I'm innocent this time too. I've never done anything to hurt anyone."

"They won't believe you," the voice on the phone says. "They've already targeted you, haven't they?"

"I spent a few hours in a holding cell," Harvey says. "They let me go so they can follow me and catch me doing something."

"So, it's already started then."

"It never ended," Harvey says.

"You should leave. Get out of there. Don't go back."

"I have to finish this."

"There is nothing to finish. Whatever you are looking for there, it does not exist." You can hear the frustration in the voice on the other side of the phone; envision the head shaking.

"It does, and I'll find it."

"Goodbye Harvey. Whatever you are looking for, I hope it doesn't find you."

The person on the other end disconnects the call.

Harvey looks down at the phone for a moment, and then puts it down.

"I'll find it," he mutters, heading for the door.

He goes out and checks the small game he left hanging for the blood to drain. He pauses, looking out to the woods surrounding the small cabin. These will be supper. He needs to catch live bait.

Blood and carcasses will attract anything that scavenges. The smell will draw an animal from as far away as the wind carries the scent of the blood, but it is the terrified quivering of live meat that titillates the hunter; the smell of fear and the squeal of an animal in mortal danger before it gives up its life.

He takes the rabbit and quail down; carrying them to a shed the size of the small cabin nestled in the trees behind the cabin, invisible to anyone approaching the cabin from most angles.

The door creaks on its hinges as he opens it, opening to the darkness within. Harvey steps inside; the blackness swallowing him. It takes him only a moment to find the light switch. It makes a soft click when he flips it on. Two florescent ceiling lights with two bulbs each flicker to life with a dull moaning hum, blinking more than they work, glowing and dimly flickering their spasmodic dance as they warm up. Finally, one bulb at a time, they snap to life and stay lit, and the inside of the shed is bathed in the sickly dim light of the bulbs that leave shadows lurking in corners and behind every barrier. Cabinets, toolboxes, and two workbenches are featured in the shed among the clutter of stacked boxes and shelves of assorted items.

Harvey goes to one of the benches, dropping the dead animals on it. He reaches up and turns on an overhead hanging light, lighting the surface like a spotlight in the dim light of the shed. The top of the bench is stained dull brown and red with the old blood of past hunts. This is where he guts and skins his prey, cleaning it to cook.

He pulls a knife out of a knife block on the bench and starts to work. First, he deftly guts the rabbit, careful not to nick the colon and taint the meat.

A fly buzzes his face and he waves it away. Two more buzz him.

He performs a few deft cuts. Putting the knife down, he digs his fingers in under the skin, holding the rabbit in one hand and pulling the skin off with the other like peeling off a tight glove. He finishes cleaning the rabbit and moves on to the bird, plucking and gutting it.

Harvey finishes cleaning the bird and sets it down next to the raw meat with bones and eyes that is the rabbit. The rabbit's mouth gapes open as if panting, its teeth now looking like it is snarling showing brighter against the raw meat of its face. He scrapes the skin and feathers and gore off the bench to fall into a plastic barrel on the floor and pressed against the bench on one side.

It plops wetly into the barrel, landing on the rotting remains of the guts, feathers, and skins of previous cleanings. Flies swarm, buzzing angrily in shock at the disturbance. The mass in the barrel writhes with pale white maggots.

The stench in the cabin must be nauseating, eye watering, overwhelming. And yet Harvey seems entirely unaffected by it.

He turns off the overhead light, picks up his meal, and heads for the door, snapping the lights off on the way.

The nonstop buzzing of the electricity flowing to the fluorescent lights cuts out and the lights cool and flicker off as he closes the door behind him, leaving the shed to its darkness.

Harvey returns to the cabin to start making his supper.

18 – Visit with the Old Sheriff

"How much do you want to bet this guy kept the files himself?"

Liam Tobin is sitting in his car in the road staring at the old house the retired sheriff lives in. The house is small, the yard sparse but neat, and an old pickup truck sits rusting in the driveway.

He looks down at the open notebook in his hand. It is small enough to fit in a sizeable pocket, bound at the top, and three quarters filled with his own hastily jotted notes.

The image of the body in the woods sits heavily before his eyes. It has the faded colorless sepia tint of old photos, as if his memory forgot the colors.

It was small, the size of a child, and curled up as if for warmth or to huddle against the nightmares that filled the last moments of life. The face stared fixatedly on something, perhaps a memory in the past the lost soul was trapped in forever, endlessly tormented at the moment of death.

The limbs and body, every part of it, were made smaller by the desiccation of the flesh, the withering of what remains of muscles after the fats have liquefied and the moisture oozed out into the ground. The muscles themselves would have partially liquefied, shrivelling and drying into ropes of hardened jerky, pulling the limbs in tighter in unnaturally twisted ways. The skin becomes a papery leather shroud after the fat layer beneath has melted away and the skin dried and stiffened.

The nails appeared long, the effect of the flesh of the fingertips and toes shrivelling away from them. The teeth jutted out in a grimace without the padding of soft lips, the eye sockets sunken and hollow; the soft eyes the first to melt away in putrefaction. The hair had mostly fallen out, leaving wispy strands still clinging to the skull.

Strangely, it did not look as if the insects had touched it at all.

He could not avoid it. He was drawn to it, focusing on the face. The face of the child refused to look at him, not all there, crisp papery skin covering a section on one side of the slack jaw, the rest bare pale bone.

It is not the body in the woods up the old Mill Road. That one was removed before he arrived and shipped off to a forensic medical examiner. He could have gone there first to see it first hand, but that was pointless.

The image haunting him is of another, older, body that he had studied the hundreds of photographs of. A body that had been found in these same woods bordering this town years ago.

Liam flips his notebook closed with a sense of finality, shoving it into his pocket.

"All right, let's do this."

He is alone, accompanied only by the nightmares of his job. They go with him everywhere, sleep with him at night, and taint his every waking moment.

Getting out of the car, he approaches the house. Raising his hand, his knuckles hesitate for a scattering of heartbeats before rapping on the door.

The wait is long enough for him to wonder if anyone is home, then he finally hears the dull echo of footsteps inside.

A man opens the door, staring at him with the worn eyes of a man who has seen too much. He is weathered with age and somewhat stooped over. He looks like he was taller once, would still be if he were not hunched over. There is a sense of frailness about him that goes beyond the ravages of age on his body.

Liam nods to him and he stares out at him, his old eyes steady and cold.

"Chester Hayes," Liam says, "I'm Detective Liam Tobin from C. C. I."

Chester looks him up and down with an unfriendly look.

"What does Cold Case Investigation want with an old man?"

"You used to be the sheriff here."

"Used to be. Not anymore. I retired a long time ago."

"You were sheriff when the remains of a child were found in the woods off Road Three Fifty-Seven. Locals call it the old Mill Road."

"That was a long time ago. Is that why you are here? That case was put to bed years ago."

"Yes, your office put it to bed, but it was never closed. Not officially, anyway. But that's not why I'm here. I was called in because another cadaver was found in the same vicinity."

Liam doesn't tell him about the other, older, body found in the same place. The body from the photo.

Staring into the old man's eyes, he knows he doesn't have to.

Chester stares him down. There is defiance in his old eyes, and something else; knowing.

"One of the officers at the station sent me," Liam says, "Malcolm Colbert. He thought you could help me."

"With what?"

"I was looking through old files to get a feel of what goes on in the area and to find anything that might be related to the remains in the woods. The thing is the files only go back so far. Malcolm thought you might know something about that."

Chester nods slowly.

"I guess I do."

"So, you know what files I'm talking about."

Chester nods again, stepping back from the door.

"I guess you can come in."

Liam follows him into the dimmer interior of the little house.

Chester shuffles through the small living room on arthritic legs, leading the way to the kitchen.

Liam takes in the worn bare home, sparsely furnished and tidy. There is nothing to suggest a wife and children ever lived in this house, or that grandchildren ever came to visit. There are no family photos or familial trinkets. The house screams lonely old man from every corner.

"Coffee or tea?" Chester asks when they reach the kitchen.

"Coffee is fine. You live alone?"

"The missus passed on some time ago. The kids don't have much use for coming back to this little shit town. Town's dying. You wouldn't think so with that foolish nonsense of putting in new houses, but it is. Has been for a long time. It just doesn't know it yet."

Liam nods understanding. From the lack of mementos and the retired sheriff's abrasiveness, he doesn't seem like he much cares if they never come visit.

"Malcolm said all the files were put into storage somewhere when the police were transitioning to the new location. But it doesn't seem any of the files were ever moved over."

Chester shrugs, his back still to Liam as he makes the coffee.

"Didn't seem much point in moving them again. In all my years on the force I never saw any call to look at those old files. No one ever did. They were sent to be archived."

"Malcolm said they have no record of that, or of where they might have been sent to."

Chester chuckles humourlessly, his shoulders moving up and down with it. He turns to look at Liam, pulling out a chair from the kitchen table and motioning Liam to do the same as he sits.

"Malcolm has no imagination," he says. "Even as a boy growing up, he never had any thoughts of his own. All the small-town forces like this use the same regional archive."

He levels a look at Liam.

"You should have figured that out."

"I learned years ago to never assume," Liam says, "especially when it comes to anything from the older generations. There are lots of checks and balances in place now for everything from how to fill out a report to how to store it. Not so much even ten years ago."

Chester gives him a brief look. He finally nods.

"You kept some of the files, didn't you?" Liam gives him a knowing look.

"You got me. I didn't send all the files off. I kept a few. Wanted to make sure they didn't get lost."

"Or you couldn't let them go," Liam says.

The coffee maker finishes. Chester gets up, pouring them both a coffee and setting them on the table before returning to his seat.

"There are always some cases we can't let go of, isn't there?"

The image of the child's body in the old photo flashes in Liam's head again. He nods agreement.

"Some years ago the remains of a child were found in the woods. They were old, have been there for some time, just like this one."

"Yes and no," Chester says.

"Tell me about it."

Chester's eyes shift, reluctant to dredge up the old memory he laid to rest years ago but could never quite let go.

"We don't get a lot of missing people around here," he says. "Folks mostly grow up here. Not many people move to little towns like this. Kids that grow up in the bush know it. They don't get lost.

We were having a dry spell. Game was scarce, probably moved on to where feed was better. A few pets went missing and no one gave it any thought. It happens. But then a couple kids went missing over in the next town."

Liam silently urges him to continue.

"There was a search of the woods. People from miles around went to help search, it being kids and all. They were not found. Not a sign of them. After a time the search was called off, although I heard the families never stopped walking the woods hoping for closure, a body, some sign, anything. Something to bury."

"But a body was found," Liam says.

"Yes sir, it was, after a bit. That was before my time. Things were quiet for a time, years, but people did not forget. And then Robbie Miller went missing."

"Another kid," Liam says.

"Another kid," Chester confirms. "Like the others, folks came from miles around to search the woods. We set up search grids."

He looks at Liam, his eyes holding the meaning of those words.

"We were organized, the search done with thought to cover every inch of these woods and not miss turning over a single leaf."

"You didn't find him," Liam says.

Chester shakes his head.

"Not at first. But then we did, after a time. Months later."

Liam stares at him expectantly.

"The thing is," Chester continues, "the Miller kid was found where he ought not to have been. We already searched that area.

He wasn't there. He wasn't there." His voice holds the gravity of a man revisiting the impossible.

"So someone placed the body there after the area was searched," Liam says.

"It's the only explanation that makes sense. But a lot of this doesn't make sense. The remains . . . he was all chewed up, torn apart, like a pack of coyotes got him."

"But you don't think that's what happened?"

Chester stares levelly into his eyes.

"Coyotes don't move a kill like that. They might drag it around a bit, but they don't move it. We'd have found it when we searched the area. It wasn't scattered either. It was set in place all nice, like he just kind of curled up there and went to sleep and died."

"But you said he was torn up, chewed on."

Chester nods. "That's what it looked like."

"Are you saying some animal or animals got the boy, killed and partially devoured him, and then someone moved the remains after you already searched the area?"

"That's what it looked like."

"You sound like you don't believe it," Liam says.

"Nothing about that case had much cause for belief."

"Who was your prime suspect? Even if you couldn't prove it, you must have had someone in mind."

"There wasn't much for crime in the area. Being so small, anything happened and everybody knew exactly who did it. Folks mostly dealt with things on their own, petty things. Teens stealing farm gas to go joyriding, that sort of thing."

"So, you know who it was."

Chester shakes his head.

"The whole town had him pegged; a young man from the area fresh out of jail. Did some stupid things as kids will do and got put away for a couple of years. He just came back to town after he was released, right around the time the Miller kid was found.

Harvey Lawson. Our best guess was someone was moving the body around to keep it from being found when we were searching the woods.

Folks were all riled up about it. We brought him in for questioning. Had to, since the whole community already decided he was guilty."

"So, he was a suspect because people around town said so?"

"It's a small community," Chester says. "Folks are usually right. And if they're not, well they won't let it go until you show them they are wrong and make them believe it."

"Was he guilty?"

"That's anybody's guess. Being the only one around who actually went to prison for anything, and that he's always been an odd bird even as a child; he was the most likely suspect. We didn't have enough to lock him up for it. But there was trouble since then. People were angry we didn't lock him up. There were a number of run-ins involving young Harvey Lawson and folks around town. It got to where you couldn't tell anymore if it was Harvey making trouble for folks in the area or the other way around.

The only thing certain was there were a lot of fights involving Harvey and his family, mostly his sister. Some of the fights got physical and we locked him up to give everyone time to cool off."

"So, he assaulted her?" Liam asks.

"Could be. Or the other way around. You know how it goes when folks are riled up and arguments get heated. He said she hit him, she said he hit her. Back then we mostly let folks sort these things out for themselves unless there was reason to lock them up. No one had injuries that I recall, so we locked up Harvey to put an end to the argument. It wasn't the first or the last time the Lawson siblings had to be split up for fighting. Harvey's sister was a firecracker. Probably still is."

"That couldn't look good for him, being a suspect in a child's death."

"No, it didn't. Didn't take long before folks decided he was behind the kids going missing some time earlier in the next town too."

"Was he?"

"No. He was in jail then, juvenile detention. I checked. That was the one thing that made me question if he was behind the Miller kid, the similarities of kids going missing all of a sudden without a trace. It's too much coincidence for me for there to be no connection.

Folks blamed him all the same. They wanted answers. Someone to blame. It took almost five years to put a case together against Harvey for the Miller boy. Then the trial. He was found guilty, probable cause, all circumstantial; mostly because of his history for being odd and the fights between him and his sister and the family.

His parents moved away. Couldn't take the shame. But his sister and her family stayed. A few years of appeals and the conviction was overturned. Harvey Lawson was set free.

"Where does Harvey's sister live? I'd like to talk to her."

"Can't say. They moved away years ago. The day he got released her and her husband packed up the kids and took off in the middle of the night."

Liam stares at him.

"Do you know why they left?"

"She was done with him I guess," Chester shrugs. "I went out to the house myself to break the news to her that he was getting out. He must have called her because she already knew. It was ugly. She was furious, Diana. Rueben, her husband, was yelling at everyone. In the morning they were gone."

"Must be some bad blood between them," Liam guesses, "from before."

"There's a lot of bad blood in this town," Chester says. "The area has a history. A dark one. And it goes way back."

19 – David's Obsession

David is agitated. He is pacing back and forth at the junction of two roads near Dusty's, an outward symptom of the thoughts swirling in his head. This is a small town and nobody keeps their mouth shut in a small town. Rumors spread fast and gossip faster.

By now the whole town and surrounding community knows someone found the desiccated remains of a child in the woods just behind the field under construction up the Old Mill Road. The body is old, years old, and little more than bones. But it is undeniably human and child sized.

Loud whispers are being shared all over town as the locals try to piece together the tragic news and figure out who the body belongs to. Despite the old wives' tales of kids and pets vanishing in the area at some mysterious time in the past, no one actually knows of any kids who have gone missing. Not recently anyway. There haven't been any disappearances of local kids in the area in the living locals' lifetime, except the Miller boy.

All fingers are pointing one way. Old Uncle Harvey.

David had done his own digging through the sludge of the rumour mills.

"When we were kids, Felicia and Nick's Uncle Harvey went to jail. More than once."

David's movements have the stiffness of a person deep in agitated thought.

For as long as I can remember all the dark rumours in this town centered around two things, the old Mill Road and their uncle Harvey. Everyone I talked to, as far back as anyone can remember stories were shared about strange things happening down the old Mill Road. Only a few of the old timers remembered anything actually happening. The rest was just stories.

There were a few others David tried to talk to, middle aged farmers Harvey's age or close enough to it who might have remembered hearing stories, but they would not talk about it.

From the people he did talk to all he got were vague over-told stories of some unknown thing, maybe kids vanishing and their remains being found. It was second or third hand, or worse.

One name was repeated. There was one man who those he questioned were sure would remember.

Old Mr. Woodstone.

David perks up when movement catches his eye, staring at the approaching man.

The old man shuffling up the road has the gait of the very elderly. His legs are somewhat bowed, his back and shoulders stooped, and he moves with the stiffness of an arthritis ravaged body. His clothes are well worn and unfashionably well-suited to how David imagines a retired farmer in his eighties would dress. Thinning wispy white hair rustles in the breeze with not enough there to cover his scalp.

David waits for him to reach him.

He can't wait any more. He is itching with impatience. He starts for the old man, meeting him on the way.

"Mr. Woodstone," David starts, jogging up to him. "Hi, I'm-."

"I know who you are," Mr. Woodstone mutters, waving him off in a gesture that is casually dismissive, dismissing the introduction, not the young man.

David is still pumped with the need to find out anything he can quickly, the sense of urgency pushing him to near rudeness.

Slow down, he tells himself. These old guys don't move fast in any way. Don't make him angry.

Trying to slow his urgency, David just jumps in.

"Mr. Woodstone, I've been talking to anyone I can to find out more about the rumours that something happened a long time ago around the old abandoned mill. I've heard all kinds of stories growing up. I know most of them were made up just to tell ghost stories, kids scaring each other and stuff. People have always said something bad happened there a very long time ago."

Mr. Woodstone's mouth works like he's chewing over the memories jumbled in his own aged mind.

"That's a pretty long time ago. I'm not sure what those old stories have to do with anything."

"I'm mostly interested in something that happened around here when I was a kid. I don't know that it has anything to do with the old ghost stories about the old mill."

"I'm thirsty," Mr. Woodstone says suddenly. Tell me what you want on the way to Dusty's. Buy me a beer and I'll think about if I know anything."

David grins. *The old codger is demanding payment for information,* he thinks wryly. He ducks his head in a nod and they walk on, the old man shuffling much too slowly for David's longer leaner legs. He has to keep consciously changing his pace, slowing to keep to the old man's shuffle.

"Everyone seems to bring up those old stories," David continues as they walk, "like somehow it's connected."

"So, what's got you all ruffled?"

"Friends of mine back then. They had an uncle who was in jail. When he got out, their family moved away all of a sudden."

The old man chuckles a dry rattle that almost breaks into a choking fit. His lips crease into a semi-toothless grin. He knows who David is talking about before David can say the name.

"Harvey," David pauses. Felicia's uncle's last name is a blank in his mind. A blush threatens to creep up his neck and he wants to give himself hell for not knowing the name before talking to people.

"Harvey Lawson," Mr. Woodstone nods. "I remember giving that kid hell more than a few times. He was always a bit odd that one."

They arrive at Dusty's. They enter and Mr. Woodstone grunts towards the bartender across the room who doesn't see them come in. They sit and David looks around, wondering if the waitress is on or if he has to go up to the bar for their drinks.

The bartender looks up from washing glasses, spies them, and immediately fills a glass with draught from the tap. He approaches the table, sets the draught in front of the old man, and turns to David.

"What'll it be?"

Mr. Woodstone grunts in form of a thank you and starts thirstily drinking the beer while David tells the bartender what he wants and the bartender walks away.

Mr. Woodstone puts the now half-empty glass down with a sigh of contentment.

"What do you want to know?"

"I want to know what happened."

"To Harvey or before?"

David shrugs. "Harvey. People said he went to jail for killing a kid. But, if he did, he should have been in jail a lot longer. What really happened? What did he really do?"

Mr. Woodstone levels his age-rheumy eyes at him.

"What's your stake in this?" His tone is serious, as if the answer will decide if he keeps talking.

"My friend. Her family left for a reason. I need to know why."

Mr. Woodstone nods understanding. "It's like that then."

The bartender returns with David's drink and another cold glass of draught for the old man. David looks down at the old man's first glass and it is empty. He is thirstily drinking the second glass.

Mr. Woodstone sets the glass down. His eyes get a far away look as he turns back to the past. So many years ago now; and yet not so long for one who has lived more than eighty years.

"A kid was found some years back," the old timer says, his eyes heavy with the memory. "It was the damnedest thing. A few kids went missing over in the next town. Some pets in the area. It was never unusual for pets to go missing. Coyotes get them usually; or a car. We sometimes get a bobcat around here too. They'll take down anything their size and smaller. We get the odd cougar too, but those are rare around here. To a cougar, everything that moves is food.

There was talk. Some folks talked about strange things said to have happened down at the old mill a long time before. Like it had anything to do with what was happening. People were a lot more superstitious then. Some said maybe it was a rogue pair of wolves, a splinter pack too small to feed itself, feeding off pets and farm animals.

Then the Miller kid went missing."

He chuckles wryly. It is not an expression of humour, but rather one of acknowledging the seriousness of the moment.

"Don't it beat all," he mumbles, his mind lost in the memory, "fitting, like a warning or something, the Miller kid goes missing and then gets found all tore up in the woods just off the road, down the old Mill Road. It took a while to find him. People came in from all over, searching the woods."

He looks at David, staring him down as if daring him to refute his story.

"Funny thing of it is that he was found where they already searched. He was all chewed up, torn apart, like a pack of coyotes got him."

"So, people didn't think it was the wolves?"

The old man shakes his head. "Wolves are particular about what they eat. They don't see people as food. Now the coyotes, they are more scavengers than wolves. They don't normally hunt people, but they'll eat anything they find dead. But there is no way. Coyotes don't hide the body and they don't move it like that. Not that far. They might drag a carcass around a bit, but if he had been left anywhere near there he'd have been found.

That body was not there the day they searched that part of the woods. The boy's body was put there after."

"What does that?" David asks, his heart pounding in his chest. His hands are clammy. He keeps flashing back to the body he and his friends found when they were kids.

The old man shrugs.

"Can't think of any animal that would move a body like that, except man and there's only one man known to bait coyotes," he says. "Harvey Lawson. I didn't think he would stoop to baiting coyotes with human flesh. Not even sure what he's baiting coyotes for. Can't sell the hides or anything. Unless they're getting to your livestock, there is no reason, and he has no livestock."

"So, Harvey used the Miller boy to bait coyotes?"

"Nah," the old man says. "I'm just pulling your chain on that. He was a suspect, though. Folks figured he killed the boy and was moving the body around to keep it from being found when they were searching the woods. Police brought him in and questioned him. The whole community pegged him as guilty. Before long they were pretty sure he was behind the kids in the next town going missing sometime earlier too.

It took maybe five years before the police had enough on him to lock him up. By then there were other problems in town. He was making trouble for some people, mostly for his sister and her family. There were some fights there. A few went physical and he got locked up a few times for hitting her."

The old man leans in. "If you ask me, though, she probably gave as good as she got when it came to blows. That girl had a temper on her.

Then Harvey got locked up for killing the Miller boy. The trial took a while. He only spent a few years in prison, though. There must have been more to the story between him and his sister than anyone knew because the day he got released she and her husband packed up the kids and took off."

David chews on this while Mr. Woodstone motions at the bartender for another beer.

Did their leaving have anything to do with the body we found in the woods? David thinks. It wasn't the Miller boy. That was years earlier. They wouldn't have just left the body there. This was another kid. Another victim of Felicia's Uncle Harvey? Maybe their leaving had nothing to do with that at all. But then what happened that night? Was it all because of old uncle Harv coming back?"

David had always sensed there was something odd there. He got weird vibes off Felicia anytime her uncle was mentioned.

I have to dig into that more later, once I figure out how and where.

"What about the old mill?" David asks. He looks up as the bartender sets filled glasses down and takes the empties away. He turns his attention back to the old man, who is thirstily drinking his beer. "I heard there were a bunch of people killed there a long time ago. That it was the reason the mill was shut down. Did that have anything to do with the Miller boy and Harvey?"

The old man shakes his head.

"That was long before the Miller boy. The mill was closed before I was born. Ghost stories about it were already being told. I was a just a kid when some odd things started happening. A few pets went missing, then more. It started to become common. Not just pets either, smaller livestock too. Chickens, goats, sheep.

Calves and weanling pigs. Some were found, some not. What was found was ripped apart. No surprise there. Whether coyotes got them, or a bobcat, or even a cougar, or if nothing got them at all. Scavengers would have got the carcasses anyway and they'd still be all torn up. You ever see a carcass after a bunch of crows got at it? Bigger mess than the coyotes.

It was a bad year for coyotes that year, wolves too. We were in the second year of a drought. Things were drying up all over. Even that weren't enough to explain where all the animals went, though."

"All the animals were gone? What do you mean?"

"Game was scarce; both big game and small. Deer, rabbits, you name it. Nobody that hunts was finding anything. It was worse than anyone remembered in worse drought years. It was like something drove them all off.

Then the wolves, they were gone too. Must have followed the game. It's not so bad for the wolves to relocate. They only have to compete with us and other wolf packs for territory. It's different for the coyotes. The coyotes don't have to compete just with other coyotes and us for their territory. They also have the wolves to worry about. A wolf pack won't tolerate a coyote pack competing with them for food. A new wolf pack moves in, and they'll either kill or drive off the coyote pack already there. Sometimes they will cohabitate an area like they do here, often not.

We could still hear the sharp yips of the coyotes at dusk. None of the low mournful howls of the wolves. That's how we knew what pack moved on and what stayed.

When animal carcasses were found ripped apart, partially eaten, it only made sense the coyotes got them. They'll eat just about anything, including dogs."

He looks down, having difficulty with the memory now.

David is not sure if the old man is having trouble remembering or with having to remember.

Mr. Woodstone continues with a heavy heart.

"Then a kid disappeared. It wasn't a local kid, so it didn't make much news in the area. The family was travelling through on their way somewhere else and stopped on the side of the road. Their car broke down or something. The family let the kids out of the car to stretch their legs and play. When they went to round them up, they were short a kid. Everyone figured the kid had wandered into the woods and got lost. Didn't hear much about it after that. A search was done then the whole thing kind of went away. The authorities still kept looking for him in the woods for a few months after, but nobody much talked about it.

While they were looking for him another kid disappeared. This one was closer to home; a family from a nearby town came into town. Some of the local kids played a prank, taking the kid up the old Mill Road towards the mill to scare him with ghost stories. They somehow managed to lose him. Another search was done; it was talked about more. But when it all died down and was forgotten everyone assumed he was found.

Then the rains came and the drought ended. The wild animals came back. The wolves too, following the game back."

He pauses, drinking long sips from his glass. He looks up at David.

David wonders at the haunted look he thinks he sees in his eyes.

The old man continues again.

"I was just married when another drought came. Four years in and everything was drying up and the game moved on, and with it the wolves again. Only the yipping of the coyotes was heard at night.

Then a girl disappeared at the old train station, young, maybe six years old. The train was still running through here then. It was maybe one of the last few trains to come through. Trains almost never came through by then. The train was stopped and her mother had taken her off the train. No one knew why. They were only passing through. Her mother last saw her chasing a butterfly in the field behind the train station, near the trees. The same bit of forest that borders the old Mill Road on the other side. She turned around and in that moment the girl was gone.

That got more attention for longer, only because the mother hung around and would not give up. Folks figured the girl wandered into the woods. A few thought maybe the coyotes were hungry enough to snatch her. More likely a cougar, I think.

Cougars are known to hunt people sometimes. She was convinced it was no four-legged animal. She swore someone took her girl.

She was the first pointing a finger at Harvey. He was young then, a kid of maybe ten, but already an odd one. Not very sociable; always hanging out in the woods and around the old mill as if he was looking for something.

People talked about what happened before, like it was somehow connected to the missing girl. But Harvey wasn't even born yet then.

It was more than a year after the first boy disappeared before his body was found in the woods, not far in from the road. The old Mill Road. They say his body was all curled up, like he was hiding or trying to stay warm. Not much to him but bones. Torn up some and some of his bones scattered. What flesh the animals had not eaten was kind of dried up like a mummy.

Six months later the other boy was found. Same thing. He was torn up and all dried up like. What was left of him was all rolled up, like he had died huddled in a ball.

A few other kids disappeared over the years too, after the girl at the train station.

The girl from the train station was found at the old abandoned mill, along with remains of some of the others. They were all torn up and partially eaten. Dried up too; probably because of the drought. Some said they thought something was holed up in the old mill.

Most thought it was someone; someone who was taking the kids and killing them then leaving them for the animals.

That was a long time ago. Everyone said the old mill was haunted. Some thought it was ghosts or evil spirits behind it all"

"What do you think?" David asks. "Do you think it was spirits?"

"Hmph," the old man snorts. "The only spirits are in a whisky bottle. There isn't nothing that kills indiscriminately like that except man and the odd predator like a cougar. Others go after the easy prey if they are weak or sick, the weak and vulnerable. There's nothing more vulnerable than a small child.

Nobody went down the old Mill Road after the girl and other remains were found at the old mill. It's a bad place."

"So if they thought it was the coyotes, what did they do?" David asks.

"Went out and shot them all, of course," the old man says. He turns and spits on the ground as if in disgust. "Worst thing you can do is drive off the pack you know, unless they turned rogue. They got the area all sorted out. They keep other packs out, whose behaviour you don't know. You can get them trained to leave your livestock alone. Did you know that? Just like dogs. Train them to leave your dogs alone too.

I figured the pack moved on like the wolves and a new pack probably moved in. That's why they started going after pets and livestock all of a sudden. Never was such a big problem before. The odd sick or injured one, but that was it. Not like this. This pack was hungry."

"After the coyote pack was killed off, what happened?"

"Things calmed down. New packs moved in, or maybe the old came back. Not too sure which. After the drought ended and the creeks filled again and everything started growing, the wild animals came back and the packs did too."

"The creek dried up?" David asks.

"Yep, every time we get a drought that lasts that long, the smaller creeks all dry up."

"So that was it then," David says.

"Until the Miller boy."

"Oh yeah, the Miller boy. That happened soon after?"

"No, it was years later. Another drought. Going into the third year on this one and everything dried up again. It was a bad time for the wild animals; livestock too. When the creeks and streams dried up and the game moved on, a pet went missing and was found all torn up and partially eaten. Everyone was worried more pets and livestock would start vanishing again.

Folks around here remembered the stories from before. They went hunting for wolves and coyotes. Never found any wolves. They were smart enough to follow the game. Trapped and shot the coyotes in the area right after that first pet went missing. But it didn't stop there. More pets vanished, and smaller livestock, just like before. Some were never found, and others found all torn up and half eaten.

Then the Miller boy went missing. A big search was organized, but no one found a trace of him. He was the only kid to go missing at that time. After a while people stopped looking.

Then one day he showed up.

He was found in the woods. The body was chewed on, of course. Scavengers would have got him. But the police didn't think it was some animal. Things about it just weren't right. Word got out and fingers started to get pointed.

And folks around here started wagging their tongues as they will do. When strange things happen it's always the strange that get blamed for it. And that strange thing was Harvey Lawson.

The police couldn't find any reason to charge him for the Miller boy. It took them a lot to piece together a case. Wasn't much of a case either. Didn't matter much, he was already guilty in the eyes of all the folks around here.

They had to take him somewhere else to try him. Couldn't find a jury here that hadn't already decided his guilt. Harvey went to prison and everyone breathed a sigh of relief."

"He didn't get long? I mean, I remember the stories about him going to jail for killing a kid, and him getting out of jail," David says.

"Yeah, he only spent, I think, a couple years if that in prison. Then they just let him out," the old man says.

"Why?" David asks. "He killed a kid, so why did they let him out so soon? Shouldn't he have gotten a lot more time?"

The old man smirks. It is a twisted grimace filled with distaste, although David is not sure if it is distaste for Harvey, the law, or something else.

"The judge decided he didn't do it. I don't know what they found, but whatever it was they just opened the door and let him go. Threw the whole thing out. Said he was innocent."

"Do you believe that?"

"That he was innocent?" The old man chews on the idea for a moment.

"Lot of people were convinced he was guilty. His own sister must have thought he was guilty. She up and packed up the family and left everything behind the moment she found out he was being let out. Didn't say goodbye to anyone. Sold the house as is. Didn't even bother coming back for their furniture and clothes and stuff."

David mulls this over. This is very interesting. *Who bought it?* He thinks. *What did they do with all the stuff?*

He tells himself he is interested because there could be some clues that would point to Harvey. Something that would reveal something about the body they found in the woods as kids.

He refuses to let himself acknowledge the real reason, that there might be something there, some small piece of Felicia left in that stuff. Something that might somehow bring him closer to her, or her closer to him.

"But what about you?" David asks again. "Do you think he killed the Miller boy?"

The old man's eyes seem suddenly older, shadowed somehow.

"You heard the old stories about the mill?"

"Yes, everyone has."

The old man nods.

"Whatever got that boy, it weren't human."

David sinks into himself. This is getting him nowhere. This old man believes the old superstitious nonsense he has heard since he was a kid. The old Mill Road monster. He wants to exhale a sharp laugh, but holds it in.

"I have to go," David says. He gets up and leaves, quickly tossing some money on the table for the bill.

*****

David stops by Ian's work. He is there behind the cashier, leaning against the wall, bored and waiting for someone to come along needing gas pumped or to buy something.

"Hey, what's up?" Ian asks, standing up when David comes in.

"Just digging up stuff on old Uncle Harv," David says.

"Are you still on that? This is really about Felicia, isn't it? She probably doesn't even remember you. I bet she's got a boyfriend. She's moved on, so why don't you?"

David throws him an annoyed look. "This is not about Felicia."

Everything with you is about Felicia, Ian wants to say. He doesn't. There is no point.

119

"So what is it about then?" Ian asks. "Why are you obsessing so much over this? It's in the past. Let it stay there."

David shakes his head, his expression only growing more intense.

"But it's not staying in the past," he says. "It's following us. There was another body found. Don't you see?"

"No, I don't see," Ian says. "That was so long ago. The body we found looked like it had been there a long time. Maybe years."

He levels his gaze at David, hoping to get through to him.

"Everyone is talking about the body. Every person who has come in here since it was found has talked about it. There is no way what we found as kids has anything to do with the body found now."

"You don't understand," David says. "It is the same body. Okay, it's not the *same* body in that sense. You would think it would be completely gone a long time ago, decomposing, animals eating it. But it could be the same body."

He is breathing heavier with the weight of what he is getting off his mind. The worry that has nagged him since learning a body was found that compounded with each new detail he learned about it.

Talking to the old man only made it worse.

"Okay, I'll bite," Ian says. "How?"

"It was found in the same spot. The. Exact. Same. Spot. Not just in the general area, but exactly. The same hollow in the ground under the same tree."

"How do you even know?" Ian asks. "That was so long ago. We were kids. How can you be sure it is the exact same place? I doubt we could have found the same place back then even if we tried."

David's impulse is to look away. He forces himself to meet Ian's look, to keep talking, to confess his secret.

"I went back," David says, his voice heavy with the weight of his confession.

"You went back." Ian feels like he is drifting all of a sudden. Those words don't surprise him. This is David, after all. It's dredging up this particular old memory that has him feeling like his feet no longer touch the floor. His body is weightless, being raised up and drawn into something he wants nothing to do with. He is being pulled into the past against his will. Or, perhaps the past is being pulled into the now. He doesn't know which. Either way it is bad and he wants no part of it.

"Yes," David says. "I went back. The next day, after Felicia and Nick didn't show up for school, I went to their house.

Their house, it looked … wrong. Stuff out of place that never was. Nobody was there. I couldn't see much through the window, but it looked like they took off in the middle of supper. Just packed up and left."

"Yes, you told me that," Ian says.

"I didn't tell you the rest," David says. "I went back again. The next day. I couldn't sleep all night. I didn't know what happened. I thought Felicia or Nick told them about what we found in the woods. But that didn't make sense with them disappearing like that, the whole family. And nobody came to talk to us. If they told, the police would have come and asked us about it. Our parents didn't ask about it. Nobody. Like no one but us knew it was there.

So, the next day I went back. I went back to the woods first. It took me a long time to find the spot, but I did. There were no police cars, no police tape. It was still there, in the dip in the ground almost under the fallen tree, just like when we found it.

It didn't even look like animals touched it. That seemed strange to me. Really strange, that even the animals were not touching it."

"They probably just didn't find it yet," Ian says. "You had trouble finding it, and you were there."

David shakes his head.

"After I found it in the woods, I went back to Felicia's house. I hoped I was wrong. That they didn't just leave. I mean, who just takes off like that and leaves all their stuff behind?"

"Someone running away from something," Ian says.

David continues.

"I remembered the basement window Felicia showed me before; a way to get in her house. I went inside. I have to tell you, it scared the hell out of me, what I found inside.

They were just gone, Ian. In the middle of dinner like something just suddenly disappeared them. Supper was on the table and they were just gone like they vanished in thin air. I remember thinking that and the strangeness of it scared the hell out of me."

There is a heavy pause. There are some things he still can't tell anyone. Not even his brother. His shoulders sag with dredging up the memory. A chill runs through him and he tries to shrug it off.

Ian opens his mouth, taking the silence as a cue to prod for more.

David continues before Ian can ask what he found.

"I didn't go back just once. I went back every chance I had," David says. "Both to Felicia's house and to the woods up along the old Mill Road; to the spot where we found it.

All that time nothing ever seemed to touch it. I never even seen bugs crawling on it like you do anything else. You see a snake or frog, even dried out and flattened by a tire in the road, there are still ants getting at it, taking pieces away.

Not this."

A chill infects Ian now, listening to this. It has to be David's imagination. Doesn't it?

"I saw him there too," David says, "their uncle Harvey, at their house looking in the windows. I saw him trying to break in. I guess he didn't know about the basement window. I don't know if he ever got in or not, or what he was looking for."

"Maybe to find out where they went," Ian suggests.

"Maybe." David sounds doubtful but willing to accept it as a possibility. It's not what he thinks the answer is. Maybe in part it is, but he is sure there is more to it than just looking for them. He is sure there is a reason Harvey is looking for them, and that it is not just because they are family.

"Then the house sold and all their stuff was cleared out, and there was no reason to go back," David says. "Around the same time it disappeared. Just like that. It was there the day before. I went back to the woods and it was gone. Not even a trace of it, except the grass and stuff being matted down. It looked more like some animal had slept there than a body laying there for who knows how long it was there."

"You think their Uncle Harvey took it?" Ian asks. This is starting to freak him out now. He suspects David is pulling his leg, playing one of his famous pranks. Except David looks genuinely freaked out.

"Something must have dragged it off," Ian says. "Or it was found and removed."

"No police tape? No car sitting in the area? Nothing in the news about it? No one around town talking about it?" David shakes his head. "If someone found it and took it, they kept it secret."

"And you think it was him." Ian says it as a statement of fact.

"Yes," David says.

Ian just breathes for a moment, David studying his reaction to all this. Finally, Ian speaks.

"So that's why you are so obsessed over him. Did you think he also had anything to do with Nick and Felicia's family vanishing?"

"I did before, at first. The whole town was talking about it back then, how strange it was that just when he comes back they vanish. I didn't know what to think. Maybe he killed them. Maybe, like some people said, they ran away, hiding from him.

There was some big fight between their mom and their uncle before he went to jail. I heard people talk about it. He was not allowed to contact them or come near them. Did you know that?"

"No," Ian says. "But there are a lot of reasons people tell others to stay away. You thought he killed them or something?"

"I thought it was a possibility," David admits. "Everybody was saying he was a killer; that he killed a kid and that's why he went to prison."

"But now Nick is back," Ian says. "Obviously, he didn't kill them."

"But they left for a reason. No goodbyes. Not even taking their stuff. They were running from something," David says. "I think it was him."

"So, you think he found it in the woods," Ian says. He still does not want to call it what it is. A body. A dried up, shrivelled up, decomposing corpse of a child. A child just like they were then.

It could have been one of them.

"You think he found it," Ian repeats, "or knew about it, and picked that moment to move it."

David shrugs. When Ian says it like that, it sounds ludicrous.

"Something like that. Even when we were kids everyone said that their Uncle Harvey was a killer. That he killed some kid. I thought maybe that was the kid he killed. When I was a kid, anyway. Now I know it had to be a different kid. So why? Why did we happen to find another kid in the woods around the time he came back?"

"The body was there a long time from how I remember it looked," Ian says.

"Yes, but maybe he just didn't get a chance to dispose of it before they locked him up. Maybe the kid got away alive and then curled up there and died. It kind of looked like it was curled up in a foetal ball, like it was trying to stay warm. He probably couldn't find it.

What if he found it only because he followed me?"

David swallows hard.

"What if he followed me, found it because of me, so now he knows that I know."

"We don't know it was him," Ian says. "That would make you a threat to him. You could put him back in prison for a very long time. So why has he never done anything about it?

You don't know what happened. He lived here all these years. If you are a threat to him, then why didn't he ever come after you? You would have been easy for him kill when you were a kid. Especially if he is a child killer like everyone says. What would be one more?"

"We have to get Nick," David says. "We have to get him to talk to us, whatever it takes. I don't care if he's on our side or if we have to bloody well tie him down and make him talk. We have to find out what he knows."

Ian stiffens. He still thinks of Nick as his friend, even though he has not seen or heard from him in all these years. The Nick that came back is like a stranger. Grown up. Not the small boy he remembers. His memory of back then is fuzzy, in bits of clear moments awash in a sea of time forgotten.

But he still sees a ghost of the boy he once played with in the face of the man. It does not matter that Nick didn't remember him at first. It has been a long time, and they were only little kids when he left.

"He doesn't want to talk to us," Ian says. He suspects it is David who Nick does not want to talk to. David has a tendency to come on too strong. Nick and David never got along.

"How do you think you are going to get him to talk to you, if he even remembers anything at all?" Ian asks.

"I'll do whatever it takes," David says. His jaw is set in determination, his eyes hard. It is a look Ian has seen before.

Just like when they were kids, and so many times in the years since, Ian finds himself forced into a spot where he feels he has to play mediator between David and someone else. David is stubborn when he sets his mind on doing something.

"I'll talk to Nick," Ian says, regretting it even as the words come out of his mouth.

How the hell am I going to get him to talk to me? he thinks. If he even remembers. He wasn't exactly happy to see us. Maybe it's David. Maybe without David there Nick will be more open."

"Make it fast," David says. "With or without his cooperation, we need to go check out his uncle's place. If he is hiding anything, if he had anything to do with that body found in the woods, if there is any evidence there, we need to find it. We need to know."

What he is really thinking is, *I need to know*. David needs to know this as strongly as he needed to know what happened to Felicia all those years ago.

"We are going to old Uncle Harv's place tomorrow night," David says, "whether Nick is on board or not. And he is coming."

"What do you think we'll find?" Ian asks. He is shocked by David's announcement. The idea of snooping around someone else's property makes him queasy. It's wrong. Apparently David has no such sense of right and wrong. Or, if he does, he has grown immune to it with the time he has spent snooping around Nick and Felicia's old house.

Ian knows David did not stop snooping around there after the house sold the first time, or after it sold the time after that.

"Something." David leaves it at that.

Ian knows him well enough to know from his expression that he won't get anything more from him. *David probably has no idea what he thinks he'll find*, he thinks. *But he'll never admit it.*

"I'll look for him after work," Ian says.

"Good." David leaves.

Nick shakes his head. "I don't know how he thinks we can force Nick to come if he doesn't want to. Hell, he might even warn his uncle if we push it. We will be trespassing."

20 – Ian Seeks Out Nick

His shift over, Ian goes looking for Nick. He has no idea where he might be staying, or if he even has a room anywhere. Dusty's only has two rooms, and he isn't staying there.

I hope I find him soon. David's obsession with Nick and his Uncle Harvey is going to get us both in trouble. Maybe whatever Nick has to say will convince David not to go snooping around the man's property tomorrow.

Ian starts with the usual places a young man might hang out, starting with Dusty's. No luck there. This could take a while, so he opts to drive.

After exhausting the usual places, Ian resorts to roaming the town. He starts with Nick's old house. The curtains are drawn and he can't see if anyone is home. There is a car in the driveway, but in a small town like this they could have walked to wherever they might have gone.

Ian doubts Nick would go as far as actually trying to go inside, so he moves on.

He goes down the old Mill Road to the construction area where the field has been scraped down and trees are being ripped out. He parks near the construction trailer and gets out, surveying the area.

Ian pauses there on the edge, not entering the jobsite. He suddenly feels drawn to that fateful spot where they found it so many years ago.

A part of him asks, What if it's still there?

Of course it's not there, he thinks. Even if the body they just found is the same body we found, it would have been removed.

There is no sign of Nick and Ian turns to leave.

He stops.

He turns back and stares at the woods. He is not sure exactly where the spot is, only that if he enters the woods at the right place along the edge of the field and walks in far enough in the right direction, he will find a tree that had fallen decades ago where a dead body not once, but possibly twice and maybe even three times now, was found in a hollow beneath the tree.

He takes a step towards the woods, and another.

"No," he shakes his head. "This is stupid. You don't even know where it is."

The sound of the crackling of dry branches snapping comes softly on the air, sending a chill down Ian's spine.

It helps him make a decision. Ian makes himself turn around and walk away. He gets back in his car, turns around, and leaves.

Behind him, across the field where police tape had recently blocked off the place where a man entered the woods and found a long waiting to be found body, the bushes move as if something had been there watching a moment before and just now let them go and turned, vanishing into the woods.

At a loss where else to go, Ian simply drives around town.

He is driving past the old abandoned train station when something unusual catches his eye. He brakes and looks.

There, on the bench against the wall of the old ticket office. He almost missed it. Someone is sitting there.

He turns around and pulls in, parking in the weed choked gravel driveway behind the ticket office.

He hasn't gotten a good enough look yet to see who is sitting there. He has an idea who it might be.

Ian gets out and walks around; hoping whoever it is won't notice him. He peeks around the corner.

"Hello Ian."

The voice startles him even though he knows the man is there.

Found out, Ian steps out and climbs the rotting steps to the platform, the wood groaning beneath his weight. He walks across, stopping a few feet away from Nick.

"So, this is where you hang out?" Ian says.

"There's not a lot of places to go."

"You've got that right." Ian climbs the stairs, joining him on the bench. Nick has to move over a bit to give him room on the remaining intact portion of the bench seat.

"So how have you been?" Ian asks.

"I'm doing all right."

"And your family? Felicia?"

"About as well as can be expected."

"David never got over it, you know."

Nick doesn't respond right away. Then he speaks carefully.

"He seems like he's managing pretty well."

It's Ian's turn to pause and think how to word this carefully. He decides to just jump in.

"He's never stopped obsessing over it all. Felicia. Your family vanishing in the night. The thing in the woods."

Nick feels like those words might knock him over. *The thing in the woods.* He wants to demand to know what the thing is. At the same time he doesn't want to admit to his long ago friend that he doesn't know. He suspects it's a body, but that's a guess. Nick has no idea why it matters. It's just one of those things that feels like what you should do, that it should matter. He thinks what to say, how to say it, without revealing that he knows nothing.

"It's been a lot of years. Maybe David should drop it," Nick says.

"I've tried to tell him that," Ian says. "He won't."

Ian has a thought. It's a long shot. But it's the only thing he can think of that might work.

"Maybe if Felicia-."

Nick cuts him off, getting protective of his sister's fragile state of mental health.

"Felicia wants nothing to do with any of it. This town, David, or what we found."

Ian bobs his head, feeling awkward at Nick's bordering on angry response.

"Sorry, it was just a thought." He looks at Nick. "David really won't drop it. He wants to go look around your uncle's property and he wants us both to go with him. He thinks he'll find something there that ties to that kid found in the woods near where they are putting in those houses."

Nick stiffens, not sure how he should take that.

"Why Uncle Harvey's place? Why does he think he has anything to do with it?" The question isn't defensive. Nick himself wonders if there is a connection.

"Probably because of all the talk of your uncle supposedly going to jail for killing a kid years ago. I mean, he was in jail when we found it in the woods, so he probably had nothing to do with that. But if he killed once he could kill again. He could have even left that kid in the woods right before he was locked up. He's been here this whole time, so he could have killed this kid too, the one they just found."

This clinches it for Nick. Now he is sure he knows what they found. It was *the remains of a child*.

Nick can't deny it makes sense, even if the idea of having an uncle who murders kids makes him feel somehow tainted by his uncle's possible crimes. *Uncle Harvey's property lies through the woods. To walk there from the old Mill Road, you would have to walk through the area where the body was found.*

Ian notices his troubled look.

"Hey, it's no reflection on you, even if he did do it. And we don't even know if he's guilty of anything at all."

"I don't think I like the idea of snooping around Uncle Harvey's place. If he didn't do anything, then we'd be invading his privacy." Nick doesn't add on that he is also still scared of his uncle.

"David is going no matter what. I tried to talk him out of it, but he won't leave it alone. He was pretty insistent on you going too. But he will go alone if he has to."

"Why does he want me there?"

"Because it's your uncle, I guess. Maybe he thinks you'll know where to look or what to look for."

"Sounds like he suspects I had something to do with it too."

The look of guilt that flashes across Ian's eyes shows he's not sure David does not suspect Nick.

"At least maybe you can help me keep David from taking this too far."

Nick mulls it over. He is torn. Uncle Harvey is family, but he's always been odd and I never really knew him. Mom hasn't spoken to her brother since before we moved in the middle of the night after we found the thing in the woods. Even I suspect Uncle Harvey. I need to know what Uncle Harvey is up to. I need to find out more about what happened, more about what we found in the woods. The kid. Was it a kid? That seems to be what we found. If we do find something, maybe it will bring out a few of the memories my mind refuses to give up.

Nick frowns. "All right, I'll come." His reluctance is clear. "But only to find out what Uncle Harvey is up to, if he's up to anything."

David would smile right now, Ian thinks sullenly. What they are going to do weighs as heavily on him as it does on his friend sitting next to him.

21 – Uncle Harvey's Cabin

David, Ian, and Nick arrive at the construction site up the old Mill Road in David's car. Work is shut down for the day and the site is deserted. David pulls up near the trailer that serves as an on-site office and turns the car off. They all climb out and pause as they close the car doors, looking around.

Ian looks doubtful. David looks determined. Nick's expression is unreadable.

"Let's do this," David says, and starts off, leading the way.

Instead of taking the shorter distance straight across the field over the rugged indents from the large tractor wheels, a route that is rough enough to make it a slow risky walk, he leads them on the longer roundabout path along the outer edge of the field. They follow the edge to the trees and walk along the tree line.

David leads the way to the point of entry into the trees. He has a very specific point where he wants to enter the woods.

"I still don't get what you think we are going to find," Nick complains.

"I don't know what we'll find," David says, turning to look back at Nick and Ian. "I'm hoping we find answers."

They arrive at the spot.

David pauses, staring at the trees and bush ahead. Once they cross this barrier, there is no going back in his mind.

He turns and looks around, police tape fluttering in the wind only in his memory.

The field is mostly one large ruined raw wound created by the tractors clearing the field and the trees. The broken trees they cleared away are still piled along one side, twisted and mangled, the mound larger now than he remembers. The police car and tape are long gone.

David sucks in a deep breath and holds it, steeling himself for what is to come. He lets the breath out slowly and steps forward, breaching the edge of the woods.

Ian and Nick follow.

It does not take them long to reach the fallen tree.

David spots it first, where they can still just make out the ruined ground of the construction site through the trees. He stops and stares at it.

The tree lies just as it did when he was here a few days ago, across the top of two large rocks. The soft spongy rotting wood sagging between them and taking a shape roughly resembling the rough ground and other fallen deadwood beneath it. The top side is a chewed open wound of soft rot that is home to an insect colony that he suspects are termites. Their destruction of the dead tree helps its slow melting back into the ground it had grown from. Ferns and other undergrowth grow around it, surrounding and devouring it as they grow in its place. A few rough stumps stick out from the trunk where the largest branches once extended out in a mighty crown of branches, all of which are now long gone.

Ian and Nick stop next to him, staring down at the decomposing tree.

"Is that it?" Ian asks, unable to help doubting his memory. He does not need to elaborate. David knows he is talking about the spot where they found the body as kids.

Nick stares down in a mix of confusion and curiosity. Is this where it happened, whatever it was, that changed Felicia? Is this where we found it?

David cannot shake the fear that fills him despite the need to be the brave one in front of his younger brother and his brother's younger childhood friend.

"It used to be further in, before they cleared all those trees. The trees used to go right to the old Mill Road. There is nothing here now," he says, trying to act casual.

He swallows the lump in his throat and walks around the tree.

Ian and Nick follow, both turning to study the fallen tree. The hollow is still there in the ground next to and beneath the tree, the tree sagging in to partially fill it. That spot where they found the body years ago.

Ian tries to bring up the image of the body exactly as they found it that day. Time, lost memories, and imagination have changed the image in his mind. It is faded and lacking in details; more a feeling than a visual of the desiccated corpse. It is larger than life, in relation to his much smaller size back then, when everything seemed so much larger. The small child's body was not so small then, made larger in his shocked horror as a child who had never seen anything scarier than cartoonish monsters created to entertain and humour small children.

In his mind, the body is larger than an adult, but as insubstantial as a fog, with little detail to it.

Nick tries to imagine what they found. Instead, he is visited with the vague memory of half-forgotten dreams, the same nightmares that haunted his sleep for as long as he can remember.

Hazy images float through him. A face; a mix of skin, bone, and exposed stringy muscle tissue looking dry and wax-like. The thought of disgusting insects crawling through moss and dead leaves rotting in the dark woods churns his stomach. He tries to remember the face of his dreams. It does not seem real, more putty than flesh and bone.

The face in his imagination swims more into focus, the world around it melting away to a blur. Just as it does in his nightmares, it looks up at him, its dead eyes weeping, mouth twisted in a grimace of pain and fear. It calls his name.

"Nick."

22 – Detective Liam Tobin

Liam Tobin stops his car in front of another small house. The house is quiet. Closed up feeling. He can see tall grassy flowering plants beyond the house in the unfenced backyard. It is the house Nick and Felicia lived in before Diana and Rueben packed them up in the night and vanished.

"So, this is the house Harvey Lawson's last known family in town lived in. Thirty-two Galving Road"

Shutting the car off, he gets out and walks around the house. The grass is a bit long, but not too bad. There is a tired looking birdbath in the back yard.

The curtain in the front window next door flutters. Moments later the door opens and a woman marches across the lawn and stops to stare at the man in her neighbour's yard with the authority of justice. She hesitates, surprised to see a stranger. *I was sure it was David coming around again.*

Feeling the presence of someone staring at him, Liam turns to see her.

"Hello, I am Detective Liam Tobin." He tries to give her a disarming smile and fails, jutting his hand out towards her for a handshake as he strides towards her.

The woman looks at his hand uncertainly, letting him take hers in its embrace and pump it awkwardly up and down a few times in a left-handed handshake. She is still in mild shock when he releases her hand and stares at her expectantly.

"Do you live here?" He motions to the house behind him.

"No, I live next door," she says a little too quickly. "I thought you were someone else." Her words ring as an excuse. "It was silly of me. You are older than him."

"Who did you think I was?" Liam asks.

The woman was coming to chase me off, he thinks. Whoever she thought I was, he is not welcome to come around.

Flustered, she blushes and hesitates to share with this strange man.

"Did the Connollys call you? Are you here to arrest David?"

"Is that who lives there now?"

"No. They own the house, but they don't live in it. No one is living there right now. The Connollys moved out because of David's obsession with the house. They considered putting the house up for rent. They did rent it out for a time. It's hard to keep renters, though, when some guy is always creeping around looking in their windows and breaking in. It's been vacant for weeks now."

"This David keeps breaking in? Does he have any correlation to a Mr. Harvey Lawson?" Liam asks.

The woman blinks at him, digesting and trying to understand.

"Harvey? Diana's brother? The kids knew him, of course, but I don't think any of the Hastings kids' friends had anything to do with him."

"So, who is this David?"

"He was Felicia's friend; one of the kids. When the Hastings's moved away David kept coming around looking for them. He's a bit obsessed with it. It's been twelve years since they moved away and he still keeps coming around, looking in the windows and such. He breaks into the house sometimes and looks around. Sometimes, I think, he just sits in there."

"That's a bit creepy."

"That's what Thomas and Marlene Connolly thought. They came home a few times to find David in the house. He did the same thing to the other owners before. Twice the house was sold because of David's obsession. I told him he won't find anything of Nick and Felicia's family in there. The place was cleaned out after the first people who bought it sold it."

"It wasn't emptied when the Hastings's moved out?"

"No." She shakes her head to show her disagreement with the decision. "When they left, they left everything behind. Sold the house contents and all."

"Where can I find this David now?"

"Twenty-five Sparrow Way. He lives there with his brother Ian."

"Thank you." Liam nods to her. "I will give David a visit."

"You aren't going to arrest him, are you?" She sounds concerned now for David's wellbeing.

"Not unless he did something to arrest him for."

Liam gets in his car and drives away, mulling over this new information.

"I'll have to check into this David character, then I'll take a look at Harvey Lawson's house. It's a small town. I'll see what whoever is on shift at the station knows about David."

23 – Uncle Harvey's Cabin

"Nick."

David's voice breaks his reverie, calling his name.

Nick shakes off the hollow disjointed feeling staring down at the fallen tree and the hollow in its shelter, the place where the rot ravaged body of a child waited to be discovered more than once, leaves him trapped in.

Nick turns to look at him, feeling startled.

"Let's go," David says.

They move on, leaving the dead tree behind and making their way through the woods. They are taking the shortest route on foot through the trees to Uncle Harvey's cottage. It is a long walk, but the drive is a long twisted route that is not always passable and David wants to arrive unseen, just in case Harvey is there.

The passage through the woods is not easy. Thick brush and low tree branches block the way and the ground is rough. They press through, getting caught on branches, until they come across a deer trail. David follows the deer trail. Able to move more quickly now, they make better time for a while.

David stops, looking around to get his bearings.

"What is it?" Ian asks.

"We are close," David says. "We need to leave the deer trail now. If he's there, he is more likely to see us if we come out the trail."

Ian nods agreement and David leads them off the trail through the thicker brush.

Sticking to the trail may have been wiser. It was quieter. The snapping of branches marks their progress.

Nick pauses before following them, feeling bad about what they are doing.

We are illicitly snooping on my own uncle's property. Uncle Harvey could be guilty of murder, but it still feels wrong.

Dry branches crack beneath their weight, snapping under their feet. Other branches crackle and snap as they push through interwoven branches. Their feet make a wet slithering sound in the layers of years' worth of fallen leaves rotting back into the ground. Every animal in the area knows they are there and have either ducked into their dens or moved off to put distance between them and these loud creatures invading their home.

If Harvey had been home and outside, he would have heard them coming too.

They arrive at the edge of the woods bordering the small clearing where the cabin sits. David waves them to stop, motioning them to silence when Nick opens his mouth to talk.

He signals them, indicating that they are to split up and circle around, staying quiet and hidden. Their first job is to make sure Harvey is not there.

Ian and Nick look at David in confusion, not understanding what his gestures mean. They know the gist of what he wants, but the specifics are lost.

"What do you want us to do?" Ian asks. "Just tell us. We made enough noise getting here, if anyone is going to hear us talking quietly, they've already heard us."

David glares at him and exhales a puff of air in exasperation.

"We'll split up," he whispers harshly. "Nick, you go that way. Ian, you go that way. Stay just inside the trees out of sight and be quiet. Scout the area and make sure nobody is there before we move in."

"Yeah, we got that part," Ian says. "The rest?"

"Nick, check out the barn hidden in the trees there, and Ian, check the shed. We go full circle and meet right back here. I'll go up to the house and check it out, make sure it doesn't look like anyone's inside."

"Why didn't you just say it in the first place?" Ian says.

"Shut up and go," David whispers, annoyed.

Ian turns away, grinning when David can't see. Getting under David's skin never gets old for the younger brother who always felt second best.

They move out, each heading in a different direction, scouting the yard and bushes.

Ian goes around the side of the cabin to the shed behind it. The moment he gets close he smells a pungent putrid stink. It worsens the closer to the shed he gets. He makes a face at the unpleasant stench. It is more than a stink now. He can taste it, the sickly rot of decay. It is strong, but bearable.

Trying not to breathe too much, he walks around the shed before trying to go in, listening for any sounds and watching for any light, anything that might give away that someone is inside.

There is a window on the back and he sidles up next to the wall, peeking into the window.

The window is smudged with years' worth of grime and is blocked by something on the inside. He can't see inside.

He moves around to the front. There is nothing to suggest anyone is inside.

Ian stops in front of the door, inspecting it.

There is no lock.

*****

Nick goes around the other side of the cabin to the barn. The trees and bush have grown in around the barn, reclaiming ground that was cleared decades before.

Now that he has a better look at it, he sees the building they assumed is a barn is really a Quonset, a half-cylindrical shaped building made out of corrugated steel like a giant label-less unopened tin can cut in half the long way and plunked on the ground open side down. The round walls and top are made from mismatched sections of metal, the result of odd missing pieces being replaced over the years. Rust stains the metal where it has been slowly consuming the roof and walls. The front and back walls are flat and made from sheets of plywood and OSB, the strands of wood in the oriented strand board sheets holding up better in the weather than the plywood sheets. The wood sections are weathered, the paint almost completely worn off, leaving the wood to the ravages of the elements.

Nick moves around the Quonset, inspecting its outside.

There are windows on both the front and back flat walls and a wide double-door on the front large enough to fit a large tractor.

Smaller square windows stick out from the sides, running down the length at sparse intervals and framed in as if added later as an afterthought.

The window frames are all soft and rotting. One small side window had at some point released from the rotting wood frame holding it in to fall out. The broken glass sits dully in the overgrown grass on the side of the structure, grimy with the dirt of years, leaving an open entrance to the inside.

Nick hears fluttering and then sees a bird land on the empty windowsill from inside.

The barn swallow looks at him curiously before taking flight and flying away, vanishing over the trees.

At the back, old wooden pallets are piled up and leaning against the structure, making a haven for rodents.

Green eyes gleam at him from an opening under the pile of pallets and he freezes, studying the rotting pallets and hoping whatever is in there stays in there.

Nick moves around and back up the other side. More detritus is stacked along the outside wall; long rotting boards in various odd lengths of two by fours, sheets of warped and rotting plywood and OSB boards, along with other rubbish. Just before the front wall a rectangular shaped add-on juts out. It's just big enough for the man-sized door it holds.

He reaches the front corner, glances around to make sure his uncle hasn't appeared, and goes to the man door. Nick tries the door. It is locked.

He moves around to the front. The large double door is chained and padlocked. He goes back to the man door and tries it again.

The knob jiggles loosely and the warped door rattles in the frame when he tries to shake it.

"It might take only a good push to open it."

He grips the doorknob with both hands and leans against the door, putting his shoulder against the door, ready to try it.

*****

David cuts across the yard straight to the house while the other two take their circuitous routes around the edges of the yard. He dodges behind anything he can on the way, hoping to not be seen if anyone is inside.

When he gets to the cottage, he ducks down, pressing himself against the wall between the door and a window. The door has a small window with four panes separated by trim. The paint is cracking and peeling from the cottage's exterior. The wood of the door is splintering, and almost all the paint has peeled from the window frames and trim. The weather here can be cruel.

He pauses, his heart pounding in his chest and his pulse racing. He is tense with the fear of being caught, like the driver gripping the steering wheel as his car slips uncontrollably into oncoming traffic on an icy highway. He feels just as out of control, caught up in his own plan and wanting to say, "Stop," but feeling helpless to end it.

David tries to take slow deep breaths, to get himself together. He rises up slowly, moving towards the window, his head rising just above the bottom window frame, and peeks in.

There isn't much to the small cabin. The living area is one room making up both living room and kitchen. Two open doors probably lead to a small bedroom and bathroom. The cottage is sparsely furnished but cluttered because of its small size.

He studies what he can see for any sign of movement, focusing on those two open doors when it is clear no one is in the main room.

When there is no movement, David moves around the cabin, staying crouched low below the level of the windows. He moves around to the back, confirming for himself there is no second entrance to the cabin.

He inches up cautiously, looking into a smaller window. It is a small bathroom. The tub looks antique, the porcelain coating worn and chipped in spots to reveal black beneath. A track hangs from the ceiling with plastic shower curtains like the privacy curtains that surround a hospital bed. The cabinet, sink, toilet, and mirror on the wall look like they were installed at least seventy years ago.

The bathroom is void of life.

He moves on to a larger window, the bedroom. The room is small, crammed with a double bed, small worn dresser, and closet. No one is in the bedroom.

Is that a flash of movement? He can't be sure. It happened so fast.

The movement that may or may not have happened is on the edge of the doorway, in the other room.

He could have gone to the other room while I was walking around, David thinks.

He edges over to the corner of the window to get a better look through the open doorway. Beyond that edge of open doorway is the living room furniture and the first window he looked through.

David tenses. It could have come either from in the house or from outside beyond the front window.

His nerves are jangling. He looks around quickly, looking for Nick and Ian and seeing neither one from this vantage point.

Where are they? He is holding his breath, trying to not make even the small sound of softly breathing.

David concentrates on breathing slowly through his nose. Just like playing hide and seek as a kid. That conscious effort only makes him need more urgently to take big gasping breaths of air that he did not need a second ago. He feels like his lungs are aching for oxygen. Holding his breath gets harder and his heart is pounding in his chest.

Stepping lightly, David moves to the corner and peeks around.

Nobody.

He moves around the corner towards the front of the cabin, stopping before cautiously looking around that corner.

Nobody.

David creeps up to the front window again, ducking below it, and slowly rises to look in.

There is no sign of anyone inside.

He looks behind him, studying the trees and bushes. He feels exposed. *Someone could be there, hiding and watching.*

Get a grip, man, he silently chastises himself. It was probably just a bird or squirrel or something through the front window. No one is here.

He goes to the door and tries it. It is not locked.

He stares down at the knob in his hand, urging himself on.

Open it. Come on, just breathe slow and open it slowly.

*****

Ian grasps the handle and opens the shed door.

The door creaks on its hinges as he opens it, and he cringes against the sound. The widening crack worsens the stink, releasing the foulness trapped inside. He freezes in the act of opening it, looking around.

Harvey could have returned. No. I would have heard a car pulling up to the cabin, even if I don't see it.

With the door partially open, he doesn't want to just let it go and have it creak loudly closed. He looks around on the ground for something to block it open with. Finding nothing within reach, he slowly lets the door close. Cautiously, Ian walks around the outside of the shed, searching all directions for movement, and returns to the front.

Seeing no sign of movement and hearing no call of anyone investigating the creaking door, he opens the shed door slowly, trying to minimize the noise. He peers into the darkness inside.

He grimaces at the stench coming from inside.

"I thought I smelled something nasty," he mutters. "It smells like death in there."

Ian gags as he enters the building nervously, vanishing into the darkness. He is disoriented in the dark, making out only vague shapes in the weak light that comes in from the open door. He is trying to not breathe. Either nose or mouth does not matter. One gives him the full stench of sickly sweet rot fouling his nostrils and lungs, the other he can taste the decay in the air like an oily coating on his tongue.

He fumbles around for a light switch, finally finding it by accident. The switch makes a soft click when he flips it on. The dull moaning hum from the electricity flowing to the two rows of florescent ceiling lights sounds too loud to him. It makes his heart beat faster with worry of being caught.

The bulbs flicker to slow life, flickering dimly more off than on, glowing orange at the ends and flickering to slow life as they warm up. One bulb at a time they snap to life with a shock of light and stay lit, filling the shed with their sickly bland light.

The light comes as a shock to Ian and he has the sudden urge to bolt and run for home.

"What? Are you a kid?" he mutters to himself, trying to shake the feeling off.

He is filled with the strong urge to shut the lights off. *Someone could see them from outside.* He looks around the shed. *Maybe I'll find a flashlight to use instead.*

Shadows lurk in corners and behind every barrier of the chaos filling the shed despite the ceiling lights. The shed has cabinets, toolboxes, two workbenches, and a host of clutter.

Ian searches the shed, more concerned now with finding a flashlight than his original, momentarily forgotten, mission.

The mission was never clear to begin with. David had some vague plan of searching the place. There was no plan, really. Just go and search and maybe one of them will find something interesting.

Ian is not sure David has any idea what his plan is. He suspects it is nothing more than a call to action without any idea what the action is.

Ian spots a flashlight and pounces on it. He flips it on, hoping it works. It blinks on to his relief.

He goes back to the light switch and turns it off, further relieved by the end of the electric hum and the lights flickering and fading off, leaving the shed in darkness.

Now I don't have to worry so much about Harvey noticing the light coming from the shed if he comes home while we are searching his property.

With his focus less on getting caught; Ian turns it to searching the shed. He is still tense with anxiety over the threat of being caught. He rummages through the nearest cabinets, finding nothing of interest.

He moves on to one of the benches, shining the flashlight on it. The bench is scarred with the straight slashes of a knife.

A fly buzzes his head.

The smell is worse here. More pungent.

There are knives laid out on one end of the bench, skinning knives and a cleaver, the kinds used for cleaning small game.

Another fly buzzes him. Or maybe it is the same one. He waves it away.

Ian is concentrating on his search. He moves sideways along the bench and kicks something on the floor. It goes skittering across the floor with a raspy scraping sound.

He looks down, but whatever it was, it has vanished somewhere in the darkness of the shed.

Ian turns, sweeping the flashlight across the floor searching for whatever he kicked. He takes a step back and bumps into something. It gives, tilting and righting itself with the dull sound of its bottom hitting the floor again as he quickly steps forward again.

There is an angry humming sound. It is not quite the same as the buzz of electricity when he turned on the ceiling lights.

He turns, shining the flashlight on the object. It is a large round plastic barrel with a black cloud swarming the opening. He leans to see inside better and regrets it immediately.

The contents are a moving slithering glistening wet hell that churns Ian's stomach. His eyes are stuck on it, unable to look away, the pale wriggling movement filling the barrel like a spasmodically vibrating fatty muscle mass. The grotesque staggered swirling movement of blackness his eyes at first reject identifying are swarming flies defending their nest of larvae.

Ian is both disgusted by it and drawn to it with a morbid fascination.

Beneath the feverish motion of flies and maggots is a putrid mass that is both leathery dry and oozing wet with rot, as if strange creatures had been mashed imperfectly and tossed in the bucket together. The oozing moving mass is barely recognizable as ever having been flesh and blood with its teaming maggots and angry flies.

The mass is gelatinous and dried at once. A slimy soup that is crusting over despite the tiny writhing worms that look like rice with black spots on one end endlessly eating tunnels through the mass.

Ian almost gags. He can make out hair and feathers, obviously from birds and small animals Harvey must have caught for food.

"Doesn't he know they sell meat in town?" he mutters.

There could be anything in that fermenting soup of rotting animal skins.

The smell in the shed seems worse, overwhelming, now that he knows its cause. He covers his mouth in revulsion and moves on to search more, glad to put a little space between himself and the brewing animal hides.

*****

Just as Nick starts to push his weight against the Quonset door, a sound makes him pause and turn his head.

"Where did that come from?"

He takes his weight off the door, still gripping the knob without realizing as he looks around for the source.

Was it David or Ian?

He stiffens with the thought it could be his uncle. What would I say if Uncle Harvey caught me breaking in?

He listens to the sound of the woods, trying to identify it. He is not sure he would recognize the sound if he heard it again. He isn't sure what he heard in the first place. *Maybe it was Ian or David forcing their way into the shed or house.*

"I hope they don't damage anything getting in," he whispers to himself. "If Uncle Harvey notices, he will know someone was here and broke in."

It feels like he is standing there for a long time, waiting and listening. Nick is unsure. "Should I get away from here? Hide in the woods and watch? Go to where we are meeting up?"

He hears a crackling sound as if something large is moving very fast through the bush with no regard for the trees and bushes it is blundering through.

He freezes. His first thought is that it is a bear.

Nick assesses his situation. What's around? Where can I go for safety if a bear charges me? If it's a black bear, it will climb any tree faster than I can. But they don't normally go after people unless there are babies around. It's the wrong time of year for that.

None of the trees nearby look large enough, or scalable enough. A larger bear like a grizzly or brown bear would be on him before he can climb the tree. If he did make it up the tree, the bear might shake him out or push the tree over by bouncing its weight on it.

The sound comes again.

It's coming closer.

Nick throws himself against the door, putting his shoulder into it while pulling up on the knob. It's a trick he learned living in many old sagging poor neighbourhood houses. With the right pressure, pulling up on the door, you can often pop it open without damaging the doorframe or leaving visible signs of breaking in.

The door holds firm.

*****

David is turning the knob of the cabin. The sound behind him makes him freeze, sending an instant chill through him.

It is the sound of something large bullying its way through the bush, moving at a fast pace.

He stands, listening motionlessly, and scanning the trees for any sign of whatever it is. He thinks he sees movement in the trees. Whatever it is, it seems to be moving past the cottage, not towards it.

"Must be a deer or something. Something must have spooked it if it's charging through the trees like that."

Still feeling tense, he opens the door slowly and peers in, half expecting to be confronted at any moment.

*****

Nick tries again, pulling up on the doorknob and throwing his weight against the door harder this time. With a dull sound, the door gives and he staggers, almost falling into the Quonset. He closes the door against whatever is out there charging through the bush towards the yard.

He takes in his surroundings.

The Quonset is sparsely furnished. Rusting sheets of metal line the floor, some with plywood laid overtop in a haphazard manner. There are birds' nests in the rafters supporting the roof. Nick spots a hole in the wall that he assumes whatever stared at him from the pile of debris outside uses to gain entry to the building. Benches line the back wall with low-sided trays filling them. The building has a musty organic stench to it, dull and earthy with tones of decay.

He walks over to the benches. The trays are lined with a crumbling drying muddy mixture. The musky stench of rot is coming from the trays filled with Harvey's homemade blood meal.

Nick steps back to examine the large jugs on the ground under the bench. Beneath the next bench are pressurized tanks of anhydrous ammonia. Nitrogen. There are some assorted old cans and jugs of other chemicals too. Turpentine, paint cans, and some the labels are so worn he can't tell what they are.

There is an old roller toolbox cart next to a workbench with a few power tools hanging from its back against the wall between the man door and the large barn style doors. Assorted boards, pieces of plywood, and partial sheets of metal are stacked against the wall across from the man door.

The Quonset is dusty and dirty, and there is nothing else of interest.

He stares at the jugs and tanks of chemicals.

"If he isn't farming crops, what does he need nitrogen and this other stuff for?"

With nothing really there to search, Nick goes back outside, making sure the door is closed and locked behind him just the way he found it. He pauses, surveying the area. Harvey could have come back while he was inside.

Nick starts moving, about to go to the rendezvous, and stops.

"Where are we supposed to meet up? David never said." He shrugs. "I guess I'll just go back to where we split up." He goes in a careful circuitous path back.

*****

The shed is too cluttered for Ian to search it thoroughly. He gives it only a perfunctory search, wanting to get out of there quickly. He looks over piles of junk, barrels, boxes, and mounds of assorted clutter without moving anything to really look inside or underneath.

"This shed is bigger than I thought," he mutters. The space feels cramped with the clutter despite the actual size of the building.

In one corner, beneath a pile of old carpets that barely cover the top, is what appears to be a pile of old scraps of metal, possibly for recycling. There is an old bicycle wheel, its spokes bent and broken, a rusting old wood stove, various cans, hubcaps and wheel rims. There is also what appears to be a stack of old cages and traps of various sizes and purposes.

Ian shrugs.

"I don't know what I'm supposed to look for, or what David thinks I'm going to find. Other than that old Harvey doesn't disposed of his skins and guts after cleaning whatever he traps, I don't see anything here."

He goes to the door and peeks out, looking around to make sure Harvey has not returned. Seeing no movement, he leaves, closing the door behind him. The door doesn't quite catch and is left ajar.

"Where are we meeting? David never said." Ian considers checking the cabin and the other building for David and Nick and decides against it. "Safer to just go around the edge of the woods back to where we split up. At least I can see them coming from there. Hopefully that's where they think to go."

He slips away toward the trees, taking a difficult trek through them around the yard to stay hidden just inside the tree line.

*****

David looks in the open door at the small room making a combined kitchen and living room and focuses on the two doors to the bedroom and bathroom. There is no sign of Nick's uncle. The interior of the cabin is as old and rundown as the outside. He slips inside, looking out through the diminishing crack as he closes the door behind him.

He turns to survey the small cabin. The closed door behind him is a physical presence in the room. His only way out and the only way in.

"If Harvey shows up, I'm screwed."

A bookcase is built into one wall. The shelves hold an assortment of books and trinkets; a few small framed photos, a chipped ceramic cat next to an action figure, a couple DVDs in worn cardboard cases among them.

David starts there, giving the books a quick search, pulling out a few random books and flipping the pages before putting them back. Nothing falls out.

He moves through the room, lifting seat cushions to look under them, looking in the few kitchen cupboards, and rummaging the drawers of a small desk shoved in a corner.

David moves on to the bathroom, finding nothing outside of the usual bathroom clutter. A closet in the bathroom has shelves. One shelf is filled with towels, the rest with an assortment of junk.

"I don't think I can risk taking the time to pull all that out and go through it." He eyes the shelves suspiciously. "There could be anything in there."

He moves on to the bedroom, doing a quick search through the drawers and trying to be careful to leave them exactly as he found them. Not finding anything, he turns to the closet. The bedroom closet is small and jammed so full it doesn't look like anything more can get in or out of it.

"I'm not sure how I'm going to search that."

*****

Branches crack despite Ian's attempts to move through the brush quietly. He keeps the clearing with Harvey's cabin in sight to his left as he makes his way through.

There is too much cracking of branches.

Ian stops, holding himself frozen mid-stride. Heartbeats later, the cracking of branches to his right and behind him stops too.

His heart thuds quickly in his chest. He has to hold his breath to stop himself from panting in fear stress. He listens.

Something is definitely behind me, he thinks.

Ian fights the urge to start moving brutishly fast through the brush. Instead he forces himself to step forward carefully, trying to be silent. He takes another step and another, concentrating on every foot placement to be as silent as possible, part of his mind focused on the unseen thing he is sure is following him.

"What if it's Harvey? What do I say about why I'm here sneaking through the woods around his house?"

*****

After a cursory look, David abandons the bedroom closet and leaves the bedroom. He stops, looking around the small cottage.

That's when he spots another door that he missed earlier. It takes very little to clutter up a small space like this, and the stuff piled next to it made the door invisible from the other direction. It looks like another closet door.

Opening the door, he is met with a small room that is packed floor to ceiling with shelves and boxes.

David hears a noise outside and turns, staring as if he can see the source through the walls. He listens.

"Something is definitely moving around outside."

He feels a sickening twist of his stomach, the fear of being caught. He is at the door in a few steps, forcing himself to stop even as his hand is already reaching for the knob.

"Slow down, look, make sure the coast is clear."

His hand is trembling as he places it on the knob. He turns it and opens the door a crack, peeking out. There is nothing to see. He opens it a little further. Still nothing.

Finally, David opens the door wide enough to squeeze out, closing it behind him. He scans the yard for Harvey, sees nothing, and starts rushing across the yard for the safety of the trees.

David dodges across the yard, hiding behind obstacles the same as he did on the approach to the cabin, and finally sprints for the trees.

He arrives at the spot where they split up to find Ian and Nick staring each other down in a standoff. Ian is panting, his eyes darting nervously and looking ready to bolt. His stance is forward, aggressive, but off to one side as if he can't decide if he should be standing up to an adversary or running. Nick's hands are balled into fists at his sides. His posture is angry. He is in a fighting stance. His face is twisted into an angry scowl, but there is something in his eyes. Fear.

More than fear. Terror.

"I'm not doing this anymore," Nick snarls at Ian, not noticing David's arrival.

"Fine, whatever," Ian snaps. Just listen to me. I'm trying to tell you something. Something is out there. Something, or someone, followed me."

"What's going on?" David looks from one to the other.

Nick's focus stays on Ian, but Ian turns to David.

"We have to get out of here now."

David hesitates and it pushes Nick past the edge he was teetering on.

"I'm out of here." Nick turns and starts off, moving quickly away through the trees.

"Wait," Ian tries to call after him.

David takes a step forward, ready to lash out and grab him.

Ian puts his hand out. "Let him go." He stares at David.

"Screw that." David stares him down. "What happened out here?"

"Nothing. Something is out here. It followed me. We need to go. Now."

"We need to stop Nick and find out what he knows. What did he find?"

"Probably nothing; like us."

"What do you mean?" David asks.

Ian stares at him steadily. "I didn't find anything, did you?"

David's expression is answer enough.

"Exactly. This was a waste of time," Ian complains.

David turns to stare in the direction Nick went in. "He's getting away."

He starts moving after Nick at a brisk walk. Not seeing him, he speeds up. He breaks into a jog.

Hearing David coming after him through the bush, Nick turns to look behind him. He starts jogging. The sound of pursuit grows in volume and intensity, speeding up. He starts running, dodging trees.

Hearing the cracking of brush ahead and the sound of Nick moving faster, David breaks into a run. Forgetting about the risk of being caught, he bulls his way noisily through the trees.

Left behind, Ian looks around nervously. He hears the sound again of whatever it was that was following him. He swallows the lump of fear in his throat and breaks into a run, following David.

Ian hears the sound of something crashing through the bush after him, chasing him. Chasing them.

He puts on a burst of fear-fuelled speed.

24 – Detective Liam Tobin

Liam steps out of the trees into Harvey's yard and looks around. Afraid he would get stuck and be unable to turn around, he left his car on the winding narrow road and walked the rest of the way through the bush.

He hears the sound of something crashing through the trees.

"Whatever that is, it sounds like there's a few of them. Probably deer." He listens. The noise is diminishing, getting further away.

Going to the cabin first, he knocks on the door and waits.

"It's the country. I bet people out here don't lock their doors."

He tries the door, finding it unlocked. Opening it a crack, he peers in.

"Hello. Anyone here?"

When there is no answer, Liam steps back, closing the door and looking around. He starts walking around the yard and spots a dilapidated building behind the cabin.

Walking around the cabin to it, he notices the shed door is ajar. The stench of rotting remains invades his nostrils before he reaches it, twisting his mouth into an unpleasant grimace. It grows as he approaches the shed.

Trying not to breathe in, Liam opens the shed door to the darkness and stronger stink inside.

"Hello."

He doesn't expect an answer and steps inside. Looking for the light switch, he spots it and flips it on, the fluorescents buzzing and flickering to life.

Liam takes a quick look around the shed. A dull buzzing attracts his attention and he follows the sound to the barrel next to the bench. He looks in at the teeming putrid mass of maggots and flies in rotting skins and feathers mixed with the remains of multiple carcasses.

The smell is overpowering, nauseating, and the sight worse. His stomach clenches sickly and he pulls out his phone, taking photos of the teeming soup.

He makes his way to the door, taking photos and scanning the shed for anything of consequence besides the barrel of decomposing remains.

Turning the light off and leaving the door ajar just as he found it, Liam moves on.

Through the trees on the other side of the house he sees glimpses of a building. He makes his way across the yard to it, discovering the Quonset rotting in disrepair when he gets there.

Uninterested in searching around it, he seeks out the man door.

Liam tries the door, finding the knob locked. He moves to a window, rising up on his toes to see better in the high window, and sees little. Returning to the man door, he tries again. This time he tries gripping the knob tight, pushing down on it, and finally pulling up while putting his back and shoulder into trying to force the door open. He could kick it open but does not want to damage anything and leave signs of a burglary.

He is about to give up when the door grudgingly pops free of the doorknob tongue holding it closed, the door opening with a groan.

Liam pushes the door open further and is startled by a flurry of feathers exploding in his face. A pair of annoyed barn swallows dive and swoop at him, crying unhappily and missing his face by mere inches before they vanish out a missing window on the other side.

He stands in momentary surprise, his heart pounding in his chest and stomach tight, before he enters the Quonset, looking around. There is room to fit a large tractor or more than one smaller tractors or trucks. The bench and roller cart with tools are uninteresting.

The benches on the other side catch his attention. They are the only other thing that could be worth investigating.

He looks down at the trays of drying homemade blood meal. Looking around, he finds an old nail; its length wicked with rust, and picks it up. Using the nail, he pokes at the contents of one of the low sided trays.

Liam pulls out his phone again, taking pictures of the trays.

Crouching down, he looks at the jugs and tanks under the benches, taking more pictures.

"Well, this is interesting."

He leans in closer and zooms in, making to get as clear of shots as he can of the labels.

Standing again, he moves to the bench on the other side, looking for something to use. Finding a box of disposable rubber work gloves, he pulls a glove out and returns to the trays on the other side.

Partially turning the hand inside out, he uses the glove to pick up a sample from the tray, turning it right-side out and balling it up to preserve the sample.

With nothing else to look at, Liam leaves, closing the door behind him, and returns to the cottage.

He knocks again on the cottage door and waits. There is no response.

Looking around furtively, he opens the door again, poking his head inside.

"Hello. Is anybody home?"

He shrugs and steps inside, looking around the small cottage.

Walking around the cottage, Liam unknowingly follows David's earlier steps, looking in the bathroom and bedroom closets, and stopping to stand before the almost hidden door. The door is not closed, just as David left it.

Opening the door, he looks at the shelves of boxes.

"What have we got here?"

Stepping into the tight space, he slips the lid off a box, pulling the box just over the edge and tipping it forward to lean on his stomach. The box is filled with files.

He takes a few pictures of the inside of the box and pulls one of the files out, quickly flipping through its contents, scanning the pages without really reading them. They appear to be old newspaper clippings, letters, and notes written on foolscap paper.

Pushing the box back securely on the shelf, he kneels, puts the file on the floor, and opens it. He takes a picture and flips the page, taking another. He continues taking pictures of random pages before closing the file and returning it to the box. Putting the lid back, he investigates the contents of a few more boxes.

"Is this guy a conspiracy theorist?" Liam puts the last box back. "Whatever he is, this Harvey character is nuts."

He leaves the cottage.

25 – Chase Through the Woods

"Nick! Stop! Stop running! What, are you five?"

David crashes through the trees in pursuit of Nick. He dodges trees, jumping over downed trees and ducking under low hanging branches.

Bent only on putting distance between them, Nick runs without thought to direction. He comes across a deer trail, thinks it is the same one they came up before, and follows it. He can move faster on the trail and puts on more speed, panting for air. Branches whip and pull at him as he races along the trail.

David follows the sound of Nick's crashing through the trees despite his own loud passage nearly obliterating all other noises.

When the crashing ahead of him suddenly stops, David comes staggering to an exhausted stop. He looks around, seeing nothing but endless bush around him.

"Where did he go?" he gasps. "Is he out of the woods?" He stands there, trying to catch his breath and trying to quiet his loud gasps, listening.

He hears the sound of Nick ahead of him, quieter on the deer trail. He also hears the cracking sounds of something charging through the trees following him.

David looks back, looking for Ian coming through the trees.

"Ian! Here!" His call is carried across the sky above, muffled in the confines of the forest.

*****

Ian hears David call to him from ahead. He tries to run faster, yearning for the relative safety of being two instead of one. He follows the sound and finally spots David through the trees. He bears down, charging towards him.

The sound of something crashing through the trees behind him is a steady reminder to keep running.

*****

David spots movement and stares through the trees. He recognizes Ian running towards him through the bush. He looks the other way impatiently, torn between waiting for Ian and not losing the chance to catch Nick.

The distance between them closes as he watches Ian push himself on.

Ian finally reaches David, grabbing at him breathlessly and giving him a combination push and tug.

"Run!"

*****

Nick is alone in the woods. He can still hear David calling him and the sound of branches breaking. He has no doubt Ian is chasing him too.

Exhausted and gasping for air, he slows to a walk. In the relative silence without the racket of his own rushed and careless race, the dry brittle crackling with every step of leaves on the ground sounds louder.

Nick looks around the forest, really seeing it for the first time.

Despite the time of year, the leaves on the trees are turning yellow. Their tips and edges show dry burnt damage from the injury of drought. He reaches up and plucks a leaf. The leaf feels dry, although not yet brittle as it would be if it were completely dead. It lacks the suppleness of a healthy leaf. Every tree, bush, and the grasses and weeds are similarly suffering.

He reaches out to bend the end of a branch with yellow-tinged green living leaves. Instead of bending, it snaps.

He keeps walking and comes to a dip in the ground that snakes off through the trees in each direction. The dip is a bed of dried cracked mud pebbled with stones and is clear of trees and bushes. The water that normally runs through the creek is gone. Now it is dry and the grasses growing along its sides are yellowing and their edges burnt dry.

Nick continues on. With no idea where he is and no direction to mark his course, he decides to follow the dried up creek.

*****

"Why are we running?" David pants, out of breath, as he and Ian race through the woods.

"There was something back there," Ian gasps back.

David looks back, almost running into a tree and managing to dodge it at the last second.

"What? I don't think there's anything behind us now."

"I don't know. I didn't see it. I only heard it. Something was chasing us." Ian's words are clipped short between ragged gasps for air.

They slow to a jog and then to a walk, stumbling with pained grimaces and gasps, trying to catch their breath. Ian keeps looking back, worried over whatever was chasing them.

"When did it start chasing us?" David asks skeptically.

"Nick's Uncle's place."

"What do you think it was? It was probably Nick's uncle Harvey."

The idea that they may have been caught snooping rings alarm in David's stomach, compounded by the suggestion he actually chased them. Harvey is odd enough to scare even David, although he would never admit it to anyone.

"Maybe? I don't know. It might have been too big," Ian says.

"If it was a bear or something, it gave up by now," David says. "Come on, we have to find Nick."

"Maybe we should just let him go. He looked upset."

"All the more reason we have to find him now. What did he find? Did he say?"

"He didn't say he found anything. He could have just been worried his uncle is going to catch us."

"If he found something, we need to know. Let's find him." David looks around, trying to get his bearings. He starts walking and Ian follows.

David keeps searching around as they walk, hoping for any sign of Nick. They come across the same dried up creek winding its way through the trees.

"Do you think he would have followed it?" David asks.

"It's possible. It's easier than fighting our way through the trees. I would."

David nods. "Which way?"

*****

Nick is walking along the dried up creek bed, picking his way over rocks. He spies something through the trees ahead on the edge of the creek, mostly hidden where the empty waterway curves. Curious, he keeps moving towards it, focusing on it and trying to determine what it is.

As he gets closer, he sees it is a small dilapidated stone and wood building. Through the trees he makes out broken and crooked leaning slats and boards on the creek side.

Coming around the curve, the old mill is revealed in all its deteriorated rot. Moss and lichen clings to the lower stones and bushes and weeds are growing up through some of the water wheel slats, the forest trying to reclaim it.

Nick hears a sound behind him and stops. A footstep crunches in the dry leaves. He turns around to face Harvey standing on the bank. He feels the heat of a flush burning his cheeks and feels startled. The thought of running crosses his mind.

Harvey is standing there, a rifle resting casually in the crook of his arm, the muzzle pointed to the ground. He holds the carcasses of a fox and rabbit slung over his shoulder, tied together by the back feet.

Nick blinks at him, shocked and afraid he must have followed him there from the cabin. He swallows woodenly, trying to think of something to say.

"What are you doing here?" he manages.

"I was just thinking to ask you the same thing." Harvey's expression is unreadable, his voice giving no clue to his mood. "I'm checking my traps. You're out a bit far from town. Just out for a walk?"

"Yeah, something like that." Nick is stiff with fear. The urge to turn and run flares hotter with the heat in his cheeks. He is sure Harvey must see his blush. "It's getting late, I need to get back."

Harvey nods. "I guess I'll see you around then."

"I guess so." Nick starts moving off, taking a few steps. He does not want to turn his back on his uncle. He turns and starts walking.

"Nick."

Nick stops, turning back to Harvey. "Yeah?"

"Town is that way." Harvey indicates the direction with his chin.

"Oh, yeah. Thanks." Nick turns and walks away again, this time in the right direction.

He has to fight the urge to look back as he walks away. He can feel Harvey just standing there watching him go.

He concentrates on keeping his pace steady, his back straight, and his walk that feels utterly miserably awkward as natural as he can. When he is sure he walked far enough that Harvey must have lost sight of him, Nick starts to run, immediately cursing the noise of the dry leaves that give his urgency away.

Harvey watches Nick go, waiting for the young man to be out of sight, and stands there for some time listening to the diminishing sound of his hurried feet crunching through the woods. He turns and walks towards to abandoned mill.

*****

"My guess is he went back to town," Ian says.

Following the creek, David and Ian make better time going back to town than they did travelling away from it through the heavy bush. They follow the creek for as long as they can, switching to a deer trail they come across that is going in direction of their destination, and finally have to push their way through the woods again until they find the field that is being cleared for construction.

They break from the trees at the far end and have to walk the distance of the field to the construction trailer office and David's car. They keep watching for signs of Nick as they go.

When they reach the car, David stands next to it looking around for Nick. David slaps the car roof.

"Okay, let's go. We'll drive up the road a bit and see if we see him. If not, then Nick is on his own to get back to town."

They get in and pull out, turning up the old Mill Road going away from town. The road is an old gravel road that is not generally maintained since nobody much goes up this way. Some distance past the field being cleared for construction the road turns to mud. The car rolls and sways with the ruts in the road and they can't drive fast without feeling like they will knock a kidney loose.

"Watch the trees. We could miss him if he's just getting to the road," David says.

*****

Nick's path back does not have the easier dried up creek or deer trails to help him. He struggles through the thick trees, going around or forcing his way through thicker brush and speeding up when it thins out.

He is starting to question Harvey's direction.

"Bloody hell, he sent me off in the wrong direction," he sputters as he pushes his way through a particularly dense area. The branches catch on his clothes and he is not sure he has not torn any holes in them. He shakes his head in disgust, trying to wipe away the cobweb he just walked through that he can feel tickling his face.

Nick pushes on through the woods and it opens up before him, the bushes and trees thinning. He almost whoops when he sees clear sky ahead through the trees.

Harvey pointed him in the direction of the road, not town. It is a longer distance, but means less time spent working his way through the woods.

Nick steps out and is approaching the road, just a few trees between him and the road, when he hears the approaching car.

"I should hitch a ride." He moves faster and then hesitates. He stops. "It could be David and Ian. I really don't want to see them right now."

He ducks behind a tree and tries to see what the approaching vehicle is.

"It's them." He ducks down lower, out of sight from the road. "They must be looking for me."

After the car passes, Nick moves deeper into the trees and starts slowly making his way towards town, slowed by the rough route.

*****

"We're getting close to the old mill," Ian says, eying the trees. He stopped watching for Nick and is now watching the trees along the side of the road ahead with a faint dread pooling in his stomach. The closer they get to the old mill, the stronger the feeling gets. "We should turn around. He wouldn't have gone this far."

"You're right. We missed him. He has to be back there walking to town. That, or lost in the woods."

I hope not, Ian thinks.

David slows and swerves to one side of the narrow road. It takes him a three-point turn to turn around and start driving back towards the construction area and town beyond that. He speeds up, the car rocking and bumping harder and leaving a cloud of dust behind them.

Ian pushes down the urge to grab onto something, gritting his teeth and silently wishing David would slow down. He gives up, gripping the dash to support his swaying body in the rough jostling of the car driving too fast down the nearly impassable road.

They pass the field with the ruined trees piled like a giant beaver dam and the little trailer office with no sign of Nick.

*****

Nick hears the car before he sees it. He sees the flash of the sun glinting off the car as it passes on the road through the trees.

"They must have given up."

He changes course, heading for the road. When he gets there, wading through the tall dry grass of the deep ditch, it is a relief to not have to struggle through bushes anymore. He starts the long walk to town.

For the first time since they met up to go to Uncle Harvey's Nick really feels the silence of the forest. The trees loom on each side of the road as if they would close in like a curtain, shutting off access to the long abandoned mill somewhere down the road behind him. The wind is a steady hissing in the trees.

Some days the hissing of the wind in the trees is a soothing sound to Nick. Not now. Not here.

A shadow passes over him, the air noticeably cooling with it, and he looks up to see a fast moving cloud blocking the sun. Everything suddenly seems muted, darker. The sun sits low in the sky and will soon set the sky on fire with the blaze of sunset if the clouds don't cover it up. The hissing of the wind in the trees is an ominous sound.

A bird cries somewhere and Nick cannot help but wonder if it cries for something bad that has happened.

Maybe it's crying over the child found in the woods.

He chuckles at the thought, smiling wryly. It is not a humorous thing. It is a nervous reaction.

"Now you're just being an idiot."

It is a long walk before he reaches the field. The line of ruined trees piled on one end sends its shadow stretching across the stripped ground, broken trunks and branches poking out like the grasping claws of a rolling mob of some strange creature, all clawing and scrabbling at the sky.

Sore and tired, Nick walks on, noting David's car is not waiting by the trailer.

"I should have brought my own car," he mutters, walking on towards town.

26 – Finding Quiet

David and Ian reach the edge of town. David stops the car, puts it in park, and leans against the door, looking at Ian.

"Now what? Do you have any idea where he might go?" David asks.

"No. I don't even know where he could be staying," Ian says. "We should just let it go."

"I'm not letting it go. He came back for a reason. There aren't many places here to go." David looks back the way they came. "He's on foot, so he can't have beaten us here. We could just sit and wait for him to show up."

"It's been a long day and I'm tired," Ian complains. "I'm out. You should be too. Just drop it for today at least. Nick isn't going to talk to you. Not the way he's feeling right now. If you force it, he'll just shut down and shut you out. You won't get anything from him."

David sighs heavily. "Fine. I'll give him tonight to sort himself out. We'll look for him again tomorrow."

He puts the car in drive and heads for home.

*****

Nick is exhausted by the time he reaches town. The sky is getting darker, the orange burn of sunset sitting low on the horizon below a band of the last light of day, the darkness chasing it across the sky. He is more than physically tired. He is emotionally drained.

"Hopefully I can get to my car without running into David and Ian."

He makes his way through town, conscious of the likelihood of running into them.

Nick stops at the sight of someone crossing the street up ahead.

"Felicia?" Nick stares. "It can't be. What is she doing here?"

He watches the distant figure. He caught only a fleeting look, but it is enough.

He has to get closer, to see. He needs to confirm.

"It can't be her. Not here."

Nick hurries to follow, breaking into a jog. He catches up, grabbing the woman's wrist just as she turns a corner, stopping her in her tracks.

"Felicia."

She turns on him with the startled look of a woman trapped and trying to decide if she is being attacked.

"Oh, uh, sorry," Nick murmurs apologetically, quickly releasing her. "I thought you were someone else."

Looking mildly panicked, the woman pulls her arm away with a scowl, her fear at being suddenly grabbed from behind by a strange man turning to annoyance. She turns away, her irritation showing in her clomping steps as she walks away.

Nick watches her go.

"How could I have thought that was Felicia? I haven't seen her in a few years, but I can't see her ever growing to the size of that woman."

Felecia tends to forget to eat. He can picture her only as the too thin emotional mess she has always been.

The only thing that the woman may have in common with Felicia is the long hair hanging down her back.

Nick turns and goes the other way. It is a small town and there is little to do and even fewer places to go, especially if you want to be alone.

Nick returns to his car and gets in. He sits there.

"What do I do now? I'm hungry, but if I go to Dusty's I'll run into David and Ian for sure. The stores are closed by now. There is nowhere else to get a bite to eat."

With an unhappy look at the passenger seat empty of any food options and still undecided on what to do, Nick starts the car. He drives out of town; not paying attention to anything but that there is road in front of his car. He goes past the abandoned railroad station and turns up the old Mill Road without realizing it is 'that' road.

He drives without thought to where he is going, just looking for somewhere to be alone.

David has been dogging him since he arrived in town.

*****

Harvey circles the old mill, not getting too close, studying the ground for any signs of human or animal trespassers. The crisp dry leaves crunch under his feet. The growth is wilted and blighted with the sickly yellow of plants dying of thirst like the rest of the region.

The old mill is an ancient wood and stone structure, stained dark with age and from the ravages of the elements. Its outer wood walls are cracked and weathered with moss and lichens growing on their lower parts on the East side where the afternoon shadows keep it moist. The lower stone part of the wall is covered with the moss and lichens. The glass is broken and large chunks missing from the windows. What remains of the window glass is cloudy with decades of grime. The roof sags and in places appears as if the wooden roof had melted inwards. Remnants of the old shingles still tease at the promise of providing a dry refuge beneath them. Moss and lichens grow on the roof where denser trees provide more shade.

On the creek side the large bladed wheel that once turned with the power of the water current sits immobilized by rot and decay. Blades had rotted free, falling to partially lean on the ground below. Long grass grows through them as though to hold them down.

Even if the creek were not dried up, the wheel would not be able to turn. The mechanism has long ago seized and rusted solid. Inside the wooden beams have rotted, letting the heavy top grinding stone shift.

On the West side the ground slopes down sharply as the land falls away. The creek would have gurgled and boiled as it fell with the land, speeding up the flow of the water until the level ground beyond could tame it. The soil had eroded to reveal a natural formation of a jumble of large rocks held by the branches of large trees that give support to the structure. Here, in what would be a deeper pool of the creek when waters fill its banks when there is no drought, the land drops steeply and a fat tangle of roots lies bare.

"Whatever that boy is doing hanging around the old mill, it's not a good place to be," Harvey mutters. "I'll have to keep a closer eye on him. Make sure he keeps out of trouble."

Harvey opens the mill door and is greeted by silence. He stares into the dim interior. A low groan moans from the ceiling, like the weight of something shifting on the floor above. He looks up and listens. No further sound comes. Harvey steps back, closing the door and leaving the mill to its unsettled silence.

Satisfied the old mill seems as untouched as ever, Harvey moves off through the forest, leaving the area.

*****

Nick slows the car and pulls over on the edge of the road. Exhaustion pulls him down like a physical force weighing down his shoulders, his limbs, his whole body. He looks around almost groggily at the trees on both sides of the road. They all blend in together. The road is deserted and darkness seems to be closing in faster with the tall trees surrounding him. A narrow dirt road branching off through the trees is all but hidden in the growing night.

"This is as good a place as any to sleep."

Feeling like he is suffocating in the stuffy car, Nick cracks a window, turns off the engine, and leans his seat back, trying to make himself comfortable.

The sounds of crickets and other night insects buzz and scree outside the car. The sound becomes a soothing drone and he closes his eyes to try to sleep, motionlessly breathing; the drone playing endlessly as darkness slowly closes in with the sun dropping below the edge of the horizon in the cloud-filled sky.

The insects go quiet.

Nick's eyes jerk open, disoriented. He blinks and sits up a little, looking around, his sleep interrupted by the silence.

Trying to get his bearings, he studies the trees, not sure where he is. He knows town is behind him but did not pay attention to where he drove aimlessly to.

Nick's eyes catch possible movement in the darkness of the trees.

He holds his breath; listening and staring at the spot he thought he saw it.

Did something move? He listens.

There is no sound. If anything is there it is moving silently. A large fierce black cat silently stalking its prey comes to mind and he pushes the image away.

"My eyes must be playing tricks on me. There's nothing there."

He settles back and closes his eyes, trying to go back to sleep. The uneasy silence weighs on his subconscious. He can't sleep.

A gnawing anxiety pulls at him. The feeling of being watched.

Nick opens his eyes and looks at the trees, just catching a fleeting glimpse of dark motion. He has the strong sense that something large and moving fast was coming at him and froze the moment he opened his eyes, vanishing in the darkness. His nerves are tense, making him feel jumpy.

He tries to place his location, thinking back to the route he paid no attention to.

"I think I'm close to the old mill." He sits upright, staring out at the trees. The knowledge sits heavy and greasy in his gut.

There is movement in the trees again. Nick stares hard, trying to make it out. All he can see is darkness veiled behind the closest trees and the suggestion of motion within.

The motion comes again, accompanied by the sudden cracking of something crashing its way through the trees without thought or care. It is gone, vanished into the woods.

His hands shaking, Nick reaches and turns on the ignition, putting the car in drive. Turning in the narrow road, he heads back to town.

*****

The drive to town feels endless in the dark with nothing but trees on both sides of the road and nothing to tell him where he is.

The moment Nick is closing in on the first buildings on the edge of town his stomach starts churning with trepidation.

"I'm not sure if I feel sick with hunger or nerves. I hope David and Ian gave up looking for me. There is no place to go in this town to hide from someone determined to find you."

As childish as running away feels, it was the only option he could think of to get away from them.

He still feels shaken from searching Uncle Harvey's property. The last thing he wants right now is to face David and his endless press for answers he doesn't have.

Nick also needs time to process what he saw after he left the Quonset.

He thinks. Where would the best place to go be?

"The train station. If I drive in behind it, right up against the trees. I might even be able to get in behind some bushes or at least try to hide the car in the tall grass there. Maybe nobody will see it. Nobody would have any reason to go up in behind that old station."

With a destination in mind, he starts driving through town. He has one problem though. His stomach is rumbling hungrily. He hasn't eaten today.

With the gnawing ache in his stomach finally making itself known, Nick subconsciously rubs it with one hand as he steers with the other.

"Oh man, I've got to eat something. I'll park the car and go on foot. At least if they're looking for the car, it won't give me away."

Nick turns towards the abandoned train station and again up the cracked road behind it. The road was built long before anyone thought little used roads around town needed to be wide enough for two cars to pass, the first cars chugging along at a much slower pace. The car rocks over the rough ground, rolling harder after leaving the warped and cracked road, the long grass slishing against the undercarriage. He gets there to see another car already parked there.

"I guess someone else had the same idea."

Nick parks and gets out, walking around the other car. It's an older model, its paint sun-bleached and the bottom panels all around rotting with rust that is eating holes through the metal. The windows are cloudy with the haze of grime and dust.

"It looks like they never came back. This thing must have been here for years."

He looks in the windows, trying to see through the grime coating them. There is little to see. He thinks he sees what might be a woman's handbag and a teddy bear on the seat.

Shrugging, he walks away, heading for Dusty's and a meal.

*****

Liam is sitting in a booth in a back corner of Dusty's squinting at the papers on the table in front of him. The dim light is not ideal for reading.

On the table before him are a couple of files, the top one spread open to the pages within, his notebook, a plate with the remains of a too greasy hamburger and fries, and a half empty glass of draught beer.

The burger sits heavily in his stomach. He takes another sip of the beer, not paying attention to the other patrons at scattered tables. Conversation is muted by the wood and cluttered decor. Rockabilly music plays at a level loud enough to drown out conversation across the room, but not too loud to be heard at nearby tables without shouting.

The door opens and a young man enters, looking around cautiously before committing himself to finding a table. He walks to the back booths, choosing one where he is not readily visible from the door and near Liam. He would be beneath Liam's notice except for two things. He looks young enough to be questionable whether he is old enough to drink, and he looks utterly and absolutely exhausted with the haunted look in his eyes of someone on the run from something.

Liam watches him surreptitiously.

Nick avoids eye contact with anyone as he makes his way through Dusty's to the back booths and slides into a booth. He ducks his head as he sits as if that will make him less noticeable.

He tenses when the waitress approaches.

"What can I get for you, hon?" she asks.

The waitress wears too tight jeans that show the round curve of her buttocks and uncomfortable high heels giving her legs an overemphasized bulge to her calves, which is revealed by the skin tight pants legs. Her blouse would probably look frumpy on a woman with a heavier set body type. The baggy shirt bottom hides the bulge of skin just above the waistband of her jeans, forced out by the too tight pants. Loose enough to contain the ample ladies up top, the blouse has one button too many unbuttoned, revealing too much round cleavage when she bends over. Her hair looks like she attempted something resembling a crossover between an updo and a messy bun, resulting in something more resembling a failed attempt to extricate large wads of chewing gum from her hair. Her makeup is too heavy and dark for her face, making her look older instead of younger as she intended.

"Burger and fries and a beer please, ma'am," Nick says.

She gives him a look, arching one eyebrow.

"Ma'am? People call my mother ma'am. I ain't no ma'am yet hon."

"Sorry," Nick apologizes, feeling the pain of unknowingly insulting a woman he suddenly suspects could beat the living daylights out of him despite her smaller size. "I didn't mean-. I was just trying to be polite."

"Clarisse," the waitress grins at him. "I'll be right back with your beer. The food will be a bit longer."

"I expect a bigger tip for that," she teases as she walks away.

Nick looks like he would vanish into the seat if he could. He was never good at confrontations. Even less when it involves a woman. The idea of a confrontation with Felicia always left him weak for as long as he could remember.

*****

Liam watches the young man at the other table, closing the file in front of him and stacking the files neatly. He absently taps the pile with a finger, thinking.

Who is this young man? It's not David or his brother Ian.

A slow grin spreads across his lips.

"Nicholas Hastings. The young nephew of our suspect Harvey Lawson. The boy who returned to town just when the body would be found.

He waits for Nick to be served his food and halfway through devouring it hungrily before sliding out of his seat and approaching him.

Nick senses the man before he realizes his intentions. The too greasy half-eaten hamburger sitting heavily in his stomach in a grease-soaked wad of bread and meat, jamming another mouthful of oily fries gritty with salt in his mouth, he looks up to see the man come to stand before his table. He self-consciously chews and takes a long swig of beer to wash the mass down, staring up at the man looking at him with a bland expression.

"I've seen you in here before," Liam says.

"No doubt. It's a small town." Nick eyes him warily.

Liam nods towards the half-eaten food. "Late supper? You must be working late."

"Something like that."

Liam's lips spread in a slight smile. "Not a lot of places to work at his hour around here, except maybe Dusty's here. Where are you working?"

Nick's unease grows.

"I work at the construction site on the edge of town. Why are you asking?"

"I'm sorry," Liam's smile grows a little, "I should have introduced myself." He holds out a hand. "I am Detective Liam Tobin."

Not knowing what to do, Nick rubs his greasy hand on his jeans and takes the man's hand. Both their handshakes are firm, Nick responding to Liam's harder authoritative grip by squeezing tighter.

"Nick," he says uncertainly.

Both hold back winces before they release the pressure on the other's hand.

"May I sit?" Liam motions to a chair, pulling it out and sitting before Nick can answer. He leans in towards Nick.

"Yes, Nick. I know who you are. No doubt you heard about the body found in the woods by the construction site." Liam's grin grows just a little more. "Of course you did. Who hasn't? I'm here to investigate it."

Nick's heart is pounding in his chest and he can feel a clammy sweat breaking out. He hopes the detective doesn't notice.

What the hell. Why am I reacting like I'm guilty? I didn't do anything. I wasn't even the one who found it.

"So, I guess you are just going around talking to people?" Nick asks.

"Only the ones I think might be relevant. You know the local police suspect your uncle, Harvey Lawson. Apparently there is some history with him and bodies being found?"

Nick shrugs. He takes another bite of his hamburger to put off responding, giving him time to think. He is still chewing and talks around the mouthful of mangled food.

"I was just a kid when we moved away. I don't know much of anything about Uncle Harvey."

"You came back just for the job? Or for old time's sake? Your Uncle Harvey is the only family you have here. You came to hook up with old friends? David and Ian Morrow?"

"You go where the work is," Nick says noncommittally. "I didn't even remember those guys."

"And yet I saw you here at this same table with them." Liam shrugs as if it is unimportant. "You must have reconnected with your uncle at least. Do you know what he does up there at his cabin?"

Nick shrugs again, taking another bite. His mind panics a little, realizing his hamburger will be gone soon and won't give him any more reason to not answer his questions.

"Hunts, traps, gardens? That's my guess," he says around the mouthful of food.

"So, he wouldn't have any need that you know of for farm chemicals?"

"Maybe he's farming?" Nick suggests. His mind immediately goes to the chemicals he saw in the Quonset.

Does he know something? Does he know we were there snooping around? How does he know about the chemicals?

"If you want to know what he does, maybe you should ask him," Nick adds. "Look, I just came here for a quick bite to eat before I sleep. I have to be up in the morning for work."

Liam nods understandingly.

"Where can I find you? I expect I'll have a few questions to ask."

"You just asked me questions. At the jobsite."

"Where are you staying?"

Nick can't keep the hot flush from rising in his cheeks.

"Nowhere really. In my car."

"It's a small town. Not many places to get a room," he adds to excuse his homelessness.

"Not to worry. I'll find you when I need to." Liam smiles and gets up, returning to his table.

Nick wolfs down the rest of his burger, shoving the fries in his mouth and barely chewing before washing them down. Leaving money on the table for his bill, he makes a quick retreat out of Dusty's.

The cool night air chills the sweat dampening his body. It is both sickening and a relief. He huddles into himself and walks quickly back to his car hidden behind the abandoned train station.

The sounds of the night insects follow him, silencing as he approaches and resuming their night serenade in his wake. Loose gravel stones from the shoulder tracked into the road crunch under his shoes.

Nick feels more chilled by the time he reaches the old train station. When he gets there, he considers mounting the platform to sit and look at the sky. Shivering with the chill seeping into him, he decides to go straight for the shelter of his car.

Walking around the platform and deteriorated ticket office on ground level reveals the rotting bases of the beams supporting the raised platform. It is at a level even with the train cars so that passengers would not have to step up or down to enter and exit the cars, so it is below eye level.

Something scurries deeper beneath the platform.

Probably a raccoon or woodchuck. I don't smell skunk, Nick thinks.

Nick takes a little wider path just in case. He can't help but look at the abandoned car. It doesn't look any different.

Getting in his car, he closes the door against the night, hoping the confined space will be enough to warm him with his body heat. Reaching over the back seat, he pulls out his pillow and blanket into the front, leans his seat back, and wraps himself with the blanket, trying to settle himself comfortably.

The sound of crickets and the breeze blowing the long grass and the leaves of the trees nearby is the only thing that breaks the quiet. That and the sound of something scuttling under the train platform, but Nick can't decide if that is just his imagination.

Settling himself in as best he can, Nick closes his eyes and tries to sleep. His mind won't stop thinking about that abandoned car.

27 – Anhydrous Ammonia and Dark Rumours

Liam looks up from his table at Dusty's when the door opens again. Being the only place open at night in a small town, most anyone stopping in for a coffee, drink, or meal is no surprise.

Malcolm Colbert lets the door close behind him, quickly scanning the room to see who is there, and nods to the waitress. He is in uniform, his police cruiser parked outside.

"Coffee and a B.L.T. please Clarisse; when you have time.

"Anything for you, hon." She gives him a wink on the way by to the bar near the order window open to the kitchen. Picking up a tray of plates with food, she expertly weaves through the room to deliver them to a table in the front corner.

Liam waves to Malcolm. Malcolm sees him but ignores the detective's attempt to get his attention.

Rising in his seat and waving harder, it is impossible to pretend he does not see Liam.

With a resigned sigh, Malcolm walks over to him.

Liam waves him to a seat and he grudgingly sits down.

"This is perfect," Liam says. "I wanted to pick your brain for a bit."

"What about?"

"Harvey Lawson."

Malcolm's facial response is a dead giveaway of his opinion of Harvey, and it is not a favourable opinion.

"What do you want to know?"

"He lives kind of remote in the bush and not very accessible."

"Yeah, what of it?"

"What kind of crops does he farm?"

"Harvey Lawson is no farmer." Malcolm shakes his head. "I'm not sure he does anything for a living outside of trapping and coyote baiting. There is no bounty on coyote, so I don't even know that he earns anything doing that."

"There is no reason for him to be keeping farm chemicals around then?"

Now he has Malcolm's interest.

"For crops? Not that I know of," Malcolm says. "I don't know that he ever farmed, so Harvey would have no reason to have anything like that. What kind of chemicals are you talking about?"

"Pressurized tanks of anhydrous ammonia among others. Some of the labels are unreadable, but if I can get a warrant we can have them tested."

"Nitrogen," Malcolm says thoughtfully. "Sales of that are restricted, since it can be used to make explosive devices."

He looks at Liam sharply.

"How do you know about this? You have no jurisdiction to go searching the man's property without a warrant."

"I was just taking a walk in the woods," Liam shrugs. "Sometimes a fellow just comes across things on a walk."

He looks levelly at Malcolm. "Do you think Harvey would be making a bomb?"

"I can't think of anything he would want to blow up."

Chester Hayes walks into Dusty's, quickly scoping the place to see who is there. He spots Liam and Malcolm, pauses to consider leaving or sitting elsewhere, and starts towards them. He catches Clarisse's eye and motions to her on the way.

Malcolm and Liam look up when he gets close to the table, sensing his approach.

Chester motions to the empty seat as he is taking it, inviting himself to join them.

"Well, if it isn't the new sheriff in town." He gives Liam a not quite friendly smile that does not reach his eyes.

"It's okay," Liam says to Malcolm. "I get that a lot."

Malcolm gives him a suffering look. He doesn't care the retired sheriff made a wisecrack meant to insult Liam.

He grins back at the retired sheriff, his own smile insolent.

"I wasn't going to say anything to defend you," Malcolm says.

Liam just chuckles humourlessly.

"The retired sheriff probably knows more about the Lawson family history than anyone at this table," Malcolm says. "Maybe we should ask him."

"Ask me what?" Chester asks. He looks up at Clarisse with a smile as she drops a drink in front of him and quickly moves on to serve another table.

Liam looks at him.

"Would Harvey Lawson be making a bomb?"

"The nitrogen," Chester says expressionlessly.

Malcolm blinks at him in surprise.

"You know about the nitrogen and other chemicals?"

"I'm retired, not senile."

Chester turns to stare at Malcolm.

"How do you not know? You're the law around here now."

Malcolm's lips tighten.

"Back on topic," Liam says, diffusing the coming fight. "Would Harvey be making a bomb? He's got the stuff for it."

Chester shakes his head, turning his attention back on Liam.

"I never rule out anything until I rule it out. Is it possible? Yes. Do I think it's likely?" He shakes his head. "Harvey is a loser. An aging hippie who should have outgrown it years ago and settled down with a family; lazy, uninterested in employment, and likely unemployable. He's not a terrorist, if that's what you are getting at. Could he ever be likely to make a bomb? Everyone could be likely in the right circumstances."

Chester shrugs.

"Maybe with the right cause, I could see that. But you need to get passionate about a cause and that isn't Harvey."

"So, you don't think he's making bombs," Malcolm says.

"No." Chester's eyes are still on Liam.

"What do you think he's making with the nitrogen then?" Liam asks.

"Poison."

"Poison." Liam looks sceptical.

Malcolm nods agreement.

"Makes sense," he says. "He's probably poisoning those coyotes."

"And other things." Chester points a finger triumphantly at him for getting the answer right.

"What do you mean other things?" Liam asks.

The retired sheriff leans forward to draw them into the story he is about to tell, and Liam has a sense of foreboding. He half expects the lights to dim to a more sinister mood.

"You heard of the old mill?" Chester asks.

Liam grins. Every small town has their own old mill.

"No, but I bet I'm about to."

Chester nods.

"As long as memory in this town holds, there's been stories of funny business going on down the road the old mill access road comes off of."

"So, the mill isn't actually on Old Mill Road."

"Nah. It's called that because everyone knows you have to go down that road to reach the mill. The access road is barely a road at all. Used to be a horse and cart road, but it's all grown in over the years. It's not more than a deer trail now. You find that old road and follow it to the creek and you will find the mill."

"What kind of 'funny business' goes on down there?" Liam stresses the two words.

"People don't go down there normally. There is no cause for visiting the mill. Only folks who live around here know it exists and they know better than to go down that way."

"This is going to be about the disappearances, isn't it?" Liam asks.

Chester nods and Liam is sure the whole story is just the old man pulling his leg, having fun at his expense.

"It only happens every so many years. Seems like each time we have a drought like we are having now. Usually farm animals and a few pets will go missing. Likely feed for the predators with game moving on when everything dries up, following the food. Sometimes it's a kid who vanishes. They probably just got lost in the forest, maybe taken down by a starving animal, but showing up the way they do years later like they've been stored somewhere gets people talking."

"I feel like someone should be going oheeeoooo all spooky," Liam grins.

Chester's lips tighten in annoyance at him.

"I'm not saying that I believe them, only that this is what people think."

"Folks think there is something out there in the woods. They think it, but not really. Nobody will admit it, but deep down they all believe."

"Why do you think that is?"

Chester looks at Liam steadily. "Because believing in a make believe monster in the woods is easier on the gut than the other option; that someone around here, one of their neighbours or kin, is preying on kids."

"Got it," Liam nods.

"Sometimes folks go down to the old mill. When they do, they come back saying they saw something disturbing."

"Do you think they are telling the truth?" Liam asks. "Do you know of anyone who actually said they saw something? Or is this more old-town ghost stories?"

"I've interviewed a few over the years who said they saw something. They couldn't say what, but it scared the devil out of them."

"Did you believe them? I mean, this area has a history of kids going missing and being found years later."

"Some years ago we had an incident. A few pets in the area went missing. People talked, making like it could be connected to the stories about the mill. Someone said they had been down to the old mill and saw something they couldn't describe. Turned out to be false. They were just making up stories for attention.

A couple kids in the next town went missing. Folks started on about the monster in the woods off the old Mill Road, like that must be what happened to them. Those boys were found, alive but looking a bit rough. Got themselves lost in the forest."

"So it was no monster from the mill. No animal hanging around."

"No sir it was not. Folks are just superstitious. But the boys' story didn't quite check out. It didn't match with the facts, but nobody could get them to tell the truth. They were lying; we just didn't know what they were lying about and we never found out. One of them committed suicide a few years later and the other still refused to talk about it."

Liam is silent for a moment, digesting this. He looks at the retired sheriff seriously.

"You think it was another kind of monster."

"It makes the best sense. Folks do terrible things to other folks. That knowledge is always in the back a person's mind. Then some time later a kid was found. It was odd because there were no missing kids anyone could account for. He was found all curled up like he was trying to keep warm. The body was old and dried out too."

Malcolm and Liam share a look.

Just like the kid just found, they are both thinking.

"What does this have to do with Harvey and the mill?" Liam asks.

"Folks always seem to go back to the fantastic when they don't know what a thing is. Talk turned to the strange things rumoured to have happened at the old mill a long time ago when animals went missing. It was likely just a rogue pair of wolves, a splinter pack too small to feed itself, feeding off pets and farm animals. When a kid went missing, folks turned to the old Mill Road monster to convince themselves it couldn't be anyone they knew."

Chester shrugs.

"There's always been dark rumours in this town about the old Mill. About Harvey Lawson, too, since he was a boy. He's always been a strange one, that boy. Folks desperate both to understand it and distance themselves from it made the leap into the implausible."

"What is that?" Liam asks.

"That maybe Harvey isn't what folks think. That something happened to Harvey in the woods years ago when he was a boy. Maybe Harvey isn't really Harvey anymore."

Liam arches an eyebrow at this.

"Harvey disappeared in the woods."

It is just a guess, but Chester's nod confirms it.

"He was found all curled up like the bodies of the others only Harvey was not all dried out or even dead. The boy was in rough shape to be sure, been missing for weeks. Nobody knew how he survived out there that long.

When another boy disappears years later it was easy enough for folks to blame strange Harvey Lawson. They blamed him.

Treated him like some kind of monster from the movies. His hanging around the old mill area didn't help.

Folks believe there is something unnatural up the old Mill Road and at the mill. Some figured whatever it is could have taken Harvey's place when the boy disappeared then suddenly turned up."

"Do you believe all that?" Liam asks.

Chester looks at him hard.

"Do you think I'm daft? These are old wives' tales. You are an officer of the law and you need to work in facts, not fairy-tales.

The boy got lost in the woods is all and was found before he passed."

Liam levels a serious look at him.

"Do you think it has any relation to the girl who vanished from the train station about thirty years ago?"

Chester looks at him stone-faced.

"Like I said, I never rule out anything until I rule it out."

"I remember the girl at the train station," Malcolm says with a mild look of wonder. "I was just a kid."

"I remember it like it was yesterday," Chester's eyes cloud into his memories.

28 – A Mother's Torment

More Than Thirty Years Ago

The train whistle blew shrilly against the loud chuffing of the wheels on the tracks as the brakes clamped against the metal wheels. The train continued to be pushed down the rail tracks by its own weight. The wheels and tracks both heated up with friction. Metal on metal shrieked and the drag could be felt throughout the train cars.

The conductor looked out the front window at the approaching train station. The station had a small worn ticket booth sitting on a raised platform that looked like it should have been shut down years ago. He gritted his teeth at a couple of kids playing around on the tracks ahead.

He gripped the pull cord by his head and gave it another couple of long tugs, the whistle shrilling with it.

The kids finally looked up at the approaching train and scampered off the tracks to safety.

Wheels ceased turning and the friction increased as the train wheels slid down the rails. The train chuffed harder in the effort of dragging the weight of the cars to a stop.

Seated in a car midway down the train, a mother and her six year old daughter stared out the window of the slowing train together. They watched the countryside passing by slow down.

The train finally hissed to a stop with the release of the pressure on the brakes and a gentle rocking in front of the train station platform. Only a few cars lined up with the raised platform. For the other cars the train crew opened the doors and folded down the stairs for passengers.

"One hour stop!" The conductor walked through the train cars repeating the cry relentlessly until he reached the last car. "One hour stop!"

The little girl looked up at her mother wide eyed with a flush in her cheeks.

"Let's get off and stretch our legs," the mother, Dorothy, said.

They got up stiffly, walked down the aisle, and stumbled down the steps unsteadily to the ground.

The girl, Maisy, looked down the length of the train.

"Do we have much further to go, Mommy?"

"Yes. We are only halfway there."

Maisy frowned and looked up at her mother unhappily.

"There is no food on the train."

Dorothy looked around, taking stock.

"Maybe there is somewhere nearby we can get something."

She stared up at the sagging weathered timber of the train platform and the small worn out ticket office. The prospects looked bleak. She turned and looked at the town.

"Maybe we can at least find some crackers at a store."

She looked down at the little girl with a smile she did not feel.

"I said we would stretch our legs, didn't I? Let's go for a walk and see what we can find to eat."

Maisy looked at the train with worry.

"What if the train leaves without us?"

"We have a whole hour. We will have to walk fast, though."

Dorothy took Maisy's hand and quick-stepped away from the train station, the little girl trotting to keep up.

Thirty minutes later they were hurrying back with sandwiches from Dusty's.

Dorothy could not help the anxiety nagging at her that the train would somehow be gone when they got back even though it was there clear as day in the distance at the platform.

They were about to board when she remembered the warning she was given when they boarded at the start of the trip. The worker stared almost accusingly at her daughter while saying it. "No food on the train Ma-am."

She looked down at the little girl.

"It's too stuffy on the train," she said brightly. "Let's find someplace to eat."

Maisy pointed up to the platform.

"All right. We'll be able to see the conductor. We'll know when he's getting ready to leave."

Climbing the rickety stairs of the platform, they sat on the bench in front of the ticket office.

As a six year old will do, Maisy became bored and restless after a few bites. She shifted and wriggled and almost fell off the bench. She stuck her feet out and twisted and wriggled and almost tripped a man.

"I am so sorry," Dorothy said quickly. She snatched at the little girl and pulled her closer.

She looked down at her. "You almost tripped that man."

Maisy gave her a long suffering stare and then her attention was gone again, pulled away by boredom.

Dorothy looked around. Her eyes settled on the tall grass of the field next to the train station. Her look shifted to the woods on the other side of the field with a vague sense of foreboding. She turned to the little girl and fixed the yellow ribbon with white polka-dots in her hair that was coming loose.

"Why don't you go play in the grass over there? Maybe you can pick us some wildflowers."

Maisy's eyes lit up and she grinned. Twirling, she skipped across the platform and down the stairs.

Dorothy watched her go. Her heart raced in her chest when Maisy vanished from sight, calming again when she came into view entering the field from behind the platform.

She wrapped Maisy's sandwich with a guilty flush, hoping they will not get in trouble for it. She would be loudly complaining of her hunger soon if she threw it away.

Maisy ran in circles, hands brushing the long stalks of grass and wildflowers, laughing at the spinning sky above.

Movement caught her attention and she stopped. She stared at a pair of butterflies that flittered and danced around each other over the stalks of wildflowers and grass.

With a giggle, she ran to them. The butterflies bounced and flittered on the air, taking off in different directions.

Dorothy watched the little girl playfully chase the butterfly in the field behind the train station. The game took her across the field toward the trees.

Standing up to call Maisy to come back closer, her attention was pulled by a small commotion at the ticket office. A man she recognized from the train was arguing with the elderly man behind the ticket office window.

She turned back to call Maisy. Her eyes scanned the field. A rush of panic filled her. Maisy was gone. She turned away and hurried across the platform and down the stairs and ran around behind the ticket office.

"Maisy!" She called the girl's name. Her eyes searched the field for her.

There was no sign of movement except the tall grass waving with the breeze and the faint motion of the leaves on the trees across the field.

"Maisy!"

She listened and heard only the hissing of the wind slapping in the trees. Even the sound of the train station seemed gone.

In her panicked state, the wind became still and the world silent and empty. A bright color across the field caught her eye. Gently fluttering in the wind against the still and silent stalks of tall grass and wildflowers was the scarf from Maisy's hair.

She stumbled forward and half ran to the center of the field, calling Maisy over and over.

"Maisy! Maisy!"

A few people looked boredly at the woman in the field calling for her kid and turned away without interest.

Dorothy stumble-ran across the field and stopped before the trees. She reached out and snatched the yellow polka-dot ribbon from the stalks that trapped it.

The moment her fingers snagged it the world came back. The trees hissed angrily with the wind rubbing the leaves and the long stalks of grass and wildflowers waved like waves washing across the field with the soft gusting wind. The scarf danced against her hand, the wind trying to pull it free from her grip.

"Maisy!" she screamed once more at the sky and the ocean of grass, the trees of the woods next to her, and the impartial people at the train station.

The shrill cry of the train whistle pulled her attention. She turned her head to stare at the train. On the platform, the conductor and crew were ushering people to board the train.

She raised her arms and waved at them as she ran across the field yelling.

"Wait! Wait! I can't find Maisy!"

The conductor turned at the sound and watched the woman run through the field toward the platform. She ran around the back of the platform and mounted the stairs out of breath, gasping from running and shouting.

"Wait!"

She ran to them, reached to grab at him, and he pulled back from her touch.

"Maisy," she panted. "We got off to stretch our legs. She was running in the field."

The conductor turned his head to look at the field. There was no sign the child was ever there. He turned back to the woman.

"You have two minutes to find her or the train is leaving without you."

She blinked at him, shocked by his seemingly callous response.

"I have a schedule to keep Ma-am," he said by way of apology.

When she turned away, he motioned to one of his staff.

"Check the train for a missing child. A little girl."

The man nodded and disappeared inside. He moved quickly through the train cars searching for the little girl.

Dorothy stumbled across the platform to people waiting to re-board the train.

"Please, have you seen a little girl? She's six."

They shook their heads mutely and escaped onto the train.

Others watched out the windows as she stumbled around the platform, down the stairs, and around on the ground next to the train, asking if anyone saw a six year old girl.

She ran back up the stairs onto the platform to the ticket office. She leaned into the window urgently.

"Sir, please. I can't find my daughter, Maisy. She's only six."

He looked at her, looked down around him, and pulled out a clipboard. He clipped a paper to it and handed it to her."

She took it and looked at it in confusion. The words and lines on the page were meaningless to her in her stressed state.

"It's a form for the missing child," the elderly man said.

She looked at him numbly.

"I don't need a form. I need to find her."

He just stared at her.

She looked around the now empty platform. Only the train conductor remained. He watched her from his place next to the train. He looked at his watch. Her time was fast running out.

She left the clipboard at the window, ran to the edge of the platform, and yelled as loud as she could.

"Maisy!"

She jumped at a light touch on her elbow.

The train conductor was looking down at her with the best he could do at a sympathetic look.

"Ma-am. I have to go now. I have a schedule. I'm sorry, but she is not on the train. I hope you find your little girl."

He turned and walked across the platform without looking back and vanished inside the train. She caught a glimpse of him looking at her as he pulled the door closed behind him.

Moments later the train brakes let out a long sigh, the engine grew louder as it gained life, and with a chuffing racket followed by shrill squeals of metal on metal, the train began its slow pull out of the train station.

She watched the slowly departing train with an emptiness filling her that expanded to fill the world.

The train getting smaller chugging away down the tracks finally snapped her out of it.

Turning, she spotted the old man at the ticket booth. He was locking the door to leave.

She rushed across the platform to him.

"Please, sir, I can't find my daughter anywhere."

He stopped and looked at her. His shoulders slumped with a sigh.

"Did you check under the platform? Kids sometimes crawl under there."

"No. I didn't have time. The train left." She added the last as a simple statement to mark the futility she felt.

He waved her to follow. Together they searched again, under and around the train platform. They walked all around and along the tree line and zigzagged through the field. The old man hobbled along, walking too slowly for the frantic urgency that filled her.

Finally, the old man stopped and looked at her with resignation.

"She's not here. I can give you a ride to the police station so you can file a report on her."

Dorothy looked at him with panic both at leaving the area her daughter was last seen in and that filing a report means she really was missing. Her heart heavy and black with fear and loss, she followed him to his car parked behind the ticket booth end of the platform.

Two hours later the train was stopped on the tracks blocking the East and Westbound lanes next to a crossroad amid nothing but fields while the authorities searched it and questioned everyone on board about the missing child. A line of searchers that started at the train platform and swept out from there worked their way into the woods that bordered the field next to the train station. If they went far enough, they would reach the old abandoned mill.

Dorothy sat desolate and alone surrounded by police and well-wishers beneath a canopy set up next to the train platform. There, large metal coffee pots and jugs of water were set on tables where local women brought sandwiches and dainties to feed the searchers.

She looked up through her misery to see a boy staring at her through the crowd. He stood motionless as though not really there. He just stared at her. His stare unnerved her. So did the sense of familiarity she got from him.

She had to look around to see if anyone but her saw him. Everyone ignored him like he wasn't there. She was uncertain if she saw him. How could she if no one else did?

Someone talking to her pulled her attention back. She looked up at the man in uniform, Sheriff Chester Hayes.

He was looking down at her with pity. He tried to hide it but failed.

"Ma-am, I am afraid I don't think we are going to find your daughter today." He looked up at the sky for emphasis and back at her. "The sky. It will be too dark to keep searching in a few hours. Do you have anywhere to go?"

She shook her head mutely. She wanted to talk, to say something, to shriek and scream that they had to find Maisy; that they could not leave her out there lost in the dark. Her voice refused to work. Her lips refused to even move in an attempt at words. She could only stare and shake her head mutely.

Sheriff Hayes found someone to put Dorothy up that night. They put her up for the next two nights too while the search expanded and continued. She stumbled wearily through the search area with the searchers and slipped out at night to continue her search alone beneath the moon and stars. Without sleep and with little hope Maisy would be found, her appearance deteriorated along with the numbing of her despair. Having her brought back in the middle of the night, watching her eerily stare off into nothing and prowl the house restlessly at night when told not to leave, the family would have her no more.

Sheriff Hayes found another family to take her in, and another when they would not have her a second night. He took her in himself after that, watching Dorothy's hollow-eyed blank stare, her shuffled movements, and her endless seeking.

Each search day ended with the group gathered next to the train platform to discuss the day's failures and plans for the next day. The volunteer searchers dropped off, returning to their normal lives, and the search lines dwindled daily until there were just a few stragglers roaming the woods with Sheriff Hayes and Dorothy.

Finally, the day came. As the search drew to an end, the deepening dusk sucking the daylight from the sky, Sheriff Hayes called the few remaining searchers together for their nightly recap and discussion of the next day's plans.

He looked at the crowd. It wasn't much of a crowd; couldn't really be called one at all.

"I'm afraid I'm going to have to call it. The search for Maisy Brown is over."

He glanced guiltily at Dorothy and looked away quickly from her empty-eyed loss.

"That does not mean we are giving up on finding her. What we are doing isn't working. Maisy Brown is still out there somewhere. She could have wandered into the woods and got turned around. Some animal-," his voice caught in his throat, "could have got at her. We won't give up-. I won't give up-. Until this little girl is found."

"Has anyone checked the old mill?"

He looked to see who spoke with that anxious quiver. It was an elderly woman. She held a trembling hand to her throat.

"It is not likely the girl would have travelled that far."

A few murmurs passed through the crowd. The words old mill and monster were repeated in the same sentences.

"Strange things happen down the old Mill Road."

Sheriff Hayes looked at the man who spoke.

"Mr. Johnstone, there is no call to start rumours about monsters that don't exist."

"Probably those coyotes," someone said.

"More likely a cougar. I heard one was spotted over by the next town," someone else said.

Dorothy stared mutely at them. When they finally quieted, she stood up and looked at them.

"It was no coyote or mountain lion." Her voice cracked and was too quiet. "Maisy was right here. Right here, where no wild animal would go in the day with people around. She was there and then just gone. It was no four-legged animal that took her."

Sheriff Hayes looked at her.

"What are you suggesting Mrs. Brown? Are you saying someone here in town stole your little girl?"

"Or someone from the train." She stared him down in weak defiance. "Maisy was there and then she was just gone. I looked away for only a moment and she was gone."

Stunned expressions met her weary loss-filled eyed.

"Mrs. Brown," Sheriff Hayes said gently, "whatever happened to your girl, I will not give up until I find her. I promise you that.

Go home to your people. Take what comfort you can from them. I will keep in touch with you."

She stared at him mutely, the world dropped out from under her, feeling hollow and untouched by anything real.

She swallowed. They were giving up the search.

"Mrs. Brown." Sheriff Hayes stepped closer. He took her elbow and steered her walking along the side of the platform looming next to them, around to the front and up the stairs, and across the platform to look out across the field.

"A train will be coming through here in an hour. It's the last train. They are closing this station."

She looked down when he placed something in her hand. She stared down at it, unable to make a noise or react. It was a single train ticket.

"Take the train Mrs. Brown. I'll keep you up on anything I find."

He walked away, leaving her alone on the platform in the growing dusk.

With nothing else and nowhere to go she stumbled over and sat on the bench outside the little ticket office. The office was closed. The old man did not bother to come on this last day to open it. The ticket was bought in advance.

An hour later the train came hissing and chuffing and screeching to a stop before the little station and left thirty minutes later, leaving the platform empty.

Mrs. Dorothy Brown left, but she did not stay. Days later she was back, having driven without rest after finding a car.

She spent the next days knocking on doors and asking if anyone saw Maisy. She begged for any scrap of information, pleaded that each person must have seen something. She was shoed away from the store and even kicked out of Dusty's. Sheriff Hayes repeatedly asked her to move on. She would get in her car and go, only to park it on another street in town.

Finally, she parked behind the train station where she lived in her car. As long as she stayed there, she did not bother anyone and they did not bother her.

Days became weeks and rolled into months. Dorothy Brown was a wraith that roamed the town and the woods next to the train station, clutching that yellow hair ribbon with the white polka-dots and asking everyone if they saw Maisy.

She told everyone she could that it was no animal that took her daughter. She was convinced someone took the girl.

When she was sitting in her car she more than once had the unnerving feeling she was being watched. More than once she looked up just in time to catch a glimpse of that same boy just standing there on the edge of the woods, not moving, staring at her, before he vanished into the trees.

"It was him, that boy. He took Maisy, I know it," she whispered, staring at the spot he was just a moment before.

*****

"No one noticed when Mrs. Brown was no longer there on account her car was still there and the whole town tried to avoid her. The car is still sitting behind the old train station."

Chester looks at Liam and Malcolm. They only look back blinking at him as if unsure the story is over.

"My best guess is she either wandered off into the forest and got lost and we will maybe find her remains some day, or she hitched a ride or walked out of town."

"The boy?" Liam asks, raising an eyebrow in question.

"Harvey Lawson," Chester says. "He's always been odd. He just hung out around there watching like he had something to say but was keeping it to himself."

"You never asked what it was?" Malcolm asks.

Chester shrugs. "He was just a kid."

29 – Night Noises

Nick's eyes open. He feels roused from sleep without knowing what disturbed him. Shifting stiffly, he sits up and looks around at the darkness closed in against the windows of his car like the world beyond the glass vanished.

His mind groggy with sleep and exhaustion and his eyes unable to see beyond the glass, he blinks numbly at the black non-world.

A pale flash of color pulls his eyes to it. A round orb that is there and gone so fast it leaves only an impression.

He leans forward, staring harder out the window.

"Was that a little girl?"

His eyes tell him he saw the pale face of a little girl outside his window, vanished before he could look more closely.

He searches the night, his eyes adjusting to the inky darkness seeing little.

Nick rummages in the clutter inside the car, pulling out a flashlight. He shines it out into the darkness, the light tunnelling through the night to reveal what it can. Moving the beam, he spotlights the abandoned car first, seeing nothing. He moves the light around the beams supporting the train platform. Seeing nothing there, he sweeps the light across the field like a ghostly apparition haunting the tall grass and wildflowers.

A fluttering motion across the field catches his eye as the light passes over it, the barest suggestion of something pale yellow flapping with the wind like a ribbon caught in the long grass. Quickly bringing the light back, he searches and finds nothing.

He continues sweeping the light across the field. It touches along the trees and he thinks he sees movement at the tree line but can't see anything when he focuses the light on that spot and stares at it.

*****

A clattering comes from the rundown shed behind Harvey's cabin. The door is open and light spills from it into the dark night to light the ground.

Harvey appears in the doorway. He vanishes back inside just long enough to turn off the light and reappears in the doorway.

He leaves the shed, closing the door behind him, and pauses to double check it is closed securely before walking away muttering to himself about people snooping. He is wearing a coat that seems a little heavy for the weather, worn and dirty, and mud-caked boots.

"Someone's been in my shed, in my Quonset, and in my house; snooping where they don't have business. Who? That old codger? No. Cops, maybe."

He walks around to the front of the cabin and in the door, his boots tracking mud inside.

"What are they snooping for? Nicholas? Nah, little Nicky wouldn't go snooping. He's a good kid."

Harvey stops, staring out into the blackness midway through closing the door. Closing it with a grunt, he goes to the closet filled with boxes and flips the light on. He stands there staring at the boxes, thinking.

Turning away with agitated motions, he finds his phone and dials, waiting through the rings for it to be answered.

"Hello. Someone's been in my place, the shed and Quonset."

He pauses while the other person talks.

"I don't know who. I got a few suspicions."

Pause.

"I don't think they found anything."

He looks around suspiciously and lowers his voice to a whisper.

"I think they're listening. They could have the place bugged."

There is a longer pause before he says with a heavy voice, "Nick is here. He's living in his car. I think he's come to figure out what he can."

Pause.

"I caught him down at the old mill. I'm keeping an eye on him, but the authorities are watching me. They are going to try and pin that kid on me like before."

He breathes heavily into the phone for a spattering of heartbeats, listening.

"I'm going to end this. Whatever it takes."

He hangs up without waiting for a response, and stalks out of the cabin, grabbing the rifle leaning on the wall on the way by.

The door bangs closed behind him.

*****

Detective Liam leaves Dusty's. He looks at his car and decides instead on a walk. He stops at the car long enough to deposit his files inside and wanders away down the sidewalk. The sidewalk ends at the next street and he continues on down the side of the road.

"That story about the little girl is interesting, but completely irrelevant. A kid hanging around the search for a missing kid sounds like curiosity. The odds of a child killer are extremely small."

His mind turns to the other files, the old faded photos grisly reminders in his mind.

"Whatever is going on here is more than Harvey Lawson. Reports of kids going missing are not unheard of. The state of the bodies found, and that those reports go back further than Harvey has been alive, that is where the mystery lies. And I think this mystery is lying to us."

He walks on, kicking a rock in the road and sending it skittering away ahead of him.

"I just can't think of anything that makes sense. What cases ever had anything like this? Could it be a family of multi-generational murderers?"

He shakes his head.

"The Lawson family doesn't match. Nothing about them says anything but normal small town farming community family. The man is a lone wolf as best as I can tell. Harvey Lawson does not belong to any group that I can find. No militant groups, left or right wing groups, religious cults, or conspiracy theorists.

Harvey is an odd duck, no doubt about that. Maybe a conspiracy theorist from all those files he keeps. If I could take possession of those files and go through them, I could learn more about what drives the man. All I got from that sneak peak is one name, Lilydale Acres. What is Lilydale Acres and what does it have to do with the mummified remains of children being found in the woods here?"

"It's probably nothing," he shrugs. "There's probably hundreds of unrelated articles in those files."

Liam looks up and realizes how far he has walked. Up ahead the darkness fills the world with the scattered lights of the small town glowing behind him. In the blackness ahead is the platform and tiny ticket office of the long ago shut down railway station.

Curiosity pulls at him and he keeps walking towards it, the darkness embracing him as he leaves the light of town behind.

"They called this a train station," he chuckles. "It's more like a bus stop."

Then he remembers.

"The car is supposed to still be there behind the platform where Mrs. Brown abandoned it. Now why would you just abandon a car like that? Why would a woman that determined to find her daughter, just abandon the search and her car?"

He is approaching the train platform now. The wood is rotten and worn even in the cloak of darkness, and the platform appears to have a slight lean to it as if its supports were growing weary of holding it up.

"Mrs. Brown did not give up the search. No sir, I would stake my life on that. She could have gotten lost in the forest and perished, but she did not simply abandon the car or the search for her daughter."

Liam stops at the base of the stairs and looks at them doubtfully. He walks around the platform instead, into the deeper black of the shadow beneath the edge with the ticket booth, swallowed by the darkness and becoming invisible until he emerges on the other side.

He stops and looks around for the car. There are two.

"It's not hard to figure out which is Mrs. Brown's," he says quietly, staring at the other car for any signs of movement or life.

"Hello Nicholas Hastings. So this is where you are living."

He turns his attention on the other car. Rust mars the sun bleached paint where years of exposure to the elements have eaten away at it.

"An empty husk like the children." He sighs. "I'll come back to check it out in the daylight."

He turns and retraces his steps. Just as the black shadow beneath the ticket booth reclaims him, Liam thinks he hears a noise coming from the grassy field beyond the cars. He turns and looks, seeing nothing but the tall grass and wildflower stalks gently swaying with the soft breeze. A scuff beneath the platform has him walking faster, the image of a rabid raccoon waddling towards him drunk on sickness flashes in his mind. The chill down his back does not leave him as he leaves the train station behind, walking back the way he came towards town.

30 – Baiting Coyotes

"Ian, come on. Let's go." David paces restlessly.

"I don't think Nick is going anywhere," Ian says, coming out of his bedroom still pulling his shirt on over his head. He looks at David. "He hasn't found out what he came here for."

"Let's just get going." David jingles the keys at Ian.

Ian hates when he does that and tries not to scowl at him. He pushes back the urge to tell him off.

It won't do any good, Ian thinks. David won't calm down over this until he solves his own obsession. He pauses his thought. Until he finds out what happened to Felicia.

He follows David out. They drive away in search of Nick.

"Do you think he's at the jobsite?" David asks.

"It's the weekend." Ian looks out his window.

"Right. I've got it." David slaps the steering wheel with one hand, still gripping it with the other.

He takes a two handed grip and the next turn too fast.

Ian grabs the dash instinctively. He thinks about asking where they are going but figures it out before he makes up his mind.

David slows the car as they approach and pulls into the cracked overgrown road leading to the train station. Parking it, he gets out and motions Ian to follow. He puts a finger to his lips for silence and closes the car door gently so it makes little noise.

Ian gets out grudgingly, closing his door with a thud.

David's head swivels around to give him a warning look and he motions him to be quiet. He leads the way around the platform to the other side where Nick's car still sits.

Insects buzz and click and the wind blows the leaves and grass. In the distance they can hear the subdued sounds of town. There is no movement at the car.

They walk through the grass, splitting up at the trunk to come up on opposite sides of the car, and stop, peering in the windows.

Nick is there, curled in an unnatural position in the confined space, a blanket partially wrapped around him and his pillow half wedged against the steering wheel, his mouth open a little like a small boy sleeping.

"Aw, isn't that just darling," David sneers, giving Ian an amused look. He puts his attention back on the sleeping man inside the car and slaps the window with an open palm.

The dull thud knocks Nick awake with a startled jolt that has him simultaneously sitting up and reaching for his blanket.

David's laughter oozes into his sleep-fuzzy mind, distant and muted through the window and cloud of grogginess.

"Nicky-boy, Wake up," David crows at him through the window.

Nick considers turning over and ignoring them but knows it won't do any good. He groans and sits up straighter, looking at David through the fuzziness still filling his eyes. He winces at the stiffness from sleeping crunched awkwardly in his car.

David tries the rear car door. It is locked.

Grudgingly, Nick reaches back and unlocks it.

David opens the door and slides in with a grin, reaching across and unlocking the other side. He waves Ian in.

Ian gets into the back seat on the other side and Nick stares at them both.

"What do you want?" Nick asks moodily.

"Why did you take off last night?" David asks.

"I'm done with your games David," Nick says.

"Fine. Let's cut the crap. Just tell me straight. Why are you really here Nick? You came back because of what we found in the woods, didn't you?"

Nick looks at Ian.

Ian shakes his head regretfully. "You might as well. It's the only way you are getting him off your back."

Nick sighs.

I'm too tired for this, he thinks. Tired from a bad sleep last night. From all the bad sleeps all these years. Tired of pretending everything is okay so Felicia can. I'm done. I just don't care anymore.

"Fine." Nick looks at them. "I can't remember what happened in the woods. I guessed what we found. It was a kid. Decomposed."

He tries to read their eyes and is sure he sees confirmation. He continues.

"Felicia won't talk about it, but it has haunted her every day since. I see it in her eyes every time I look at her. She's there but not really. Whatever happened, it damaged her. Inside. I came to find out what took my sister away all those years ago. I don't know, maybe I hope to put her back together again. Or maybe I just want answers for myself."

David nods. "Fair enough. We found a kid. It was all mummified like. Just like the stories we grew up hearing about kids vanishing and being found months later."

A humourless smile curls up the corners of Nick's mouth.

"The old Mill Road monster."

"The old Mill Road monster," David agrees. "Seems kind of odd that just when you come back they find another body just like the one we found twelve years ago."

"You think I had anything to do with it?" Nick is in disbelief.

"No. But it is a coincidence, don't you think?"

"Why do you keep harping on this?"

Nick turns away, ready to abandon his own car to get rid of them. He turns back, his voice heavy.

"What happened that day? I won't tell you anything unless you answer my questions too."

"We found a body, that's it." David meets his stare.

He caves after a long moment of staring each other down.

"We were just kids. We thought we would get in trouble, so we made a pact to not tell anyone."

Something flashes in Nick's eyes, an uneasy question. He hesitates before asking.

"Whose idea was it?"

"To keep it a secret?" David asks. "Mine."

Ian is shaking his head.

They both look at him.

"I'm not so sure it was your idea." He blinks at them. "I could be wrong, but I think it might have been Felicia's."

Her name sends David's heart pounding rapidly in his chest. The memory of his dream resurfaces. He can almost smell her perfume in the stale air of the car. He shakes it off and looks at Nick.

"Nick, what is it?"

Nick looks down. "I don't know that it's anything."

He looks back at them.

"Felicia was determined to keep this a secret. I remember her grilling me to stay quiet about it. I thought it was just because she didn't want to break your stupid pact. We should have told someone. Whoever that was, were they ever found?"

The flush of guilt rising in both Ian's and David's faces is answer enough. They never spoke of it.

"As far as we know it was never found," Ian says.

"What happened to the body then?" Nick asks.

"Animals probably ate it," David says. "It's been twelve years."

"It's kind of funny," Ian says, his face as sick looking as his voice sounds, "that twelve years later another body is found in the exact same spot and they found nothing of that first one."

David looks intently at Nick.

"So, you really ran away just because you were sick of us?"

Nick's eyes shift, giving him away. Betrayal burns hot inside him, a flush rising in his cheeks when he speaks.

"I felt guilty snooping in my uncle's property. And he has all these chemicals like you might use for crops, only he's not a farmer."

"What do you think he's doing with them?" David asks.

"I don't know. But there were these trays of blood and I think blood mixed with mud."

"It has to be animal blood, I'm sure of it," he adds after a pause.

David looks at Ian. "What do you think?"

Ian shrugs. "Harvey is one weird guy. Everyone knows he baits coyotes. I don't know why since there is no bounty on them."

"What would he be doing with all those chemicals then if he's making some kind of blood and mud coyote bait?"

Nick looks at them, a memory tickling at the edge of his thoughts.

"What is it?" David asks.

"I don't know. Something, maybe nothing. It's like it's just right there, but I can't quite remember."

Nick pushes the teasing almost memory away. Something about the other day is sitting heavily on his chest too.

Do I tell them? It will probably just make trouble. Hell, it's probably nothing.

Reading his look, David presses. "What is it?"

Nick hesitates and reluctantly tells them.

"The other day, after Uncle Harvey's, I ended up at the old mill."

"Wow, you really did want to run away from us. No wonder we couldn't find you." David smirks. "We were going to give you a lift back to town. We didn't plan to just leave you out there, you know. We looked for you. We really did."

"I know. I saw you. I didn't want to be found."

David grins. "Same old Nick." He chuckles.

Ian is staring at Nick. Nick has a sickly look to him now. A chill passes through Ian.

"What did you see at the mill?"

"It was more what I felt than what I saw," Nick says. "It felt . . . wrong somehow. I don't know how to explain it. Like the area was just . . . off. All I wanted was to get out of there."

"You saw something," David says.

Nick looks away, nods, and turns back to them.

"Uncle Harvey was there."

"He made you feel off?" Ian asks.

"I don't know."

David slaps the top of the front seat back. His face breaks into that sly half grin that is often a dead giveaway he is up to no good.

"We have to go check out the mill!"

He looks at them with an almost hungry eagerness.

"Let's go."

I want to ask Uncle Harvey about the mill, Nick thinks.

"Let's go to Dusty's and get something to eat first," Nick says, turning around and starting the car.

He drives slowly around the train platform to the service road. Nick can't help staring at the trees across the grassy field and the abandoned car as he drives.

*****

When they arrive at Dusty's they make their way to a table, ordering coffee and what passes for the breakfast meal; two partially cooked runny eggs that look like they were angrily scrambled with a mash of partially charred flattened pre-cooked potatoes that could have been hash browns or maybe leftovers from last night's French fries, and cubes of what is probably canned ham.

"So, you think he could be baiting coyotes with that stuff he's making?" Nick asks.

"More likely poisoning them," Ian says. It is meant as an offhand joke. The others stare at him. He shrugs.

"I saw a few cage style small animal live traps in the shed. Nothing you can trap a coyote with. I don't think it's even legal to trap coyotes around here."

"Nah," David grins. "He probably just shoots them. That's the whole point in baiting."

He focuses on devouring a few large bites of food, washing it down with coffee, before speaking again.

"Soon as we eat we go check out the mill."

"If Uncle Harvey is baiting coyotes around the mill, we should be careful." Nick looks at each of them. "I'd rather not get shot by accident if he's there hunting."

I'd rather just not go to the mill, he thinks. Coyote baiting or not, that place was creepy as F and Uncle Harvey is just off. Hell, if he's hunting them there then that must be where they den. We'll be coyote bait.

*****

The sound of footsteps crunches through the woods. Harvey comes into view walking up the deer trail, a rifle and sack slung over his shoulder hangs on his back. Not far ahead the path brings him to the crumbling stone and wood structure, the old abandoned mill.

The wood is stained dark with age, spoiled by the elements, and cracked and weathered. Moss and lichens grow on the lower stone part of the small building on the East side where the afternoon shadows keep it moist. The window glass is cloudy with decades of grime. Some of the windows are broken and large chunks of glass are missing. The sagging roof melts inwards in spots, remnants of the old shingles still teasing the false promise of providing a dry refuge beneath them. Moss and lichens grow on the roof where denser trees provide more shade.

The large bladed water wheel sags, immobilized by rot and decay. Some blades rotted free and partially lean on the ground below. Long grass on the edge of the dry river bank grows through the wheel as though to hold it in place.

On the West side the ground slopes down sharply. A natural formation of a jumble of large rocks held by the branches of large trees in what would be a deeper pool in the creek when water fills its banks is laid bare. The creek is empty and silent except for the hissing and clicking of insects and a few birds singing to each other.

Harvey pauses next to a tree across what was once a clearing for the mill, pulling a wad of burlap from his sack and hanging the small worn burlap sack with twine next to the remains of a ruined string of twine. Whatever is inside it makes a small ball shape inside the sagging fabric. The fabric is stained brown-red from the contents leaching through it.

He moves through the trees around the mill, always keeping some distance from the building, hanging similar little sacks, some higher and some lower. The highest is low enough that a large dog could jump to reach it. The other trees also have remnants of sack hung before, some just what remains of the twine and others tattered shreds of burlap still caught in the twine.

Returning to one of the sacks, he pulls on the twine, testing it.

He stops and turns to look towards a noise in the bush behind him. His eyes rove the foliage but see nothing, no sign of motion. Whatever it is now stands still and silent, perhaps waiting for him to turn away from it again.

On a low bush a shred of burlap caught on a bush ruffles with the wind picking up. The branches of the trees and bushes sway and the rubbing leaves hiss.

Harvey shifts his foot, crushing the partial footprints of an animal left in the mud and making them unidentifiable.

A low groan comes on the wind. Harvey pauses and listens. When the sound comes again, he follows it.

Minutes later he finds the source of the sound. Pulling back the branches of a bush, the dog face hidden there looks up at him with pain-filled sickened eyes. Its mouth is partially open and discoloured tongue protruding. Its cheeks puff and relax with rapid panting. It makes no attempt to move.

Harvey pulls back more branches. The sick coyote had crawled weakly into the bush and curled up, later lying sprawled out on its side in its agony. Its side moves with the rapid stressed pants.

The coyote only watches him with the one eye it can see with without lifting its head, too weak and sick to do anything more than lay there with its laboured breathing.

He puts the sack down slowly and unslings the rifle from his shoulder. Racking the slide to chamber a round, he brings the business end to point down at the dying animal. He aims, takes off the safety, and the crack of the rifle echoes off the sky sending birds scattering in a flurry as the neat hole appears in the coyote's head with a jerk of impact and a spray of red and bits of fur.

The coyote lays still and silent, no longer suffering, the remnants of the rifle crack still echoing off the sky.

Harvey bends and grabs it by a leg, dragging the limp lifeless carcass from the bushes. Leaving it, he slings the rifle over his shoulder again and moves to the rotting abandoned mill.

Pushing the door open, he enters the cool darkness within. It takes his eyes a moment to adjust to the sudden change in light.

The small building is empty except for a wooden chair with one leg snapped off and a pair of large grinding stones, one resting on top of the other. The large wooden beam above the stones sags, the wood looking chewed with rot where it snapped. The heavy top grinding stone is shifted from where it should be, sitting lopsided atop the other and pulling down the wood beam meant to hold it in place. The mechanism that turns the stone has long ago seized and rusted solid.

Littering the floor, scattered dry leaves and grass skitters across the rotting floor planks with the breeze blowing in the open door. The dust is thick and heavy in the air, coating every surface.

Harvey studies the floor for any sign of tracks running across it. The only marks in the dust are his own boot prints at the door from repeating this ritual each time he comes.

Satisfied nothing and no one has entered the mill, he steps back, closing the door behind him.

31 – Felicia

The crossroads sits accusingly in front of the stopped car like an unwanted X. The X that marked the spot they left behind twelve years ago. Felicia stares out the windshield at the road ahead of her with a frown. The space where the cat carrier was feels conspicuously empty and it adds to the unpleasant feeling.

He'll be happier, she thinks. The little bastard deserves a proper home with someone capable of loving him. Not some manic human roommate who serves as nothing more than a source of food and cleaning up his shit.

She tries to stiffen her face and her heart.

"Damn, I miss the hairy bastard," she mutters, only half wishing she didn't give the cat away. "I never planned to keep him anyway. It was just temporary until I found him a home."

In some ways the cat reminded her of her brother Nick. He was a little sad and broken himself and always annoyingly trying to make her feel better.

"We're better off without each other," she sniffs.

Squeezing the steering wheel tighter, she starts lifting her foot off the brake and stops before the car starts rolling forward. She grits her teeth and closes her eyes, opening them to stare at the empty crossroads ahead of her.

"Damn you Nick. I should just turn around right now. Take a different road and see where it takes me; anything but going back there. I should just leave you there on your own. Why are you doing this? Why are you dragging me back there? Why did you go back?"

A rough sigh exhales from her, her shoulders sagging with it. Her head drops forward and she shakes it slowly.

"Why do I always have to look after Nick?"

She lifts her head and starts driving, turning left down the road to her past.

Memories of that past push forward, haunting her, clamouring to come back with the spinning of the tires bringing her closer with every passing minute.

In her mind the house she only partially remembers echoes hollowly with her mother's voice. The words are lost, an audible echo she hears in her head but does not remember what they are. It's the tone of voice she remembers, the anger and fear, her voice strained like she has never heard it before.

Light and shadow play tricks, showing her glimpses of the house and furniture as if that is normal.

I don't remember what my bedroom looked like. I remember the blanket. We took the pillow that matched it with us. But I don't remember what the bed looked like. I don't even remember what Mom and Dad looked like then. What did the living room furniture look like? I think there was a big vase with sticks. Was the kitchen table speckled? Or was that the counters?

Other memories push their way in. Being forced to follow Nick around with his friend so they could play outside.

"Mom didn't want them to play in the house and make a mess, so I had to follow them around, and his annoying brother. He was stuck following Nick's friend around too."

Walking through long grass, roaming the town, four kids hanging around outside the school because they had nowhere else to go.

Walking through the woods. So many times they walked through the woods.

Felicia can smell the leafy muddy odour of the woods. Feel the breeze on her skin.

Darkness creeps in and she closes her eyes.

A sense of carelessness lacking anything carefree comes over her. Recklessness. Out of control. Fear.

She opens her eyes, pulling the car back, tires skidding and fishtailing with a dull grinding on the gravel kicking up a cloud of dust around her. The car veers dangerously towards the ditch from her overcorrection and she manages to straighten it out.

Her heart is pounding in her chest and her breath is coming in ragged pants. Felicia is less afraid of the near accident than of losing control. She focuses on the road, pushing the memories away.

*****

Felicia drives into town with a sense of being out of place in time and place. It holds an old familiarity and yet she does not quite recognize it.

She drives past places that should be burned into her memory; the stores on Main Street, Dusty's, and the school. Finally, she stops in front of their house.

The house looks the same and different all at once. It has been repainted a new color and the curtains are different.

"It seems so much smaller than I remember it."

Felicia has the urge to walk around the house; to go inside and look around.

"I don't think the new owners would let me in to look around."

She starts the car moving again, driving around until she comes across the construction site on the edge of town. Stopping in the road, she stares at the ruined earth, the trees torn out and piled on one end of the field, and the hulking machines sitting motionless in the field like dozing behemoths fallen asleep while grazing on the raw mud.

The trees across the field pull her attention. She can't take her eyes away from them.

"Is that where they found it? Was it in the exact same spot?"

She shivers with the chill filling her and finally forces her eyes away.

"I have to find Nick. Where would he be staying?"

Felicia thinks for a moment.

"Knowing him, he probably just parked his car somewhere and slept in it."

Turning the car around in the road, she starts back towards town.

"Before I find Nick, I need to see Uncle Harvey."

32 – Mrs. Brown's Car

Liam walks up the abandoned service road to the old train station, walking past the rotting platform with the ticket booth to the field behind it. Only Mrs. Brown's abandoned car is in the field now.

The car rests in the shade of the ticket booth and platform, long grass grown up around it. It looks even more abandoned in the light of day. The faded discoloration of the sun-bleached paint is worn unevenly, as is the rust mottling the body. The grime of decades coats the windows with a smudged hazy finish. Bird droppings have splattered randomly on the car, dried and worn off, and re-splattered to repeat the cycle, leaving traces of the old droppings amid the newer.

Moving past the platform, Liam approaches the car.

Insects buzz and click in the long grass that seems to trap the heat of the day and dampen the sounds of the town as if the car is entombed in some kind of snow globe, out of time with the world.

He leans in, looking in the window through the film of grime. There are a few discarded items in the front of the car. On the passenger seat is a doll, its face and dress sun-bleached and eyes staring blankly ahead as if mocking him for not knowing the secrets they have seen. The hair is dishevelled as though brushed with care then hastily grabbed and tossed onto the seat. The doll lies on what looks like a folded highway map.

It is what sits on the driver's seat that interests him more. Bleached and cracked from years sitting in the dry car with the sun beating in on it is a lady's purse.

"Curious that wherever Mrs. Brown went, she didn't take her purse."

Liam walks around trying the doors. They are all locked. He stares at the car, thinking. He looks around for something to break into the car with. His eyes move up to rest on the old ticket booth on top of the train platform.

Walking around it to the stairs on the other side, Liam mounts the stairs. The wood sags and groans under his weight but holds him. He goes to the ticket booth.

The window is shuttered and single door padlocked. The rusting lock does not look likely to give without at least a crowbar to use against it. He studies the wood of the door and its frame. The wood is chipped and crumbling with rot.

"Shouldn't be too hard."

Grasping the doorknob, he leans his shoulder into the door and pushes. He increases the pressure, feeling it give a little, but it holds.

Letting go, he steps back and lashes out with a solid kick. With the soft crack of rotting lumber, the door pulls from the padlock hasp, crumbling at the strike plate, and bangs against the wall.

He looks around to see if anyone noticed. The insects have gone momentarily quiet and begin their nonstop song again.

Stepping inside the tiny shack, Liam is pleased to see a coat hook on the wall with two wire hangers abandoned by the clerk who once worked the ticket booth.

Taking a hanger, he exits, stopping long enough to try to close the door. When it won't stay closed he shrugs and hurries across the platform and down the steps, retracing his way back to the abandoned car, untwisting the wire as he goes.

Liam pushes against the window and slides the end of the ruined coat hanger into the door. He fumbles around with it until he thinks he feels what he wants and yanks on the wire, and fails. It takes five more tries before he snags the lock mechanism inside the door and is rewarded by the little knob inside the window popping up.

Pulling out the wire with a grin he tosses it away and opens the door. The hinges cry out with the agony of years of disuse and rust.

The first thing he checks is the purse. It contains no surprises other than its abandoned state. There is a small round compact with a mirror, pressed powder, and round applicator pad. The lipstick long ago melted out of its tube to be mostly absorbed into the purse's fabric interior, leaving a bright red mess behind that has dried and hardened.

He pulls out the wallet and opens it. The wallet is little more than a change purse with a spot for the driver's license. There is a little money, not much even by the standards of the day Mrs. Brown last used it, and a yellowed driver's licence stained with lipstick.

Removing the license carefully, he reads the name on it.

"Dorothy Amelia Brown. So, Mrs. Brown has a first name. That will help with finding out who she is."

He carefully replaces the licence into the change purse for safe keeping and searches the purse for anything else. He finds a small flat metal tin of Anacin. A folded fabric handkerchief is stained by the red lipstick, looking suspiciously like it had been used to wipe off blood that will never fade brownish from its bright red. Unfolding it reveals nothing hidden within its folds except a carefully embroidered "DB", likely done by Dorothy herself.

Liam almost misses the tiny motion and catches it by accident with his quick reflexive grab. He holds out his hand to show the item in his palm that was hidden inside the cloth after all. It is small enough and its ivory-white a match to the kerchief. A small tooth. He studies it a moment and carefully folds it back into the fabric and sets it on the seat.

"Maisy must have lost a tooth on their train ride. I guess the tooth fairy didn't find her before she went missing."

The final items of the purse are a small address book and a pen. The book's cover and pages are stained red from the melted lipstick seeping into it on the spine, worn and dog-eared. He flips through it. The ink has faded with the years, but the elegant swoops of her handwriting are still partially legible.

Liam grins like he just won the prize.

"Looks like I have some calls to make. With luck one of them remembers Mrs. Dorothy Brown."

Carefully replacing the contents into the purse, he pulls the map out from under the doll on the passenger seat. The paper is crisp and brittle, sun-faded where the sun touched it to leave a morbid shadow impression of the doll. It is a highway map for the area.

"I'll study this later where I have room to open it up. Maybe she left markings on it."

He puts the doll and map with the purse and opens the glove box to search its contents. There is little there; the car registration, another map, and a pair of gloves. He looks at the registration quickly. Glenn Anthony Morrison. It is not Dorothy's car. Leaving the gloves, he puts the other two with the purse.

Popping the trunk latch, he goes around and opens it. It opens stiffly with a squealing cry like the door.

The trunk contents look innocuous at first. A spare tire and jack, a blanket tossed carelessly into the trunk, and a suitcase. Shifting the suitcase, he pops the latches and opens the lid to reveal carefully folded woman's clothing. He shifts a blouse. The tidy blouse on top hides the disorganization beneath. Beneath it is smaller clothes for a little girl. He shifts the clothes around. It is all for a woman and small girl, the kind of items you might hastily pack to travel.

"Why do I have the feeling you were running away from something when Maisy went missing?"

Liam retrieves the items from the front of the car and carefully places them in the suitcase. Latching it, he lifts it out of the trunk.

Carrying the suitcase, Liam closes the trunk and walks back the way he came across the rutted road and then cracked concrete towards Dusty's where he got a room.

Each small room has its own door along the back wall of the building.

Liam fumbles for his key and enters the room. It is as seedy and rundown as would be expected for a room at Dusty's. The worn bedspread and carpet and out-dated décor scream small town fifties and may have been modern when it was last updated. The room has the unpleasant stale odour one would expect from a room rented by the day on the back of an aging small town bar; musky with stale cigarettes, mold, sweat, and odours Liam would rather not try to identify.

Closing the door behind him, he carefully sets the suitcase down on the small table in the room and sits in the only useable chair. The other chair leans against a wall to keep it from falling over on its cracked leg.

Opening the suitcase, he pulls out the purse and retrieves the small address book. He flips through the pages again. There are a lot of empty pages and only scattered names with addresses and phone numbers.

Liam calls the first couple numbers with no success. The first is disconnected and the other re-circulated into use by a new phone customer years ago. They never heard of Dorothy Brown.

"I would rather not call every number, but I will if I have to," he mutters, staring at the address book.

He starts leafing through the pages more slowly, looking at the names. He stops at one. Its familiarity strikes him.

Mrs. Glenn Morrison (Helen).

"I never could understand why they referred to wives by their husband's name back then, as though she lost her identity as a person the moment she married."

He looks at the suitcase then pulls out the car registration, checking the name again. The name is a match, Mr. Glenn Anthony Morrison.

"Hello. Who loaned our Dorothy Brown the car? Was it the missus or the mister? My bet is on the missus. Will you still be there at the same number after all these years?"

Liam dials the number and listens to it ring and ring and interminably ring.

"They must not have an answering machine," he mutters.

He is about to give up when the ring is cut off mid sound with an almost inaudible pop and then silence. He listens and is not sure if he hears anything.

These old land lines are like listening to a seashell. You know it's impossible to actually hear any sound out of it, but your ear still hears that quiet hissing that is supposed to be an echo of the ocean it came from.

There is a subtle sound of rustling as of the phone being shifted and then an age-cracked voice comes weakly through the years and miles of the phone line.

"Hello?"

Liam determines the voice to be a woman.

"Hello, Ma-am. I am Detective Liam Tobin. I work out of a department that solves cold cases. Is there a Mrs. Helen Morrison at this number?"

"Oh dear. I am Mrs. Helen Morrison." Her voice is strained with concern over receiving a call from a detective.

Liam smiles.

"Mrs. Morrison, I found your name and phone number in an old address book I believe belonged to someone who knew you."

"That would be a lot of people." He hears a hint of humour in her tone.

"Mrs. Morrison, do you know a Dorothy Brown?"

Only the sound of laboured breathing comes through the phone and Liam is afraid the woman is going to hang up.

Finally, her voice crackles through the receiver again, quivering with age and stress.

"Yes, I did, I mean I do."

"I found an abandoned car registered to Mr. Glenn Morrison with items inside I believe belonged to Dorothy Brown."

There is a sharp intake of air on the line.

Liam gives her a moment to digest the information.

"Did- did you find Dorothy?" Helen asks, her voice raised an octave and quivering more.

"Ma-am do you know anything about how a car registered to Mr. Morrison may have come to be in Dorothy Brown's possession?"

"That's my husband. He passed."

"What do you know about your husband loaning Dorothy his car?"

"I lent it to her." She pauses. "You found the car?"

"Yes ma-am."

"You didn't find Dorothy?"

"The car contained Dorothy's purse and a suitcase with her belongings." Liam intentionally leaves out mention of the children's clothes.

"Maisy," Mrs. Morrison says hesitantly.

"Pardon ma-am?"

"Did you find Maisy?"

"Maisy?"

"Her little girl. Please, I have prayed all these years for them. Please tell me you found Maisy."

"Mrs. Morrison, you need to tell me everything you know about Maisy and Dorothy Brown and how your husband's car came to be abandoned with their possessions in it.

The old woman chokes on the other end of the line. Liam pictures her clutching at her chest in shock from the gasping sounds coming through the line.

"Ma-am, I need you to tell me everything you know about Maisy and Dorothy Brown."

The old woman gasps and murmurs unintelligibly before she clears her throat and starts. Her voice comes weak and quivering, shaking with strain and the misery of her assumption her friend and her daughter are likely dead.

"I remember Dorothy Brown and Maisy. Dorothy was my best friend. Her husband Peter was so tall and handsome; quite charming to the ladies, and the gentlemen too. He could have sold any man a thing he neither wanted nor had any use for."

He can hear the wistfulness of times long gone in her voice. She continues.

"Dorothy was quite taken by him. But something about him just didn't feel right. He was a terrible man. Peter showed his true self after they were married.

At first, I was only suspicious. Dorothy showed the signs of a woman hiding that she was being abused. She couldn't always hide the bruises though, and she became increasingly withdrawn, a shell of who she used to be. She stopped going to the Ladies' Auxiliary club and started avoiding everyone she knew. It was a push to get her just to let anyone in or leave the house."

Liam has to interrupt.

"Mrs. Morrison, can you tell me about loaning Dorothy your husband's car?"

"Yes, I was just getting to that. You need to know the story. I was sure he was abusing Dorothy. I suspected he was abusing that little girl too. I didn't imagine how bad it could be.

A few of us convinced Dorothy to come out. We had to tell Peter it would make them look bad if she didn't go just so he would let her out of the house. Before long he was encouraging her to go out more. Dorothy never wanted to, but we pushed her to come. We didn't know."

The sorrow in her voice is heavy with remorse.

"Dorothy seemed to be coming just a little out of her shell, but you could tell she was always worried leaving Maisy home. We all thought it was just a mother's separation anxiety. She was more than old enough for her father to mind for a few hours.

And then one day I was dropping off Dorothy. We had a grand time that afternoon and Dorothy was unusually happy and invited me in to show me something, I don't remember what now.

We went into the house and she hushed me right away. She had this funny kind of smile on her face, like not a smile at all but more of a sickly grimace trying to hide behind a smile. She'd heard a noise, you see.

We crept down the hallway to the bedrooms and stopped in the doorway to Maisy's room. What we saw can not be unseen. I felt instantly sick and raced to the washroom to throw up. That moment I saw and he stared back at me will be burned into my eyes until the day I die.

There was Peter and that little girl in a compromising position. His red-faced reaction revealed his ill intentions towards the little girl. He stared at us with shock and fear. Right when I moved to run for the toilet, I caught a look of such a rage and hatred as I have never seen before.

I returned, shaking and weak, to Dorothy still standing motionlessly in the doorway staring at him. Seeing me again must have broke him from his shock at being caught at it.

Detective Liam Tobin, that man was abusing that little girl in ways one would not want to have to imagine.

He came at me then, not even having the decency to straighten his self out. He grabbed me hard about the upper arms and forcefully turned me about and walked me out the door. He kicked me out of the house and slammed the door, and before I was off the stairs, I could hear him screaming at Dorothy and the sound of what I believed was him hitting her.

I was terrified, but I went back and banged on the door and yelled at him to stop. He came to the door, his face ugly with rage, and ordered me off or he would beat me too. Behind him I could see the frightened tear-streaked face of that little girl a moment before she darted away to hide, and the already bruising unhappy face of Dorothy, her lip dribbling blood.

I pushed her to leave him. To take that little girl and go."

"Did she leave him?" Liam asks.

"She did, finally. Dorothy called me all in a flutter one day. She was at the bus depot and there was a problem with the bus. She could not go back home. I went to pick them up and there was Dorothy and Maisy standing there with one suitcase for them both. I put them on the train myself," Mrs. Morrison says. She pauses. "She was going home to her mother."

"Her husband would have guessed where she was going?" Liam asks.

"Women always run home to their mothers, don't they?" Mrs. Morrison says reflectively. She continues her story.

"They got on the train, but then days later Dorothy returned alone and frantic saying that Maisy vanished and no one would help her. The sheriff put her on the train home, telling her they would contact her if they found anything. She could not return to that house and to him. I loaned Dorothy the car to go back. She never returned."

The moment of silence on the line is heavy. He hears the deep shuddering breath the old woman takes to collect herself.

"I never heard from her again. My Glenn reported the car lost or stolen and Dorothy with it and we never heard anything on the matter."

She pauses again, the line crackling with her raw nerves.

"You have not answered my question Detective Liam Tobin. Did you find them? Dorothy and Maisy, did he kill them? Did he catch them and take them to that little town with the old mill? He always said he would, that monsters lived in the woods there and if he took them there and left them in the woods no one would ever find their bodies. He said the monster lives at the old mill, and nothing can stop the monster."

"He threatened to kill them and leave them in the woods?"

"Just to leave them. He said the old Mill Road monster would do the rest and his hands would be clean. Monsters aren't real, Detective, except monsters like him, people with something ugly and nasty inside. He grew up there and told them the stories about the monster as if that would somehow keep them in line. He said he couldn't be charged with their murders that way. He was a wicked evil man who controlled and abused Dorothy and that little girl."

"What town?"

"Havenwood."

Liam turns and stares out the window at the water tower across the field on the edge of town. The faded letters painted on its side are partially scrubbed off by the abrasive winds and time.

Havenwood.

A chill slithers through him.

"I need to go check out that mill."

"Pardon?" the elderly voice wavers into the phone.

"Thank you Mrs. Morrison, you have been very helpful."

Liam hangs up the phone and stares at the water tower.

"A woman and child don't just vanish on their own. My money is on Peter Brown coming after them. Why would Dorothy go to her abusive husband's home town? She wouldn't. Not of her own choice. Was she just passing through? Did the train just happen to stop here? Did he bring them here? The old sheriff said nothing about the husband.

Peter may not have known they took the train the first time. The little girl's disappearance may have had nothing to do with him. But if he knew Dorothy came home and borrowed her friend's car . . . if he saw her . . . he could have followed her back here.

I need to go check out that old mill."

He looks at the time.

"For now, I need to learn more about Peter Brown."

33 - Felicia and Uncle Harvey

Felicia's car travels along the winding trail that is barely a road through the woods to Harvey's cabin. She pulls into the yard, parking next to a rusting truck that has seen better days and getting out.

She looks around. The yard is silent except for the sounds of the woods surrounding it. A squirrel chitters at her angrily and scampers up its tree, leaping to the next, across the branch, and to the next tree after it.

Going to the cabin, she opens door, not surprised to find it unlocked. She walks in.

"Hello, Uncle Harvey?"

She moves through the few rooms, finding them empty of her uncle.

"His truck is here. Maybe he's outside."

Felicia goes to the Quonset. The man door is ajar and she walks in. Harvey is not there. She walks through the building, looking at things curiously. She runs her fingers idly across the tools on the workbench, the disturbed dust showing they are used regularly, but the bench never dusted.

She moves across the building to the other benches with the trays laid out and drying. Pinching some of the blood and dirt mixture between her fingers, she brings it to her nose to smell it. The rich copper smell of dried concentrated blood fills her nostrils so that she imagines she can taste it. She brushes it from her fingers and kneels to look under the bench at the chemicals. She reads the label on the pressurized tanks.

"Anhydrous ammonia." Felicia frowns. The other labels are unreadable, but she has her guess what is in them.

"Using nitrogen to make the blood meal more potent. Oh Uncle Harvey, what are you doing? You aren't making blood meal as a deterrent to keep animals away. You are poisoning them, aren't you?"

Felicia leaves the Quonset, walks past the cabin, and goes to the shed. It is the only other building. She opens the door and gags at the stench of putrefaction it releases. Holding her nose, she quickly closes it. She shakes her head.

"This is why you are alone Uncle Harvey," she mutters.

Turning back towards the cabin, she catches motion through the trees. She watches it pass behind trees and bushes, hearing the rustle of movement through the woods, until Uncle Harvey materializes through the trees.

The moment feels unreal as she watches him approach, expecting him to vanish with the next breath and not be real. He looks rugged and worn, his hair and beard long and scraggly and his clothes having seen better days. A burlap sack hangs at his hip and a rifle is slung over his shoulder hanging at his back. Tail and head lolling limply down his back, he wears the carcass of a coyote like a stole over his shoulders, gripping the front and back legs tied together to keep it from falling.

Felicia's eyes light up as he emerges from the woods.

"Uncle Harvey!" she squeals just like when she was a little girl, and she races to him, throwing her arms around him.

"How are you Felly Silly?" Harvey asks.

"As good as you Silly Nilly," Felicia says, her voice lacking the playful tone the childhood response normally required. She pauses seriously, staring off into the woods behind him, still gripping him in a hug. "I'm good, Uncle Harvey. How are you doing?"

Harvey awkwardly tries to hug her back without dropping the carcass.

"What are you doing here Felicia?" he asks when she releases him and backs away.

The moment of excitement gone, she has returned to her usual quiet sullenness. She looks him up and down, her eyes stopping on the coyote.

"You are poisoning coyotes again." Her tone is accusing.

"We're in a drought again. The streams are all dried up and the woods are dry and brittle. The game has moved on and their food is scarce," Harvey says. "They are hungry enough they will eat just about anything."

"You could still let them be." She reaches out and gently strokes the dead coyote's fur.

"It's not for the coyotes. You know that. They just eat it too."

Felicia looks at him levelly.

"You just won't let it go, will you?"

Harvey looks away.

Felicia continues.

"This whole community is stuck on this make believe game, this idea they have of a monster in the woods. But you, you are consumed by it."

"You haven't seen what I have," Harvey says quietly.

And you haven't seen what I have, Felicia thinks.

He looks at her again and he can see the troubled look in her eyes. They have a darkness in them.

They have always had a little bit of darkness in them, haven't they, he thinks. That little bit of darkness has always been inside Felicia, even when she was little.

"You didn't answer my question," Harvey says. "Why did you come back here?"

"You know why Uncle Harvey." She looks at him levelly.

Felicia turns and looks at the cabin.

"It's in worse shape than I remember. Like I said before, you should leave here. It's not a home. It is an old cabin that isn't even liveable."

"It's still my home."

Felicia turns to him.

"How long can you keep going like this? You have nobody here. The whole town hates you. Those who don't are scared of you."

Harvey starts to respond. Felicia speaks again first.

"Yes, I know; unfinished business." She shakes her head. "I told you not to come back here and you did anyway. Small towns don't forget. They will only look at you with suspicion, and I was right. They already picked you up for that thing they found in the woods, didn't they?"

"They held me for a few hours and let me go. They can't charge me with anything because I didn't do anything."

The weight of the coyote seems to be growing. Harvey walks past her to the shed. Felicia follows.

"Uncle Harvey, you did do something. Years ago, I know, but they will never forget." She waves her arm to indicate the community. "They would rather string you up than find out the truth."

"They tried that before," Harvey shrugs. "Had to let me go then too because I didn't do anything."

"You didn't do what they think, but you did something. You are weird, Uncle Harvey, scary weird. And you got in trouble lots. This town will never forget that, and they will never let you forget it."

"They don't matter to me." Harvey pushes the shed door open and finds the light. The lights flicker on with their sickly stutter.

Felicia plugs her nose and tries to hold her breath. It doesn't help.

Harvey drops the coyote on the bench and grabs a knife. He starts working at skinning it.

She watches him until she can't take the smell any more.

"This smell is disgusting," she mumbles through her pinched closed nose, trying to open her mouth as little as possible.

Harvey drops some gore into the barrel next to the bench, sending an angry swarm of flies buzzing around it.

"I'm going inside," Felicia says, leaving the shed more quickly than she entered it.

She walks purposely, her legs long and angular like her too long legs of her childhood. Halfway to the cabin she stops and listens.

The crackling sound of something moving through the bush is undeniable.

"Who is out there?" Felicia calls out, her voice shaky and trying to sound confident. "What are you doing out there? Are you watching? Stop watching Uncle Harvey. Just leave him alone."

Felicia takes a few steps towards the woods and the sound stops. An irrational fear slithers up her spine and she scans the woods for any sign of movement. There is none.

"Probably just a deer or bear," she mutters.

Felicia turns and retreats to the cabin, entering and closing the door behind her.

The sound of something moving through the woods resumes when the door closes; growing fainter as it moves away.

Inside the cabin, Felicia looks around. This time she takes in the condition and contents of the cabin, something she paid no attention to when she was looking for Harvey.

The cabin is small, making it neatly cluttered. Everything about it is old and worn. She looks around at the eclectic collection decorating it. Walking through to the other room, Felicia stops at the narrow almost hidden door. She opens it to reveal a mudroom sized space filled with shelves of boxes. Easing the lid off one, she flips through the carefully printed labels of the files standing up like a filing cabinet. She pulls a file out and looks through it, reading partial entries.

"You and your conspiracy theories." She shakes her head, putting the file back.

Felicia is interrupted by the cabin door opening and Harvey's entrance. He stares at her and she feels caught in the act of something.

"I told you to get rid of this stuff," Felicia says, leaving the boxes to stand in the living room.

"I need it. It's my proof," Harvey says.

"Proof. That you didn't kill those kids? What it is, is proof that you are crazy, and that will just convince people you did do it."

Harvey walks past her, closing the closet door.

"It's proof that what is out there is real. Not just here. Other places too."

"Uncle Harvey, I can't help you if you keep this up."

"I don't need help. I just need to be left alone."

He moves to the bathroom, leaving the door open while he washes the coyote gore from his hands.

Felicia notices he left a blood smear on the closet doorknob. It sends a faint sick feeling tickling down inside her stomach.

"You aren't allowed to hunt or trap coyotes. What are you going to do with the hide?"

"Use it."

"For what?"

Old Mill Road

He steps from the bathroom and looks at her.
"To make me invisible so I can get closer."
"Closer to what?"

34 – Going to the Mill

David's car kicks up a cloud of gravel dust following behind it down the old Mill Road. The car slows then slows more to a crawl, all three occupants peering out the windows.

"Are you sure this is it?" Ian asks. "I don't see anything that looks like a road."

"Nobody has driven down it in so long it's going to be all overgrown," David says.

He stops the car and they stare at the bush.

"Doesn't look like there was ever a road here," Nick says.

"Look at the ditch," David says. "There is no ditch there." He points. "It's level with the road and just wide enough for a single lane. That's the road."

Ian shakes his head skeptically.

David turns the steering wheel as he takes his foot off the brake, angling across the road for the bush.

"You are going to just drive into trees," Ian complains.

"There's no trees there. Just bushes," David says.

"At least it's not my car," Ian mutters.

The front bumper pushes its way into the bushes, leaves and branches crackling, thumping, and hissing against the car pushing them to each side and flattening them beneath its undercarriage. The whole car is enveloped in the bushes, branches bouncing back into place behind it and leaving a trail of partially broken bush noticeable only if you knew to look.

David presses on, driving slowly over the ground roughened by the bushes overgrowing it. He concentrates on the trees standing taller to each side, the only signs showing where the road once was. The heat and buzzing insects make it feel more closed in, the world outside gone.

"This is too far in," Ian says. "This isn't the road. There should be something, a deer trail at least."

"Even the deer won't go there," Nick mutters quietly.

"It's there," David says. "This is the road."

The bush melts away in front of them, opening to a clearing. David parks the car and shuts off the engine. The air seems still, the forest silent. The only sound is the ticking of the cooling engine and distant buzz of what must be a single insect.

"Behold; the old mill." David grins.

The mill sits silent and eerily still in all its deteriorated rot, the stone and wood structure crumbling and its water wheel motionless and even the trees silent and unmoving.

The wood is stained dark with age, spoiled by the elements, and cracked and weathered. Moss and lichens grow on the lower stone part of the small building on the East side where the afternoon shadows keep it moist. The window glass is cloudy with decades of grime, some of the windows broken and large chunks of glass missing. The sagging roof melts inwards in spots, remnants of the old shingles still teasing the false promise of providing a dry refuge beneath them. Moss and lichens grow on the roof where denser trees provide more shade.

The creek bed is dry, not even a trickle of water running down it. Moss and lichen clings to the lower stones and bushes and weeds are growing through some of the water wheel slats, the forest trying to reclaim it. The large bladed water wheel sags, immobilized by rot and decay. Some blades rotted free and partially lean on the ground below. Long grass grows through the wheel from the bank of the creek bed as though to hold it in place.

On the West side the ground slopes down sharply. A natural formation of a jumble of large rocks held by the branches of large trees in what would be a deeper pool of the creek when water fills its banks is laid bare.

"Let's check this place out," David says, breaking the silence. The squeal of the car door opening is too loud in the dead silence.

With a glance at each other, Ian and Nick reluctantly get out of the car and stand looking around.

"What do you expect to find?" Nick asks.

David looks around hopefully, his eyes lighting when he spots something. His grin is triumphant. He moves eagerly to the trees, grasping a balled wad of worn burlap sack hanging from the tree with twine and tugging in a quick rough tug, snapping the twine.

"This!" He holds out his prize for them to behold. The round wad of tattered burlap sack looks like a circle of sack wrapped around something and tied off around the opening. The same thin twine used to tie it was used to hang it from the branch. The fabric is stained brown-red from the contents leaching through it.

They look around them and now notice more hanging from the branches of the trees and bushes around them, each sagging with the weight of the ball shaped contents within.

They hang at varying heights, all within arm's reach. Among them hang remnants of sacks hung before, some just what remains of the twine and others have tattered shreds of burlap still caught in the twine.

The breeze picks up, blowing through the clearing and making the sacks sway like pendulums on their twine amid the hissing of the leaves rubbing.

A fast moving cloud passes over the sun, the sudden shadow wrapping them with a chill that still grips them after the cloud moves on and the sun warms the clearing again.

"What are those?" Nick asks, not really expecting an answer.

Nick and Ian move closer to watch as David picks the twine apart to release the bundle. He unfolds the burlap to reveal its contents.

"What is that?" Ian echoes the question, staring at the lump in David's hand with a mix of curiosity and disgust.

The lump is only roughly round, its contents not all identifiable. They make out what appears to be the head of a small bird with the beak still attached, its severed feet and hair and feathers mashed together with unidentifiable animal bits. The whole thing looks like it was dipped in what could be blood; either soaking through the burlap or after the sack was tied around it. David brings it closer to his nose to sniff it and makes an unpleasant face.

"It stinks like rot."

The unexpectedness of it makes the discovery feel more shocking.

"It's disgusting," Ian says.

David throws it on the ground with a scowl, going to another branch and snatching another one. Picking the twine off, he opens it to reveal the same thing. This one appears to have parts of one or more small rodents. The desiccated flesh is shrivelled and dry with a grey fuzz of mold.

He tosses it on the ground and grabs another. Nick and Ian join him, yanking down the blood dipped tattered balls of burlap and opening them to reveal their grisly secrets.

Each makes them feel more disgusted and shocked, the contents varying remnants of small heads, bones, and dismembered flesh and innards of small animals and birds.

When they cannot find any more, they stand there looking at the scattered shreds of burlap and ruined carcasses surrounding them.

Pieces of burlap ruffle and flutter in the breeze, a few picked up on the wind to roll and blow until they snag on a branch, impaled and fluttering there.

The scene is disjointed and unreal, menacing.

"What is this?" Ian says, his face pale and expression grim. "Some kind of pagan or witch shrine?"

Nick can't shake the chill gripping him or the feeling of déjà vu tickling at his memory.

A small choked guttural sound rises in his throat; the three of them standing in a circle looking down at the gruesome spectacle on the ground. There is an empty space in their circle, filled with an echo of a memory that one more should be there with them.

Felicia. David almost whispers the name, catching himself.

David catches Nick looking at him as if reading his thoughts and knowing his sister's name is on his lips.

A cloud moves over the sun, dark and heavy, sending a deep shadow washing across the ground like darkness is creeping across the sky and chasing the late afternoon sun away.

"No one says anything about this." David's voice is hollow and cold, empty. No one meets David's eyes. No one looks up, their eyes locked on the scattered animal parts.

The breeze picks up, the gust of wind invading the woods to rustle the leaves, picking up and swirling a few loose leaves. It teases at a piece of burlap, making it sit up and dance for a moment, and then the gust of wind is gone and the burlap settles to lay still.

Ian shivers harder under the onslaught of the wind despite the lack of chill on it.

"Let's get out of here," Ian says.

"I still want to check out the mill." David turns his attention on the rotting structure.

Nick looks up. A crow on a branch above stares down at them from its perch.

*****

"You should go," Harvey says, looking at Felicia with the heaviness weighing him down. "Go find your brother. He's hooked up with the Morrow boys. He needs your help more than I do."

Felicia blinks at him. It takes a moment for the name to register. *Morrow. David and Ian.*

"You didn't answer my question. What are you trying to get closer to?" She stares him down, trying to look and feel more authoritative than she does.

"Whatever is in the woods," Harvey says. He can't meet her eyes.

"You still think there is something there that is taking kids, vanishing them, and then leaving them years later to be found."

Harvey shifts uncomfortably.

"Uncle Harvey, please, you have to stop this. If anyone knew about this they would lock you up forever. They already think you are the one who took that kid, and the other one, the little girl when you were just a kid."

His eyes flash surprise. They fill with remorse and suffering.

"You know about that?"

"It's a small town Uncle Harvey. Everybody knows about that."

"I don't want to talk about it," Harvey mutters, turning away.

"Uncle Harvey."

He won't look at her.

"Uncle Harvey."

He won't answer.

Felicia sighs.

"Fine. I'm going to look for Nick, but I'm coming back."

*****

Nick and Ian reluctantly follow David to the old mill, wanting only to leave this place. Nothing about it feels right and their discovery of animal parts hanging from the trees only makes them feel worse.

David pulls the door open, the rusted hinges crying in protest at the unaccustomed movement.

They step into the ruined structure and the darkness within, immediately enveloped in the cooler air inside. Their eyes quickly adjust, the grimy windows letting in enough light to see, like stepping into a gloomy basement with small dirty windows.

The small building is empty except for a wooden chair with one leg snapped off and a pair of large grinding stones, one resting on top of the other. The large wooden beam above the stones sags, the wood looking chewed with rot where it snapped. The heavy top grinding stone is shifted from where it should be, sitting lopsided atop the other and pulling down the wood beam meant to hold it in place. The mechanism that turns the stone has long ago seized and rusted solid.

Scattered dry leaves and grass litter the floor, the floor planks stained with rot and age. The dust is thick and heavy in the air, coating every surface.

The dust on the floor is disturbed by the footprints of one or more people who had been there before.

David walks over to the grinding stones and looks at them. He tries pushing the top one, but it is too heavy for him to budge. He braces his feet against the floor, putting his back into it and pushing as hard as he can. His muscles strain and tighten with the effort, a grunt escaping his lips, and he manages only to push his feet back, leaving a pair of skid marks in the dust coating the floor.

He gives up, standing and rubbing his dusty hands on his jeans.

"That thing is heavy."

He looks around.

"Stairs."

David points at narrow wood stairs of questionable safety against the back wall leading up to the second floor. The railing sags, a piece of it hanging broken. The stairs are worn down in the middle where they were trod on the most over the generations of feet using them.

He walks to them and stops, testing the soft looking wood of the first step. It gives a little under his weight but holds.

"Let's see what's upstairs."

David starts climbing the stairs. They groan and sag under him but hold.

Ian and Nick exchange an unhappy look and follow him up one at a time, both testing the stairs before putting weight on them.

Just as Nick steps up one more step, putting his head above the upper level floor boards, a shadow passes the open doorway of the mill.

They breach the second floor and look around. The space is not empty as they expected it to be. Above where the grinding stones are below a thick rod is bent and broken, hanging over a hole in the floor they did not notice before.

Ian walks over, looking down the hole at the shifted grinding stones.

He looks at the heavy rod. It is displaced from the gear mechanism that was once turned by the turbine powered by the slow rotation of the water-powered wheel now sagging uselessly into the empty creek bed.

An old wood table with three chairs matching the one below sits under an undisturbed coating of dust. An old oil lamp sits on the table, its oil long ago evaporated to leave a sticky looking dried residue discolouring the bottom. A film of undisturbed dust coats it.

David turns to Nick and Ian.

"Do you remember the story about why this mill was shut down?"

Nick only looks at him, suspecting he will tell them anyway.

Ian shrugs. "You told it enough, how could I forget?"

David grins wickedly at Nick. "Come on Nick, ask. You always fell for this. Felicia would always get mad at me for telling you the story, saying it would give you nightmares."

He hesitates at the memory of Felicia, some of the playfulness slipping from his eyes with a shadow of unhappiness.

"Fine," Nick says with a hint of exasperation, "I'll bite. Why was it shut down?"

Not feeling the thrill of instilling fear from his childhood, David leans forward for dramatic effect and talks in a voice lacking enthusiasm for the game.

"Because there were bodies all over the mill. The floors and walls were painted red with their blood. It was the worst killing in the history of the world. A mass killing, blood and gore and body parts everywhere."

He pauses for the reaction that is supposed to come. Nick only stares at him unblinking. David continues flatly.

"The night it happened, it was a full moon and no one saw or heard a thing. No one even knew why they were there in the middle of the night. Some say they might have been Devil worshipers there to summon demons." His voice trails off in his practiced soft hiss on the 'S', trying to dredge up the old memories of the thrill he once got terrorizing Nick and Ian as kids with the story. "But, to this day, some people still say you can hear their screams echoing in the sky at midnight on a full moon."

He lapses into silence and they just stare at each other as if waiting for the long ago screams to echo once more through the woods.

"Yeah, whatever," Nick mutters, turning away. "There is nothing here, so let's get out of here."

"Nothing except dismembered animals tied to the trees by some crazy person," David mutters. "Someone crazy like your Uncle Harvey."

Nick stops; almost turning to say something, clenches his jaw, and goes to the stairs, making his way down.

Ian gives David a suffering look of disapproval and follows Nick down the stairs.

David grins, but the smile is off, uneasy. He follows a little too quickly to be casual, not wanting to be left behind in the abandoned building.

They cross the floor to the door, unknowingly walking across a square of wood flooring with a pull ring mostly hidden beneath the layers of dust, dry leaves, and grime.

"Maybe we should look around the building," David says when they are outside.

Ian turns on him.

"Enough of this, David. We have both had enough of this. If you want to stay and search the woods, that's fine. We are going back without you."

He stalks off angrily towards the car. The door squeals loudly when he yanks it open, slamming it closed when he is seated in the driver's seat.

Nick looks at David, David not meeting his eyes, and follows Ian, getting in on the driver's side in the back. Ian looks down at the steering wheel glumly.

"I have the keys," David calls after them.

Ian glares at him moodily and slides over to the passenger seat and just sits there.

David stares at them waiting in the car and shrugs.

"Fine. I'm getting hungry anyway."

He walks to the car, gets in, and starts it. It takes a few tries to turn around and then the long grass and bushes are once again hissing and scratching against the undercarriage and sides of the car as he slowly drives back out the way they came in.

They drive in sullen silence for a bit.

"Say, you guys didn't think you saw any blood stains back there inside the mill, did you?" David asks carefully.

Ian and Nick both have the urge to punch him.

Their unease does not lessen with the growing distance between them and the old mill.

35 – Felicia in Town

David pulls up outside Dusty's, putting the car in park and shutting off the engine.

"Let's get a bite to eat and figure out what we do next," he says, getting out of the car and heading inside without waiting to see if they follow.

Ian and Nick follow him in.

David nods to the waitress, Clarisse.

"Beers, burgers, and fries." He points to himself and the two following him to a back booth.

Clarisse gives him a wink and moves to put the order in at the kitchen. By the time they are seated in the booth she is setting their beers on the table.

"Here you go boys. I hope you are hungry." She smiles and moves on to another table.

"That was really odd," Ian says, "that stuff hanging at the mill." He looks at David and Nick. "Who do you think did that?"

David focuses on Nick, making him feel uncomfortable.

"You said you saw your uncle at the mill. You said seeing him there made you feel off."

"I didn't say he made me feel off," Nick says defensively.

"You didn't not say it," David says. "Ian asked you and you didn't deny it. What else did you see there? Were those things already hanging in the trees?"

"I don't know. I didn't look all that closely at what was around. I found myself there and then he was there. I was looking at Uncle Harvey, not the trees."

"So, they could have been there or not. What was he doing there?"

"Hunting, setting traps. He said he was checking his traps. I guess he traps around there."

"He has a barrel of animal parts in his shed," Ian says, feeling sick at the memory of the sight and smell, the flies buzzing and maggots crawling over the cesspool of decomposing hides and intestines.

"Jesus Nick, your uncle is some kind of witch or devil worshipper," David says. "Everyone in town knows he's some kind of whack-job conspiracy theorist. I didn't figure him as a witch or Satanist too."

"Conspiracy theorist?" Nick is surprised.

"You didn't know?" Ian asks.

"I knew he went to jail a few times."

"Your uncle has always been weird," David says. "He's got some crazy idea weird stuff happens whenever there's a drought. He goes off on it every so many years."

Nick looks at Ian for confirmation, unsure he can trust anything David says.

Ian nods. "He was in town ranting about it just a few days before we saw you at the construction site. The whole town knows about his conspiracy beliefs."

Nick doesn't know what to make of it.

"It's a drought now," he says.

"We have one about every twelve years," David says, as if that justifies his suspicions. He is about to continue, but Ian interrupts.

"Wait." Ian looks at them both, then focuses on David. "Every twelve years?"

David nods. "It was in the paper after that body was found in the woods by the construction site. Apparently the Farmers' Almanac lists us having a drought about every twelve years too."

He looks around, spots Clarisse, and waves her over.

"Another round?" she asks.

David nods and focuses his attention on her.

"Clarisse, do you have any old newspapers?"

"There's a stack of them in the back that didn't make it to the garbage."

"Great! Thanks!"

David is up and gone for the back room, leaving her staring after him curiously. She moves away to get their beers and is back setting them on the table as David comes back.

He tosses the paper down on the table. It's not a large newspaper, just a handful of pages catering to the community encompassing theirs and the surrounding towns and rural area.

David flips a few pages and jabs his finger at the article. "Twelve year drought hits on cue," he reads the headline.

He looks at Nick.

"This could have been written for your uncle. It's right up his alley."

Nick bristles, feeling defensive even though he doesn't really know or like his uncle. But he is family.

"It says we get a drought about every twelve years and with everything drying up game animals move away looking for food or maybe aren't reproducing and are dying more. With less game, the predators like wolves and coyotes are hungrier. They get braver and could be more likely to hunt pets and farm animals."

He looks at the other two seriously.

"Pets and small livestock have been going missing and it's probably the wolves and coyotes going after them."

"Jake Bronson was out shooting them in the woods the other day," Ian says. "He got ticketed for illegal hunting. He was angry about it; said they killed some of his livestock and his cattle dog."

"What does a drought have to do with anything?" Nick asks.

David looks at him, his eyes steady and cold.

"It's not just livestock and pets. Every drought some kid goes missing somewhere and shows up someplace else months after they gave up searching."

A chill fills Nick. He glances at Ian to see his shocked expression and knows he feels it too. He is drawn unwillingly back to David's unwavering stare.

"Every kid is found in the woods somewhere along the old Mill Road and just like that one at the construction site, all curled up like they died trying to stay warm and dried out and decomposed like they rotted away and dried up all like they were mummified halfway through decomposing."

A sickly half grin plays at Nick's lips, uncertain and feeling like it does not belong.

"You are just playing your old games," Nick says, his voice lacking any will. "We aren't kids anymore David. Your stories were never funny then either."

"These stories have been told over and over," David insists. "Us, our parents, our grandparents, and their parents. Kids now tell the same stories about the old Mill Road monster. How many generations have told the same stories? What if it's not just ghost stories to scare kids with?"

"He's got a point," Ian says, his own voice sounding weak.

Nick looks at Ian and realizes how pale he looks.

"Lots of cultures used to pass down history in oral stories. It's where a lot of our fairy tales came from. The stories change over time from being retold over and over, but some believe there is still a grain of truth behind them."

"What does any of this have to do with my uncle?" Nick asks.

"His cabin is in the woods off the old Mill Road," David says. "He spends all his time in those woods." His expression and tone make his suspicion clear. He believes Harvey is behind the kids' deaths.

"It's his obsession," Ian says.

"There's also the rumour he was behind a little girl going missing from the train station when he was a kid," David says.

Nick gets up angrily.

"This is ridiculous. You guys are ridiculous."

He walks away, heading for the door. David gets up and follows him. Ian pauses long enough to toss some money on the table for their bill before half jogging to catch up.

"Why are you always chasing me out of Dusty's?" Nick mutters. He keeps going, David on his heels, not holding the door for him as he bursts outside.

Nick heads down the sidewalk with David still on his heels and Ian jogging to catch up.

"We have to go back to your uncle's," David says. "There has to be something there we missed."

"What are you trying to catch him on anyway?" Nick whirls on him. "Something we found in the woods twelve years ago? That body found a few days ago?"

David and Nick stare each other down. A slow cruel smile teases at the corners of Nick's mouth.

"Felicia leaving?"

David's change of expression is telling.

"So that's it," Nick says. "This is all about Felicia, isn't it? Wow. I remember now. You didn't think we would notice with you always going out of your way to be such a jerk to me all the time, pretending you were mad that you had to follow your baby brother and me around to watch him. You were mooning over my sister. She knew it too. She chose to ignore it."

A red flush is rising up David's face, his eyes flashing anger and his mouth hardening with his hands clenching into fists at his sides.

Ian puts a restraining hand on David's shoulder. David turns to look at him and Ian sees the anger and violence simmering in his heated stare.

David's face goes slack and for a moment alarm flashes through Ian.

What's wrong with him? He thinks. Ian realizes David is not looking at him. He is looking past him.

Ian turns around.

David stares at her. He can't blink. Closing his eyes might make her go away. Vanish. He has the irresistible urge to reach out and touch her to make sure she is real. He has to force his hand to stay. The need is a physical pain.

"I'm dreaming," he whispers without realizing he vocalized the thought.

Still feeling the heat of anger, Nick is still staring at David, expecting a response. He turns to see what they are staring at.

Felicia is standing on the other side of the street. She doesn't smile. She doesn't have any reaction to seeing them. She simply starts walking across the road to them, stopping just a few feet away as if to keep that small barrier of space between them. To keep just a little apart as if she is not one of them.

"Felicia, I told you not to come," Nick says.

"My little brother needs me," she says. "Why did you come here Nick? There is nothing here for you."

The bottom half of Nick's face reddens with the heat flushing up it.

"I had to find out," he mumbles, looking embarrassed.

"Find out what?" Felicia's face still holds no expression, except for the empty haunted look that never leaves her eyes.

Nick looks down, trying to put it into words when he himself does not quite understand what he is really looking for.

"He came back to find out what happened," Ian says. "What we found."

David is still staring dumbly at Felicia.

"Hello David," Felicia says without looking at him. She keeps her attention on Nick.

"There is nothing to find, Nick. We didn't find anything."

Nick looks at her, staring at her with the defiance of a little brother trying to stand up to his older sibling who always seemed above him by right of age.

"Just because you wouldn't talk about it doesn't mean it never happened. Something happened in the woods. Something that changed us all. It changed you. I had to look at that haunted look in your eyes every day, had to see you act like a part of you died, and you would never tell me why."

Oh Nick, what happened to me happened long before we found it in the woods. Felicia keeps her silence, just standing there without expression.

"Felicia," Ian says to get her attention. She looks at him.

"Another one was found," Ian says, "or maybe the same one. I don't know. But they found a body in the woods off the old Mill Road. We heard it was all decomposed and dried up like a mummy. Just like before."

Felicia says nothing.

David finally breaks from his shock of seeing her again. He tries to sound calm and mature. He doesn't feel it. He feels like that little kid who thought he was so mature at only ten years old but felt so hopelessly like an immature kid staring at the girl he was in love with.

"They already decided your uncle is behind it," he says and immediately regrets it when Felicia turns to look at him.

Way to go, David, he silently curses himself. Not the first thing you say to her when you see her for the first time. Dumb, dumb, dumb.

"Nick told me," Felicia says. "That's why I'm here." She looks at each of them in turn. "What are we going to do about it?"

"David is trying to find proof of Uncle Harvey's guilt," Nick says.

David flashes him a warning look. Felicia looks at him in time to catch the look and, catching her eye, David almost looks sheepish.

"Let's go somewhere we can talk," Ian says, glancing around to see a few people looking at them curiously.

*****

They arrive at David's and Ian's house, settling themselves into the living room.

David is burning to talk to Felicia. To find out what she knows, how much she remembers. He can't stop looking at her and feeling like she has to know he's staring at her even though she does not look at him.

Of course she does. Just like when they were kids and she chose to ignore the knowledge of his burning crush on her, she chooses to ignore his staring now.

Felicia focuses on Ian and Nick.

"What do you know about what they found?"

"Nothing," Nick says. "Just that they found the body of a kid in the woods just inside from where we were digging the trees out."

"It's like before," Ian says. "Decomposed and dried up. A kid."

Are they talking about the drought yet?" Felicia thinks. Has anyone figured out the connection between the drought and the kids?

"You disappeared after," David says. His tone is almost accusing.

Felicia finally looks at him.

"The day after we found it, you came to my house. You were crying. You said everyone was going crazy, your mom was crying,

245

your dad was yelling at everyone, at the police. You didn't come to school the next day. I went to your house and you were gone."

David swallows. He is fighting the pain welling up from the memory.

"It was like your whole family was snatched up. There was still dinner on the table. You never even said goodbye."

"That wasn't her fault," Nick says, misunderstanding the accusation in David's voice and expression.

David turns to stare at him.

"You told. One of you told," he says. "We had a pact to keep the secret."

"Nobody told," Felicia says, bringing David's attention back to her.

"Then what happened, Felicia?" David demands. "What happened that night your family took off?"

"What do you remember?" Ian asks more gently.

Felicia looks at Ian and back at David.

36 – What Felicia Remembers

"The day we found it," Felicia starts. She stops and starts again. "The day we left, everything was kind of crazy. It had nothing to do with what happened in the woods. What we found. It was Uncle Harvey."

David expects, almost asks, if she is talking about the kid they found that day, if that was Harvey.

Felicia continues.

"Everything was already weird. Off. Nick and me trying to hide how we felt, like the world just stopped spinning, like a horror house fun ride that wasn't fun stopped but we couldn't get off. We were trapped in it; inside the nightmare that we couldn't wake up from."

She glances at Nick.

"Nick was barely holding it together. It's okay Nick. You were so young then. He was holding up pretty good, considering.

We didn't even finish supper that night. The phone rang in the middle of supper. Dad answered it. He was angry as soon as he did. He put mom on the phone."

Felicia's memory:

Felicia and Nick stared at their father, Felicia's expression not revealing the turmoil inside while Nick's bordered on panic.

Their father pulled the phone receiver away from his ear and turned to their mother with an angry glare. He held the phone out to her.

"It's your brother, Diana."

She blinked at him and her face fell into a sickly panicked look that made Nick's face pale more.

Felicia only stared at the exchange.

Diana got up from the table and went to Rueben standing where the phone was attached to the wall. She looked at the phone receiver in his hand like it was somehow going to bite her. She took it hesitantly and held it to her ear.

"Hello?" Her voice had an uncertain tremor to it.

Rueben returned to the table and sat, glaring at her as if it was her fault as he passed her.

"Harvey?" Diana said into the phone. She listened as he spoke on the other end. Her face flared red and she blinked.

She stammered and stuttered.

"You can't come here," she finally managed. "Don't even think about it. We don't want you here."

She listened again. They could hear Harvey's voice small and far away coming from the receiver but could not make out what he was saying.

"Diana, please," Harvey begged. "I don't have anywhere else to go."

"You did that to yourself. You are always doing these things. How many times did you embarrass Mom and Dad? How many times did you get arrested? Go to jail? And this last time-." Diana broke off, almost choking on the words.

She looked at Nick and Felicia staring at her, not touching their dinner. Little Nick who looked scared and Felicia; Felicia always with that dark look in her eyes, expressionless, like something inside her was already lost. Looking at them was a physical pain.

Whatever happened to Felicia. . . Whatever haunts her. . . Does it have anything to do with Harvey? They used to spend so much time together, out there in the woods.

She sees too much of her brother in Felicia, Harvey as a kid reflected back at her in Felicia's eyes, two kids the same age in her daughter's haunted eyes.

Is that what haunts her? That he's gone to jail and she can't see him again? Or is it something else?

Harvey was saying something to her on the phone, but she didn't hear. She turned her focus back to his voice on the phone, sounding so far away with a little static that crackled on the line.

"After what you did this time Harvey, don't even think of coming here," Diana said. Her face flushed with the heat of her mixed feelings. She was scared. Scared of what Harvey did, of how the neighbours would react if he came back, of Harvey.

"Diana please," Harvey begged again. "I didn't do it. Everybody has it in for me. Yeah, I messed up. I made mistakes. I was a kid then, just a dumb kid doing dumb things. That kid . . . it wasn't me. They realized that, the judge let me go. The courts, they are going to overturn the guilty verdict. I know it. That's why they let me out."

He paused, desperate.

"Diana, I'm coming home."

"No, don't come here!" Her voice shook with the strain that twisted her face into an ugly grimace. She burst into tears.

She stared at Rueben across the room for help.

Rueben was on his feet pouncing on her. He snatched the phone from her and barked into it.

"You are not welcome here! Don't you come here! We won't let you in!"

Diana shook and her voice trembled with the tears she could not stop. She turned to the table and shooed the kids away.

"Felicia, Nick, go to your rooms."

Felicia and Nick just sat there and stared at her, their father yelling at Uncle Harvey on the phone with such vehemence that it frightened them.

"Go on, go to your rooms and close the door." Diana tugged at them to get them on their feet.

Rueben turned on them, his face a mask of fury. He barely pulled the phone from his mouth to yell at them.

"GO TO YOUR ROOMS!" he bellowed. He turned away to yell into the phone again.

"We've had enough of your games Harvey! When will you ever grow up? Never! You will never grow up! Act like a man for Christ sake!"

Diana took the phone again.

"Never come back here, Harvey," she said, sobbing into the phone. "You just stay away from me and my family."

She pulled the receiver away from her ear and reached for the cradle to hang it up when Harvey's voice came rough and tinny.

"I'm coming home anyway. I have no place else to go." Anything else he said was lost when she hung up the phone.

Diana turned to the kids still hovering in the doorway.

Felicia looked back at her father as their mother pushed them from the room and down the hall. He paced angrily in the kitchen. He looked like he was ready to tear someone apart. Like a caged beast that did not know what to do with its rage.

Why are they so mad at Uncle Harvey?

Nick gave no resistance. He sped up to escape the frightening angry scene in the kitchen. He looked back at his mother's teary face as she closed his bedroom door, scared and confused by his parent's reaction to a simple phone call.

He stared at the closed door.

"What did Uncle Harvey do? He's weird and scary, but does he deserve this?"

Nick stuck his hand in his pants pocket, gripped his action figure that made a small bulge in his pocket, and released it and pulled his hand out in a jerk when he heard the angry thump when his father pounded his fist on something in the kitchen. He stared at the door, scared.

Diana pushed Felicia into her room and started closing the door. Felicia didn't fight, but she turned and stared at her mother.

"What did Uncle Harvey do?"

Diana's eyes were full of guilt when they met hers.

"Nothing. He didn't do anything," Diana said.

"Then why are you mad at him?"

In the pause, the sound of Rueben on the phone sounded like he was talking to someone else now. He was angrily telling someone about Uncle Harvey's phone call.

Diana glanced backwards towards the kitchen and then looked back at Felicia.

"You keep this door closed no matter what."

She closed the door and to Felicia it was like the world closing on her. She stood alone in her room. Outside the window the sun was starting to fade and the afternoon moved into evening.

Felicia stood at the door and listened. Her father was yelling at her mother now about her uncle, threatening to call the police. Her mother was crying openly.

"He's going to come here," Diana sobbed. "I know it."

"He better not," Rueben spat. "I told him not to come here."

"So did I. He's coming. He's going to come and there's nothing we can do to stop him."

Felicia could hear sounds like her parents were walking around, relentless pacing, like her mother did when she was in a frantic cleaning binge when company was coming, even though the house was always spotlessly clean as far as she could see.

"If he comes, I'm calling the police," Rueben growled.

"We have to go." Diana's voice was a high tremor of fear. "Remember what happened last time? Before the trial?"

Felicia could hear her mother's frantic movements around the house, past her bedroom door. The sound of someone rustling around in their bedroom.

The phone started ringing and Rueben answered it.

"Hello." A pause. "Diana! Diana! It's your father!"

Felicia heard her hurried movement past her door again, then her mother on the phone.

Felicia turned away from the door. Her eyes brimmed with tears and her chest felt tight and heavy like it was stuffed with an old wet towel.

"What's happening?"

She heard yelling from her window. She went to it and looked out, trying to see what was happening. She couldn't see.

Felicia went to the door and opened it slowly. Her head poked around the doorframe. There was no sign of her parents. She crept down the hall towards the kitchen, walking lightly. She froze when the floorboard creaked under her slight weight. She heard the clatter of the phone being hung up and saw the shadow of her mother move past the kitchen doorway.

Diana emerged from the kitchen and Felicia almost yelped. She stood there frozen, staring in wide-eyed fear at her mother, caught.

Her mother didn't look in her direction. She rushed the other way into the living room. The front door opened and banged closed behind her. In that moment the door was open, sound of her father viciously yelling at someone came loudly and was quickly muffled by the closed door.

Blue and red flashing lights came through the front window and strobed across the living room walls.

Felicia continued down the hall to the kitchen and slipped out the back door.

Outside were more cars than just the police car. Her dad was yelling at the people and the police and her mom was sobbing.

The heat of tears reddening her face, Felicia ducked her head and ran down the street away from home.

Present:

"I went to your house, David," Felicia says, her voice heavy with the burden of the memory.

David nods. "I remember. You were crying and shaking. Then your mom was calling."

"When I got back home, there were people standing around in the street just watching, and the police. There were people in the house. Mom acted like I'd been kidnapped. We were both sent to our rooms and told to go to bed. I don't know how late it was when I finally fell asleep. I could still see the lights of the police car and hear people outside and in our living room. Dad kept yelling at people and Mom kept Crying." Felicia breaks off.

Nick looks at them after Felicia finishes talking. He reaches in his pocket, pulling out the small action figure and looking at it. It is small enough to hide in his adult sized fist.

"This was one of very few things from our life here that I was able to bring with me." He looks sheepish.

"I forgot most of it. I didn't remember much of what happened for years. It's starting come back now, some of it. Like little pieces of dreams you can't quite remember. Disjointed bits.

I remember the police being at the house and Mom outside running around calling Felicia. She was missing. Mom was going crazy crying and calling Felicia. Calling and calling. I remember that. The police were there and Dad was yelling at them. I feel like other people were there too. I thought it was because Felicia ran away."

He swallows, trying to pull up the memories.

"I remember being woken in the middle of the night; Mom grabbing clothes and shoving them into bags, clothes from my drawers, from the floor. I remember her shoving clothes at me, telling me to get dressed. She was scared and it scared me to death. I was half asleep and confused.

They were the same clothes I wore that day. That stuck with me.

I remember how strange that was. My mom, who kept the house cleaner than any other mom, who always made sure everyone wore clean pyjamas every night and clean clothes every day. She made me put on the clothes I played in all day.

That scared me more than anything I can remember in my life. My mother, tears in her eyes, looking frightened, urging me to put on dirty clothes while she frantically grabbed random things and shoved them in a bag.

I remember that moment more vividly than any other memory.

Everything after that is vague. I know I found the toy in my pocket when we were driving. It was very dark, the middle of the night. Felicia sat next to me in the back seat."

He glances at her and looks back down at the toy.

"She didn't look out the window. She never looked back. I was surprised to find the toy. I forgot I left it in my pants pocket.

"I remember these two things because I reminded myself every time I looked at that toy. Felicia never looked back and I found the toy in my pocket in the back of the car while we drove away."

Nick's voice is rough with emotion.

"I don't remember much of that night. I remember feeling like nothing would ever be okay again. I remember Felicia's haunted eyes. The telephone ringing. Mom crying. But not why."

"We left because for some reason Mom was scared of Uncle Harvey and he was coming back," Felicia says quietly.

Ian looks at her. "You remember what we found in the woods?"

Felicia nods. "The kid."

"That's why your mom was scared of him," David says, "because of the kids in the woods. Your Uncle Harvey's kids. The kids he killed."

Felicia gives him a hard look, but it is softened by the emptiness inside her and the haunted look in her eyes.

"You never understood David." Her voice is a soft whisper.

"What is there to understand?" David is getting frustrated. "Your uncle killed the kid we found. He just got out of jail for killing a kid. Everyone says he killed that little girl that disappeared at the train station years before."

"He was only a kid when that happened," Felicia says.

"So? And he did it again. They found another one. He was gone for a while and now he comes back and another kid shows up dead."

Felicia looks him in the eye, her stare steady and cold.

"Who is it?" she asks. "Whose body is it? Do you now of any kids that went missing? It looked like the one we found? Old? If he just came back how is it his?"

David has no answer. He only blinks at her, thinking.

"I didn't think so," Felicia says.

"What do we do now?" Ian asks, afraid of what the answer will be.

37 – Telling Old Tales

Liam walks into Dusty's, looking around for a familiar face. He spots the one he is looking for and smiles, walking over and sliding into the seat across from the retired sheriff.

Chester grunts and squints at his beer in acknowledgment.

"Sheriff Hayes," Liam grins.

"Retired Sheriff Hayes," Chester grunts, taking a swig of beer and setting the bottle back down without looking at him.

"Retired Sheriff, yes, but does one ever truly retire?"

Chester ignores the question.

Liam turns to the other elderly man sitting with Chester, extending his hand.

"Detective Liam Tobin, C. C. I. That's Cold Case Investigations."

He reaches out his left hand to shake hands with the elderly man. The old man looks at the offered hand.

"That old thorn in my side is Barry Woodstone," Chester says around another swig of beer.

"That's Mister Woodstone to you," Mr. Woodstone mutters, finally reaching out awkwardly with his right, pulling it back, and then with his left to shake Liam's hand.

"Mr. Woodstone, I'm told you know more about the history of this town than anyone, except maybe for Chester here," Liam says.

"That's because he's one of the longest lived residents who is still of sound mind," Chester coughs out a stale laugh.

Mr. Woodstone downs the beer in front of him and motions towards the bar for another, his eyes steady on Liam.

"Between the two of us, if there were any goings on back then we don't know about, it never happened. What are you looking for?"

Liam nods.

"Good, good. There are a few things that just aren't quite sitting right with me. A few things I won't find in the police department files." He winks at the old man.

The waitress, Clarisse, drops a beer in front of Mr. Woodstone and another in front of Liam without asking what he wants and is already on her way to another table before he looks up after her.

"That construction site up the old Mill Road, Acting Sergeant Malcolm Colbert told me it's not the first time that area was surveyed for the construction going on," Liam says. "They had problems with the first survey?"

Chester and Mr. Woodstone exchange a look.

"That site's been surveyed more than a few times for different purposes," Chester says. "People around here aren't much for change." He shrugs. "Sometimes they tamper with the stakes, sometimes it gets a little more extreme."

"Extreme? How?" Liam asks.

Mr. Woodstone starts chuckling. Liam looks at him.

"Once, they were looking at building a new church on that lot. We already have a perfectly good church and folks around here don't see the need for competition for our little church. Some of the old ladies in town got together and sewed dozens of voodoo dolls and set them about the property with some witch symbols. Nobody had the heart to tell them they were mixing religions that don't mix. It didn't matter, it did the charm. Next thing we knew the church put a for sale sign on the lot and the survey stakes had been all pulled up."

"Never did find out whose goat that was," Chester chuckles.

"Goat?" Liam looks confused.

"Severed goat's head. They left it right on the hood of the surveyor team's car parked outside Dusty's."

"That's sick," Liam says.

"Like I said," Mr. Woodstone says, "folks around here are set in their ways. They don't like change or anything that doesn't fit."

"Is that where the rumours about that old mill come in?" Liam asks.

Chester and Mr. Woodstone exchange a serious look. Chester leans forward.

"Those are just stories the kids tell each other to scare the wits out of each other."

"So, there is no monster living in the woods by the mill?" Liam asks.

"If you believe that horse sh-," Chester starts.

Liam cuts him off.

"I don't believe in the bogeymen of bedtime stories, if that's what you mean. Only the real bogeymen, people."

He looks at them seriously.

"There is a lot of history in these old towns," he says. "The remains found by the construction site, they aren't the first, but if I can I will make them the last. There was a similar case in this town years ago."

"Everybody knows that," Chester says, "whether they grew up here or are new to town. Everybody's heard about it."

Liam nods. "No story dies in a small town."

"There were others," he says.

"The Miller kid," Chester says.

Liam nods. "Robbie Miller. And two kids from the next town over."

Mr. Woodstone nods.

"There was an older case of a little girl going missing at the train station," Liam says. "Maisy Brown. Her mother and her were just passing through town when the train stopped."

He looks at the two old men, catching their reactions. They both stiffen at the name.

Liam looks down at his beer bottle, methodically turning it slowly on the table with a dull sound of glass on lacquered wood.

"You never found that little girl, did you Retired Sheriff Chester Hayes?"

The use of his title and full name ring a warning bell in Chester's head and his face stiffens.

"You probably remember the Brown family," Liam continues. "The girl's father grew up here. Some of his family probably still live here. I find it odd of all the places that lady could take her kid, she would just happen to be on a train passing through the town of Havenwood and that little girl would just happen to go missing here."

"It does seem unlikely," Chester says slowly, "considering what that little girl went through and all."

Liam looks at him and back down at his bottle, still slowly and deliberately turning it.

You know about that, he thinks.

"You figure her father had anything to do with her disappearance?" Liam asks as if it is the most casual question in the world.

"We suspected someone, but it wasn't that little girl's father, Peter Brown. Oh, we all knew what he was. He had to leave town just to start a family. The whole town knew. There wasn't a woman in a hundred miles in any direction that would have him. Peter Brown grew up here, but he knew better than to ever come back to Havenwood."

"Who did you suspect then? People tend to believe these things can run in a family, like some people are just born with a bad gene. The police are eying Harvey Lawson pretty hard right now."

He looks at Chester.

"You suspected someone in his family in Maisy Brown's disappearance? Is that why they are so sure he's behind this latest body?"

"Harvey Lawson," Chester says, nodding. "No, we never suspected anyone in his family of anything but him. Lawson is a good family; a good family name. Sometimes when that apple falls from the tree it doesn't just fall far. Sometimes it falls wrong. Sometimes it's just plain rotten.

I figured he was good for that little girl's disappearance. He was always and odd kid. I couldn't find enough proof though."

"He would have just been a kid then too," Liam says.

"That boy hung out too much in those woods. That and his odd behavior made him look pretty guilty."

"What odd behavior?"

"He was just plain odd. Secretive and always out in the woods. While the other kids told stories about the old Mill Road monster to scare each other, Harvey seemed to actually believe it was real."

"Seems a coincidence too that every time that Harvey boy comes back to town another body is found," Mr. Woodstone says.

"They are found right around when he comes back?" Liam asks.

"Shortly after. Days or weeks."

"The remains were older than that. By my estimation, they would have had to have died months at least before Harvey came back to town. They could have died years before they were found; depending where they were stored."

Chester leans forward.

"You think they were stored?"

Liam grins at him. It is a humorless twisting upwards of the corners of his mouth.

"Someplace dry. They were not left in the woods after they were killed; they were planted there months or years later like it was time for them to be found."

He blinks at Chester, feigning surprise at his stunned expression.

"You didn't know? You were the sheriff then. I just assumed that would have been part of your investigation."

"You bastard," Chester mutters.

Liam settles back in his chair, looking at Chester.

"I'm just trying to get behind these older bodies. It seems odd to me how they seem to pop up about every twelve years, and always with striking similarities."

Mr. Woodstone leans forward with interest now.

"Do you think we have a serial killer?"

"A serial killer who hits every twelve years?" Liam asks. "It isn't unheard of. I keep my mind open to any possibility. I have to."

"Harvey Lawson a serial killer," Mr. Woodstone shakes his head with mock wonder. He looks at Chester. "I guess we should have seen this one before."

He turns to Liam. "I was involved in trying to solve these cases back in the day. I grew up here. Went federal instead of the local police. A man could make a career just out of trying to solve the Havenwood town slayings. I came back here to retire."

"I know," Liam says. "That's why you're sitting here, Retired Detective Barry Woodstone. Just remember, I didn't call him a serial killer, you did. Is that what you called them? The Havenwood town slayings?"

"Officially we didn't call them anything," Mr. Woodstone says.

"You also came back and retired before retirement," Liam says casually.

He turns his attention to both old men.

"You really like Harvey for these children; you and the current police. But I'm just not seeing it. Sure, he's odd. He's a loner and a conspiracy nut. That doesn't make a man a killer, or a serial killer. What do I not know about Harvey?"

Chester and Mr. Woodstone exchange a look. Chester seems to think about it, weighing his options, before he speaks.

"You already know it," he says.

"You mean the story you told me about Harvey getting lost in the forest as a kid?" Liam asks.

Chester nods and Mr. Woodstone's head does a slight bob in agreement.

"Like I said before, there's always been dark rumours in this town about the old mill," Chester says. "And about Harvey Lawson for as long as that kid was big enough to wander off that first time."

Liam smiles.

"I remember. You suggested that Harvey isn't what people think he is. They seem to think he's a killer, so you don't believe it?"

"That's not quite what I said," Chester says. "I have no doubt something happened to Harvey in the woods when he disappeared as a boy; something that changed him."

"Maybe Harvey isn't really Harvey anymore," Liam repeats Chester's words from earlier.

Chester nods.

Liam looks at Mr. Woodstone. His expression is stony, revealing nothing.

"We thought he was one of them," Mr. Woodstone says quietly, "when we found Harvey. He was only about ten." He looks at Chester for confirmation.

Chester nods. "About that old. Maybe a bit younger."

Mr. Woodstone continues.

"We'd been combing the forest for weeks. We gave up on ever finding him. We were in a drought for months, just like we are now. Everything was all dried up and crisp. We couldn't run any off road vehicles because of the risk of starting a fire. It was just like when the others were found before him. Game was scarce. Hell, everything was scarce except the coyotes."

"Before him," Liam says.

Mr. Woodstone nods. "Last one was twelve years before Harvey."

He takes a breath.

"Young Harvey was found all curled up in a hollow under a fallen tree, like he was trying to keep warm. He was dirty, half buried in dried up rotten leaves like he'd been buried there for some time and half dug up.

The boy was cold to the touch and not moving. Ralph McKinley found him when he was out hunting. Thought for sure the boy was dead. It shook him to the core."

"Is Ralph any relation to Tucker McKinley? If game was scarce because of the drought, what was he hunting?" Liam asks.

"Tucker's his son. Prairie chicken, he said." Chester snorts. "More likely he was hunting the coyotes that had been going after the smaller farm animals. It was a bad year for hungry coyotes with their natural prey mostly gone."

"So, Ralph McKinley was shaken finding what he believed were Harvey's remains and rushed back to town."

Chester shakes his head.

"He didn't rush back. That's what shook him up so much. He figured the boy was already long dead, so he took his sweet ass time about it. Figured what would a few more hours hunting do. Sent him into a tailspin when he found out he left that boy like that, still alive. He's been hitting the bottle hard every day since."

"That would be the drunk gentleman I've seen in Dusty's every day," Liam observes.

Chester nods. He looks a little haunted himself at the memory.

"So, Harvey was found alive after being missing for weeks," Liam nudges.

"He was in rough shape," Chester nods. "Catatonic. Couldn't get him to talk for a year. Nobody knew how he survived out there that long and when he finally started talking, he claimed he couldn't remember."

"You didn't believe him," Liam says.

Chester shrugs. "The boy didn't want to talk about it. He was strange after that. Kept taking off in the forest. Would never say where he was going; only that he was looking for something he lost."

"Why did you think he had anything to do with Maisy Brown?"

"His odd behavior. He was seen staring at her in that weird way."

"You think he-," Liam doesn't finish.

"There was anything sexual? No," Chester says. "He was twelve when that little girl went missing. Old enough, but I never pegged him as that. He was odd in a different kind of creepy way."

"Harvey kept talking about a monster in the woods," Mr. Woodstone says. "I probably spent more time questioning that boy than anyone else; after he was found, he seemed to barely know I was there, when he would finally talk after a year, and later when Maisy Brown disappeared. That kid listened too much to people's talk. People talked like he was a monster when he acted different after he was found. It was like some part of him was left behind in the forest. People started to talk like something had taken a part of him."

"What kind of monster did he see?"

"He wouldn't say. I thought maybe he didn't just get lost after all. Maybe he'd been kidnapped, had things done to him. He just kept saying the monster is in the forest. The kid walked around town like a ghost since he was found. People saw darkness in him. They were disturbed by the haunted look in his eyes, the emptiness there. People said there was something unnatural about him. His family started trying to keep him home where no one could see him. He kept taking off into the forest, for days at a time sometimes; hanging around that old mill."

"So, when Maisy Brown vanished-."

"The whole town blamed that kid," Mr. Woodstone says.

"Do you think he did it?" Liam asks.

Mr. Woodstone meets his stare, both unwavering, the weight of the accusation hanging heavy in the air.

"We sure did when another boy disappeared years later," Mr. Woodstone says. "We just couldn't find any proof. We searched up around the old mill too. We thought that was as good as any other place to find the body."

"You never found it," Liam says.

"Twelve years later," Chester mutters. "All curled up, decomposed, and dried out just like the one just found."

He looks at Liam.

"Harvey isn't the only one to go missing and come back."

"Who else?" Liam asks.

"Felicia Hastings went missing too, her and the younger kid, Nicholas, Harvey's niece and nephew. The kids were probably too young to remember it. But their family was crazy over it. Harvey showed up with them like he just found them. Everyone suspected he took them.

We never found out what happened out there, but that little girl was never the same after. You always saw a darkness in her eyes when you looked at her. It sent a chill down my spine every time I looked at her."

Liam stares at him. "You're serious."

"Some things folks don't joke about."

38 – The Mill

Harvey stands in the clearing staring around speechlessly, his mouth open in a slack expression and his face a mask of shock. The remains of his bits of burlap sack hung in the trees and their contents are scattered all over. Behind him, the old mill sits silently brooding in the late afternoon light.

He closes his mouth and his eyes harden. He scowls. Kneeling, he lays his rifle on the ground and picks up a scrap of burlap and a lump of hand-pressed desiccated feathers and small bird and rodent bits. He shakes his head.

"What have you done?" he mutters.

Harvey moves to pick up another, his motions jerky and his hands shaking.

"What have you done?"

He picks up another and another, shoving them in his pockets when he can't hold more in his hands, and moving on to pick up more.

Harvey paces angrily, looking around as if for the guilty culprit, looking like he is ready to tear them apart.

"No. No. Nonononononono. What have you done? What have you done? WHAT HAVE YOU DONE?"

He raises his head to the sky and screams, clutching at his hair and pulling it. Harvey falls to his knees and screams again. They echo off the sky, sending birds bursting from their roosts as his screams echo into the distance.

Harvey falls on his hands and knees, crawling around collecting up more of the grisly remains of blood-soaked burlap and their disgusting contents scattered on the ground.

"Nononononononono," he keeps moaning.

He falls back heavily, sitting on the ground, dropping them and emptying his pockets into the pile.

He screams again.

"Nonononononono," he keeps moaning as he starts trying to piece them back together.

Somewhere in the brush a branch snaps.

He freezes. His head comes up, looking around sharply.

Harvey's head drops again, focused on his task piecing the blood-soaked burlap and desiccated flesh and bones together again. His hands move in hurried jerky shaking motions.

39 – Seeking Answers

"You are so quick to believe the townies' rumors." Felicia looks at David coldly. She turns her gaze on Ian, then Nick, and back at David. "You really have no idea David." She stares into his eyes.

David looks away from her, breaking the spell of her eyes staring into his.

"We need to go back to Harvey's and search it again, maybe ask him questions," David says.

"I feel like if we are going to find anything it will be at the old mill." Nick looks sickly at the idea.

Ian looks at each of them then at Felicia.

"What do you think Felicia? Harvey's or the mill?"

"You don't even know what is out there in the woods," Felicia says softly. "You have no idea what you are looking for."

"The woods," David says. "Maybe we should start with where we found it twelve years ago."

"We've already been there," Ian says. "That's where they just found it, or a new body. There is nothing there."

"We thought it is," David says. "We need to go look again."

*****

David's car slows and turns into the entrance of the construction site, bouncing over the rough ground and parking by the construction trailer.

Across the field police tape still flutters where one end is still tied to a branch. The other end and half the tape have broken free and are long gone.

They get out of the car and stand there for a moment looking across the field to the trees.

"Are you sure about this?" Ian asks.

"No," David says. "Let's just do this. We'll check it out then decided what to do next."

They cross the field and vanish into the trees. With the forest closed in around them, the outside world seems years away and muffled out of existence.

David leads the way, stepping over downed trees and skirting heavy brush looking for the deer trail.

With all four of them there together it feels like they have been sucked twelve years back in time.

"There," Ian points, "the surveyor's pole."

They go to the pole. They stop and stare at it next to the rotting downed tree.

"It's been a lot of years," David says. "I just can't say for sure it's the same spot or even the same area."

The image is burned into his eyes. The downed tree. It wasn't hard to find with the abandoned surveyor's pole jutting crudely from the ground like a flag pole marking the discovery.

Every moment of their walk out of the woods twelve years ago is burned into his memory as fresh as if they are still there. He feels like they are. Still there; trapped forever in that moment, the feel of the rough ground beneath his shoes, the smell of the forest, green and leafy and rotting.

He has to force himself to see past the memory to the rotting tree before him.

The remains of the large fallen tree are little more than an elongated mound, limp and sagging with the rise and fall of ground and rocks beneath it, melting into the ground. Ferns and other undergrowth crowd in to take its place, as if to erase its existence but failing. A few rough stumps stick out where the largest branches once extended from the trunk. What is visible of the tree looks chewed down and soft with rot.

His mind flashes to the memory of the image years ago.

The softly rotting tree lays straight, its trunk still strong and sturdy and partially leaning against another tree. It does not quite touch the ground except at its base. Beneath it are two large rocks, rough ground, and other fallen deadwood. Its dead and brittle branches are partially caught up in the branches of other trees as though it had reached out to its brethren with bony knobbed branches, reaching for them and they catching their fallen brethren, snagging its branches with their own and forever frozen in time in that position.

"It's the right spot," David says. His voice is rough. "It has to be. The very same exact spot we found that body when we were kids. I've seen the image of it in my mind every day. It's burned into my memory as fresh as the day we saw it."

David has the cold undeniable urge to look up for the crow he remembers hearing that day. He is a little surprised to not see one.

It takes every ounce of willpower David has to make himself walk around that God damned tree.

The others follow wordlessly, looking down. The ground beneath the tree is scraped raw. There is nothing there now to see, but he can see the body as if it is still there exactly as they found it twelve years ago. The face of the child stares back at him, not all there, soft skin covering a section from the nose down on one side of the slack jaw. The rest is part flesh covered, part pale bone, as if the skin and tissue were slowly melting away like an ice cube left in the hot sun. The rest of the body is lost in the dimness of childhood memory, only the grisly face staring at him, clear and accusing. He can't tell if it was a boy or girl.

"I don't think it's the same spot," David lies.

Felicia stares at the scraped spot, accusingly bare of any grisly remains; its memories scraped away with the crude blade of a shovel.

"That's it," she says. "I remember the rocks. The rocks are the same."

David looks at her. Her face is pale and her eyes hollow.

"There is nothing here," Nick says. "I'm telling you, I feel like whatever we are looking for we will find it at the mill."

"Fine," David says, his eyes still on Felicia, "let's go to the mill."

Felicia does not look at Nick or at any of them. She just stares at that scab of earth scraped bare where the grisly face, partially covered with dried thin flesh, part pale bone, as if the skin and tissue had slowly melted away like an ice cube in the hot sun, is supposed to be staring blindly back at them with its hollow empty sockets and slack drooping jaw.

40 – Old Photos and Older Cases

Liam reaches into his pocket and pulls out an undersized photo. He places the photo on the table between them. Its image captivates the old men, its faded sepia tint as hollow as the hole its horrifying image opens up inside them.

Chester reaches a hand for it and stops, unable to bring himself to touch it.

"How old is this?" Mr. Woodstone asks, staring at the photo.

"Old," Liam says.

The image is of a body in leaves and dirt, the faded colorless sepia tint lost some details like a faded memory, the colors forgotten. It is small, a child curled up as if for warmth or to huddle against the nightmares that filled the last moments of life. The eyeless face stares fixatedly at something, perhaps a memory in the past the lost soul is trapped in forever, endlessly tormented at the moment of death.

The limbs and body are made smaller by the desiccation of the flesh, the withering of what remains of muscles after the fats have liquefied and the moisture oozed out into the ground. What remained of the muscles and connective tissues partially liquefied, shrivelled, and dried into ropes of hardened jerky, pulling the limbs in tighter in unnaturally twisted ways. The partial skin is a papery leather shroud, dried and stiffened, covering yellowed bones.

The nails are claws jutting from the fingertips, the effect of the flesh of the fingertips and toes shrivelling away from them. The teeth jut out in a grimace without the padding of soft lips, the eye sockets sunken and hollow; empty. Wispy strands of hair cling to the skull and lay beneath it. Shreds of rotten fabric melted into the dry skin partially cover the grisly corpse, giving evidence to clothes.

Liam does not look at it. He does not have to. The image is burned into his memory forever; the desiccated face of the child refusing to look at you, not all there, crisp papery skin covering a section on one side of the slack jaw, the rest bare pale bone.

He pulls out another photo, dropping it on the table, one corner partially covering the edge of the other. This one is black and white and also faded.

"Older."

The image is eerily similar to the sepia photo. Another child, curled up and desiccated, the corpse decomposed until it dried up, mummifying before the decomposition was complete. This one appears to be lying on a cold metal table, broken off cadaver pieces carefully set next to where they belong.

Liam points to the sepia photo. "Nineteen thirty-five."

They look at him in surprise, only the fading of the photo holding back their disbelief.

Liam points at the faded black and white. "Eighteen eighty-seven. They pulled it out of storage for another look."

He pulls out a folded paper from his pocket, unfolding it and laying it on top of the photos. The grisly image is ruined through the imperfection of photocopying a very old drawing. It is another child, like the others.

"Undated."

"What is this?" Mr. Woodstone looks at him in numb shock.

"This is the history of Havenwood," Chester says heavily, his eyes on the pictures on the table. "I told you this area has a history. A dark one. And it goes way back."

Liam looks at him.

"Your family, Hayes, is one of the oldest families around here."

Chester just nods.

"You can't be saying this goes way back to the eighteen hundreds." Mr. Woodstone looks at them.

"I need you both to tell me everything you know about the history of Havenwood, its twelve year drought cycle, and kids going missing and being found," Liam says. "Then I'll be checking out that old mill of yours."

"I'm too old for this," Chester mutters, suddenly feeling much older.

"No one is asking you to come," Liam says.

41 – Into the Woods

The leaves above and around them hiss with the breeze rubbing them against each other as if trying to warn them away. The clicking buzzing of insects and cloying warmth making them sticky has Nick looking back wishfully the way they came. The cooling breeze does not touch them here, in a world separate from the rest of the world inside the woods bordering the old Mill Road.

Nick leads the way with Ian following, David and Felicia bringing up the rear, pressing their way down the wavering deer trail that is sometimes barely there.

"Are you sure this is the way to the mill?" Nick asks, pushing a branch blocking the path aside and holding it for Ian behind him. "We should have gone back to the car and drove around."

"This way is faster," David says, "straight across the woods instead of taking the road all the way around."

They press on, David and Felicia falling a little behind as they pick their way through the woods.

David feels Felicia's presence next to him without looking at her.

I have so many things I want to say to her, he thinks. So may questions I want to ask.

"Do you still think Uncle Harvey did it?" Felicia breathes into David's ear, startling him with her sudden nearness.

Her soft scent is heady, her closeness intoxicating. She is as perfect as . . . *In my dream.* The thought is on the edge of his conscious thoughts, hovering, almost tangible.

David itches to touch her, to make sure she is really there. To hold her hand. Something.

She moves away. He can feel her presence like a tangible pressure as she moves behind him. She comes close again, whispering into his other ear.

"It's been a long time." The words are soft, breathy, barely there. "What are you doing here in the woods David? What are you really looking for?" His name almost caresses off her tongue.

David swallows, a hard dry knot in his throat. He feels like he will choke on his own throat.

"Are you scared they will find out what we did?" Felicia is on his other side now, whispering in that ear, looking ahead at Ian and Nick.

They are paying no attention to David and Felicia behind them as they talk about old times while trudging through the woods.

"We-we didn't do anything." David's whisper is hoarse.

"Are you sure?"

She moves past him and ahead, catching up to Ian and Nick. Felicia does not look back at David.

He can only stare after her mutely, feeling off kilter.

*****

Harvey knots the broken twine with shaking hands, re-hanging the last of the repaired blood-soaked rodent and bird remnants-filled burlap pieces. He rubs his hands on his jeans, looking around as if for something or someone that could be watching.

Walking over and picking up his rifle, he circles the clearing by the old mill, ending on the edge of the dried creek bed, staring at the ruined water wheel slumping off the side of the little building.

Stepping carefully over the rocks, he climbs down into the creek bed. With a last look downstream, he starts making his way upstream.

The low sound of something moving through the bush follows from above.

*****

Liam slows his car, stopping on the side of the road and putting it in park. He peers out the window at the wall of trees and bush on the other side of the ditch.

"Are you sure this is it? It doesn't look like anything is there."

A gnarled hand reaches forward from the back seat, past his shoulder to point at the ditch.

"There," Mr. Woodstone says.

"Where?" Liam asks.

Chester leans forward in the front passenger seat.

"It's there."

Liam sees it, the spot where the ditch rises level with the road, the hole from the culvert beneath almost invisible in the long grass choking it.

"Is that actually a road?"

"Used to be," Chester says.

"Never was much of a road," Mr. Woodstone says.

"You know there's a backwoods travel ban right now, right?" Chester says. "Just so you know, with the drought and all and the risk of the hot exhaust starting a fire."

"We can park it and walk," Liam says, still staring at the trees.

"Did you not hear me say I was too old for this?" Chester mutters.

Liam looks at the two old men. Mr. Woodstone nods to him.

With a grim look, Liam creeps the car forward and turns the wheel towards the wall of bush. Leaving the road, the car drives over the long grass swooshing against its undercarriage and noses into the bushes to be swallowed by the branches swaying back into place behind it.

*****

David can't stop staring at Felicia ahead. This all feels wrong. He dreamt of seeing her again, fantasized about their reunion. She would be so happy to see him. Somehow it would complete him.

Instead he feels empty. She is a void, indifferent and distant.

Realization dawns as a surprise when they break through the trees into the clearing that is the old mill. David blinks at the aging sunlight no longer blocked out by the trees. The sun sits far to the West, not quite setting yet.

They all stop and look around. The old mill draws their attention, the rotting building sitting silent and still with the sound of a few birds in the forest singing in muted apathy.

"Does anyone else get a weird feeling about this place?" Nick asks.

"Like it doesn't want us here," Ian says.

"And still is pulling us to it," Nick finishes.

"It feels heavy," David says.

They look at him. He looks back at them and his eyes are pulled away again to stare at the mill.

"Like the air is heavy. Stale, the air is stale. Smell it." David takes in a deep breath through his nose. "The air smells stale. Old."

Nick and Ian oblige, taking their own breaths and nodding.

"It smells like a tomb," Nick says.

David pushes away his uneasiness and the vague sense of doom, putting a false grin on his face.

"How do you know what a tomb smells like? I was just playing you."

"You are still a jerk," Nick says, shaking his head and turning away. He stares at the bushes around and the bulbous scraps of blood-soaked burlap hanging from them with their gruesome contents.

Ian gives David an annoyed look and looks away from him. His attention is drawn to the motion of one of the burlap talismans dangling from a branch.

David watches him walk to it, reaching one hand out to take it and stop just short of touching it. Ian's hand drops to his side and he turns to look at David.

"What the Hell," David mutters.

Felicia turns to him curiously.

"We took all these down," David complains. "Every one of them. Tore them apart too. Looks like your uncle Harvey was busy putting them all back up."

He walks over, reaches past Ian, and grasps the burlap. He snaps it free with the faint sound of the string breaking and tosses it away into the trees with a grimace of distaste.

Nick is staring at the burlap bulbs hanging from the branches. A chill dread fills him with a sense of uneasy déjà vu. A memory teases at the edge of his mind.

Darkness. Night. Trees. A trembling hand held out one of those things to him on a string.

"Go on, take it." The voice was a man's. His own hand reaching uncertainly was a small boy's hand. It had some weight in his hand and left a smear of wet blood.

"Hang it. Like this," the man said. He watched the man's hands tie it to a branch.

He watched his own small hands fumble awkwardly to hold the burlap bulb and tie it. He dropped it and it hit the ground with a dull wet sound and broke open. He looked down at a sickening ball of moist flesh and feathers broken apart on the ground. A rodent face sneered at him from it, its dead eyes glaring sightlessly at him.

"You broke it." Felicia, young and thin, her legs not yet grown to the long lanky things he remembers her childhood body having. Little Felicia stooped before him and picked up the pieces. She looked at him sternly.

"You will never learn to do it right if you break it," she scolded.

She sounded wrong. Her words too mature for her young age. He thought she might be six or seven. But that would make him, what? Four? Three? He did not know. His own thoughts felt too old for his age.

"What is wrong with you Felicia?"

"You are forgetting, Nick, like you always do. You will forget today too."

A shadow passed over them and he looked at the old abandoned mill rotting in the woods. The gurgle of the creek was missing, the water silent with barely a trickle meandering slowly down the middle of the creek bed.

The groan that pulled his attention repeated itself. It sounded like something was moving inside the old mill, its weight on the softening floor boards making them creak.

"Do we have to go in there today?"

"You can stay out here today," Uncle Harvey said.

He turned and walked towards the old mill and that sent a chill down Nick's spine.

Uncle Harvey grasped the door handle and began to open it. Nick wanted to cry out to him to stop. Don't go in. Don't let it see him. He opened his mouth and was voiceless.

The shadow moved, now in the trees. It was as large as a man, maybe larger, and made no sounds of an animal. Nick stared at it, trying to see it through the trees, willing himself to not see it.

"If I don't see it, it won't see me." The thought was irrational.

"It's coming Nick," Felicia whispered. "I think it's coming for you. Nick. Nick. Nick."

"Nick." Felicia's voice, different, older.

Nick blinks and looks at her, grown up Felicia looking almost bordering on emaciated in her thinness, her eyes serious and clouded with a darkness that never goes away staring at him intently.

"Where were you Nick?" she asks, and he has a sense she knows.

Ian and David are staring at him.

"I think someone is coming," Ian says quietly, looking towards the trees. "I think I heard a car. We have to go."

"Go where?" Felicia asks.

"This way, come on," David urges them in a rough whisper.

Nick looks at the old mill, unsure if he hears the soft sigh of a groan coming from the mill or the woods, or if he hears it at all. He sees a shadow of movement, maybe the size of a man, maybe larger, silent. A shadow passes over them all and he looks up to see a cloud passing over the sun. He follows the others into the trees.

*****

The long grass swooshes against the undercarriage of the car, branches crackling and breaking as it pushes its way through.

"I hope that buffs out," Liam mutters, pressing on. He looks in the rear-view mirror at the path behind them. You can barely tell they were there.

He is driving on what he hopes is a trail. There is no trail.

"I don't think I could turn around and go back if I wanted to."

"It's a one way road," Chester says.

Liam glances at him.

"Whatever way you are pointed, that's the only way you can go," Chester adds.

The nose of the car breaches the edge and the trees and bushes drop away. They have reached the clearing.

Liam stops the car and looks at the old mill.

"So, this is it, huh?"

"This is it." Chester and Mr. Woodstone get out of the car.

Liam follows, walking halfway to the mill and stops, looking around. He spots the burlap pieces hanging from the trees and walks over to one to take a closer look at it.

"What is this?"

Chester and Mr. Woodstone join him, staring at the bulbous burlap hanging from a branch.

"Looks like burlap," Chester says.

"Have you seen this before?" Liam asks, looking around and seeing them hung all over the branches around the clearing.

Mr. Woodstone steps forward and yanks it free, weighing it in his hand. He makes a face at it.

"Is that blood?"

He pulls the burlap apart to reveal the insides. Fur and feathers pressed together with flesh and intestines, a small bird head staring up at him with rodent paws, one curled like it is sleeping the other in a twisted claw grotesquery of pain.

He drops it with a grimace of disgust, wiping his hand on his pants as if that could make it feel clean again.

Liam moves closer to see it better, bending and then kneeling to study it. He pulls out his phone, taking pictures of it. He pulls out a pen, poking at it and rolling it over, taking more photos.

He stands, walking along and taking photos of the burlap bulbs hanging from the branches, finishing with photos of the mill.

"These strings look like they've been broken and retied," he says, studying some of them.

Chester walks over, staring at it.

"You're right."

"I've seen this before," Liam says, indicating the bloodied burlap pieces hanging from the trees surrounding the clearing.

"Like this?" Chester points to the mutilated and pressed remains now lying on the ground."

"Lilydale Acres," Liam says.

"Never heard of it."

"You don't want to."

He turns towards the mill.

"So, this is it? The mill where the bloodbath was supposed to have happened?"

Chester chuckles. "People believe what they hear a little too much. A lot too much. The place got old. Irrelevant."

"That's not why it shut down," Liam says distractedly.

He starts walking towards the mill.

"This place has quite the history."

"It sure does," Chester says.

Mr. Woodstone is looking at his hand, rubbing it on his pants, looking at it again, rubbing, trying to get the blood staining it off.

Chester looks at him.

"Your hand's fine."

"I can't get it off." Mr. Woodstone looks at him and walks over, showing them his hand.

"The blood was dry. There's nothing there," Liam says. He turns his attention back to the mill. "I want to take a look inside."

Mr. Woodstone is standing there looking at his hand and rubbing it on his pants while Chester follows Liam to the door of the rotting stone and wood building.

Liam grasps the door handle and opens the door, releasing the musty smell filling the place. They step through the doorway, vanishing into the relative darkness inside.

Still trying to clean his hand, Mr. Woodstone looks up, staring at the trees where he heard the sound of something moving. He hears it again and is drawn to it, to see what it is. He starts walking toward the trees where it came from.

*****

The memory won't let Nick go. He moves mechanically through the trees, Ian beside him his guide, not seeing where he is going.

Walking through the woods. Dark, so dark. It was night. Hardly any moon to see, just the stars. Lights flashed ahead, moving. Blinding light. On them. Yelling. People ran at them. "We found them!"

People grabbed them. Pulled them. Urged them to move faster. It felt like they were running from something, but he didn't know what. They were running to something. More people, more flashlights. They lit the forest in spasms of flashlights that bobbed and swung recklessly.

His mom and dad were on them, grabbing them. They held them too tight. He couldn't breathe. His mother was crying. He looked at his dad, he was crying too. Somehow that made it real. Something happened and his father's tears were what made the whole thing suddenly scary.

He looked back at the forest behind them. Looked for Uncle Harvey. He was nowhere.

Felicia pulled his face close to hers, noses touching, staring into his eyes in the dark.

"You remember nothing Nick. Got that? Nothing," she whispered sternly.

He nodded. "Where is-."

"Nothing Nick."

"-nothing Nick. Hey, Nick." Ian tugs at him, pulling him back to the present and leaving the memory in the darkness where it belongs.

"What?" Nick asks.

"I said I don't think anyone was there. Did you hear anything? I'm not sure I did. We probably heard nothing, Nick."

"Did Felicia and me go missing when we were kids?" Nick asks. "I mean before, you know. Years before."

"I don't remember anything like that," Ian says.

Nick veers off, changing direction.

"Hey, where are you going?" Ian calls after him.

"I'm not sure. I just feel like I need to check something out."

Ian looks back at David and Felicia. They fell far enough behind he almost can't see them through the trees. He shrugs and grins.

"Just like old times."

He follows Nick.

*****

David keeps looking behind them, trying to see who is coming.

"It's probably your uncle." The accusing tone in his voice is unmistakeable.

"He wouldn't be coming by car," Felicia says. She looks at him. Ian and Nick have gone ahead of them, wanting to put some distance between them and the mill. Felicia moves closer to David.

He feels her closeness, the soft almost touching of her body. It feels unreal. He has to turn his head to look at her to see if she's really there. It still feels unreal to him to have her back again, the four of them walking through the woods, the two of them side by side following their younger brothers.

"It's like when we were kids," David says. "You and me following them through the woods."

A small smile plays at the corners of Felicia's lips. It makes David's turn up in a small half smirk.

Felicia's smile vanishes.

"You still won't stop about Uncle Harvey."

David looks at her. She is looking ahead, not looking at him.

Old Uncle Harvey. The words echo in his head, her voice softly whispering, her breath tickling his neck with her closeness, a flashback to his dream. *Bad bad Uncle Harvey? Do you think he did it? Do you think you will find something after all this time to incriminate him? We all knew he was a bad man, that he did bad things, didn't we? Everyone in town said so.*

David swallows the lump in his throat. "What we found as kids," he starts and hesitates, "do you think. . ."

"What?" Felicia stops and looks at him, making him stop too. "That he killed that kid? That bad bad evil Uncle Harvey is at it again?" She shakes her head. "You are as bad as the rest of them. You don't know anything about Uncle Harvey."

She turns away from him, pacing, walking around him. She passes so close she almost touches him. She stops behind him, so close he can feel her presence although he can no longer see her.

David swallows.

"You don't remember as much from that day as you want everyone to believe," she says. "You are missing so much David. So much that you just don't understand."

David's mind can only focus on one thing, Felicia. The rest of that day does not exist, just her.

"I remember we found it," he tries to answer. "We were scared and kept it a secret. You came to my house the next day. You were crying. Then you were gone."

She starts walking again. Her body barely brushes against his as she circles him, her perfume wrapping him in its heady blanket. She stops in front of him, looking at him.

Are you scared they will find out what we did? Her words from his dream echo in his head followed by his reply. *We didn't do anything.* He is expecting the rest to come from her lips.

"It wasn't Uncle Harvey," she says softly instead. "It was-."

"David! Felicia!" Ian's voice cuts over whatever she said, sounding alarmed.

They both look, not seeing them.

"Where are they?" David asks.

"David! Felicia!" Ian's voice comes again, strained.

Felicia takes off running in the direction his cry came from. After a moment's pause David follows.

*****

With the rise of the land above and the heavy bush, Harvey does not hear the car breaking through the bushes. The sound of the car doors thudding closed is a muffled sound lost in the calls of a pair of birds chirruping at each other. The breeze in the leaves, causing them to rustle and hiss, covers the sound of people walking in the forest.

He steps carefully over the rough rocky bottom of the dried creek bed, stepping higher over and going around tangled roots sticking out into the air as if to suck moisture from it. Ahead, the cut-out from the stream into the ground rising above jots off to the side, an opening in the stream bed that continues on ahead of him.

The sound of something crashing through branches comes from ahead and Harvey stops, listening. He hears a dull thud and grips his rifle tighter. He starts moving forward and is stopped by the sound of something moving in the woods behind.

Harvey turns, searching the trees above with his eyes. His shoulders sag and his head drops, shaking back and forth slowly. He starts walking back the way he came.

*****

Liam and Chester stand inside the old mill, its musty air enveloping them with the dimming light of the waning afternoon coming in the broken dirty windows filling corners with deep shadows.

Scattered dry leaves and grass litters the floor of the small building. A single wooden chair leans forlornly with one leg snapped off. On the other side is a pair of large grinding stones, one resting lopsidedly on top of the other. The large wooden beam above the stones sags, the wood looking chewed with rot where it snapped, the chain of the heavy top grinding stone pulling down the wood beam meant to hold it in place.

Cloying and heavy in the air, thick dust coats every surface. The stain of rot and age discoloring the floor planks shows through.

Multiple sets of footprints cross the floor back and forth.

"Someone has been here," Liam says.

"Harvey. He hangs out around here," Chester says.

The ceiling groans with the weight of something shifting on the soft rotting wood floor above.

They both look up, and then exchange a look. Liam points towards the stairs going up and Chester gives him a resigned nod.

Trying to walk quietly, they make slow progress toward the stairs.

Liam pauses at the bottom, one hand on his holstered handgun, and looks up the stairs. He sees no sign of movement.

The stairs are discolored and worn down the middle where they had the most traffic over the generations and the soft rotting wood of the railing sags, a piece of it hanging broken.

Putting a cautious foot on the first step, Liam tests it before putting his weight on it. He feels it sag under him, but it holds.

Setting his feet carefully against the wall, he slowly makes his way up.

Chester follows, freezing when a few steps up the stair groans too loudly, sagging under him.

Liam looks back at him with alarm, motioning him to stop.

Chester sighs. "Harvey, if you are up there, we are coming up," Chester calls up the stairs.

Liam rolls his eyes at the old man. There is no point in trying to be quiet now. He mounts the stairs faster, no longer trying to avoid creaking stairs, hand still ready on his handgun.

He stiffens when his head reaches floor level and moves more quickly, taking the second floor and scanning it as he steps away from the open stairs.

Chester appears a moment later, joining him.

"There's no one here," Chester says.

The second floor is empty except for an old wooden table with three chairs matching the one below. An old oil lamp sits on the table, its oil long ago evaporated to leave a sticky looking dried residue discolouring the bottom. Above the grinding stones below, a thick rod is bent and broken, hanging over a hole in the floor. Thick dust coats everything, the dust on the floor disturbed by the footprints of those who came before.

Liam walks over, looking down the hole at the shifted grinding stones. He looks at the heavy rod displaced from the gear mechanism. He looks at Chester.

"We would have heard them hit the floor below if they jumped."

Chester looks around the room. "There's no other stairs or door. There's no place up here to hide."

"You think it was Harvey," Liam says.

"Has to be; or local kids messing around. They'd have a better time fitting down that hole, but like you said, we'd have heard them hit below."

They make their way back down the stairs to the main floor, going to the off-set grinding stones.

"There's no footprints. No scuffs. It doesn't look like anyone came down that hole," Liam says.

The ceiling above groans with the shifting of weight on the soft boards.

They look at each other and then up at the ceiling.

"We'd have seen them if there was anyone up there," Chester whispers. "Even if it's a kid."

A dull thud sounds above, followed by two more. Distinctive. Footsteps.

Liam is moving across to the stairs, Chester still trying to react.

Chester takes a step after him as Liam starts up the stairs.

"Stay there," Liam says, taking the stairs quickly.

Chester's hand flinches at his side, suddenly missing his own handgun that hung at his hip for so many years on the job. He stares at the opening in the ceiling above the large stones, listening to Liam's weight creak the floorboards above, his footsteps a dull thud, and another and another and more, thudding and the wood boards groaning with his moving back and forth above.

Chester sees movement at the hole in the floor above and moves to stand near the grinding stones. He looks up to see Liam peering down at him through the hole.

"There's no one bloody up here," Liam says, his face grim. "No other door or stairs. Nowhere down or out."

"Nobody came down through here," Chester says. "Wait, I'm coming up."

Moving across the floor, he goes up the stairs, meeting Liam at the top. They stand there looking around with puzzled expressions.

Downstairs, a shadow passes the open doorway of the mill. The wind picks up, sending leaves and debris scittering across the floor when a gust blows in, swinging the door on its rusting hinges with a loud cry.

Liam races down the stairs, stopping in the middle of the room and looking around. Another gust comes, dancing leaves and moving the door with another cry of its hinges. Unseen beneath his feet is the square of wood flooring with a pull ring mostly hidden beneath the layers of dust and grime.

"I think it's just the wind," Liam calls up to Chester, going to the door and looking out. He scans the trees, seeing no sign of movement except the braches swaying in the wind. The afternoon is growing darker, dusk only hours away slowly closing in.

Chester makes his way down the stairs, moving more slowly, growing tired. He looks at the square of floor, its pull ring hidden by debris.

"Where is Mr. Woodstone?" Liam asks, turning to look at him.

Chester moves across the floor to join him looking out the door. "We left him outside.

The floor above groans as they step outside.

They wander the clearing looking for Mr. Woodstone.

"Mr. Woodstone!" Liam calls, looking for movement in the trees.

"Barry!" Chester shouts.

*****

David and Felicia run through the trees, following Ian's voice. The sound of their crashing through the trees drowns out the sound of Liam and Chester's calls, their shouts muffled by the trees.

"There," David says breathlessly, spotting someone through the trees. They run towards him, slowing when they are approaching Ian, panting to catch their breath.

Felicia looks around. "Where's Nick?"

Ian is looking down a deep cut in the ground, one that would be filled with water normally, the stream feeding the water wheel sagging off the mill when it could still turn.

They stop at the edge and look at Ian. He points down. They look.

"Nick!" Felicia cries, an edge of panic in her voice.

Below them, Nick is moving, getting up stiffly.

"I'm okay," he calls up. "Just a little banged up."

Felicia looks around anxiously.

"Get out of there!" she cries down to him, her voice shrill with stress. She is moving, looking for a way down.

David moves to stop her. She pushes him off, glaring at him.

"We have to get him out of there. Now."

"What's the panic?" David asks. "He's fine." He looks around. "We'll have to walk back to find a way down."

"You don't know anything David," Felicia says, pushing past him. She looks down again.

"I'm coming Nick! Follow the creek back and meet us!"

"All right," Nick calls back.

Felicia starts making her way along the raised cliff above the creek bed running below.

David stares at her retreating figure in confusion. "Maybe you can enlighten me Felicia." He starts following her.

With a final worried look below, Ian follows.

"That was a long fall," he mutters, shaking his head in shock.

*****

"Mr. Woodstone!"

"Barry!"

The shouts echo to Harvey through the trees. He falters, looking ahead, and speeds up.

42 – Beyond the Mill

Barry Woodstone follows the crackling of something moving through the forest, still rubbing his hand on his pants. He glances at the blood staining his hand and rubs it on his pants again as he focuses on the path ahead.

He is following an almost non-existent deer trail. He falters, noticing a red smear on one of the tree trunks ahead.

Stopping to stare at it when he reaches it, he stretches out his hand, stopping just short of touching it.

"Blood." His voice is quiet, uncertain, yet it is unmistakeable what is on the tree, a bloody partial hand-print.

Stumbling forward, he follows the trail, finding another bloody hand-smear on another tree trunk. Staring past it, he sees there is more. They trail through the woods, marking the deer trail.

The sound of branches snapping ahead comes through the hissing of the leaves rubbing in the wind. The light is growing older, the afternoon subtly fading with the shadow of the coming dusk creeping up the horizon.

He stumbles forward, following the trail, speeding up. He keeps rubbing his blood-stained hand on his pants as he goes.

Mr. Woodstone stumbles into a clearing and stops, looking around. The car is gone. The mill is there, the water wheel sagging into the dried creek bed.

"No. no no no. This looks wrong. It doesn't look as old, as weather-beaten."

The door is ajar.

He stumbles across the clearing, passing wet blood-soaked burlap balls hanging from the trees. Single droplets of blood slowly drip to spatter on the ground. He stops in front of the door staring into the darkness inside the mill.

Pushing the door open, its hinges squealing, he enters the dimly lit mill and stands there looking around the empty room.

The ceiling groans with the weight of something moving above.

Looking up, he moves to the stairs, looks up them, and slowly starts going up.

He pulls his hand away from the railing, staring at it. The railing is wet, red and sticky with congealing blood.

Putting a trembling hand on the railing for support, he starts slowly up the stairs again.

*****

David catches up to Felicia, working to keep up with her anxious pace.

"He's okay Felicia," he says.

Felicia stops, turning on him, glaring at him. He stops, staring at her in confusion.

"I'll meet you there," Ian says, pushing past them and leaving them behind.

"You don't get it," Felicia says. "He's not okay. Nick is not okay." Tears are burning in her eyes. "After that day-," she chokes off.

David feels weak at her nearness, numb. He is exhilarated and terrified all at once. He wants to touch her, to wipe her tears away and hold her, to show her everything will be okay.

"He was up, walking. He said he was okay," David says.

Felicia steps closer and puts her hands on his shoulders, looking up at him. She rises on her toes, leaning in, and for a brief panicked couple of heartbeats he thinks she is going to kiss him.

She brings her lips to his ear, whispering softly.

"You remember, don't you," she pauses, "what we did, what we all did that day?"

"We did nothing," he stiffens, confused.

"We … did … nothing," she barely breathes the words into his ear.

Her words bring back the vision of his dream again. David expects her to move around him, circling around, and the bite of her knife stabbing him.

Felicia pulls away, stepping back, and walks around him. He turns with her, a sudden rush of fear filling him, not wanting to let her out of his sight.

She walks past him, following Ian's path to find Nick.

David blinks after her. It feels surreal, dreamlike. He isn't sure if he is dreaming or awake.

He follows her.

"Nick!" Ian's voice comes back to him, calling his friend.

*****

Liam and Chester search the woods bordering the clearing, not finding Mr. Woodstone.

"Mr. Woodstone!"

"Barry!"

They keep calling, circling around to the other side of the old mill and coming back. They stop next to the dried creek bed, next to the mill and its sagging water wheel.

"Where could he have gone?" Liam asks. "Do you think he decided to walk back?"

Chester shakes his head. "He wouldn't make it far and he knows it."

Liam turns at the sound of something moving in the bushes.

"Mr. Woodstone!"

He looks at Chester. "That has to be him."

"Mr. Woodstone!"

He jogs to the edge of the clearing, staring into the trees, searching for any sign of movement.

The crackling of dry branches comes again and he starts forward, pushing his way into the trees.

"Liam, come back!" Chester says. "I don't think that's him."

"Mr. Woodstone!" Liam shouts again, following the sound deeper into the trees.

Chester sighs heavily. "I'll wait here for you then."

He looks at the mill and a chill passes through him.

Liam presses on, leaving the mill behind as he moves deeper into the woods calling Mr. Woodstone.

The hissing of the leaves and crackling of something moving through the growth ahead is the only answer. The trees fill the sky above; the sky above that is growing darker with the shadow of dusk, making the shadows of the forest deeper. The buzzing ticking of insects silences and the birds' calls stop, but he does not notice.

He breaks through the trees into a trail, looking up and down it. It looks like the ruts of an old road, tall grass grown in to take it over, meandering away through the trees.

"Which way?"

The sound of something moving through the trees decides. He follows the sound, jogging along the overgrown road. The road keeps going, his breath coming harder as he continues until he has to stop and walk again.

"How far could the old man have gone?"

The narrow road opens to a small clearing. Liam stops and stares.

"There's more than one? No, it has to be the same mill. It looks the same, but I don't remember a road. Where's the car? Wasn't the car there?" He hesitates. "Where the road was."

He steps into the clearing looking around. The blood-soaked burlap balls hang from the trees, but there is no sign of Chester or the car.

Liam stumbles forward, looking around.

He hears a noise coming from the creek. Walking towards it, the creek bed comes into view, the steady flow of the water filling its banks running through it with a soft gurgle. It washes around the sagging water wheel as though urging it to turn once again.

Turning to the mill, he hears something inside.

Liam follows the sound, opening the door and stepping inside. The mill looks the same, leaves and debris scattered across the dusty floor. He hears a groan in the ceiling, the weight of something shifting on the floor above.

He jogs across the room, taking the stairs quickly and breaching the second floor. It is empty. He goes back down, walking halfway across the floor to the door and stopping.

Liam listens. There is another sound, a soft guttural sound. He looks at the floor.

"It's coming from below."

Eyes on the floor, he moves, listening, stepping sideways.

He feels something under the edge of his foot and stops, looking at his foot. He lifts it and sees the ring in the floor.

Using his foot to sweep away the leaves and debris, Liam reveals the square of wood floor, its edges almost indistinct with the years of grime filling in the crack around it.

Drawing his handgun, he moves slowly, placing his feet carefully to be quiet. Kneeling to one side, he grips the ring and slowly lifts. It pulls up and the square floor follows with a groan, opening a trap door in the floor.

Liam gently lifts it up and over, cringing when the unused hinges squeal loudly, and lets it rest quietly on the floor.

He shifts, looking down into the blackness below. A ladder hangs straight down into the darkness. The soft guttural sound is louder.

Pulling out his phone, he opens the flashlight app, flicking the image of the switch. The light sprays out instantly across the floor. He swings it to the square hole, lighting below.

Leaning forward cautiously, handgun ready, Liam takes another step closer and looks down into the hole.

Light shines back at him, a dancing reflection of his light on the water below. His face mirrors back at him behind it, waxy and deathlike. The water is rolling and gently lapping at the ladder a few feet below.

"Whatever is down there, it's flooded."

He leans closer to take a look.

A shadow passes across the open door of the mill behind him.

Liam stands up, replacing the square of floor.

"We'll have to pump that out to get down there and take a look."

*****

Chester turns at a sound behind him. He stares at the empty creek bed. Another sound comes, the soft clatter of a stone on stone.

He moves, walking towards the creek, looking upstream where the sound came from.

A man appears, his clothes as worn and tired as his beard and unkempt hair. The man is looking down, making his way over the rocks in the dried creek bed, holding a rifle ready in his hands.

Again, Chester's hand twitches at his side, missing the weight of the handgun that hung on his hip for so many years as part of the uniform he hasn't worn for so long now.

As if sensing he is being watched, the man stops and looks up.

"Harvey," Chester says.

Recognizing the old man, Harvey starts walking again, making his way past the sagging water wheel and towards the bank. He comes up the bank to stand before Chester, looking at him.

"What are you doing here?" Harvey asks.

"Just checking out the old mill," Chester says. "Probably the same as you." He has to make himself not turn and look at the grotesque talismans hanging from the branches.

"I doubt that." Harvey scowls and looks around.

He nods towards the car.

"That's that out of town cop's car. So, he's here too. Who else is here?"

"Mr. Woodstone."

Harvey chuckles wryly.

"Two old jokers and a cop from out of town. He couldn't find anyone else to come out here with him? Or did Mr. Woodstone sucker you both into his crazy ideas?"

He looks around, stiffening, and listens. He turns back to Chester.

"Where are they?"

"Liam, the cop, and I were inside the mill. Barry stayed out here. He wasn't here when we came out. Liam thought he heard something in the bush and went looking for him."

"Bloody Hell," Harvey mutters, shaking his head.

"You do all this?" Chester asks carefully, nodding towards the burlap wads hanging from the branches. It's more of a statement than a question.

"You know that makes people think you are crazy," he says. "You know that, right?"

"Nobody comes out here," Harvey says. "Besides, it doesn't change what people think of me."

"What are you baiting with out here? You're baiting coyotes, right?"

"I'm not baiting coyotes."

"Come on Harvey, the whole town knows you bait coyotes. I can see the baits hanging from the trees. What are you using?"

Harvey looks down and away, staring off into the bushes.

"It's not for coyotes and it's not bait."

"So, it's poison then," Chester says. "You're poisoning them."

"It's meant to keep it here." Harvey's voice sounds like his mind is far away. He is listening. He thinks he hears something moving out there.

He turns to Chester.

"You said they're inside?"

"No, they're out there. In the bush."

The sound of boards groaning comes from the mill followed by a thud, the sound of footsteps.

They both turn to stare at the mill.

A shadow passes the partially open door.

"Then who is inside?" Harvey asks.

"One of them must have come back when I wasn't looking," Chester says. "Maybe both."

A cold dread fills him.

Bloody Hell, I'm going nuts now. There's nothing here to be afraid of.

One hand gripping his rifle reflexively, Harvey starts towards the mill.

Chester stays where he is, feeling the urge to not go any closer.

Harvey stops and just stands there, staring at the mill.

"What if it's not them?"

"What?" Chester scowls. "Who else would it be?"

Harvey doesn't answer.

After a pause, Chester speaks again.

"What happened Harvey? Out in the woods years ago when those kids went missing? Your niece and nephew, did you really just find them, or did you have them out here?"

"Shut up," Harvey says quietly.

They both turn at a sound coming from up the dried creek bed.

*****

Mr. Woodstone blinks and staggers when he reaches the top of the stairs, all color draining from his face, leaving it an ashy wreck. He grips the railing to keep from falling back down the stairs.

"The stories are true," he manages, his voice not sounding like his own in his ears.

The greasy dust coating the floor is scuffed and ruined. Footprints move and slide in the dust like twisted tentacles as if there had been a struggle. The lantern on the table is tipped on its side with dark liquid pooled beneath it like lamp oil. The oil inside it coats the bottom where it dried to a sticky residue. Dark liquid dried where it dripped down the tipped oil lamp.

He stumbles forward, releasing the railing to leave behind the smudge of his hand in the thick dark dust coating it, and sidestepping to avoid the puddles on the floor. They are dark and dried pools, drops, and spatters. His focus on the horror filling the room, he steps in a dried puddle, his foot scuffing it to loose powder that clings to his shoe, leaving his smudged footprint behind.

Mr. Woodstone rubs his hand on his pants leg without realizing it, still trying to rub off the blood that will not come off. He feels soiled with it, bathed in the dust of ancient carnage, the blood of a century ago coating him in its dust.

It is everywhere, the pool beneath and drips down the tipped oil lamp, pools and spatters covering the floor and walls. Ruined partial limbs and chunks of gore look like a room full of people exploded or were torn to shreds, pieces of them carelessly flung out in the violence. They are dried, shrivelled in the twisted lumps and shapes they landed in.

He moves to the hole where the grinding stone was once hooked to the beam above, leaning forward and looking down.

A round orb flashes in his vision for barely the blink of an eye and is gone. All he sees is the dried desiccated remains of what is left of the long ago dead, blood pooled and splattered and dried to dust.

"Was that a child?" he barely can breathe the words out, his chest tight with shock. The world feels miles away.

It takes a moment to react, to let the numbing shock melt enough to be capable of moving. He staggers across the floor, scuffing through the dried puddles and spatters, spreading the blood dust. His hand smudges the blood dust coating the railing, gripping it to keep from falling and he stumbles too quickly down the stairs.

Mr. Woodstone stops at the bottom of the stairs, his breath coming in rapid pants in his stress, looking around.

"Little girl," he whispers, hoping only she will hear. "Little girl, where are you?"

He can't stop seeing that pale moon-face staring up at him in that briefest flash, can't be sure he even saw it or that what he saw was a girl child. He stumbles across the floor to stand in the middle of the old mill. There is no little girl.

A shadow crossing the open door pulls his attention to it, sending a chill slicing down his spine.

"She must have gone out."

He does not make it to the door before a low groan of wood settling beneath weight freezes him in his tracks. Turning slowly, his eyes stop at the dark square pit in the floor. It takes a moment to register.

"A trap door. That wasn't open just now. I walked right there."

The hint of motion in the darkness, pale and round, brings back the impression of a small girl's face.

Willing himself to leave, his feet instead bring him towards the black hole in the floor. Stopping on its edge, he looks down. A ladder descends straight down into darkness.

He kneels then sits on the dusty floor. Turning around, he puts one foot down, finds the rung, then the other. Mr. Woodstone slowly descends, swallowed by the blackness below.

*****

Nick limps his way along the dried creek bed. He can year Ian calling him and now and then Felicia and David arguing. He doesn't call back. He doesn't feel like it.

Sound really travels out here with nothing around, he marvels.

The suddenness of the world dropping out from under him was as startling as the ground rushing back up at him before he could mentally process what just happened.

The jarring collision of his body with that ground knocked both the senses and air out of him, leaving him feeling battered, bruised, and like he had just been hit by a car. It took a moment gulping like a fish out of water before he could suck air back into his lungs, choking on the dust raised by the concussion of his landing. It took another moment before he could shake it off, get painfully to his feet, and call up that he was okay.

He doesn't feel okay. Every muscle and limb is sore and even his lungs feel bruised. Having taken the brunt of the fall, his legs and feet are worse. A hot spot of pain is alternately flaring and throbbing in one leg where he landed on the rocks, a sharp shock of pain radiating down to his foot each time he puts his weight on it.

It's his mind that has the bigger problem.

There was a cave in that gully. A cave that would be under water when the creek isn't empty and that pool is full. I feel like I know it. Why? I feel like I've been there before, in that cave. I feel like I have to go back and check it out. Not alone. Why the hell does the thought of going back there scare the hell out of me?

He forces himself to turn his back to the gully with the cave and follow the dry streambed the other way, back towards the mill.

Every step is pain, the rough rocky bottom of the dry creek making it worse. Nick presses on, his shoes crunching on the rocks grinding against each other under his weight, concentrating only on the path ahead. He is startled when he limps past the down-sloping ground running next to the creek to suddenly come upon Ian.

Ian stares at Nick with relief.

"You look a bit banged up," Ian says, looking down at Nick.

"Just a bit."

Nick walks a little further where the bank is only a few feet high with the gradual upslope of the rocky creek bed against the downslope of the bank.

Ian puts a hand out, helping Nick up onto the bank. He looks behind him.

"David and Felicia were just behind me."

"They'll catch up," Nick says. "They weren't far behind."

"You could hear them?"

"Clear enough."

The sound of David and Felicia making their way through the brush arrives before they do, Felicia walking in the lead. They stop before Nick and Ian, Felicia looking at Nick with concern.

"How did you manage to fall off a cliff?" she asks, checking him over for injuries.

"It wasn't a cliff," Nick complains, trying to ward off her prodding. "It was just a bank."

"It was far enough. Anything broken?"

"I'm fine. Just a bit sore." Nick winces when she pokes the sore spot on his leg.

Felicia gives him a pained look. "That's going to hurt for a while."

"What do we do now?" Ian asks, hoping the answer is go home.

David is staring ahead in the direction of the mill.

"We go back."

He looks at the others to find them staring at him with mixed expressions of shock and regret.

"We have to," David insists. "We have to find out who is there."

"It's just Harvey," Ian says.

David focuses on Nick.

"Did your uncle drive to the mill or walk?"

"What?" The question catches Nick off guard. "Why?"

"Just answer. Did he have his truck there or did he walk? Harvey isn't known to drive around the forest. He walks."

"I don't think," Nick is hesitant, trying to remember. "He walked? I'm pretty sure."

"Are you asking me?" David frowns.

Nick shakes his head uncertainly. "I think he walked. I don't remember seeing his truck."

He looks at Ian for help, then back at David.

"I don't remember seeing it in the yard at his cabin either. Was is there?"

"I don't remember," Ian says.

"It doesn't matter," David says. "If he's hanging around the mill and driving there, there'd be a trail down the old road. Going over it once or twice, that will bounce back. Going down that again and again in a truck, it's not coming back from that. There was no path. He walked."

"Why does that matter?" Felicia asks.

"Because, whoever showed up at the mill drove." David looks at each of them. "We are going back to see who it is."

Nobody moves. They all look at him skeptically.

David's lips tighten. He points to Nick.

"Besides, Nick there is injured and probably won't get far on that leg. Going past the mill is the quicker way home with Gimpy's leg."

He waves them to follow and starts walking without waiting to see if they are coming.

They stand there silently watching David go.

Minutes later David hears them following and smiles.

Ian walks faster to catch up to David.

Felicia closes in on Nick.

"You up to this?" she asks.

"I guess I have to be," Nick shrugs.

He thinks, almost says nothing, and decides to ask.

"Do you remember being out here? Not the day we found it, before that."

"Sure," We've been out here lots.

"When the creek was dried up?"

Nick notices her stiffen. Felicia answers after some paces.

"We weren't really allowed out here during the droughts, but we sometimes came out anyway."

"Back there, do you remember a cave?"

Felicia's eyes flash a warning, but she stares straight ahead, not turning to look at him, trying to keep it to herself.

"Maybe. I don't know. I remember a few dens. Could be bear or coyote or wolf."

"They don't den under water. This would be under water when the creek isn't dry. Back there it drops; it's a deeper pool when the creek fills. Deep enough."

"I can't say I remember that cave in particular."

She's lying, Nick thinks. I can see it. Felicia has her little tells when she is lying. Why is she lying about it?

"I feel like I remember it," he says. "Like I've been there. Like we've been there."

Felicia flashes him a look.

"You probably forgot it because it wasn't safe. We won't go back there. It's not safe."

How does she know it's not safe? What is she not telling me? Nick keeps the thought to himself.

"Let's catch up to the others," Felicia says, taking Nick's hand and pulling him along just like they were still kids exploring the woods against their parents wishes. She is grateful it shuts Nick up.

David and Ian stop, David motioning back to Felicia and Nick for silence. They catch up to them.

"We should be almost there," David whispers. "From here on no sound. Walk as soft and slow as you have to. I don't want them to hear us. Keep out of sight. I want to see who is there before they know we are here."

"We should take the creek bed," Felicia says. "It will be easier for Nick."

"It will be too noisy," David says.

"Quieter than breaking dry branches and the water wheel will hide us."

David looks at her, sighs, and nods. "We'll stick to the edge where we'll be less visible.

43 – The Old Mill Road Monster

Mr. Woodstone reaches the bottom of the ladder. The floor beneath him has that soft woodsy texture of dirt. He looks around in the darkness, seeing nothing at first, the light from the open trap door all the light that exists down there. Slowly his eyes begin to adjust.

The walls and floor are crudely dug out in mostly straight lines, wood beams pounded in to offer support from the dirt and rock walls caving in. A few spots are bricked in where the ground failed and crumbled in, the bricks themselves cracking and bowing out in a few places where the weight of dirt behind them pushed them in.

He looks back up to the square of dim light.

A sound draws his attention, his head snapping back to peer through the darkness.

"Wish I had a proper light," he mutters.

He pauses, thinks, and fumbles around in his jacket pockets, finding his old battered Zippo lighter.

"Almost forgot that was in there. Always keep a lighter on you; you never know when you'll need it. Learned that on the job forty years ago."

He shakes the lighter next to his ear, trying to hear if it has and fluid. Flicking it open, he tries lighting it, barely getting a spark flashing feebly in the dark. It finally sputters to life on the fifth strike of the wheel on flint.

Mr. Woodstone holds the lighter up, trying to spread its small light further. The walls and floor continue. On the other side is a rough dark area. He walks forward, approaching it, the light showing more as he goes, leaving shadows closing into darkness in his wake.

The dark area reveals itself to be an opening dug into the wall, tall enough to stand in and wider than a doorway.

He stops at the entrance, holding his arm out ahead of him to light it. The light fades to deeper shadows fading to darkness.

"It's a tunnel."

Feeling like it is the most foolish thing he has ever done, Mr. Woodstone steps forward into the tunnel. The dirt floor remains relatively flat going from dirt to stone, the stone walls curving up and around into a roughly rounded ceiling.

"What could have dug this? It doesn't look like they'd have got any heavy equipment down here."

He follows the tunnel, the Zippo heating up in his hand from the feeble flame.

After some distance the Zippo sputters out, dead, out of lighter fluid. Mr. Woodstone flicks it, burning his fingers on the hot wheel and muttering, almost dropping it. In that brief flash of spark something seems to hover behind him in the dark.

He flicks it again, sucking in a breath against the heat causing pain in his fingers, and the faintest motion behind him is revealed by the weak spark that flashes and is gone.

Mr. Woodstone keeps trying to light it. Dim light flares briefly each time he tries flicking the wheel against the flint, just a spark of almost life that won't light. In each spark movement in the darkness comes closer, shadowy, indistinct, and vaguely human.

After the last spark dies there is a rough guttural grunt that is quickly cut off. The lighter clangs dully against the stone floor; sparking and briefly lighting with a last gasp of life from the empty fuel reservoir.

Barry Woodstone's mouth gapes, blood leaching to the stone floor where his head rests, his eyes unfocused. There is an indistinct sound beyond the weak light. His body shifts, pulled by something unseen, vanishing into the dark just as the Zippo gives up its last breath of life and plunges the world to black.

*****

Liam goes to the door and looks out. The light outside seems heavy, as if a subtle curtain of shade had been drawn down across the world. The first thing he notices is the road is gone and the car is there.

He blinks, feeling off kilter.

"My eyes are playing tricks on me, or my head is."

Harvey is still facing the creek. The hairs on the back of Chester's neck rise with the hairs on his arms, as if a chill breath barely touched him. He has the unsettling sensation of being watched.

Chester turns towards the mill, his old eyes roving to see what gave him a chill. Dark clouds loom on the distant horizon behind the mill. It takes a moment for the man standing in the mill's doorway to register. It takes another moment for the haggard face and slumped shoulders to register.

"Liam."

Harvey looks at him quickly then looks around, quickly spotting the man in the doorway.

Chester looks at the trees where he last saw Liam vanish, chasing after Barry Woodstone. He turns his gaze back to Liam.

"How'd you-," he cuts off, "never mind." He raises his voice, "Did you find him?"

Liam spotted them when he heard Chester say his name. He is walking to them.

"Not a sign. I followed him back here. I could hear him, but never got even a glimpse. You didn't see him come back? Where he went?"

Chester shakes his head. "Haven't seen or heard anything. Just you showing up just now."

The chill that filled Harvey, setting the hairs on the back of his neck and arm hairs standing up when Chester's did is now ice in his veins. He watches Liam as if unsure he should trust him.

Liam stops in front of them.

"Does everything seem a little off to you?" he asks. "Have you seen anything that didn't make sense?"

"No," Chester says. "Like what?"

"The car, I swear it was gone. And that road that isn't there anymore was there." Liam walks past them to stand staring at the dried up creek bed. "The creek, I remember it being dried up then I swear it was full."

"It's bone dry," Chester says, "and that road hasn't been there, it's been grown in, since before I was born."

"We should get out of here," Harvey says.

"Not until we find Barry," Chester says. "You can go on, but I'm staying and looking for him."

"He's gone," Harvey says.

"What the Hell, how do you know?" Chester looks at him suspiciously.

"I'd swear he went inside the mill," Liam says. "I followed the sound of him back here."

"But you didn't find him in there did you?" Harvey looks at him.

"No," Liam admits. "I heard something upstairs, but there was nothing. It was just the building settling. I found a trap door, but it was full of water. Probably what's making the building shift and groan so much."

"No way," Chester mutters. "There is no way there is water under that thing. Even if there were a spring-fed pool under the mill, everything's been so tinder dry for so long there couldn't be more than a trickle."

"I'm just telling you what I saw," Liam says.

"Well then we're going in to check it out," Chester says.

"That's a bad idea," Harvey mutters.

"Come or stay," Chester eyes him balefully; "I'm taking a look."

He starts for the mill, leaving Harvey and Liam behind. Liam shrugs at Harvey and follows. Harvey watches them go with a scowl.

The two men vanish into the deepening shadows inside the mill.

"Where's this trap door?" Chester asks when they get inside.

Liam looks around with a puzzled look.

"It's there, but the leaves were cleared off from opening it."

The floor is littered with windswept leaves and tree litter. There is no cleared spot.

"Doesn't look like you found any trap door," Chester says.

Second guessing himself, Liam walks over, using his foot to sweep away a curved line of leaves. He pushes some more away, revealing the embedded pull ring.

He looks at Chester.

"I'll be damned," Chester mutters.

Liam crouches and pulls the ring tab, pulling the square of wood up and over, laying it on the floor to reveal a square of blackness beneath it.

"I don't hear anything," Chester says, stepping closer but still keeping a few feet distance from the hole.

Liam pulls out his phone, switching on the flashlight app, the light spraying out from the phone to light the floor and wall. He brings it to bear on the square hole in the floor, both men stepping closer to it together.

The ladder descends straight down into the darkness below.

"Shine that light around," Chester says.

Liam obliges, revealing little but a glimpse of a dirt floor some distance below. He frowns.

"I could have swore-."

"There's no water now," Chester says. He looks at Liam. "I guess we have to check it out."

With a regretful look, Liam positions himself, sits on the floor, shoves his phone in his pocket, and gets his foot on the ladder, starting the climb down. The ladder sags a little under his weight. He stops with his head level with the floor, looking up at Chester staring down at him. The image of Chester's face grinning wickedly as he slams the trap door closed on him, locking him in blackness, flashes in his mind.

"I'll be right behind you," Chester says.

"I hope so."

Forcing himself to not keep looking up, Liam continues the climb down. He's halfway down before he hears the soft scuff of Chester's shoes above and feels the sag of added weight on the ladder. The sound of Chester's shoes on the ladder and his breathing through the exertion as he follows him down are a relief.

Liam pulls his phone out when he reaches the bottom, shining his flashlight around at the dry dirt and stone walls shored up with timber and dirt floor.

"That's hard on the old knees," Chester groans when he reaches the bottom. He looks around. "I never would have imagined this was here."

Liam's light slides across the opening in the wall and past it before it registers. He brings the light back.

"Looks like there's more to this place."

They follow the light to the hole in the wall, Liam shining the beam into it to reveal a tunnel fading away into blackness. They look at each other.

"I guess we go in," Chester says. "But I got to say I have a really bad feeling about this."

They follow the light in. Chester's feet shuffle along behind Liam's slow steady steps, moving deeper into the tunnel beneath the ground.

"Do you hear something?" Liam whispers.

They stop and listen, standing motionlessly.

"Did I just hear something move?" Chester whispers, nodding towards the tunnel ahead of them.

"Mr. Woodstone?" Liam asks quietly.

"Barry," Chester's voice echoing down the tunnel is like a slap in the face to Liam, shocking him and feeling vulgar in the uneasy silence.

They listen to the echo quickly die off to silence.

"He's not calling back," Chester whispers.

They start moving forward again. Some distance in the walls spread away, the tunnel widening. They stop and Liam swings the light around, following the walls around. The tunnel has widened, but also ended. Clusters of rock litter is strewn against the walls surrounding them. A couple of sharp jagged outcrops of rock hide deep shadows behind them.

"Might be another tunnel behind any of those," Liam whispers.

Something pale in the darkness catches his attention.

"What's that?"

He swings the light to shine on it. They both take an involuntary step forward, staring at it, and freeze, staring at it. Liam moves closer to get a better look, Chester reluctantly following. They stop three feet away, staring at it.

A dirty pale yellow ribbon with white polka-dots.

They stare at the faded soiled ribbon.

Liam's soft words and Chester's thoughts echo each other.

"Maisy Brown."

They stare at each other in shock.

"What's that it's tied to?" Chester asks, his old eyes not seeing well in the poor light.

Keeping the light trained on the ribbon, Liam closes the distance, stopping to stand over it. After a moment pause, Chester follows, coming to stand next to him.

The dried up husk of a body is curled up in a foetal ball as if trying to find warmth in the last moment of life. Its head is bowed to its chest. It is part flesh covered, part pale bone, as if skin and tissue slowly melted away before drying into hard mummified flesh.

What little flesh of the face is visible looks strangely soft and putty-like but hard and waxy at the same time. The jaw hangs slack, drooping towards the ground.

A single insect sits atop the corpse, a beetle, paused in the act of feeding off it. It skitters away through the partially decomposed face, vanishing in the darkness beneath the desiccated flesh.

It seems small, shrunken, and even smaller huddled into itself in the dark cavern. They cannot tell if it is male or female, child or adult. The faded and dirty now pale yellow ribbon with white polka-dots is clutched in what remains of its bony hands, wrapping them loosely so that they cannot see the size of the hand and finger bones.

Chester gags, bringing a hand up to stop the hot vomit that does not come.

"It's Maisy Brown, isn't it?" Liam asks softly.

"It could be Dorothy Brown, her mother," Chester manages to utter quietly. "She had the ribbon last, when she was looking for Maisy."

Feeling like the world is reeling, Chester staggers away to brace his hand on the wall for support. He hangs his head, his eyes close against the vision he cannot wipe from his memory.

Liam kneels for a better look.

"Maybe it is both Dorothy and Maisy together."

"What?" Chester looks up.

"There's two heads," Liam says simply.

He sees it now, one curled within the other, mother giving warmth and comfort to the little girl in the cold dark silence of the cave beneath the old abandoned mill.

"She found her," he says softly. "She found her. Do you think she found her like this? Already dead?"

"I hope not."

Chester pushes himself off the wall, coming back to stare down at the entwined dried up corpses. He scowls and has to spit on the ground. It hits with a wet sound, splattering.

"Harvey Lawson." The name is poison on his tongue. "She said it. She knew. He was there, always hanging around, being weird, staring, watching. The whole time we searched for that little girl."

Chester looks at Liam to find him staring at him.

"It's him, the old Mill Road monster. Harvey Lawson," Chester says.

*****

Harvey is still staring at the empty doorway of the abandoned mill when he hears the clatter of a rock behind him.

He turns to stare at the creek bed behind him and is met with silence, only the sound of the wind whispering the leaves in a dry rustling and the ticking buzzing of insects.

Slowly unslinging his rifle, he takes it in a ready two-handed grip, muzzle pointing to the ground.

"Who's there?"

After a pause the sound of another rock shifting comes from behind the sagging water wheel.

"If I have to come in there I'm going to shoot you." He raises the rifle, aiming for the rotting wood wheel with its failing blades.

After a pause there is movement. Felicia steps clear, standing next to the edge of the wheel.

"Felicia, what are you doing here?"

"Looking after Nick. I'm not alone." She motions behind her, waving someone to come out.

Hesitating, Nick steps out behind her.

"Who else is back there?" Harry asks, lowering the rifle muzzle to point to the ground.

David and Ian step out into view. Harvey shakes his head and sighs.

"How many times have I told you kids not to hang out around here?"

"We heard people, a car. Who is here?" David asks.

Harvey indicates the mill.

"Some out of town cop and the retired sheriff. They're in there, gone down into its lair."

David gives him an odd look.

"You know the monster isn't real, right?"

Felicia looks at the sky. Dark clouds are rolling in fast, filling the sky and the world with gloom. The wind picks up.

"It's going to rain."

She looks at Harvey.

"Are you going to stop it?"

The first heavy raindrops begin to fall, cold against the dry warmth and splattering the dry ground.

Harvey looks up just as the clouds open, dropping a torrent of rain. He looks at her and sighs heavily.

"Not this time."

"It's pouring, let's get out of here," Ian says.

Nodding, David moves past Harvey, Ian following, to take the shortest route home through the woods.

Nick stares at Harvey and Felicia, trying to measure them against his vague childhood memories.

"Something happened here when we were kids, didn't it?"

"Maybe someday I'll tell you about it," Harvey says.

He looks at Felicia. She is staring at him, her face pale.

"How many?" she asks. "How many disappeared?"

Harvey's expression is hollow.

"None. Maybe one, Mr. Woodstone. Three if it got that cop and Chester."

Felicia closes her eyes and stands there. She opens them slowly.

"Not enough. It's not enough."

"Time's up," Harvey says, pointing to the sky. "The rains have come."

"Come on," David shouts over the rain in the distance, waving at them to come.

Felicia turns to stare in the direction of his voice, her face expressionless.

"We can help it happen."

"It still won't be satisfied," Harvey says. "It likes innocence."

"What are you talking about?" Ian asks, looking at one then the other with frightened concern.

"It will only be worse the next time," Felicia says quietly. "Hungrier."

She starts forward, walking mechanically after David and Ian. The pouring rain closes behind her like a curtain as the distance grows between them, Harvey and Nick staring after her.

David stumbles on through the woods, the trees giving little cover against the downpour.

We didn't find out anything, he thinks unhappily. This was all just a waste of time. No, not a total waste. Felicia came back. Maybe for good? Will she stay?

In his heart he knows there is nothing to keep her here. Nick is planning to leave as soon as the construction is done. That only leaves her crazy uncle.

Would she stay for me? David barely lets himself think it.

His mind turns back to the last dream he had about her; him finding the body and then Felicia showing up, acting weird.

He can almost smell her perfume, a dream scent that was eerily accurate, intoxicating. He can almost feel the bite of the sharp blade stabbing him in the back. It is a hot pain, itchy, between his shoulder blades. David has to push back the urge to try to reach around, to scratch, but really to see if his hand comes away wet with blood.

Her words echo in his head. Coming softly from her mouth just before she attacked him in his dream, 'Gone. Weren't we all gone that day, one way or another?'

Maybe we were gone before that, David thinks.

His head still rings a little from the sudden blow to the side of his head. He reaches up absently rubbing it.

"It was only a dream, so why do I feel like I really got my skull rung?" David mutters.

Felicia's frenzy haunts him, the memory of the words she shrieked accusingly at him in the dream.

'I did it! I killed the boy! It was all my fault!' Those were her words, spat out as if he was somehow to blame.

"Maybe we all were to blame in a way," David says.

Trudging through the woods ahead of him, Ian doesn't hear him over the hissing of rain pounding the leaves and ground.

*****

"We have to get out of here," Chester says, his breath coming faster with the realization the old Mill Monster is real and he is outside.

"Hang on," Liam says. He gives Chester a look suggesting there is something he isn't seeing in the bigger picture. "Taking a few more minutes to check around won't change anything."

Liam indicates the craggy outcrops of rock, deep shadows gently dancing behind them with the subtle movement of the phone flashlight in his hand.

The motion intrigues him, pulling his eyes to it. Then he realizes, the light is moving with his own breathing coming harder and faster too. He makes a conscious effort to slow his breathing and fails, the shadows still softly swaying behind the outcrops.

Chester stares at him like he's crazy.

"We don't know if there are any other openings down here," Liam shrugs. "Can't see what's behind those."

"Good idea. There might be another way out. We could come up behind him."

They start moving towards the first craggy outcrops of rock, the light in Liam's hand moving with them leaving the darkness following. Chester surveys the cave as they go, half expecting Harvey to step out from the black void beyond the light's reach.

He pauses, staring into the shadows along the floor against the wall.

"Bring that light closer."

Liam comes, the cave brightening with him, shadows scurrying after him. He stands next to Chester.

Against the wall are more bodies just like Dorothy and Maisy, dried, petrified after putrefaction. Only they are all small and huddled alone against the chill darkness of the cave.

"You got it wrong, Chester," Liam says.

There is a hollow pause between them.

"It's not right," Liam says. "This has been going on here for hundreds of years. If it is Harvey Lawson, he's only the last in a long line of monsters haunting the old mill."

They go back to stare at the bodies of Maisy and Dorothy. "Things get muddled with time," Chester says. "It's been a lot of years. Maybe we had some of the stories wrong."

"Let's get the hell out of here," Liam says.

"We didn't check that way," Chester grunts towards the shadows hiding behind the other craggy outcrop. "Just in case there's another way out and he's waiting for us to come out that door."

Staying closer together, they move across the cave, shining the light on the other side of the outcrop.

The black hollowness of the opening to a narrow tunnel is both a relief and sends cold watery dread through them.

"Guess we got to try it."

"Guess we do."

Liam pulls his handgun from his holster and leads the way, his shaking hand making the light dance ahead of them through the tunnel. The ground slopes up at a gradual incline. After some distance the incline becomes severe, forcing them to crawl up it on hands and knees, their hands searching for purchase to pull them up. Cresting the rise, the floor drops away again, first a sudden drop of a few feet, then a gradual decline.

"Do you hear something?" Chester asks.

Liam stops in front of him, looking at him. They both hold their breath, listening. A steady sound is coming from somewhere.

"Is that water?" Liam asks.

"Could be. I can't tell if it's coming from ahead or behind us."

"Let's go. I'm starting to get claustrophobic."

They start moving forward again, at a faster pace this time.

The sound is getting louder and after some distance their shoes are sloshing in water.

"Maybe we should go back," Liam says. "This water is getting deeper."

"We've gone quite a ways already," Chester says. "We have to be getting close to the end. That's probably why we hear water. It must be a stream, but it doesn't make sense. The only stream around here is the dried up creek."

"If we drown going this way, I'm not going to be happy with you," Liam mutters, pressing on. The water is shin deep now and icy. He can feel the pressure of the flow against his legs, pushing him back.

"We have to be close to an entrance. The water is flowing towards us. And I think that's rain."

"That promise is the only thing keeping me going," Chester says. He shakes his head. "Sounds like a lot of rain," he mutters doubtfully. "There wasn't any rain in the foreseeable forecast."

They push on, their shoes sloshing loudly in the water in the cramped space. The ceiling is getting lower, forcing them to crouch awkwardly to avoid crawling on hands and knees through the water.

The steady hissing rushing of falling water grows louder and the wall ahead seems to be moving. They stop when they reach it, crouched low looking out the mouth of a low cave.

The sky has turned dark with heavy clouds and they can see little through the heavy rain. They emerge in a low pool off the creek close to where Nick fell. They both stand, stretching their backs, grateful to be standing again.

The torrential downpour is already filling the pool with the runoff streaming down from above in every direction.

"It looks like we got out just in time," Chester says, squinting through the rain looking around. That cave is going to be under water in no time. No wonder nobody knew it was there. It's under water if there's any water in that creek."

They wade out in already knee-deep water, stepping up to reach the creek bed and climbing out to higher ground.

Liam's phone flashlight dims and flickers; the phone unhappy with the wetness beginning to seep into it. He turns it off with a frown and shoves it in his pocket.

"Let's get back to the car," Liam shouts over the sound of the pounding rain.

"We never found Barry," Chester shouts.

"We won't find him in this. I can't see more than a few feet in front of me."

They start working their way back to the mill and the waiting car. When they reach the car, they climb in, grateful to be out of the rain.

"Let's get out of here while we still can," Chester says, trying to peer at the mill through the rain. "We won't get through that trail soon. It might already be too late."

Liam starts the car, puts it in reverse, and starts carefully backing out. He guns it when he feels the tires slipping and sucking at mud. Halfway down the trail the tires start to sink. Stopping, he tries rocking it out, gunning the car forward and in reverse, the tires miring deeper in the mud until he has to admit defeat.

He shuts off the car and looks at Chester.

"I guess we're walking."

Chester groans. They get out and start the long walk back to town in the pouring rain, chilled and soaked through.

*****

The rain comes harder, obliterating the world outside of Nick and Harvey.

Nick looks at Harvey.

"What is she going to do?"

Harvey's eyes are full of regret.

"What happened here when we were kids, Uncle Harvey?" Nick asks.

"Nothing happened," Harvey says, his mind lost thirteen years in the past. The year before the kids found 'it'.

"Nothing is going to happen this time too," Harvey mutters under his breath.

"We have to stop her." He says it to himself, to Nick, as if Nick is nothing more than a thing to talk to yourself to. The words come with a feeling of finality, as if it might already be too late.

Harvey starts off after Felicia, walking with a fast purpose.

Shaking his head in confusion, Nick limps after him, trying to keep up.

David's head is still filled with the images of his dream, Felicia, the biting at his back, Felicia stabbing him, killing him

He does not hear her catching up to him.

In her focus and his lost state, neither hears Harvey and Nick.

Nick limping after, Harvey breaks into a run when he sees Felicia through the pouring rain. Almost running right into her, he grabs her upraised wrist, turning her to look at him, a knife clenched in her fist.

She stares at him, her eyes cold and hard, hair plastered to her with the rain pouring down her.

"Not like this, Felicia. It won't work." Harvey carefully pries the knife from her hand.

The wild shriek fills Felicia, her head, her chest, bursting to break free. Silently, she turns her head to stare with empty eyes after David's retreating back; David who is blissfully unaware.

Somewhere behind them a shadow moves away with the soft hiss of the breeze rubbing dry leaves together. It slithers back through the forest to the clearing and into the darkness inside the open door to the old abandoned mill.

The rain pounding it, a low moaning creak comes from the mill. A trickle of water is running down the creek alongside it, widening and slowly filling it with the runoff from the torrential downpour.

The wind gusts the rain in billowing sheets, swaying the branches of the trees.

The door swings shut, closing out the rain, the old abandoned mill sitting still and silent against the pounding rain.

END

A guttural scream tears through the darkness with a shrill edge of fear.

A sharp deafening crack of thunder tears the night with a brilliant flash of lightning that is gone almost instantly as the thunder continues to roll across the sky, leaving the afterimage burnt in your eyes. David, sitting up in bed, pale and haggard, sweating, gulping for air, panting ragged breaths.

His dream envelopes him in the memory of its cloying scent.

David trying to blink out the image burned in his eyes in the flash of lightning; thin and pale, standing in the corner of the dark room in a sun-faded dress.

"Felicia," he gasps.

Other books by L.V. Gaudet:

<u>The McAllister Series:</u>

Where the Bodies Are

Are you ready to step into the twisted mind of a killer? What kind of dark secret pushes a man to commit the unimaginable, even as he is sickened by his own actions?

A young woman is found discarded with the trash, left for dead. More bodies begin to appear.

The killer's reality blurs between past and present with a compulsion driven by a dark secret locked in a fractured mind. Overcome by a blind rage that leaves him wallowing in remorse with the bodies of victim after victim, he is desperate to stop killing.

The search for the killer will lead to his dark secret buried in the past.

The McAllister Farm

Take a step back in time to meet the boy who created the killer and learn the secret behind the bodies in Where the Bodies Are.

William McAllister is a private man who does not like to have attention on his family. His family history is as dark as the secret hiding in the woods.

Just as he begins to bring his troubled son into the family business, a serial killer starts preying on local young women. The McAllisters quickly find themselves drawn into the spotlight when the town decides William McAllister is the killer.

The attention is a threat to both William McAllister's profession and his family. He has no choice but to find the killer himself.

He might not like what he learns.

Hunting Michael Underwood

Step deeper into the twisted mind of a killer as he slips further into madness.

Hunting Michael Underwood follows on the heels of book one, Where the Bodies Are, bringing the first two stories and their characters together as the search for the killer continues.

Michael Underwood has vanished and Detective Jim McNelly will not stop until he finds him. Working with the detective, Lawrence Hawkworth is still chasing the bigger story he knows is behind the bodies.

Jason McAllister knows he must stop the killer he created before he goes too far. He may be the only one who can stop him.

Unable to let go of his barely remembered past and the search for his sister, the killer goes looking for Jason McAllister's past and his family.

Killing David McAllister

Sometimes the only way to stop a monster is to kill it. He has gone by many names, but he was raised as David McAllister, and finding what he is looking for is not enough to quiet the darkness inside him.

Other Books:

Garden Grove

Who wants to stop construction at the new Garden Grove residential development? Garden Grove is a hotbed of complications from costly mistakes and vandalism to sabotage and the poisoning of the work crew.

While the construction crew struggles to stay on schedule, they face growing problems and, with them, a growing sense of unease.

A group of local housewives drawn into the growing mystery uncover a secret that brings Garden Grove deeper into a new mystery connecting all the suspects.

The mystery deepens with the discovery of old human remains that have their own dark past recently planted at the jobsite.

When all attempts to shut the site down permanently fail, two long time elderly residents step up their own efforts. Each with their own family secrets, the pair of quirky old birds are pitted against each other and their longstanding family feud is brought to the boiling point.

The Gypsy Queen
(1952)

When a young man with an enthusiasm for get rich quick schemes discovers a rotting abandoned paddle wheel river boat, he has dreams of the riches and glamour she will bring rebuilt as a floating casino. His best friend and unwilling business partner sees only rot, decay, and their ruination in the old boat.

Struggling to rebuild her, they are pitted against everyone from the Shipbuilders' Union to the local casino boss. Meanwhile, strange accidents and a sense of dread falls on those who enter the boat as she awakens with a hunger for her ounce of blood.

The Gypsy Queen's dark past will not be forgotten.

Old Mill Road

Twelve years ago four kids found something in the woods that tore their innocence away. They made a vow to keep it secret. Now, impossibly, someone found it again.

The abandoned mill off the old Mill Road has a dark history that has been told for generations, a story about something sinister haunting the woods.

Unable to remember the events of twelve years ago and troubled by the haunted look he sees every time he looks at his sister's eyes, Nick has returned to learn what happened when they were kids.

Still obsessed with Felicia and Nick's family suddenly vanishing in the night after their childhood discovery, David is determined to get answers from Nick, while his brother Ian tries to temper his obsession.

Felicia's return to help Nick will trigger new revelations about the mummified bodies of children appearing in the woods decades apart.

About the Author

L.V. Gaudet is a Canadian author, a member of the Manitoba Writers' Guild, the Horror Writers Association, and Authors of Manitoba.

L.V. grew up with a love of the darker side; sneaking down to the basement at night to watch the old horror B movies, Vincent Price being a favorite; devouring books by Stephen King, Dean Koontz, and other horror authors; and has had a passion for books and the idea of creating stories and worlds a person can get lost in since reading that first novel.

This love of storytelling has this author working writing and editing into a busy life that includes work, family, and supporting the writing community. L. V. Gaudet volunteers with the Manitoba Writers' Guild, is the editor of the MWG newsletter, proofreads for the HWA newsletter, and visits schools for I Love to Read month.

L.V. Gaudet currently lives in Manitoba with two rescue dogs, spouse, and kids.

Follow L. V. Gaudet:

Facebook: https://www.facebook.com/LVGaudet.Author/
Instagram: lv_gaudet
Twitter: @lvgaudet
Wordpress: https://lvgaudet.wordpress.com

Old Mill Road

Stories have been told as far back as stories existed about monsters in dark places. Old Wives' tales to scare children into behaving. Stories kids tell each other with willful glee to see how much they can scare the other.

When Nick, Ian, David, and Felicia go wandering in the woods, the kids stumble on something so terrible they are afraid to tell anyone about it. They make a pact to keep it secret. Two days later Nick and Felicia's family vanishes in the night.

12 Years Later

David has never forgotten Felicia, the long-legged girl he was forced to spend time with looking after their younger brothers as they roamed the town and surrounding woods.

Stuck growing up in that town, David and Ian could not forget that day in the woods that changed their world.

Was what they found left by the rumored old Mill Road monster?

Nick returns to dig into the past and learn the forgotten childhood memories that still haunt Felicia and him. Right after his return something shocking is found in the woods.

Detective Liam Tobin with C. C. I., Cold Case Investigations, comes to investigate the discovery in the woods and the town's dark history.

With Nick and Felicia's strange uncle Harvey suspected to be behind the new gruesome discovery in the woods and Nick's return, Felicia is forced to come back to the place where it all began, Havenwood.

Everything centers around the old abandoned mill, where the stories of the old Mill Road monster were born.

9 781999 282332